MURDER IN THE TREMBLING LANDS

Also by Barbara Hambly
from Severn House

The Silver Screen Historical Mysteries

SCANDAL IN BABYLON
ONE EXTRA CORPSE
SAVING SUSY SWEETCHILD

The Benjamin January Series

DEAD AND BURIED
THE SHIRT ON HIS BACK
RAN AWAY
GOOD MAN FRIDAY
CRIMSON ANGEL
DRINKING GOURD
MURDER IN JULY
COLD BAYOU
LADY OF PERDITION
HOUSE OF THE PATRIARCH
DEATH AND HARD CIDER
THE NUBIAN'S CURSE

The James Asher Vampire Novels

BLOOD MAIDENS
THE MAGISTRATES OF HELL
THE KINDRED OF DARKNESS
DARKNESS ON HIS BONES
PALE GUARDIAN
PRISONER OF MIDNIGHT

MURDER IN THE TREMBLING LANDS

Barbara Hambly

SEVERN HOUSE

First world edition published in Great Britain and the USA in 2025
by Severn House, an imprint of Canongate Books Ltd,
14 High Street, Edinburgh EH1 1TE.

Paperback edition first published in Great Britain and the USA in 2026
by Severn House, an imprint of Canongate Books Ltd.

severnhouse.com

Cover and jacket design by Jem Butcher Design

British Library Cataloguing-in-Publication Data
A CIP catalogue record for this title is available from the British Library.

ISBN-13: 978-1-4483-1485-0 (cased)
ISBN-13: 978-1-4483-1831-5 (paper)
ISBN-13: 978-1-4483-1486-7 (e-book)

All Severn House titles are printed on acid-free paper.

FSC
www.fsc.org
MIX
Paper | Supporting responsible forestry
FSC® C013604

Typeset by Palimpsest Book Production Ltd.,
Falkirk, Stirlingshire, Scotland.
Printed and bound in Great Britain by
CPI Group (UK) Ltd, Croydon CR0 4YY

The manufacturer's authorised representative in the EU for product safety is
Authorised Rep Compliance Ltd, 71 Lower Baggot Street, Dublin D02 P593
Ireland (arccompliance.com)

Praise for the Benjamin January Series

"Outstanding . . . Consistently surprising"
Publishers Weekly Starred Review of *The Nubian's Curse*

"Hambly is a terrific storyteller; she builds a world that feels very real with fully realized characters. In the Benjamin January novels, we feel like we've been transported to a different time and place. Wonderful"
Booklist on *The Nubian's Curse*

"A hauntingly atmospheric mystery with a complex and exciting storyline"
Kirkus Reviews on *The Nubian's Curse*

"The historical backdrop is vivid, and the writing is exquisite. One of the best in a not-to-be-missed series"
Booklist Starred Review of *Death and Hard Cider*

"This masterly portrayal of smoldering racial tensions deserves a wide readership"
Publishers Weekly Starred Review of *Death and Hard Cider*

"One of Hambly's best mysteries combines historical detail, intense local color, and ugly truths about slavery and politics"
Kirkus Reviews on *Death and Hard Cider*

About the author

Barbara Hambly, though a native of Southern California, lived in New Orleans for many years while married to the late science fiction writer George Alec Effinger. Hambly holds a degree in medieval history from the University of California and has written novels in numerous genres.

www.barbarahambly.com

For Brother Ed

With special thanks to
Jennifer Navarre of the Historic New Orleans Collection

ONE

Sometimes after walking home from playing some Mardi Gras entertainment – an hour before sunrise with the fog thick off the river and the trapped smells of scorched sugar and burning bagasse in his nostrils – Benjamin January would dream about Chalmette.

1815

He'd been twenty-one when the British forces had landed in Louisiana, wild manhood stirring in his heart and his loins and his hopes. In the freezing darkness above the old Rodriguez millrace, he had smelled rather than seen the muddy up-river field of the de Chalmet plantation, had felt the dank cold on his cheeks. He remembered feeling calm, though he'd been aware that his heart was racing.

His arms had brushed the shoulders of the men on either side of him – the men of the Second Battalion of the free colored militia – and he had tried to forget every gunshot wound he'd ever seen in his life. And had failed.

Listening with the whole of his being, all he could hear was the dim crying of invisible gulls.

For five years – since the age of sixteen – he had studied surgery with Rubal Gomez, and every Carnival season had assisted that sturdy, deft-handed surgeon in dealing with the aftermath of pistol duels, sometimes two or three in a week. Six feet tall when he'd come to Gomez – he had grown another three inches since then – and muscled like an ox, it had been January's job to hold the patients down while his teacher dug lead out of their chests or thighs or abdomens. He knew the frantic strength of their struggles. Even muffled by leather-wrapped gags, their screaming bled into his dreams.

When they died under his grip, the dreams were worse.

All this had flooded back into his mind, waiting in the dark atop that ten-foot redoubt, waiting for the fighting to begin.

Somewhere behind him he was aware of blurry pinpricks of

yellow light, the windows of the de Macarty plantation house. Somewhere to his right, barely visible lanterns on the sloop *Louisiana*, lying still on the river, pirate guns trained on the field that the redcoats would have to cross. The faces of the duelists he'd helped operate on returned to him: young men, as he was young. Men with mothers and sisters like his own, who loved them – in many cases, who depended on them for the whole of their livelihood. Mothers, sisters, wives who would lose with their sons or brothers or husbands all their means of support.

Men who had looked forward to years ahead: to sweethearts, wives, children. To evenings spent with friends: laughter, music, talk. The joy of knowing you weren't alone. All those small, exquisite islands of peace gone, never to return, in one crimson splash of agony.

In the darkness, a man would cough, or he'd hear the crunch of boots on wet gravel and shell. The ghostly shape of General Jackson on his white horse passed behind them along the line, a soft creak of saddle-leather and the grind of hooves.

Will I survive this day?

Then far off in the silence, the beating of the British drums.

1841

Not quite a month after the twenty-sixth anniversary of that clammy dawn – on the fifth of February, 1841 – Benjamin January played at a public ball in the Orleans Ballroom on Rue Orleans, where he had played every Carnival season since his return from Paris eight years before.

During Carnival, every ball was a masked ball. Even before his departure for Paris – even before he'd turned eighteen – January had presided over the ballroom's green-and-gold six-octave Broadwood, leading the other musicians in the complexities of waltzes and quadrilles, olivettes and passe-pieds, while the white folks danced. Planters who owned miles of sugar and cotton, along the river or on any bayou big enough to carry freight; wealthy townsmen who owned the cotton presses, the brickyards, the sugar mills and steamboats that made New Orleans the economic heart of the Mississippi Valley. French and Spanish, and the Americans who'd come flooding into the city in the years after that battle.

Merchants and slave owners. Some nights, their mothers, daughters, sisters, and wives.

But this wasn't one of those nights.

The mothers, daughters, sisters, and wives were in attendance tonight at a subscription dance in the Théâtre d'Orléans, a venue owned by the same man – Pierre Davis – and in the same complex of buildings on Rue d'Orléans. And indeed, these ladies had been squired to that event by their husbands, uncles, brothers, sweethearts . . . whose mistresses, free women of color after the Caribbean custom, were in the Orleans Ballroom less than a hundred feet away. During his years in Paris, January's friends had all shaken their heads over the 'custom of the country' – just as if most wealthy Frenchmen didn't have mistresses, though not, to be sure, simply at the end of a discreet passageway from one ballroom to the other, which not a white woman in New Orleans would admit existed.

The old Orleans Ballroom had burned down in the years that January had spent in France. But upon his return, and for the eight years thereafter, he had played, turn and turn about, for the so-called 'Quadroon Balls' – or 'Blue Ribbon Balls' – or for the respectable subscription dances held in the Théâtre or in the new Ballroom above the gambling rooms. The custom remained the same after twenty-six years, but he could see the changes that time had wrought.

The whole world had changed since 1814. The town in which he'd grown to manhood – the town for which he'd fought against an invading army – was no longer what it had been.

It was odd, to miss a place when standing in it.

Beside the piano, Hannibal Sefton – the only white man on the musicians' dais, like a dilapidated elf in a coat that had probably seen the inauguration of Thomas Jefferson – caught the melody of the piano's bright Schubert gallopede and with his violin embroidered a galaxy of golden lace around it. On the other side, the alto voice of Cochon Gardinier's viol and the sweetness of Jacques Bichet's flute touched each note of piano and violin with a counterpoint like shadow and roses. Not the men January had played beside in his first years as a musician, but the joy of the music, the beauty of Mozart and Schubert and Strauss, remained. New waltzes, new mazurkas, new tunes from new operas and from New York . . .

For January, that beauty – beauty that had saved his life and his soul more than once – would never change.

Other things had. There were more Americans present, for one thing. Even with everyone attired as imitation Ivanhoes, pseudo Musketeers, spurious Bedouins and courtiers of every French king from Charlemagne to Louis XVI, he could see how the crowd around the edges of the ballroom divided itself, like a badly made béchamel sauce, and smiled. Along the 'lake-side' (or 'swamp-side') wall – as directions were reckoned in New Orleans – he recognized fancy dress from years past: sturdy Hercule Lafrennière always wore that silver-gilt pasteboard armor, and the elderly Spanish Creole planter Xavier Peralta invariably trotted out the gold-trimmed black velvets of the court of Philip II, complete with a starched neck ruff so wide it prevented him from sampling the cold ham and fried oysters, the honey-gold sherries and ruby clarets, spread on the tables of the buffets. On the other – the 'river' – side of the ballroom were the Americans. That overly elaborate Indian chief outfit (or what some theatrical agent had imagined an Indian chief would wear) would be the wealthy contractor Jed Burton. And Henry VIII was always the banker Hubert Granville, complete with a bevy of present and former mistresses done up as his wives.

His real wife, of course, was at the subscription ball for the New Orleans St Cecelia Society, being held tonight in the Théâtre d'Orléans, at the other end of that discreet passageway – and was almost certainly saying to her friends there, 'Oh, Mr Granville's probably just stepped out into the courtyard for a cigar . . . A terrible habit, cigars!' And her friends – the wives of Jed Burton, of the planter Fitzhugh Trulove, and of half of the French and Spanish Creole gentlemen here as well – were nodding and exclaiming, 'Yes . . . Oh, Basile? He's just gone down to the gambling rooms for a few hands of tric-trac . . .' or, 'Oh, Jean's just stepped out for a few words with M'sieu Trulove – he'll be back for this next dance, or the one after . . .'

Couples advancing, couples retreating; January's hands floated across the piano's keys. Around the punchbowl near the ballroom's doorway, a Turk, a Chinese mandarin, an Elizabethan courtier wearing trunk-hose like pumpkins – roared with laughter over a joke that couldn't possibly have been told at the festivities next door. A little cluster of plaçées in gypsy scarves or medieval hennins or fairy wings whispered gossip behind their fans: 'Can you imagine? At the opera she actually *followed him* up to my box . . . Did she really think he was going to leave me just because he married that cold fright of a daughter of hers?' And the younger girls, smoky-eyed damsels of sixteen and seventeen, there with their mothers in quest of a 'place' of their own, eyed the younger planters, the sons of the bankers and brokers and merchants: 'He said he'd buy that cottage in Marigny for me, but Mama says that place is clear back on Florida Walk, almost to the swamp. She says I can do better . . .'

Many of them, like their mothers, were no darker than Spaniards or Italians – two of them January recognized as girls to whom he'd given piano lessons when first he'd returned to New Orleans eight years before.

'M'sieu de la Chaise!' All the plaçées – and all their hopeful daughters – dropped into curtseys like a meadow of flowers at the wind's caress, as a smugly smiling planter came through the curtained passageway from next door, his dazzled seventeen-year-old nephew in tow.

The gallopede wheeled to its close, tied up with a bow of cascading notes; laughter and chatter among those around the ivory-painted walls. January watched the descent of pretty damsels and provident mamas upon the wealthy M'sieu de la Chaise ('. . . shares in the Natchez and Balize Steamboat company and four cotton plantations in Avoyelles Parish . . .!').

'*Pallas his form with grace divine improves*,' murmured Hannibal Sefton, from Pope's *Iliad*. '*The gazing crowd admires him as he moves*.'

'I suspect,' returned January, shifting the music on the piano's rack, 'that it isn't Pallas Athena but Plutus whom young de la Chaise has to thank for his popularity.' He glanced back at his friend, who in his opinion shouldn't have been on his feet at all. He looked chalk white in the gaslight, his breath wheezing in a way January didn't like. 'Are you all right?'

'*A heart unspotted is not easily daunted*.' Hannibal coughed like a dying horse, his hand pressed to his side. Five years ago, January remembered, his friend would have made it through the evening on the steady consumption of sherry and laudanum. An encounter with a moneylender's hired bravos a few weeks before hadn't helped matters. How he could play at all, sober and in pain, January couldn't imagine, much less how he could make music that the Olympian gods themselves would have quit their quarrelling to dance to.

'There,' Hannibal added, nodding across the ballroom to the group of Americans. 'Observe the gent in the Robin Hood togs . . .'

January turned his head to look. 'You mean the one with the smoke coming out of his ears?'

'Bastien Damoreau.' Cochon Gardinier resettled his three-hundred-plus pounds on his tiny gilt chair and picked up his viol again, studying the saturnine young planter who, moments before, had been talking desperately with the elegant gray-haired banker Mr Chew. 'Sweet on Manon Figes . . .' He swiveled with surprising delicacy to regard the giggling group around the wealthy de la Chaises. 'Ah, yes, there she is. The houri in the white and gold veils.'

'Five cents says Damoreau calls de la Chaise out before one,' Jacques Bichet offered, shaking the spit out of the reed of his instrument.

'Ten cents says Mama Figes murders him if he does,' contradicted Hannibal promptly, digging in his pocket for a coin. 'She's not going to let anything interfere with *that* match.'

'Won't do Damoreau any good if he does call the boy out,' opined January. 'According to my mother' – a woman renowned throughout Orleans Parish for the accuracy of her gossip – 'the Damoreaus haven't got a pot to piss in and Bastien's up to his hairline in gambling debts. Mamzelle Manon's mama wouldn't even look at him.'

'Oh well,' Cochon agreed with an elaborate shrug, 'I guess *that* settles it. He looks like a man who's willing to be reasonable.'

The other musicians – Philippe duCoudreau and old Uncle Bichet – laughed at that. January shook his head, and with a flourish of notes led his colleagues into a lively mazurka: conscious as he did so of Jacques slapping two fragments of a silver Mexican real down on the lid of the piano, while the smiling Uncle de la Chaise took Mamzelle Manon's hand to lead her to his nephew.

'*I have set my life upon a cast*,' quoted Hannibal grandly, '*and I will stand the hazard of the die*.' His violin swung into the melody without missing a note.

An unfortunate choice of epigram, reflected January, considering the fate of the man who'd spoken that particular line in Shakespeare's play.

And indeed, the whole minor drama on the fringe of the dance floor was to him – as many others over the years had been – like something Shakespeare would have cooked up in act one. White folks' business. Nothing to mar the lingering afterglow of seeing his niece married, three weeks previously, to another young man whose family hadn't a pot to piss in. But the young harness mender's apprentice who had led the glowing Zizi-Marie to the altar would, he knew, cherish her to the ending of the world, and to hell with the gifts that the gods chose to shower on white planters and the pretty daughters of financially provident plaçées.

God, the best maker of all marriages, Shakespeare had elsewhere said, *combine your hearts into one . . .*

'All very well for you to talk, Chew,' growled the white-haired patriarch of the Aubin family, as he and the banker passed the musicians on their way to the gambling room downstairs. 'Hardly pays to get the crop in these days. Thirty-seven cents a pound for cotton five years ago – thirty-seven cents! With the bank crash in '37 I couldn't get but ten cents for it today, and I can tell you my niggers don't eat one mouthful less than they did in '36 . . .'

Times had, indeed, changed since the banks had failed (*Thank you, President Jackson . . .*). The ladies clustered around M'sieu de la Chaise and his nephew, smiling and laughing at his jokes, were only being provident. There wasn't a woman among them who didn't know of at least one friend who had been dismissed by her protector ('I know you'll understand that we all need to retrench, my dear . . .'); or who had discovered, upon that protector's death, that he had not, in fact, gone through the legal complexities to circumvent the statutes that forbade a white man to give property to a woman of color. ('I'm sorry, Madame, but legally the house belongs to Monsieur's surviving family . . .' '. . . annuity to remain in effect for the lifetime of the testator only . . .')

All along the Rue des Ramparts, the Rue Burgundy, and all the little streets between, those small, stucco dwellings were being sold, with increasing frequency, to house saloons, or bordellos of two or three girls. Too often, the men who bought them up were either on the municipal council, or had relatives who were, so the complaints by neighbors – January included – about noise, drunkards, and declining property values were disregarded ('You're welcome to file a complaint, Madame, but the original deeds say nothing about the use of the property . . .'). Other cottages still belonged to the women who'd received them as gifts from long-ago protectors, but the owners now took in pro tem 'protectors' for a week or two, a month or two. ('Cheaper than a hotel . . .') The women who were still 'plaçée' – 'placed' – with a regular protector did not speak to these part-timers, some of whom still came to the Quadroon Balls.

'One can still make profitable investments,' argued a visiting French businessman, with a bow to the gray-haired landowner, Bernard de Marigny, 'if one knows where to look.'

'Of course!' The little aristocrat, who had chosen to attend the ball in the cloth-of-gold robes and golden crown of Jove, king of the gods, brandished his gilded lightning bolt. 'Of course!'

The Frenchman glanced around him, lowered his voice, and stroked his beard. 'I understand that it is possible to purchase land—'

'By all means!' Marigny put a hand on the Frenchman's elbow, as if to draw him away from the noise of the musicians' dais to a quieter corner. The mazurka had ended, and the circle of dancers crumbled into couples and clusters. The noise of conversation swelled, and several of the plaçées who had been eavesdropping on M'sieu de la Chaise's tête-à-tête with Madame Figes pricked up their ears at the words *purchase land.* Others, January observed as he shifted his music to a new German quadrille, seemed to be asking M'sieu Froissart, the ballroom's master of ceremonies, who that bearded Frenchman was and (January was willing to bet) if he was by any chance going to remain in New Orleans for any length of time . . .

Both Marigny and the bearded French businessman bowed to these ladies and pressed on determinedly towards the privacy of a corner away from the doors. Their retreat, however, was thwarted by the approach of Marigny's beautiful half-sister 'from the other side of the family' (as the French Creoles said of their mixed-race half-siblings) and her wealthy white protector, magnificent as the King and Queen of Hearts and intent upon an introduction to a prospective investor.

'Madame Eulalie de Mandeville,' Marigny introduced, with a courtly bow, 'please allow me to present M'sieu Edouard-Georges Couvillier of Bordeaux—'

'Get your hands off that woman!' bellowed Bastien Damoreau, as the Frenchman bent to salute the silk-fine kid of the plaçée's glove. 'You lying nigger fraud!' He lunged from the window niche where he'd lingered after the banker had left him, and strode not towards the lovely Mademoiselle Figes and the enamored Nephew de la Chaise, but straight at the Frenchman, catching the man by the shoulder and thrusting him away from Madame de Mandeville's side.

The couples already assembled for the quadrille froze in their tracks and like the mechanically synchronized figures in a clockwork – in near unison with everybody else in the ballroom – all turned their heads.

In an aggrieved voice, Cochon protested into the ensuing silence, 'Hold on, he's got the wrong man!'

Nowhere in the United States – and certainly not in New Orleans – was there an accusation more damning than that a man with so much as one drop of African blood in his veins, no matter how European his features and complexion, would masquerade as a white. At a quadroon ball, it was understood that the women, fair complected as they might be, were of the 'lesser race,' the men (with of course the exception of the waiters, musicians, and servants in the kitchens) were – must be – white. The bearded Frenchman stared at Damoreau in disbelief – 'Here, now—!' protested Marigny – then stepped back and bowed formally to the furious young man.

'I believe you mistake me for someone else, sir.' He took a silver cardcase from his vest pocket – he was one of the dozen men in the ballroom clad in simple evening dress – and produced a card. 'My name is Couvillier – Edouard-Georges Couvillier of Bordeaux. I have only just arrived in your country—'

Damoreau slapped the little pasteboard rectangle away. 'You *hope* everybody'll mistake you for someone else, you sneaky musterfino bastard.' Even in the silly garb of the Thief of Sherwood Forest, he seemed to give off waves of red rage. 'You think you're passin' for white, palmin' yourself off on decent white folks an' thinkin' if you wave enough money around, nobody'll notice that kinky hair an' them nigger lips!'

Couvillier – whose full lips within the luxuriant brown whiskers were definitely more Praxiteles than Congo – said nothing, his expression that of a man who can think of nothing *to* say. Under the shine of pomade, his hair, like his beard, was definitely curly, but without the slightest trace of what the whites called 'kinky' or 'nappy.' January guessed the man might just possibly be Jewish, or of Jewish descent.

But every gentleman in the vicinity of the little group drew back. With a scowl of distaste, Madame Eulalie's protector urged her away, as if mere proximity with a putative man of color – no matter how fair of complexion – would make her less desirable. Only Marigny remained at Couvillier's side.

'See here, Damoreau—'

The infuriated – *intoxicated?* January wondered – young planter ignored him. At the top of his lungs he went on, 'If I wanted to put somethin' over on decent folk, I could walk into any printer in this town and for three dollars get a ream of cards provin' I'm Andrew Jackson – or the Czar of Russia, or some lyin' Frenchman from Bordeaux – an' who'll know the difference? But the likes of you can't go around sayin' you're a white man—'

Talk began to buzz among the men. January saw the glances that went back and forth, while the women – who knew the provenance of every libré family down to cousins (like the queenly Eulalie de Mandeville) who could 'pass' with one African great-grandparent out of eight – whispered among themselves about who Couvillier might actually be related to, tallying up family connections on their fingers. Two of January's fellow musicians – and half a dozen of the waiters – could easily have 'passed,' but for their African features.

Framed in the rich forest of beard, the Frenchman was now very pale, as it sank in on him what such an accusation could mean to any chance of establishing himself in New Orleans society. But his voice remained firm and calm. 'I believe you are mistaken, sir,' he repeated.

'And *I* believe you are a liar.' Damoreau deliberately left off the word *sir*. 'And a damn fraud.'

'Easy for you to say, sir,' returned the Frenchman, 'to a man who has but yesterday stepped off a boat from France and has no friends in this town.'

'Yet some of us are ready' – the Prussian fencing master Augustus Mayerling stepped from the crowd – 'to stand beside a man accused with no proof but a drunkard's spite.'

At that point – even as two or three of Damoreau's young cronies, likewise in Robin Hood green, crowded up around their friend – the ballroom's master of ceremonies, M'sieu Froissart, hastened in from the lobby. 'Messires – Messires . . .'

At the same moment, the curtains sheltering the passageway to the Théâtre were slashed aside to admit Pierre Davis, the owner of both properties, in a fluster of calming words. 'Messires . . .'

What looked like every man who'd still been at the St Cecelia's subscription ball in the Théâtre piled through in his wake, and January had to stifle a grin at the thought of what the wives and mothers and fiancées left behind would be saying.

Froissart checked in stride for an instant before joining Davis – while half the Americans clamored for explanations of what had just happened from those who understood French – and gestured imperatively to the orchestra: *Play something!*

January's signal swept his colleagues straight into the German cotillion, bright music covering the rising hubbub of speculation all around. But he wasn't at all surprised when, two dances later, Davis came over to the musicians' dais and asked if he would be willing to act as one of the surgeons the following Monday morning, at a duel.

TWO

Monday, the eighth of February, was chosen for the duel because the challenge had been issued on a Friday night. After being called a liar and an imposter, M'sieu Couvillier had no choice but to request Damoreau to name his friends, and at least a day had to be allowed for the seconds to attempt to settle the matter without bloodshed. (Nobody would even bet on that one.) The following day was Sunday, and though the French of New Orleans would dance, drink, and gamble through the Sabbath night as readily as on any other, both parties drew the line at dueling, possibly out of concern that such behavior might result in bad luck.

January had been hired to play Sunday night, for a birthday ball at the town home of one of the Duverger family, an event he knew (given the entanglement of the Duvergers with the other prominent French Creole clans) would last until dawn. Turning down either the engagement or the call on his medical services immediately after the ball was out of the question. Owing to another calamitous drop in cotton prices, the fathers of two of the five students at the school his wife Rose operated had regretfully concluded that they must withdraw their daughters ('temporarily,' one of them had politely written) from the establishment. Both letters had arrived Saturday.

January's house itself, for five years now the school which was the center of Rose's life, had been robbed only a few weeks before, and the quarter's fees stolen. Reimbursing a large percentage of those fees to Mr Eustace Simmons in Mobile, and to M'sieu Raoul Fossat of Baton Rouge, had thrown the school's finances into a precarious position. Even the few dollars January would earn bandaging up bullet wounds at the crack of dawn Monday could not be foregone.

'And no sign of Couvillier?' January inquired, as the musicians took their places for the Sunday night pre-ball reception, with servants lighting the hundreds of candles in the second-floor ballroom – what the French and Spanish Creoles referred to as the 'first floor': the 'noble floor' – and the queenly Madame Duverger, in green fairy wings and a flowered wreath, stalking like Napoleon from ballroom to parlor and back with the family's major-domo hurrying in her wake.

'He's rented a cottage on Rue Craps.' Cochon Gardinier picked his way to the dais around the fanciful design of flowers and arabesques that had been freshly chalked on the ballroom floor to mitigate the danger of dancers slipping on the beeswaxed oak. 'Nobody's seen him—'

'That's no surprise.' Jacques Bichet blew an experimental trill. 'They toss him out of the Iberville?' He named one of the French Town's finest hotels – one which, January knew, couldn't afford rumors that they'd allow a putative black man (masquerading as a French businessman from Bordeaux and visibly as white as any legitimate French businessman) stay beneath their respectable roof.

'He – and his wife – left the Iberville of his own accord Friday night.' This much January had learned from his nephew Gabriel, who up until last summer had worked as sous chef in the Iberville's kitchens.

'I seen them on the levee.' Uncle Bichet raised his head from his cello strings, candle-gleam gilding the thick lenses of his spectacles. 'Couvillier and that pretty young wife of his, an' every white man an' lady that invited the pair of 'em to parties an' dinners this month lookin' every which way pretendin' they don't see 'em, an' prayin' they won't show up.'

'Serve 'em right.' January fingered chords on the Duvergers' iron-framed English grand, the mellow tones like sunlight on his heart. 'And if Couvillier shoots and kills Damoreau tomorrow morning, does that mean all those hostesses and planters are going to suddenly start inviting him to dinner again? Or are they still going to worry about their friends whispering that they'll invite an "Ethiopian imposter" into their homes?'

Jacques immediately set aside his flute and produced a quarter of a silver real. 'This says they don't.'

'*They* bein' who?' queried clarionettist Philippe duCoudreau, digging in his own pocket.

It still amazed January that nearly fifty years after the United States began striking its own coinage, most of the silver in Louisiana was still a combination of whatever came through the town in trade – British, Austrian, or French – and Spanish or Mexican: pesos, of the same value as a dollar, or reals, worth a little more than a dime. Or, in these tight-money times, chopped-up fragments thereof.

'All of 'em? Just the French? Just the Picards?' (Bastien Damoreau was related to the Picards, who were related to the de Macartys, the de la Rondes, the Almonasters, and the St-Chinians.)

Speculation was cut off by the appearance of Agrippa, the Duverger major-domo, in the double doors that connected the ballroom with the parlor, as the last servants were reeling the last of the three Venetian glass chandeliers into place. (January didn't know whether the absence of gas in the house was dictated by the expense of piping or Old Gran'père Duverger's objection to the new illuminant on principle.)

Dignified as a king despite Old Gran'père's insistence on dressing all the servants as fairytale mice during the Carnival season, Agrippa bowed in the doorway and said politely, 'Gentlemen, please begin.' Meaning that the first carriages had arrived before the courtyard carriageway on Rue Bourbon.

Bastien Damoreau, at least, had not been invited to the ball. This didn't prevent everyone within earshot of the musicians' dais from discussing the upcoming duel, and at least two other challenges were issued by that hot-tempered young gentleman's supporters and detractors. Before the night was over, both January and Dr Ker, the trim, elderly chief surgeon at the Charity Hospital, had been asked to preside over these additional affairs of honor as well.

'Honor,' sniffed Ker, when he met January at six thirty the following morning, in the black cold and fog along Bayou St-John. 'Like it's an honor to let yoursel' be killed – leavin' that poor little wife of yours alone in a foreign land – 'cause every white in the town's going to believe a drunken ne'er-do-weel when he calls you nigger—'

'Why?' asked January.

'Because not a one of 'em has the stones to stand up against—'

'No – if you'll pardon me, sir,' he added, since Ker, though a hard-headed Scot, after twenty-six years in Louisiana might well have picked up some of the local touchiness about being contradicted by a black man. 'Why did Damoreau force the quarrel on him in the first place? So far as I can tell he has no family connection, no business connection, with Couvillier. Couvillier only arrived from France Thursday. He's never been in America before, and from everything I hear, Damoreau never laid eyes on the man before Friday night. Yet

Damoreau deliberately picked a quarrel with a stranger, whose capabilities with a pistol he has absolutely no way of knowing—'

'It could be that.' A trace of sadness touched the older surgeon's gruff voice. 'I hear now and now of a man ruined on 'Change, or whose life came to smash over a hand o' cards, ridin' to break his own neck. Times have been hard, and by all I've heard, Damoreau's eye-deep in debt.'

Gold seeds of light in the distance. As the two men waded closer through the long, wet grasses, the clinging weeds of these low acres along the bayou, threads of topaz outlined the dark trunks of trees, the moving shapes of men. As always at this season, the air was heavy with burned sugar and the gritty smoke of torched bagasse in the fields.

'In that case, wouldn't a man tired of life pick someone he knew was a dead shot and a bad-tempered bastard? God knows there's plenty of those in town.'

'If the man was known in town, the lad couldn't make his accusation stick.' Ker shrugged. 'Too many people'd know him – and his family.'

The voices of the men beneath the trees carried across the sodden field, changed by the fog that was already lifting. As if the mist were a warming blanket, the air seemed to grow more chill.

'Maybe.' January's eye picked out the tall form of Couvillier, the deep brown of his beard spread out over his breast as he huddled into a dark greatcoat several sizes too large for him. Damoreau, too, January observed, had borrowed a coat from one of his stouter friends, its buttons either blacked over a candle flame or replaced by those made for garments of mourning, covered in black bombazine that wouldn't catch light. Pierre Davis held a lantern up over the pistol box supported by the sword master Mayerling and a dandy named Evard Aubin, as the two seconds compared the weapons.

The sky was graying above the oaks.

Beside him, January heard the surgeon mutter, 'Daft, the pair of 'em.'

As required by the 'code duello,' both seconds went first to Damoreau, then to Couvillier, in what was supposed to be a last attempt to get them to settle their grievance without bloodshed. No Louisiana gentleman, January was well aware, and precious few French ones, would step back at this point. Of all possible accusations, it was one that *had* to be met, if a man was not to be shut out of New Orleans society. To simply pass it by without a challenge to bloodshed would be tacit admission that his opponent spoke truth – that Edouard-Georges Couvillier was of African ancestry trying to pass himself off as white. Or that Bastien Damoreau was a liar.

Morning light widened. Crows cawed. A horse shook its head in a faint jingle of buckle and bit, bringing to mind again the ghostly shape of Jackson on his white steed. Feet crunched on the gravel of the bayou path. January's first wife, the beautiful Ayasha of his Paris days, would have been able to distinguish a black thread from a white one, to determine that it was time for her prayers.

The two men, old and young, took their places, back-to-back – feeling what? January wondered. Fear? Anger? Anxiety for those who depended on them for shelter, for food: Damoreau's mother and sister on their thrice-mortgaged plantation, Couvillier's young wife, as Dr Ker had said, alone in a foreign land?

But a part of January's mind asked grimly: *How about anxiety over something real? Like, 'Am I going to be sold to cover my master's stupid gambling debts?' Or, 'Will my daughter, or my wife, get sold to a whoremaster in town over those same debts?' Or how about, 'How will I feed my family if the Man cuts our rations again?'*

After thirty-nine years – although he'd been only a very young boy at the time – January remembered clearly how *that* had felt.

Pierre Davis counted off the paces as the men stepped away from each other: *One, two, three . . .*

Or how about only, 'Will I die, my life unlived?' he thought as the gray fog lifted from Chalmette's northernmost field, the scent of burned sugar and sodden earth mingling in the air with the steady beat of those oncoming drums.

One of those men – January glanced sidelong at the bloodhound face, the tight jaw, of the man beside him – had been Dr Ker.

. . . eighteen, nineteen, twenty.

The roar of the pistols was instantaneous. White smoke belched from the barrels, and Damoreau seemed for a moment to curl over on himself, as if he'd been hit, but he stayed on his feet. He had simply flinched in terror as he'd fired.

Couvillier spun half-around to his left, arms flung wide, his body almost twirling as it dropped. His spasming hand released the pistol, and he hit the ground before it did.

Men went running to both duelists. Ker strode to Damoreau, who was still bent half-over, shaking and sobbing; January went to Couvillier. The Frenchman was dead, blood already soaking through the breast and the back of his dark coat, where the ball had plowed straight through.

Davis had arranged for a small wagon, transport back to town for whoever might need it. Two of the waiters from the Orleans Ballroom – free men of color who had worked for Davis's late father – lifted the dead man in and covered him with old, but clean, blankets. Tradition allowed as many as three seconds for each duelist, but such had been Damoreau's accusation that only the fencing master Mayerling had stepped forward to act on the older man's behalf: the Prussian didn't care what anyone in town thought of him.

Now he said to January, 'Take him to Quennell's,' naming the best undertaker in the French Town. 'I shall take it upon myself to inform Madame Couvillier.'

'Thank you.'

The fencing master looked down at the old man's face, as the waiters straightened the body on the cart and folded the strong, brown, calloused hands on his breast, and started to say something else. But he thought better of it and went to speak to the driver instead.

January, however, saw him glance in the direction of the dark wall of oaks that fringed the bayou. And while Mayerling was giving his instructions – interrupted by Pierre Davis with some inquiry about Couvillier's business connections, if any, in town – January turned back the blood-soaked right front of the dead man's coat. The bullet had gone straight through the body, but the wound in the front looked to him too large – not like an entry wound at all and certainly not the entry wound of a pistol ball.

Gently and quickly, he slipped his hand under Couvillier's back and raised him a little, confirming his suspicion. The wound in his back was close to the spine, marking an oblique course through the ribcage, heart, and lungs.

Either Couvillier had been shot from behind – from the trees along the bayou – or from the front and to his right, at an angle of some thirty degrees from the direction he'd been facing.

In either case, he had not been shot by Bastien Damoreau.

He laid the body back down and was wiping the blood from his hands with bandages from his satchel when the waiters came back to put the blanket in place. He stepped aside and said nothing, as Mayerling mounted his horse and Davis climbed into his gig. Evard Aubin, himself a renowned duelist, helped the young planter into his own sporty fiacre.

Young Adrien Lafrennière stopped Dr Ker, tugging him imperatively by the sleeve. 'Is he all right, sir?'

January crossed to the older surgeon's side.

In English – which January was fairly sure the young gentleman didn't know – Ker muttered, 'Swoonin' like a lass. They want me to come along an' bleed him – as if that poor warroch hadn't set out to do just that! The Frenchman's dead, isn't he?'

'Quite dead.'

'And for what?' Ker's voice was bitter. 'Fools – an' more than fools – all right, damn you,' he added, as young Lafrennière stepped forward again. 'Hold your water.' But he said it in English. 'Mayerling going to tell the man's poor wife?'

January nodded.

'You need a ride back to town? 'Tis a fair walk in the cold.'

'Thank you, yes.' January glanced at the carriage, already crowded, knowing that even had it been empty he'd be relegated to standing on the footman's perch at the rear. Better, though, he had long ago learned, than walking some three miles alone through the fog of early morning. For a black man, that had always been asking for trouble: another of those situations which had worsened with the passage of time. For several years now, January had kept to the streets of the French Town when he could. At least, if someone tried to kidnap him to sell in Texas or the Territories, people were likely to come if he yelled for help.

So he took one last look around him, at the trees along the bayou, where he guessed the real killer had crouched, almost certainly with a rifle; seeing again the way Couvillier had spun around – anticlockwise, as if someone had shoved him hard and obliquely from behind.

And reminded himself that this was white folks' business, and not his.

He told himself this again, a few hours later, when – returning from a piano lesson with the Savonnière girls in the Faubourg St-Mary and hoping to get a few hours of sleep before another lesson at four – he was intercepted by Augustus Mayerling at the foot of the steps to his house on Rue Esplanade.

'I was hoping to speak to you,' said the fencing master, who didn't look a hair the worse for not having any sleep the previous night. (*And he proposes to give* lessons?)

But January saw in that cool, thin face the reflection of his own questions, and only said, 'You saw the way Couvillier fell, sir?'

The Prussian nodded. 'I went on to Quennell's after I had broken the news to Juliette Couvillier of her husband's death. The wound in his back is smaller, the fabric of his coat, vest, and shirt driven inward into the hole. Have you any idea who this Couvillier was, and why Damoreau would lure him to a place where he could be killed with impunity?'

January shook his head. 'I've heard nothing. And I only know Damoreau by sight, from seeing him at balls and the opera. I think everyone in town knows he's in debt. And I'd be curious to hear if Couvillier, or anyone connected with him in a business way, was buying up those debts, but that's not something I could easily learn. And it's not my business.'

'Nor mine.'

'Did you know him, sir? Before Friday night, I mean.'

'Neither before nor after, save a meeting Saturday to arrange matters.'

An open fiacre rattled by in the street, the three men in it costumed rather improbably as two of the Three Musketeers and Cardinal Richelieu. They – and the brightly clothed women with them – were clearly returning from the festivities of the night before (it was nearly noon), and singing:

> *My ol' lady, she mad wid me,*
> *'Cause I wouldn't go wid her into Tennessee . . .*

Mayerling's gray glance cut sidelong, identifying the sound behind him and evaluating it – *dangerous or not?* – then returned to January. 'I knew the man was a stranger in this country, without friends, as once I was. He was forced to accept the challenge, and I will watch no man put in such a position, without coming forward to act on his behalf.

'I make my living teaching men to kill,' he went on in his soft alto voice. 'I see many quarrels that end in bloodshed. Couvillier swore to me that he and his wife had only stepped off the *Dame Blanche* from Bordeaux on Thursday, and that he had neither met nor heard of Bastien Damoreau in his life. He would go through with it, he said, because he must. If he did not, any undertaking in this country – he said he planned to import fruit from Spain – would turn to ashes in his hand. But what we saw this morning was murder.'

'I agree, sir. Damoreau set him up.'

'This afternoon I will escort Madame Couvillier to Quennell's, to identify her husband's body and make arrangements for a funeral. She may know who, or why, or any number of things that she will be willing to speak of, that before neither would admit. If you hear anything, of Damoreau, or of Couvillier, or of anyone who would wish the man harm . . . might you let me know?'

'I will, sir.' January liked the sword master, and they had helped one another out of difficult situations in the past. 'Has Madame Couvillier any resource – any relatives or acquaintance – in this country?'

'I will ask.' Mayerling hitched the gray fur collar of his coat closer around him, for the wind blew cold off the river, stirring his short-cropped pale hair. 'I did not receive that impression. If that is the case, my wife has said she will offer her the shelter of our house and passage back to France.' And the cool hardness of his face softened at the mention of the woman who had been one of January's pupils back in 1816.

'I'm very glad to hear it, sir,' said January, answering his smile. 'And if I may say so, not at all surprised.'

Other carriages, now, were beginning to appear in the street, as people paid calls to celebrate the Carnival spirit. Even the servants, on their way down to the markets, whistled or sang snatches of tunes. As he climbed the steps to his house – calculating how many hours of sleep he could get before setting forth for Carrollton and the Walters children's piano lesson – his mind caught another verse of the minstrel song the Musketeers had been singing as they passed.

We all hear of the Battle of New Orleans,
An' how ol' Andy Jackson gave the British beans;
Them Yankee boys do the job so slick,
They catch ol' Packenham an' rowed him up the crick . . .

THREE

'Cur Caesar in Galliam iter fecit?' inquired Germaine Barras's gentle, well-bred voice as January slipped quietly through the French door into his study – the room that in Spanish or French Caribbean houses was traditionally reserved as the bedroom for the master of the house.

There was a long pause from beyond the closed door that led into the parlor – and the dining room beyond it, which was where most of the lessons took place. Still more distantly, like the calling of birds, came the treble voices of January's sons playing in the yard, and that of his two-year-old niece Zéphine. Mondays, Tuesdays, and Wednesdays were the days the children played here, and he smiled, loving the sound of them, the wild life of them, even when (as today) they had the tin whistles that some god-cursed plague-festering grass-biting couyon (Philippe duCoudreau) had given them for Christmas. *May the fleas of a thousand camels infest his underclothing* . . .

Then, hesitantly: 'Caesar fectus ab . . . in . . . in Galliam est ut fortuna sua . . . ut fortunam suam quaere. Quaereret.' Aglaëa was almost nine, and labored long hours over declensions and cases.

'Optime,' enthused Rose, as January opened the door and tiptoed through the parlor towards the bedroom door. At the same moment that January noted that only two of the boarders – Germaine and Aglaëa – and one of the day-students (Coralie Chardin) were present, Rose got to her feet.

'Ite in opere tuo.' As a teacher, she was strongly in favor of speaking nothing but Latin during the designated Latin hour. 'Mox redibo.'

'Gratias tibi valde, magistra,' the girls chorused, and Germaine even managed – getting to her feet and curtseying to January – 'Salve, magister.'

January bowed gravely. 'Salve, Germanica,' which made Coralie and Aglaëa giggle. Germaine managed a smile at the pun, but he thought she looked as if she'd been crying.

He held the door open for Rose, who preceded him into the bedroom.

'Cosette Gardinier's grandmother is taking her out of the school,' said Rose, when he had shut the door again behind him. 'She's upstairs packing now.'

The fairylike Germaine and the more businesslike Cosette were inseparable friends.

'Damn it.' The words were spoken in distress for Germaine's loss of a friend – though Cosette's Gran'mère Poucet lived in Spanish Fort, January guessed the old lady would keep the girl home to do housework rather than let her continue at the lower rates for a day-student. But in a dark corner of his heart he wanted to shout, *Stop this!* at the universe that was now demanding of him the reimbursement of Cosette's school fees as well. *And where the hell am I going to get another twenty-five dollars on top of what it costs for us all to eat?* That 'us all' included, these days, his newly wed niece Zizi-Marie and her new husband Ti-Gall L'Esperance, who had taken up residence in one of the house's three attics rather than start their married life in the crowded four-room cottage of Ti-Gall's mother and four siblings.

Most afternoons, the January table also included Zizi-Marie's eleven-year-old sister Chou-chou, and Hannibal Sefton, who contributed his earnings as a fiddle player to the family exchequer by 'accidentally' leaving them on the kitchen worktable.

'We have until Friday to come up with the money,' went on Rose in a neutral voice, as January dropped down on to the bed. 'Clarice Picard' – she named the woman whose husband had been Cosette's grandfather, the protector of 'Gran'mère' Serafine Poucet back when Spain had ruled Louisiana – 'found a way to recover the investments that had been settled to care for Cosette's education.' Cosette's plaçée mother had never forgiven her daughter's stubborn pleas for what she called a 'real education' (and her refusal to accept the proposals of a young white planter); January had often wondered how long it would be before the white side of the Picard and Gardinier families found a way to claw back the settlement. 'Serafine Poucet sold her housemaid to cover immediate expenses—'

January raised his hand wearily. 'We'll think of something.'

He had not the smallest idea what.

He and Rose exchanged possibilities for a short time – they had already borrowed from his sister Dominque's protector, Henri Viellard, to cover the reimbursements for the departing Alicia Simmons and Marie-Evaline Fossat, and though he was fairly sure Viellard would lend more if asked, he was wary of being indebted to the corpulent planter's family. Even when Rose left to resume the lessons in the dining room, he lay listening to question-and-answer sessions about the events of the Gallic Wars ('Vercingetorix Romanis non placet . . .') and was still wide awake when footsteps clunked on the gallery outside the bedroom's French doors. Hurting inside, he heard Cosette's tearful leave-taking from her much-loved schoolmistress, the friends and the study of mathematics and steam engines that had been for a year the center of her life. He was hurting, too, with guilt that his thoughts were as much on where he was going to get an additional twenty-five dollars – the cost of food and fuel for his family (not counting the students) for a month – as on the human pain of loss.

Damn it, damn it, damn it . . .

Then when the porter and Cosette were gone, the fleeting scamper of feet running to the attic stair, stumbling as they climbed, as if the climber was half-blind with tears.

In the street, the noise had increased. Tambourines, tin trumpets, pots and pans. Voices caroling:

Tap, tap, tap
Who taps there?
'Tis my own self, love,
Open the door for me. . .

He was still awake an hour later when boots thumped again on the gallery, and he heard a knock at the French doors of his study at the other end of the house.

'Mr J. in, m'am?'

Lieutenant Abishag Shaw's scratchy voice and appalling French. The Kentuckian City Guard spoke softly, knowing that at two o'clock in the afternoon on any day before the start of Lent, any musician who could afford to would be sound asleep.

January couldn't hear Rose's sotto voce reply but guessed what she was saying.

'If'n you'd be so good as to let him know I called, I'd appreciate it, m'am. I need to talk to him 'bout that French feller what got hisself killed this mornin' in that duel . . .'

Damn it.

January got to his feet, slid into trousers and shirt and socks – though bright, the day was freezing cold – and dragged the spare quilt from the foot of the bed to wrap around his shoulders as he stepped through the bedroom's French doors on to the gallery. Shaw was just turning from the closing door at the other end. 'I'm not saying there *was* a duel, sir . . .'

Dueling had been outlawed in Louisiana in 1812.

'Well, let's say it's about that French feller what got hisself shot this mornin' down by Bayou St-John.'

At the sound of January's voice, Rose reopened the study door; January walked the length of the gallery and gestured Shaw inside. The policeman looked as he usually did halfway through Carnival season, with a cut on one cheek and a bandage wrapped around his right hand and wrist, and the haggard complexion of a man who hasn't had eight hours of sleep since Twelfth Night.

'Have you talked to Mayerling, sir?' January asked, as Rose disappeared into the parlor and closed the door. He gestured to the worn leather chair beside the desk; himself took the bent-willow one close to the cold hearth. There was no fire in the room – wood was two dollars a cord – and Shaw's breath puffed visibly in the light from the door's glazed panes.

'I did. An' I hear tell from the fellers down at the Broadhorn Saloon that Bastien Damoreau went around this mornin' payin' off near to three hundred dollars' worth of gamblin' debts. When I asked him about it, he said there hadn't been no duel, an' he'd got the money from a man what owed him, name of Tom Jackson, from Philadelphia. Just only came today. An' no, he'd sort of burned the note it come with, by accident like.'

January patted his pockets like a man searching for something, then heaved an exaggerated sigh. 'And me without my smelling salts. Did you look at the body? Sir,' he remembered to add. His mother wouldn't have admitted the policeman to her house, but he was, after all, a white man.

'You mean the entry hole in his back an' the exit hole just short of his right armpit in the front? Bigger'n anything you'd get with them Manton pistols Mayerling brung to the party?'

'Yes,' said January. 'Those holes. Sir. Did Madame Couvillier have anything to tell about who might have wanted her husband dead? Wanted it badly enough to follow him to Louisiana and pay a sorry debtor like Damoreau three hundred dollars to stand him up like a fairground "Aunt Sally" to be shot at?'

Shaw shook his head. 'When Mayerling got to the house they's rentin' in Marigny, to take her to Quennell's, M'am Couvillier was gone.

'All her plunder was left there,' he went on, into January's startled silence. 'Clothes an' hairbrushes an' sech, though if there was money in the room, it'd been took. I get to spend the rest of the day along the docks, askin' if she's by any chance sneakin' out of the country for some reason, but this time of year we got no men to spare lookin' for her. You wouldn't by any chance be willin' to ask around a little, Maestro, among them as might have heard of what became of her, would you?'

January hesitated for a long time over that. It was possible, he knew, that the Frenchman's wife herself – whom he had never seen – could have been the one to pay Damoreau, for reasons best known to herself. He had known – and still knew – women capable of killing a man in cold blood with a rifle at a hundred yards, and perfectly willing to do so if they felt themselves threatened. But he knew, too, that there were men in New Orleans who would think nothing of blotting out a murdered man's wife if they thought she might connect them with the original victim's death. So far as he knew – and Juliette Couvillier was only a name to him – the vanished wife had no connections or friends in New Orleans, no family. Nowhere to flee.

Was she hiding in the corner of a warehouse somewhere, listening for the sound of boots approaching in the silence? Or was she instead dickering for a first-class cabin with the captain of a ship bound for Cuba or France, with a copy of her husband's will in her reticule?

And if she *had* hired the killing done – and killers came cheaper than sugarloaves in the market, in New Orleans these days – what were the chances that the man (or men) she'd hired would simply shrug off the news that a big black man was asking questions? And what were the chances that if said big black man were shot, some night during the tawdry confusion of Carnival season, that the overworked City Guard would give a tinker's damn who pulled the trigger?

The same argument went doubly for anyone else who might have wanted Edouard-Georges Couvillier dead.

As someone clearly had.

He took a deep breath, whispered, *I'm sorry*, in his heart to that terrified woman who had fled from her rented lodgings that morning with only what money she could find in the dresser. That woman who might not even exist.

His sister Olympe had often told him, *You can't save everybody, Ben.*

But four weeks later, faced with the horrifying outcome of subsequent events, he would wonder whether some saint – or voodoo loa – had disapproved of his choice and set out to teach him a lesson he'd never forget.

He repeated, aloud, 'I'm sorry, sir. I'll keep my ear to the ground, and if I hear anything about Damoreau's debts, or Madame Couvillier, or who might have known anything about Couvillier's enemies, I'll let you know. Beyond that . . .' He shook his head. 'I don't know who was behind what happened, but calling their attention to myself is not a risk I can afford to take. Whoever paid Damoreau's debts would probably be able to hire someone to shut me up, if word got around I was asking questions. This isn't my business.'

Shaw nodded, clearly understanding. 'Worth a try,' he said. 'An' I 'preciate whatever you might just pick up in passin'. There's scoundrels enough in this town without you go pokin' around lookin' for more.'

He stood, resumed his hat, and fished in his pocket for his twist of tobacco, having politely blown out his previous wad over the gallery rail before coming into the house, January was sure. 'All well with you otherwise, Maestro? Newlyweds still billin' an' cooin'? I meant to thank you, by the way, for askin' me to the festivities. Your sister an' her son between 'em sure cooked up a storm.'

'I'll tell them you enjoyed it, sir.' He smiled, remembering: Zizi-Marie's wedding was the first time he'd ever seen his friend completely relax.

'Oh, hell,' said Shaw. 'My praise ain't worth gettin' into a state over. I'll eat corn husks an' red-eye gravy, an' ask for seconds. But that was somethin' special.'

He shook hands, a little shyly, and departed, rattling down the gallery steps like a broken limberjack toy and ambling riverward along Rue Esplanade towards the wharves, his thin corduroy jacket flapping in the sharp wind. January finished dressing, then collected his music satchel, and took the steam train to Carrollton, to instruct the blind daughter of a brickyard owner and the girl's tiny brother in the wordless wonders of music. All the way there – and back, with a payment made in bartered eggs from the Walters family chickens – he wondered if he should have asked Shaw, *What will you pay me, to seek that information?*

Wondered, too, where he was going to come up with twenty-five dollars beyond what he needed for beans and rice, an onion and firewood, not to speak of paper and ink for Rose's students and soap for the laundry that was part of the girls' school fees, and new shoes (again!) for little Professor John and tiny Xander . . .

That night he played for the birthday celebration of the Lecoq brothers, notaries born four years and one day apart whose vast tribe of nieces and nephews, grandsons and daughters, were related to nearly every other French family in the parish. Speeches were made and toasts drunk by the men who'd served with jolly Alain and dour Laurence twenty-six years before at Chalmette. King cake was eaten, and – the usual procedure at such French Creole gatherings – everyone danced holes in their slippers until nearly sunrise.

Perhaps it was the speeches, or the recollection of the drunken carriage load of pseudo Musketeers the previous day singing 'Old Zip Coon,' but upon his return home, January dreamed of Chalmette.

1815

Dreamed of the wet crunch of the clamshell road underfoot, as they marched out of the camp around de Macarty's plantation and into position along the redoubt. Of his friends Gilles and Davy Gignac silent at his side: *Thinking what?* At the time, his own doubts had kept him from asking, from even considering the question.

Of the weight of his musket on his shoulder and his pack on his back.

Of the question in his own heart: *What happens after this?*

And if I survive this day, what road will I take then?

Images of that day merged strangely in his mind. The rolling thunder of the guns on either side of him, the stink of the powder smoke that mixed with the thinning mists as the sun rose over the greenish-gray wall of the swamps. The yelling of the red-coated men floundering in the mucky ditch below the embankment. How one man, and then another, slithering in that mud, had flung up their arms as crimson splattered over their faces and throats, or darkened the bloody hue of their jackets. Tired, unshaven faces furious with the self-roused fury of battle – he remembered their faces later, wondering if it was his shot that had ended their lives or someone else's?

Men's shoulders jostling his arms as he stepped back to reload, the men behind him crowded forward. The heavy *putt*! of British musket balls into the wet cotton bales of the redoubt. The thunder of the *Louisiana*'s guns.

The stink of the hospital tent that night, as he and his teacher Gomez had gone to help with the captured British wounded. The pain in his own grazed arm. His first meeting with Dr Ker, the hook-nosed Scot unhurt but bloody to the biceps from tending the hurts of others. The British surgeon had turned himself over to the American troops, so that they'd have another healer on duty: 'Doan stand there gawpin', lad – hold this one whilst I cut for the ball.'

The reek of blood and of feces shit out in terror or in death.

That first overwhelming understanding, that each man was a man like himself. *What will become of those who live? What will happen to the wives, the sweethearts, the brothers, and the children of those who died today?* The sudden knowledge that it all mattered.

Clearest of all, his own sense of surprise that he himself was alive.

So what happens now?

1841

He opened his eyes, and by the angle and degree of the light through the closed jalousies he knew it was late in the morning (and six-year-old Flora McCullen had her piano lesson – in Bayou St-John – at noon damn her). Silence in the dining room. Rose, Germaine, Aglaëa, and the two remaining day-students – Coralie and Lalage – would be in Rose's workroom above the laundry for a science lesson. No sound from the yard either. Zizi-Marie would have taken the boys (and their Satan-inspired tin whistles) for a walk. At this hour, Gabriel would be at Alciatore's boarding house and restaurant on Rue St-Louis, washing vegetables.

He wondered if there were hot water still in the kitchen.

He had just put on his shirt and trousers when a swift, firm step bounded up the gallery stairs outside, and a moment later knuckles rapped briskly on the French door of his study at the other end of the house.

I hope this is someone offering me money . . .

Slipping into his jacket, he passed through the parlor and opened the door.

'Ben,' said Dagobert Janvier, and warmly shook his hand.

FOUR

During the fifteen years that he lived in Paris – as a student, as an ill-paid junior surgeon at the Hôtel Dieu, as a musician – January had several times tried to explain to his friends the relationship between himself and Dagobert Janvier.

On the rare occasions in his childhood that January encountered young Michie Dagobert, cordial friendliness had prevailed on both sides. He had always addressed the son of his mother's protector by the polite pronoun 'vous,' or as 'Michie' or 'Michie Dagobert,' though the boy was three and a half years younger than himself, a substantial difference when one is ten. Michie Bertie (as his friends called him) in his turn had addressed the son of his father's mistress (albeit by an earlier union) as 'tu.' Most whites spoke to blacks thus, whether the black person in question was slave or free. When they became adults, he had switched to the more formal, polite 'vous,' though his stepmother – the legitimate white second wife of St-Denis Janvier – never did. Had there been a less respectful pronoun than 'tu' (designed perhaps for sea-sponges or bedbugs) January guessed that Madame Marie-Hélène would have used it.

In Paris – and indeed in liaisons among the French and Spanish Creoles of New Orleans – January had often observed cold rivalry between a man's legitimate offspring and the children of a white mistress, even children by a different father. But in New Orleans, the white wife might seethe in well-bred silence every time her husband came home for breakfast with his shirt smelling of his plaçée's perfume, but at least she knew that there was no chance – *none* – that her husband would put her aside and marry the woman on whom he spent money and fathered 'libré' children.

Such unions were utterly forbidden by Louisiana law.

His Parisian friends had shaken their heads, but his wife of those years, the beautiful Ayasha, had understood. Her mother had been the second wife of a merchant in Algiers, and she had spoken of 'Ostaaza Samar' as 'um muhtarama' although she knew perfectly well that that aloof gray-haired lady was not the woman who bore her. Ostaaza Samar's children, those of the second wife, and of the concubine, were all brothers and sisters together.

Rose, too, was on perfectly friendly terms with her white father's white children. The white side of the Janvier family – with the exception of Madame Marie-Hélène – treated January as 'a member of the family' (as French Creole euphemism had it) 'from the shady side of the street.' Most Sundays, his mother had coffee with her late protector's mother, much to the unexpressed annoyance of Madame Marie-Hélène.

Now he said, 'Come in!' and stepped back to usher Janvier through to the parlor. 'Please forgive me—' He gestured self-consciously to his stockinged feet.

'Oh, Lord, no—' Janvier waved the apology aside. 'I know how late you must have been out this time of year! All the way here I was passing carriages full of people who looked like *they* were just coming home, so I'm a little surprised to even see you awake.'

'What gives you the idea I'm awake, sir?' January grinned. 'There should be coffee in the pantry. Can I get you some?'

'Thank you.' Janvier laid his hat on a side table and settled into one of the chairs beside the hearth.

Before continuing his errand, January stooped to add a log to the fire (at two dollars a cord . . .) and poked the low-flickering blaze to renewed life. Dagobert Janvier, at forty-four, was nearly a full head taller than his short, paunchy father had been, mousy-fair where St-Denis Janvier had been dark, with features that were nondescript without being precisely unhandsome. Since the wine merchant's widow Janvier had married when January was twelve looked not unlike her stepson in height, build, and coloring, January assumed the first Madame Janvier had been similar in appearance. Like his stepmother's, Dagobert's light-brown hair was thin and silky, now retreating from his spreading acreage of smooth pink forehead, and like hers, his features were what men called 'rugged' – though without the strong chin and hard, square mouth of Madame Marie-Hélène's. A modest second chin was beginning to manifest itself below the first; a small paunch now subtly altered the fit of his well-cut broadcloth coat.

To January's relief, Rose had left a jug of coffee above the low flame of the pantry veilleuse. Beneath a glass cover, three orange tarts and a half-dozen pralines (all that had survived January's return to the house six hours previously) remained. Another cover guarded a small dish of butter and a dessert cup of Gabriel's ambrosial apricot jam. All this January assembled on a yellow Queens Ware plate, with two cups, the sugar bowl (*Is this the last of the sugar?* He feared it was), and what he hoped wasn't the last of the milk on a tray. These he bore out through the dining room to the parlor again and set them on a small table more or less equidistant from the two chairs by the hearth.

'What can I do for you today, sir?' He settled in the other chair.

Dagobert Janvier's dark-blue eyes grew soft, his shoulders relaxed. January could almost hear old Gran'mère Sidonie Janvier sniff – as she had at their last brief meeting during the visit he'd paid to his mother on New Year's Day – *God help us, the poor noodle's in love again.*

Janvier leaned forward and said, 'I need your help, Ben.'

'Of course.'

'And it must be in confidence. Maman' – meaning, January knew, Madame Marie-Hélène – 'and Gran'mère simply wouldn't understand.'

He said again, 'Of course.' He and Madame Beatrice – Dagobert Janvier's brisk, pretty wife – never crossed paths, and he guessed that she would consider it beneath her to ask questions about her husband's activities. Particularly of a musician on 'the other side of the family.' He drew his chair a little closer, and when Dagobert tonged two pieces of sugar from the half-empty bowl, he flicked a surreptitious glance at the camel-back clock on the other side of the room.

Half past nine. Plenty of time to wash, get breakfast, and walk to Bayou St-John.

'What is it?'

Janvier sighed and was for a moment silent, with the air of a man about to disclose the contents of his love letters.

'Do you remember Bartolomé de Cedillos?' he asked at last. 'He was a planter, a Spaniard. He had three arpents of land along Bayou Joyeuse and back into the swamp.'

'Alegre,' said January, a little surprised that he could recall the name of the place. Bayou Joyeuse had at one time been the largest of those subsidiary waterways in the marshy miles behind Bayou

Sauvage, downriver from town. 'And there was a scandal, wasn't there? Didn't he try to raise a slave uprising to attack Jackson's troops during the battle at Chalmette—?'

'That was a lie!' The angry jerk of Dagobert's hand sent coffee slopping into his saucer. 'You see? Everybody in town – in Louisiana! – believes that!'

'He was killed.' January groped to sort out recollections of blood and noise and the smell of gunpowder, of grief and disillusion. 'Wasn't he? Shot by the rebelling slaves—?'

'That's another lie!' His not-quite-relative's quick anger dropped from boiling to a passionate simmer. He leaned forward, blue eyes ablaze with passion. 'And that business about the rebels burning three plantations—'

'But they *were* burned,' pointed out January. 'We were ordered – d'Aquin's battalion was ordered – to patrol the swamps east of the battlefield looking for runaways and for British stragglers. We camped near one of the burned plantation houses.' Someone – probably the slaves themselves (*What the hell was the name of the place?)* – had stripped the plantation's storehouses bare, and twice, on guard duty at night, January had glimpsed what he was pretty sure had been runaways slipping back through the sodden labyrinth of bayous, islets, and ponds to glean straying poultry and swine from the surrounding woods. He had neither challenged nor reported those cautious movements in the dark.

'De Cedillos had nothing to do with that!' Dagobert's forefinger stabbed the tabletop beside his second apricot tart. 'And just by *purest coincidence*' – sarcasm dripped from his voice – 'his neighbor, Icarus Pelerine, who'd had claims in the court for years to the best part of the Alegre land grant, brought up the case again *immediately* after all those rumors began to circulate. He went on to claim the whole of Alegre. The Negroes there ran off during the battle, and de Cedillos's wife and two daughters, Paloma and Felicita, were left destitute.'

Something about the way the white man's voice cracked when he spoke the names of those ladies triggered a suspicion in January's thoughts; he saw Dagobert's fists clench.

'Paloma was my first love,' Dagobert continued, after long silence. From his watchpocket he took a miniature painted on ivory: a dark-eyed girl, innocent face surrounded by the fluffed halo of short curls – and the extravagant topknot – in vogue during what had been called Mr Madison's War. 'I was seventeen, when I fought at Father's side.'

This January remembered well. St-Denis Janvier had visited January's mother the night after Gabriel Villeré had ridden into New Orleans with the news that the British troops had emerged from the swamps and seized his plantation, only a few miles below the city. Janvier had embraced January – with whom he'd never been terribly demonstrative – and his own tiny daughter, Dominique . . . 'In case I don't return . . .'

Dagobert, January recalled, had stood awkwardly in the doorway, in the uniform of the New Orleans Volunteer Rifles . . .

'Paloma was sixteen,' Dagobert went on. 'Beautiful beyond what I or any man can describe. She, her mother, and her sister Felicita, made their way to Cuba, where her mother's sister had been raised. But when they arrived there, penniless, the aunt was gone. It cost them two years of backbreaking hardship before they could raise passage money to return to Spain—'

'You stayed in touch with them?'

'Good God, no!' Anguish twisted the younger man's face. 'Had I known – had I had the slightest intimation of what they were going through – I would not have hesitated to go to them, whatever my father might have said. No.' He sighed again, staring ahead of him for a time, the coffee cup forgotten between his hands.

'The hardships of those years, living with the remnants of the de Cedillos family in a few rooms of what had been their townhouse in Seville . . .' He shook his head, and January recalled, during his years in France, what the Spaniards of his acquaintance had said of the chaos in a country that had never recovered from the Peninsular War. Juntas, coups, a second French invasion, then civil war again. His Spanish liberal friends in Paris had said, "the Devil has the people by the throat."

'Paloma . . . died' – Janvier's hands trembled so that he had to set down his cup – 'three years ago. With their mother's death last year, Felicita sold the last fragments of her mother's jewelry, took the few remaining reals her sister had saved, and returned to New Orleans. If she can clear her father's name, she hopes to have that long-ago, unjust court judgment reversed, and regain the plantation granted to her grandfather by King Ferdinand of Spain.'

'You've seen her, then?' *That must have been where he heard her story . . .*

Dagobert's eyes closed, and he groped again in his pocket for the miniature. 'She is the image of what Paloma was, when I beheld her last.' He spoke like a man in the depths of prayer. 'Not only the shape, the tenderness of her eyes, the delicacy of feature and frame. Like Paloma's, hers is a spiritual beauty, like a lamp of alabaster at twilight.'

He turned to January again, something that was close to a plea in his face. 'That is what I cannot – and will not attempt to – explain to Maman, or to Gran'mère. Maman is a woman of the highest character and the noblest temperament, as I have no need to tell you.'

Recalling Madame Marie-Hélène's attempts to have him expelled from the school in which St-Denis Janvier had enrolled him – while Janvier himself was out of town – January said nothing. But he remembered every lie she had told her husband about his honesty, and the occasion on which she'd accused him of theft and taken him to the City Guard to be whipped.

Dagobert went on earnestly, 'For twenty-six years, she has heard nothing but those calumnies, put about by old Pelerine to justify his seizure of the de Cedillos land. All her friends are related to the old sinner, and to the Dufresne and Lafrennière families, whose plantations along Bayou Malheur were burned in the uprising. And Gran'mère . . .'

He paused again, clearly loath to come out and say that old Sidonie Janvier was a cynical octogenarian beldame who would invariably put the worst possible interpretation on phrases like *spiritual beauty, delicacy of feature and frame,* and *lamp of alabaster* in accounting for her grandson's attachment to Felicita de Cedillos.

At last he asked, 'Do you understand? *Can* you understand?'

Slowly, January returned, 'Does Mamzelle de Cedillos really think a Louisiana court is going to reverse – or even take up – a property case twenty-six years old?'

'That's why we need proof!' His fingers clenched tight around the miniature. 'Proof of her father's innocence! Proof of what really happened, during the battle! Proof of who really stirred up the slaves to rebellion. Of who really planned to have our battle line weaken at a critical time, in a critical place, so that the redcoats could break through.'

He leaned closer, as if he would grasp January's arms; shake him into seeing the truth. 'Icarus Pelerine hated Paloma's— Felicita's— Mademoiselle de Cedillos's,' he corrected himself quickly, 'father. He would have done anything to get the title to Alegre, and he hasn't changed. He will do anything to keep those lands. His own plantations on Bayou Sauvage and Bayou Joyeuse are played out, the soil exhausted. He needs the Alegre lands, even half-flooded as they are. It's why we need proof of what really happened. Of how those slave revolts – only in that one place, along Bayou Malheur, right behind our lines – got started. Who was really behind them?'

January half-opened his mouth to reply that men and women who have been kidnapped, beaten, raped, driven to exhaustion, and have seen their children sold away from them, frequently do not need further incentive to burn down their captor's house and run away – particularly not during the back-breaking labor of roulaison, the cane-grinding season.

Then he closed it, seeing that such a comment would not change his relative's mind.

Instead, he asked, 'Do you think such proofs still exist?'

'We have to find that out. Palo— er . . . Felicita— Mademoiselle de Cedillos . . . has staked everything she has, her last hopes of survival, on finding those proofs, on regaining that land. On re-establishing her father's name and honor. I'm her only hope, Ben, her final hope. I can't let her down.'

January remembered what it had felt like to lose . . . *Everything*? *No*, he reflected. Even when the banks had crashed, he'd still had the house, and he still had his piano. He'd still had Rose and his friends.

To be so desperate that you'd sell the final few things you owned, to take ship back to New Orleans in pursuit of . . . what? Something that could have been just a family tale?

Dagobert was watching his face, as if by the force of his own desperation he could will January to say yes.

In the four years since the bank crash, January had undertaken a number of tasks – rather like the labors of Hercules – to keep the roof over the heads of Rose and his sons. He had sought missing persons in New York State, the Republic of Texas, Washington City, and the distant wilds of northern Mexican territory. He had retrieved pilfered information for the British consul in New Orleans and hunted missing treasure in Haiti.

In the course of his work with the so-called Underground Railroad, which smuggled escaping slaves to the free states, he had encountered a number of formerly free black men who had taken on freelance jobs of one sort or another and who had subsequently discovered that not all prospective employers were what they said they were: men who had woken up naked in slave pens with an opium headache and the ashes of their freedom papers cooling in the nearest stove. January had always been very careful to take on no job unless vouched for by someone he knew – and knew well.

Dealing with Dagobert Janvier, he knew, would involve no such risk. For one thing, it wasn't something a gentleman like Dagobert did. For another, Dagobert knew jolly well that Gran'mère Sidonie would kill him if he brought 'one of the family' to harm.

'What sort of help do you need?'

'I need a strong right arm.' Dagobert clenched his fist again and 'made a muscle,' as the schoolboys said, as if baring his own arm for combat. 'I need someone to watch my back, against whatever threats Pelerine may bring against us. To guard the door when I enter a room; a reserve force in case of danger.' He took a small sack from his pocket, counted out three ten-dollar gold pieces. 'I need a Patroclus, a Horatio, a Man Friday. Will you be my Patroclus?'

January's mind boggled momentarily at the thought of the paunchy, balding Dagobert in the role of Achilles. *On the other hand, that will take care of Cosette Gardinier's father . . .*

'I understand that you have your commitments,' Dagobert went on when January hesitated. 'And I respect that we shall need to work within those limitations. I'm sorry that it will cause you the hardship of some lost sleep. I'll do what I can to spare you that. I just need to know that there will be someone to help me, someone who believes in my . . . my quest, I suppose you could call it. My quest to help a wronged woman retrieve what her family has lost. I need someone I can trust.'

January picked up the money. 'You can trust me.'

FIVE

In point of fact, January would have been grateful to lose more sleep that Carnival season. Prior to the bank crash, Carnival had more or less paid the household expenses for the remaining forty-six weeks of the year. There had been a subscription ball, a private party, a children's dance, or an opera every night from Twelfth Night to Mardi Gras – Fat Tuesday – itself. *You can sleep during Lent*, the musicians would say, and even that wasn't entirely true: six weeks without a celebration of some family birthday or somebody's saint's day was to the French and Spanish Creoles unthinkable. ('God did not intend for us to behave like Protestants,' January's mother declared.)

These days it was different. People still held parties, or processions in costume, and ran around the streets all night garbed as knights or Greek gods, blowing flour into one another's faces and banging tin pans – and crammed the gambling halls as if vingt-et-un and poker were going to disappear forever with the onset of Lent. Carriages decked with flowers and filled with Columbines and Pierrots, Lancelots and Gueneveres, rattled through the French Town trailing snatches of song and the fumes of wine. But the St-Charles Theater presented fewer operas than before and had cut down the number of musicians for its melodrama performances. Cotton that sold for ten cents a pound on the wharves, sugar that brought no more than sixty dollars per hogshead, with corn at forty cents a bushel and bacon at six cents a pound ('Ahhh, the niggers don't really need no bacon . . .') meant fewer balls as well as fewer white men willing to pay for an illegitimate quadroon daughter's education.

January – and his partners on the musicians' dais – were spending two or three nights a week at home. Or, in the case of some of them, selling their days of sleep time to roll cigars.

So it was without repining that he joined Dagobert Janvier three nights later, where the street optimistically called The Elysian Fields petered out into rutted dirt and puddles, and in moonless darkness followed him – and very quickly led him (despite Dagobert's insistence that their destination lay to their left) – to the Gentilly Road along Bayou Sauvage.

Men of color – particularly on the plantations – were actively discouraged from learning to read or make maps, for obvious reasons. Still, in January's childhood, every person in the quarters on Bellefleur Plantation had learned the location of each small bayou, each dead tree, each Indian mound within fifteen miles: fishing spots, hideouts, caches where pilfered tobacco could be concealed from The Man. The habit of making mental maps had persisted, in freedom and in adulthood. January had never been to the de Cedillos plantation of Alegre, but he knew where Bayou Joyeuse, on which it lay, branched from Bayou Sauvage in the watery cypress wilderness of the back swamp. And he had a fair idea of how to get there even on a clouded and moonless night.

The house still stood.

'Gran'mère says Pelerine put his son in to live there after he turned poor Madame de Cedillos and her daughters out,' said Dagobert, as they turned their mounts into the overgrown track along the little watercourse. 'Then after Pelerine fils was killed in a fire – in one of the stables, I think it was . . . it was just before Jackson was elected, so it must have been in '28 – Pelerine used the house for storage. Like Pelerine's plantation at Sept-Anges, the Alegre land is almost exhausted, and after the big hurricanes in '31, a lot of the land became too swampy to plant.'

January remembered, in his Paris days, reading about the 1831 hurricanes, but beyond writing to his sister Dominique to make sure she and their mother were safe (not that his mother would have written to him had God wiped three-quarters of Louisiana from the face of the earth), he had been far more occupied with the unrest in Paris following the takeover of the government by Louis-Philippe d'Orléans. Upon his return from France, he had seen Icarus Pelerine at a wedding reception, his garb the black coat of mourning and the left side of his face a twisted mass of scar tissue.

Bayou Joyeuse, on which the house at Alegre fronted, still looked deep enough here to admit small barges bearing hogsheads of sugar down to Sauvage, whence they could be hauled to the river. But even in darkness he could tell that the fields on the 'town' side of the house had not been planted in years. A decade after the disaster, ruin lingered in many places in the south of the state. These lower fields smelled of wet foliage and standing water, and the weeds that encroached on to the narrow track slapped January's legs and the flanks of his rented riding mule. When they neared the house itself, the feeble glow of the candle within his lantern showed him that only a few bollards choked in reeds and scuppernong remained of the plantation wharf, so he guessed that Alegre's sugar mill had been left to decay.

'Pelerine's land isn't producing more than a hogshead an acre these days, if that,' Dagobert went on. 'I don't know how much of that comes from Alegre, but from what I hear at the Exchange, he's still using the old kettle-battery equipment to refine it at Sept-Anges, so he needs the swamp timber. I think they use the mill here to store wood.'

Easier than using the house, January reflected, as they drew nearer and he tried to calculate what it would be like to haul wood up the gallery steps. Presumably Pelerine had stripped the Alegre mill of whatever equipment the man thought he could use, even before his son's death. The old Caribbean method of kettle batteries used vast amounts of fuel, and the newer vacuum-pan equipment needed significant investment. In either case, a second mill was an unnecessary liability.

They drew rein before the grayish shape of the house, and Dagobert gazed vaguely around him in the dim glow of the lantern. 'Felicita – Mademoiselle de Cedillos – said her father had a strongbox buried under a belvedere in the garden, where he kept money and copies of sale papers on the Negroes,' he said. 'Pelerine bribed some of the house servants to spy on him, especially once the war started. She said he hid everything of importance.' His eyes returned to the house, flanked on the 'lake' side by a field of sugar cane that came up to the wall, and on the 'town' side (as directions were reckoned in New Orleans) by a shaggy, soggy wilderness of palmetto, standing water, and tangles of swamp laurel and vines. 'Could you go look for that while I take the house?'

He had brought two spades and a couple of crowbars, tied on to the back of January's rented mule, and carried a big canvas satchel on his shoulder. As Dagobert hitched the horses among the willows beside the old landing, January reminded himself of how much five dollars would improve the tiny cushion of emergency funds – barely a pincushion, Rose had observed – buried in an oil jar in the cellar. The money was for doing whatever he was told. He took up lantern and spade while his employer made for the house itself, and surveyed what he could see of the surroundings in the heavy darkness.

A belvedere meant a formal garden, and a formal garden would lie at the front of the house, where it could be seen from the bayou. The arable land along Bayou Joyeuse was narrow – hence the use of every available foot of it, up to the wall of the house itself. But he winced, knowing what that would have meant to the inhabitants in terms of cane rats and snakes invading their bedrooms. It had probably been like that twenty-six years ago as well: these smaller, bayou-side plantations were like islands in what were called the 'trembling lands.' Even a few inches of elevation made a difference in the crop.

Behind the house, and on the lower ground in the direction of the Gentilly Road, Bayou Sauvage, and eventually New Orleans itself, would have been the kitchens and the stables. In competition for space with the sugar fields, the kitchen garden would have been small; the 'shell-blow grounds,' as the private vegetable patches of the slaves were called, smaller still. Even so, no plantation mistress would forego the pleasure of a formal garden – which guests would admire – for mere mundane considerations like fresh greens, fresh corn, tomatoes, and runner beans for the 'hands.' ('Hell, they get plenty salt pork and parched corn! What else they want?')

In the summer, even on a moonless night it would have been possible to locate the formal garden by the scents of honeysuckle and roses. Rose thorns attacking his legs like malicious dragons merely confirmed the fact that the granny knot of foliage between the bayou and the river-side front corner of the house had, in fact, been a garden, once upon a—

What was that?

He froze.

Stillness. Wind rattled the wall of cane on the other side of the house; brought the rank pong of water in the irrigation trenches between the cane rows.

Nothing, he told himself. Dagobert's horse had whinnied, that was all.

The sound came from the wrong direction. The horse – and the mule his relative had rented for him (*God forbid a mere henchman should ride a horse like a white man*!) – had been left near the landing, and he was ready to swear the sound had come from the hackberry thickets that had engulfed the one-time quarters, back beyond the kitchen.

In the chalky rectangle of the house, dim lantern-glow bobbed behind a window. Moved on. *Dagobert.*

January stood still and listened, almost sick with the pounding of his own heart.

No sound.

In the birdless silence of winter woods, when frogs and cicadas and every other thing with half a brain was asleep (*including snakes, thank God*!), that silence meant nothing.

But he knew they were there.

Or were they?

Who?

It didn't matter.

After what felt like half an hour and was probably only a few minutes, January resumed his cautious progress along the line of what had once been the box-wood hedge surrounding the garden. Where the dense box wood gave way to a looser screen of shoulder-high swamp laurel, he turned inward and to his left, forcing his way through the laurel but conscious of what had at one time been a clamshell path underfoot. Listening – straining his ears as if with sheer muscular force he could detect indistinguishable sounds.

To judge by the chunks of fallen pillars, the belvedere in the garden's center had been exactly like every other such ornamental structure January had seen in a hundred gardens in France, in Italy, in Britain. The feeble glimmer of his candle lantern showed him barely shapes of dark gray, black, and stygian-abysses-of-hell black, but his fingers told him that the obligatory pillars, instead of being marble, had been faked up from lathe and plaster. The little temple's foundations had been the soft New Orleans brick that crumbled with the onslaughts of a tropical climate. It was easy to find, beneath the matted blanket of weeds, the broken tiles that had covered the small, square pit in the center. Easy to pry apart with a spade. Despite the certainty that snakes, spiders, and scorpions were generally asleep at this time of year, January wrapped his hands in bandanas taken from his pockets before reaching down and lifting a small iron strongbox, which he scraped carefully on all sides before tucking under his arm.

As he did so, he never ceased to listen, barely dared to breathe. Not another sound.

Yet he knew he hadn't been mistaken. He had grown up, it seemed to him, listening, stretching his senses for some whisper of peril: a crazy-drunk and violent master on Bellefleur, and when he was free, and a grown man, listening for the threat of slave stealers, black-birders, kidnappers who could always find a buyer for a black man who couldn't prove he *wasn't* a slave.

And for sixteen years – from the moment he'd set foot on the wharf at Le Havre – the relief of not being afraid of every sound had been almost more than he could get used to.

Except of course when he and his friends discussed politics and had to keep watch against the secret police . . .

Even in a land dedicated to liberté, égalité, and brotherhood, it didn't do to talk too loudly about such things in connection with the government.

Crouched in the weedy thickets of what had been the garden, he knew himself invisible, his lantern hidden by the foliage. *When I cross to the house, they'll see my lantern.*

That knowledge clenched like an iron band around his chest.

But if I make it, I'll have a white man to vouch for me.

He didn't even know where they were, who they were . . .

Go . . .

He edged to the limit of the heavy shrubbery, spotted the grayish ghost of the plantation house, took a deep breath.

Stood and walked – fast – the strongbox under his arm, to where he knew the stair up on to the gallery had to be. (*Jesus, what if they're under the house*?) It was as if the corpse-pale hulk of rotting planks and gaping window holes sat on top of an eight-foot block of darkness. Weeds had invaded from the kitchen-garden side. On the lake-side, shoulder-high cane (Pelerine's crop, cut last year, he could tell, and not ripe for this year's harvest) formed a rustling wall. Anything could have been hiding there. Like every other French or Spanish plantation house in Louisiana, Alegre faced the waterway that would carry the crop to market, and extended two wings back to funnel what breeze there was, the whole surrounded by galleries.

The steps up to the gallery creaked ominously as January sprang up them. Even twelve years of neglect, in a climate like Louisiana's, had its effect. The overhang of the gallery roof made the gallery itself a pocket of night, nothing visible within. An army of slave stealers could have been standing there . . .

From the dark of the porch, January glanced behind him, trying and failing to pierce the overcast night. Quickly he turned back to the broken shutters of one set of French doors, reflecting how typical it was of Dagobert that even to enter a ruin, he had forced open the doors 'on the river side,' closest to New Orleans. The 'man's' side of the house, by French Creole reckoning.

We have to get out of here. There's something wrong . . .

He didn't know what.

Yet, he told himself, even as he slipped through the door. As Dagobert had reported, the parlor was still half-full of cut slats of wood stacked along one wall (*future barrel staves*?) and thicker chunks of tree trunk intended to be split into shingles. The dismantled limbs of what were probably looms huddled like monstrous spiders in the town-side half of the room. (*Does* anybody *in this country weave their own cloth anymore*?)

A footfall creaked somewhere overhead.

Attic. If Pelerine's son – and his family, presumably – had occupied the house up until 1828, surely the children (given the nature of children) would have found whatever was there to be found?

Had the de Cedillos women left trunks of their clothing, their dishes, their household goods, in the attic, when they'd been 'turned out'? How much time had Madame de Cedillos had to prepare for their departure? To search, herself, for whatever her husband may have left when he vanished?

At the creak of the ladder-like stair in one of the little 'cabinet' rooms at the sides of the house, January dodged behind a door into darkness. Moments later, Dagobert's voice called out, 'Is that you, Ben?'

January felt immediately better. His relative might not have the brains to claim, *Oh, yes, Ben here is my valet* – most kidnappers wouldn't steal a slave out from under the nose of his owner, no matter how much they thought they could sell him for in Texas; a lawsuit over title wasn't worth it. But at least he'd be a witness, to discourage swamp-rat bandits.

'It's me, sir.' He half-emerged from hiding, keeping his eye on the door out to the gallery. 'Did you find anything?'

He kept his voice low, hoping Dagobert would get the hint, but Dagobert called out excitedly, 'I did!'

Lantern light in a doorway, followed at once by the man himself. In triumph, Dagobert brandished his satchel, which now bulged with papers and what looked like ledger books. 'Cita was right: her father did hide plantation records in the attic, in two or three— Oh!' He stopped, eyes widening at the sight of the filthy, rusted box under January's arm. 'Oh, good job! Cita – er – Mamzelle de Cedillos – said . . .'

'I think we need to get out of here, sir,' whispered January firmly. 'I can't tell, but I think there's someone out there, watching us from the woods. We're close enough to the swamps that there's a good chance river pirates have seen our lights.' If they were pattyrollers – men hired by the local planters to ride the roads by night and capture night-wandering slaves – they'd have showed themselves by this time . . . And in any case, pattyrollers seldom ventured into the trembling lands of the back swamp.

Certainly they didn't do so during Carnival season.

'Pelerine's henchmen!' Dagobert's jaw thrust forward.

January thought it unlikely that Icarus Pelerine had maintained nightly guard on a half-ruined house full of barrel staves for the past thirteen years on the off chance that de Cedillos's daughter would attempt to search it – *for what*? Slave stealers on the hunt for runaways was a more likely guess. 'That could be, sir.'

Dagobert drew a pistol from his pocket, cocked it, his eyes grim in the shadow. With a peremptory wave for January to follow, he crossed the parlor, pressed himself against the side of the doorway, and looked out – beyond the dim puddle of lantern light, everything past the gallery's pilasters was pitch-black – then signed January to follow him across the gallery and down the steps.

January felt it again, that stabbing realization, *Something's wrong*, an instant before he understood what it was.

The horse and the mule were gone.

He would have heard them, smelled them – he would have seen the reflection of their eyes as they turned, startled, towards the light . . .

This he knew in a second, and in that second he flung his lantern from him, swatted Dagobert's from his hand, and as two shots cracked from somewhere in the darkness in front of them, he was already shoving the white man into the dense choke of shadow and cane beneath the house. In the next second, he grabbed the pistol from his companion's hand: they were invisible in the darkness and the muzzle flash would show them up. With all his strength, he pounded the underside of the gallery steps with the pistol butt, jumped up to hit the gallery boards above them, then dragged Dagobert deeper into the black abyss of foliage under the house.

Men's boots pounded the steps, thundered on the gallery overhead. 'Door open,' said a voice in English. Footsteps creaked into the house.

Keeping a firm grip on his companion's wrist, the strongbox jammed tight beneath his arm, January dragged Dagobert into the wall of sugar cane on the swamp side of the house. Shoved his head and shoulders down into the cover of the half-grown crop, and, stumbling among the ridges and the standing muck of irrigation trenches, they made their way into the swampy margins of the trembling lands.

SIX

It was dawn before they reached the Gentilly Road along Bayou Sauvage, daylight when the carriage of Dagobert Janvier's good friend Arnaud Chauvin – encountered by chance on the road – deposited them on the banquette before the house of Lollo Lemâitre, where Felicita de Cedillos had taken a room. ('You sure you won't come back to Bon Chance for breakfast, Bertie?' Chauvin had asked, pushing the wreath of golden laurel leaves out of his eyes. The four other gentlemen in the carriage – Praetorian Guard to Chauvin's blood-beslathered Caesar – had chorused approval: 'Ben won't mind walking back to town, will you, Ben?') Since they had met the returning revelers barely a hundred yards from the Chauvin plantation of Bon Chance, Chauvin had thrown the Praetorians bodily out of the vehicle and ordered the coachman to turn around and drive Dagobert – and only incidentally January – back to town.

The coachman, beside whom January sat, expressed no opinion of this addition to what had probably already been a very long night's work.

Both January and Dagobert kept a weather eye on the shell road behind them, and the wasteland of cypress and tupelo that made up most of the landscape on both sides of the bayou. January neither saw nor heard any sign of pursuit, but that, he knew, meant nothing. He had been watching, first through the coal-sack darkness of the night in the back swamp and then on the cautious retreat to Bayou Sauvage as soon as it grew light enough not to run into trees. At the moment, he was so tired he doubted he'd have seen a company of British grenadiers closing in on them.

A night spent listening to his companion's speculations about the evil machinations of Icarus Pelerine had not improved his mood.

He reminded himself firmly that he had made thirty dollars, of which he had already repaid twenty-five to Jules Gardinier for his daughter's uncompleted school term.

It was the kind of thing people remembered, when times improved.

Slave stealers. I refuse to believe even the archvillain Icarus

Pelerine has had watchers stationed around Alegre for the past twenty-six years.

Lollo Lemâitre, still handsome at forty-five, was cooking breakfast for the men who boarded in the two wings she'd had built on the back of the cottage her protector had left her. She kept the two rooms above the old kitchen for women, unusual in a world where a woman traveling or boarding alone was universally assumed to be an adventuress. She knew both January and Dagobert, however, and only nodded when Dagobert asked would she be good enough to see if Mamzelle de Cedillos was awake and, if so, announce his presence? He handed her a card, damp around the edges from a night spent in the ciprière along Bayou Joyeuse.

'You keep an eye on that cocoa, Ben.' She smacked the ladle into his hand. 'See it don't burn.'

'Yes, m'am.' January bent his head obediently, and she crossed the cramped yard to the stair like the warrior-queen Boudica on her way to – as a Louisiana song might have put it – give the Romans beans. No man in town would have had the temerity to attempt to climb those steps or knock on the doors of those rooms Mamzelle Lollo kept for women. There were rumors that the landlady had murdered the last man who'd tried, and sold his bones to the voodoos.

She was back almost at once, her narrow ivory features grave. 'She's not there, Michie Bertie.' Her light, gray-turquoise eyes went from January to Dagobert and back again, under brows drawn together with concern. 'She didn't sleep in her bed. Some of her things are gone – her hairbrush, her toothbrush, the dress she had on yesterday. This was on her pillow.'

She held out a bandana, which had been carefully knotted around a twenty-five-cent piece and an assortment of dimes and half-dimes. 'Her week's money, short fifteen cents. And this.' With her other hand she gave Dagobert the title page torn from *The Corsair's Bride*, on which was written Dagobert's name, followed by the word *Monina*, and a string of numbers.

'It's a code,' said January, seeing his employer's puzzled frown. 'A book code, by the way the numbers are hyphenated: 6-40, 7-93, 39-22 . . . But what book it is—'

'It's Shelley's *Fortunes of Perkin Warbeck*,' cried Dagobert. '*Monina* is the clever half-Moorish damsel who befriends its hero! We talked about it the other day, 'Ci— Mamzelle de Cedillos and myself. It was Paloma's favorite,' he added, features softening with the name. 'Mine, too. Mamzelle de Cedillos said there was a copy in Madame Lemâitre's parlor – she knew I'd understand! And I have a copy at home!'

The message, deciphered a half-hour later on the loggia beneath the rear gallery of the yellow-brick Janvier townhouse on Rue Royale, was short. *Steamboat carol town after noon eclipsed* . . . 'Eclipsed by what?'

'The steamboat *Eclipse* leaves this afternoon,' said January. 'It stops at Carrollton – they all do – and I'll bet you five dollars to the hole in a donut she'll be watching from the wharf.'

'You're right!' Dagobert's face kindled with admiration. 'That's my smart girl!'

The Janvier houseman and the gardener, engaged in digging fragments of moss and stray plumes of resurrection fern from between the paving bricks of the long courtyard, turned their heads at this outcry but immediately went back to their chore, evidently well used to their master's enthusiasms. The maid – who had paused in her mopping of the loggia's flagstones to glare at Dagobert when he'd pulled two chairs in from the garden beyond – icily ignored him. Behind the French doors that led indoors into the dining room, other servants could be glimpsed, polishing the glass of the doors, rubbing beeswax on the floor on hands and knees.

Great events were clearly afoot.

Dagobert's brow clouded again. '*Noon*? But she's in danger *now*! How can she get to Carrollton to meet us? If she had to flee from her rooms—'

'She had time to write out a message in a book code,' January pointed out, laying a hand on the Morocco-leather binding of the novel that lay on his knee. 'That's not something you do in a hurry, sir. You count pages and words. That tells us that something frightened her, but it wasn't an attack. And Madame Lemâitre's room is at the end of one of those wings, beside the gate into the yard. As tiny as that yard is, you know Madame would have heard men coming in. And she didn't say the room had been searched,' he added, as his relative opened his mouth to object to this temperate view. 'You know what kind of a housekeeper she is. She'd have noticed a pillow out of place, or a drawer not properly closed.'

The French door behind them opened and old Madame Sidonie's pug Thisbe catapulted forth in protective fury, to challenge the gardener – whom she had seen, January guessed, every day of her pampered life. Madame Marie-Hélène Janvier, following her, stopped in the doorway when she saw January. The pause was only for a moment; the tightening of her lips infinitesimal.

Then she said, 'My son,' as if January weren't present. With the death of her own son from her first marriage, and that of Dagobert's younger brother Clovis a few months after that, she had passionately claimed the nine-year-old Dagobert as her own and never referred to him as anything else. 'M'sieu Morrell is here with the preliminary contracts from M'sieu Forstall, M'sieu Livaudais, the Aubins and the St-Chinians.'

January and Dagobert, both already on their feet, bowed. She acknowledged Dagobert's greeting with a warm smile. January recognized the name of the Janvier family's business manager, whose father, back in 1803, had arranged the purchase of a handsome cottage on Rue Burgundy from a free colored labor contractor in his own name, the property being then conveyed to January's mother by deed of gift – it being against the law at that time for a white man to give property to a woman of color. Aurelian Morrell was a dry, thin man in his fifties, his eyes a light gray-hazel and his features little darker than the unfortunate M'sieu Couvillier's had been, though their shape was classically African.

In the presence of Madame Marie-Hélène, January knew better than to acknowledge that he even knew the man, who was in fact his mother's business manager as well. The man would be waiting for Dagobert, January guessed, in the townhouse's library, which was just as well. On those rare occasions when they did meet in her presence, Morrell would ignore him, both accepting the fact that it wouldn't do to remind Madame of the connection – though both knew perfectly well that she knew.

January picked up his rusty iron strongbox, tucked it under his arm, and bowed again. 'Madame,' he murmured in polite leave-taking, to which the widow of his mother's protector responded with the flicker of an eyelid and another, almost undetectable tightening of her thin lips.

To Dagobert he said, in a perfectly neutral voice, 'Until we meet again, sir.'

Dagobert nodded absently, as if they were not meeting again in a few hours on the steamboat wharves, to take the *Eclipse* to Carrollton.

But it was more than discretion, thought January, as he watched the son of St-Denis Janvier turn from him to follow his stepmother back into the house. The man's whole bearing and expression changed, as if the muscles that clothed his bones and made up the fabric of his face had shifted their orientation slightly, like an actor stepping out of a role . . . or into one.

'I shall inform M'sieu Morrell you'll be with him in half an hour.' Madame Marie-Hélène's voice faded into the house. 'You'll want to change clothes and wash – I'll send Strawberry upstairs with water and soap. I won't ask where you were last night, son, nor what you were doing, but I would like to think you had better taste than to bring that woman's children to my house . . .'

As he stepped into the brick-paved carriageway that led to the street, January couldn't make out the words of Dagobert's reply. But the tone of voice was that of a reasonable middle-aged man placating his mother, a man who dealt competently with the business of buying sugar from the planters and arranging fair prices from European middlemen. A man who knew how many hogsheads of sugar any planter in the parish was getting from his land, who managed the American side of his grandfather's wine import firm and made sure that the profits were soundly invested in shares of cotton presses, city real estate, banks, and land speculation. A man who would never think of riding to the midnight rescue of a girl in trouble.

'Benjamin.' The door to January's left – from the enclosed dimness of the carriageway into the dining room – opened, to reveal the thin, silver-haired shape of Sidonie Janvier, the actual head of the Janvier family, whatever Dagobert – and Madame Marie-Hélène – liked to think.

January bowed and removed his cap again. 'Madame.' This time he smiled with pleasure.

'Have you an engagement to play on Mardi Gras?' The old lady descended the shallow step into the carriageway. 'As you can hear from here,' she added, nodding back towards the courtyard, 'or would if you had poorer manners – Governor Roman has accepted my daughter-in-law's invitation to dinner and a ball on that evening, and she has decided to make it the social event of the season. Are you engaged?'

'No, m'am.' Generally his services were spoken for well before Christmas, but among other things, the drop in cotton prices had caused a number of the planter families to put off making plans for the end of Carnival.

'Good. I'd have thought Anna Marigny would have asked you by this time, since she's holding the wedding of that whey-faced niece of hers at the mansion that night. I daresay she's held off to see if she could get anyone cheaper.'

Having played at the Marigny mansion on the river – or at Marigny's plantation on the far side of the lake – for handsome sums, January only inclined his head and said, 'That wouldn't be for me to say, m'am.'

'The six of you, then,' said Madame. 'Yourself, Sefton, Cochon, the Bichets, and duCoudreau; sixty dollars. And if Marie-Hélène tries to talk you down, tell her that I said she was to speak to me. If she's determined to make Governor Roman's ball the most elegant affair of the season, you can't do that without decent music. You can tell her I said so.'

'I haven't the courage, m'am.' January bowed again, and the old woman laughed. 'Thank you. That's extremely generous, and I'll speak to the men today.'

'Nonsense, Benjamin. Despite what *some* people have to say, you *are* one of the family.'

January held out his hand to help her up the shallow step to the dining-room door again – one of the few circumstances under which it was proper for a black man to touch a white woman. As she laid her hand on his wrist, she turned to look through the bright archway into the courtyard and called out peremptorily, 'Thisbe!'

In the courtyard, the little dog sniffed all around the area newly mopped by the maidservant, defecated on the damp flagstones, and then dashed to her mistress's side with the air of a dog who has accomplished her duty.

1814

The only time January had ever known St-Denis Janvier to act out of character – to behave as something other than a respectable, reasonable French businessman – had been in the brazen heat of the autumn of 1814.

Only days previously, word had reached New Orleans of the British invasion force that had landed in Maryland, advanced virtually unopposed on Washington City, and burned the Capitol, the Navy yards, and the President's mansion, narrowly missing capturing President Madison himself in the process. Britain's primary ally in the war was Spain, and the only reason, January guessed, that Spanish troops had not invaded already from Mexico was because the Spanish were still trying to put down the uprisings in that portion of their empire.

He guessed also that many of the Spanish who had settled in Louisiana during the fifty-odd years of Spanish rule – mostly Isleños from the Canary Islands – would not have minded such an invasion in the slightest.

'*There shall be wars and rumors of wars*, as Our Lord warned us,' Rubal Gomez would reply, to January's questions. '*See that ye be not troubled*, he said, *for all these things must come to pass, and the end is not yet*.'

Gomez – a free man of color, a libré, the son of one of those Isleño settlers – had been out of the little surgery on Rue St-Pierre on the day, towards the end of September, that St-Denis Janvier had come in with General Jackson's *Proclamation to the Black Men of Louisiana*. 'I have volunteered in the New Orleans Rifle Company,' said the sugar broker quietly, as January ran his eye down the block of text: the Tennessee general's expressions of regret at the Congress's failure to recruit 'Negroes' into the militia. (*With the British arming and training the Red Sticks* – the anti-American, warrior faction of the Creek nation – *I'll just bet he regrets it.*) 'Jackson needs men. The word is that fifty British ships are on their way to the Gulf. Jackson has barely four thousand men, to stop them from taking the whole of the Mississippi Valley.'

January refolded the *Moniteur de la Louisiane* in which the *Proclamation* had been printed, then set it down on the long oak counter that divided the little office in two. The door stood open in a vain attempt to catch the river breeze, but the only thing that came in was flies, droning in the high ceiling or buzzing noisily in the three glass fly catchers set on the end of the counter. The smell of the gutters outside was almost palpable in the heat. 'I thought Congress sent men to Ghent to discuss a treaty,' he said.

'And if the British can get troops established on the Louisiana

Territory before that treaty's signed' – Janvier's dark eyes were grave – 'you can bet they're going to claim that the whole territory is part of the Spanish Empire still. Parliament will argue that the treaty that turned La Louisiane over to France in '03 wasn't valid. Spain is in chaos. King Ferdinand needs the British if he's going to keep his throne. If the British take New Orleans – if they take the mouths of the Mississippi – do you really think they're going to pull their troops out and hand nearly a million square miles of land back to the Congress?'

Too many things flickered through January's mind, as if he thumbed through a stack of reports, accumulated not only over the course of 'Mr Madison's War,' but for the whole of his short lifetime. British Canada. The money to be made from furs in that territory, as well as that of New Spain beyond the borders – which had been left deliberately unclear – of Louisiana. The ongoing chaos in what had been called New Spain. Royalist troops fighting those who had followed the priest Hidalgo y Costilla towards an independent union of Mexican states . . .

Britain's alliance with the Shawnee confederation, with the militant Creeks and the other native nations . . .

And what does any of this have to do with me?

White folks' business . . .

'Last spring,' he said slowly, 'when Napoleon abdicated – when it was clear that Britain could now turn her attention to us – you remember I joined the Orleans Volunteers, sir. And what we ended up doing – what the black members of the Volunteers ended up doing – was being sent out to look for runaway slaves in the ciprière. Most of the white men in the Volunteers didn't even want us to be given weapons. They were afraid it would "give us ideas."'

Even the men of color – the lighter-complected men of color, the quadroons and the octoroons and the musterfinos – had seemed uncomfortable with the idea of men who looked like they should have been slaves walking around with rifles in their hands. (How many times had he heard his mother declare – among her fellow plaçées – 'We're not *black*, we're *colored*!')

'Things have changed,' said Janvier. 'He needs help. Jackson has fewer than a thousand regulars. Maybe another two thousand militia troops added to that. Plus volunteers. Our country needs help.'

'And what,' asked January quietly, 'is "our country," sir? The

United States? Whose Congress paid Napoleon – who doesn't even rule France anymore – fifteen million dollars for the privilege of telling us who can vote and who can't? Who can hold property and who they can give it to? Who you can sell sugar to and for how much? I've lived under four different governments and I'm only twenty-one. When you were born, this country was French, ruled by the same king who ruled over your family in Bordeaux and then later in Saint-Domingue. By the time you came here, this country, this city, this street outside the door there beside you, was Spanish, and you had to swear your allegiance to the King of Spain. I was born under the flag of Spain, sir. And then when I was a little boy somebody told me that I – and this building and that street and this town – were French instead, though the King of France was long gone. And then three weeks later I was told that suddenly I was – everything was – a part of America.'

For a time Janvier said nothing. Even in his childhood, January had regarded this man – this neat, tubby white man who had lived for three and a half years like a husband in the cottage on Rue Burgundy – not as a substitute father but as his mother's business partner. But he knew well that this white man had been under no obligation whatsoever, when he'd bought the beautiful Livia from her master, to buy her two children as well, lest she pine. (*And he didn't know her very well if he thought she'd do that*!) St-Denis Janvier had always treated him, and his sister Olympe, with an adult civility, as if it were a matter of course that he would pay the fees for the St-Louis Academy for Young Gentlemen of Color – not that anyone in the academy had ever regarded a boy as African-black as Ben January as a gentleman or anything close to it. Later he had seemed to regard it as an accepted part of the purchase price, that of course he would pay for January's apprenticeship to Rubal Gomez, and for his lessons with the Austrian musician Herr Kovald. He had paid Olympe's school fees at the Convent of the Ursulines as well, for as long as she could be forced to attend.

In his well-cut plum-colored coat and discreetly stylish waistcoat, St-Denis Janvier looked as he had always looked: a good man, not a great one. A respectable, unimaginative man whose whole heart was given to the making of money. Not a man to pick up a gun and put his plump flesh out where it could be torn apart by British musket balls.

'Our country is Louisiana,' he replied at last. 'It is the people we live with, work with. It is, as you say, this building, this city, the street outside the door. Your mother. Your sisters. Your friends.' He laid his hand on the folded newspaper, with its advertisements already heralding sale of Alabama land taken less than a month ago from the Creeks, or offering cut-rate prices on English and Spanish goods without any clear mention of how these enemy wares had been acquired. Proclaiming Niggers For Sale or promising rewards for runaways.

'More than that,' the sugar broker went on, 'General Jackson is willing to pay a fair price – finally – for what he asks of the men of color in this state. He's offering a bounty of one hundred and sixty acres of farmland – government land – to any who'll sign up.'

January fell silent at that, his breath caught behind his lips.

A hundred and sixty acres.

Land.

'My son is joining with me,' continued Janvier. Even then, January had wondered what Madame Marie-Hélène had had to say to that. 'I hope you'll reconsider, and add your strength, your arms, to the fight, Ben. We need every man.'

As his mother's protector left the shop, January reflected on what his own mother would say, should he decide to step out in front of that hail of death for the benefit of a Congress that was perfectly happy to leave men in slavery – men like his father, whom he had never seen again. ('Oh, don't be silly, Ben . . .')

While he was an apprentice to Gomez, he earned what he could, giving lessons on the piano for two Spanish reals per hour and playing at the local subscription balls – both for whites and the so-called Blue Ribbon balls for the white men and their mistresses of color. But he had continued to live in the garçonnière at his mother's house, the room – traditionally separate from the main dwelling – in which the grown son of a household slept before his marriage. Before he became quite an adult.

A hundred and sixty acres.

When St-Denis Janvier had bought the beautiful slave woman Livia from her owner – with her two children thrown in casually, for what was called in this country *lagniappe* – January had been told that, like his mother, he would now be free. But as long as he lived in the garçonnière behind the cottage that Janvier had given

Livia – as long as he depended on Janvier's generosity for books, for clothing, for any extra expenses above Gomez's bare support – he had not felt free.

A hundred and sixty acres would make him free.

SEVEN

January saw Mamzelle de Cedillos while Dagobert was still scanning the Carrollton landing and biting his fingernails on the upper 'boiler' deck of the big side-wheeler *Eclipse*. The only prospective passengers in sight were a grouchy-looking American and his wife – the man checking his watch repeatedly and chewing his cigar as if he would break it in half. Their valet and maid stood a little back from them with enough luggage to see the King of France through a Rhineland military campaign. There was a nursemaid also, and two small children whom their parents stolidly ignored, and no wonder: some Satan-inspired relative had gifted the boy with a toy drum, the girl with a tin whistle. January made a bet with himself as to which of the boat's other passengers would steal these instruments en route and drop them overboard, and how soon.

There was no sign of a woman waiting to board alone.

'I knew it!' Dagobert's fists tightened convulsively on the rail. 'I knew we should have gone after her this morning! Pelerine *did* trace her somehow—'

He moved towards the steps to the lower deck, and January scooped up the flour sack that held the iron strongbox and strode after him. One didn't grab a white man by the arm, no matter how long you'd known him . . .

'Sir, if we go ashore here, what can we accomplish? If she misses the boat, she'll find a way to follow it—'

'No!' He turned an anguished face to January. 'She's in trouble, I know it! His men found her—'

Down below on the bow deck, the deckhands were taking up the gangway, unshipping the long poles that lay beside the rails, ready to push away from the wooden platform of the wharf. Smoke belched afresh from the *Eclipse*'s twin chimneys, and the nursemaid shouted, 'You children get away from them boxes!' as her charges disappeared into the labyrinth of crates and barrels at the front of the boat.

Dagobert opened his mouth to call down to the deck boss to replace the gangway, and at that moment a slight, dark figure stepped around the corner of the woodpile at the foot of the levee, and darted across the open ground in a flutter of skirts and cloak, frantically waving a passage receipt in one gloved hand.

Still halfway up the steps, January glanced automatically at the whole view of the landing, and could see no one either following her or taking any visible notice of her progress. What the deckhands said, as they pushed the *Eclipse* the few feet back to the wharf and ran the gangplank out once more, was fortunately in the 'gombo' patois of the cane patch and unintelligible to anyone but January and Mr American's valet. The valet put a hand quickly to his mouth to hide a grin.

But the deckhands knew damn well they'd be in for a couple of licks across the shoulders with the end of a rope, if not worse, if they left a white lady on the dock. Hard, sweaty hands reached to grasp the daintily gloved fingers and take her satchel. The deck boss even managed jocular congratulations.

If anyone had pursued Mamzelle de Cedillos to the landing, they didn't show themselves.

'Thank God!' Dagobert plunged down the remainder of the narrow steps.

Following him more slowly – and watching, from the elevation of the steps, whether anyone on the bow deck seemed to be taking an interest in the meeting – January didn't precisely recognize Felicita de Cedillos. But her resemblance to her sister Paloma's miniature was accentuated by the old-fashioned frizzle of tiny, dark curls that framed her forehead and temples, beneath a high-crowned bonnet twenty years out of date. The cloak that she huddled about her in the sharp chill of the river breeze was faded and shabby, and topped with an equally dilapidated paisley shawl. Yet he had an impression of fawn-like lightness beneath the somber garments, and when he came closer, he saw that her face was thin, a delicate oval beautifully shaped. Even the lines around her eyes – which were dark beneath a bower of lashes – seemed somehow elfin, and her pert little nose was red with cold.

Dagobert was already gripping her hands. 'Felicita – Mademoiselle de Cedillos . . . You're freezing!'

She shook her head quickly, as if the cold were the least of her concerns. 'M'sieu Janvier, thank God! All the way here I was praying . . . Did you see if anyone followed me? Watched me?'

Dagobert looked nonplussed at the question. January shifted the flour sack on his shoulder and touched the brim of his hat. 'If you'll excuse me, m'am, I watched you cross the batture and saw no one come after you.'

'Thank you!' Her smile was indeed the glow of an alabaster lamp at dusk. 'Thank God!' Then she glanced inquiringly at Dagobert, who seemed to wake from an enchanted daze.

'Mademoiselle de Cedillos, Ben Janvier.'

January bowed and handed her his card, the easiest way to establish that yes, he was a free man and not his companion's valet. Below his name on the pasteboard were the tiny letters FMC, and he guessed that nobody needed to explain to this planter's daughter how he happened to have the same last name as the white man at his side. Had he been a servant, he would have been introduced as Ben or possibly not introduced at all. 'May I take your bag, Mamzelle?'

'Thank you – if it's no trouble.' She laid her kid-gloved hand on Dagobert's proffered elbow, let him lead her up the steps to the boiler deck, and along the narrow walkway to where the deck widened over the stern of the boat. The sharp wind lifted back that nondescript cloak to show a schoolgirlish blue dress at least twenty years out of fashion. Yet it was unthinkable that two men – and one of them black – would enter the tiny Ladies' Parlor, or that a man of color would even contemplate crossing the threshold of the larger Main Saloon. It being Carnival season – the time of business and of buying in the city – even that small area at the rear of the boat was crowded with barrels of flour, cornmeal, and salt pork, for the plantations upriver. Dagobert removed his coat and, shivering, laid the garment over the top of a crate for Mamzelle de Cedillos to sit on.

'And thank you' – Mamzelle raised trusting dark eyes to Dagobert's – 'for meeting me. I knew you would understand.'

January dutifully swallowed any repetition of the comments Lollo Lemâitre had made about people who tore the title pages out of their landlady's books.

'Were you attacked?'

In the harshness of the pale spring light she was definitely no longer a young girl, but there was an innocence about her gaze – as well as the skillful application of rice powder and rouge – that made her seem much younger.

'Not . . . not really.' The delicate brows tugged together. 'Men stepped suddenly out of a doorway and tried to hustle me into a closed carriage on Rue de l'Hôpital. Thank heavens there were so many people all around that I was able to pull clear of them, and a couple of sailors came to my rescue. I was able to disappear into the crowd.' She shuddered at the memory. 'But it was planned. It had to have been. One of the men, I had noticed on the pavement behind me several times as I came up the street from the market.' Her French was good, though with the trace of the Spanish 'I' and 'R'. And she used the Spanish word – acera – rather than the New Orleanian's word for the brick footpath, banquette. 'They have been watching me, I know it. I left a note, fled the house where I had been staying . . .'

'*Pelerine*.' The muscles of Dagobert's jaw bulged with anger. 'His men were watching Alegre. They shot at us, too.'

Her gloved fingers flew to her lips, her eyes aghast with guilt.

'Nevertheless,' he continued and held the satchel out to her, stuffed with the papers and ledger books he had found in the plantation attic. As the woman's expression changed to wonder and joy, Dagobert fairly snatched the flour sack from January's shoulder, opened it, and set the iron strongbox on top of the nearest barrel with the air of Galahad pulling the Grail out of his waistcoat pocket.

'Oh!' Countenance radiant, she turned upon him eyes brimming with tears of gratitude, as if she assumed that it was he who had unearthed the box and had simply had January carry it.

January hoped she wouldn't be disappointed in its contents. He hadn't mentioned to Dagobert that when he'd scraped the rust and dirt off the box and oiled its hinges (when he could have been sleeping upon his return from the Janvier townhouse that morning), he'd had a look inside it as well. From his mother's long-ago efforts to get him work at Mr Chew's bank, he recognized that other than a fire insurance policy and a couple of gambling markers, most of the dozen sealed packets of paper inside were drafts or bills of exchange on various state and private banks. He recognized the names of about half of them, jotted on the outside of the packets in pencil: the Imports Bank of Mobile, the Planters Bank of Natchez, Finlay's Exchange Bank of Louisiana . . . a common means of paying planters for cotton or sugar, facilitating the transfer of funds from buyer to seller. Most of them – with the exception of the Bank of Louisiana – hadn't survived the crash of '37.

In other words, worthless, thanks to President Jackson's fiscal policies. Given that planters lived on credit, from crop to crop, he guessed that this fragile woman would be lucky if even one of the drafts would repay her fare from Havana.

Yet she breathed, 'Thank you!' as if box and satchel brimmed with gold. Tears flooded her dark eyes. 'Oh, Monsieur Janvier—'

'Dagobert,' he corrected, smiling down at her gently. '*Monsieur Janvier* did for me when you were six, Mamzelle. Surely I've earned a mark of your regard?' He almost kissed her hand.

She turned her eyes aside and would have blushed, January guessed, had she not been shivering in the cold. 'Monsieur Dagobert,' she murmured. 'I am . . . eternally in your debt.' Then she smiled through those preposterously long lashes at January. 'And you, also, Monsieur Janvier.' Like Dagobert, she used the polite 'vous' with his name: Et vous aussi . . .

Dagobert she called 'tu.' As a sister would a brother. Or a maiden her fiancé.

'When I fled Madame Lemâitre's I went and took a room on the Rue Crozat, near the turning basin,' she went on after a moment. January frowned – and Dagobert scowled – at mention of that grimed and rowdy neighborhood. 'I don't think anyone followed me. Cresson Joubert is the woman's name. I paid her almost everything I had to keep quiet—'

Dagobert dug instantly in his pocket.

'No—' Mamzelle protested but didn't pull away when he dropped five silver dollars into her lap. She pulled a handkerchief from her sleeve; pressed it to her trembling lips.

'You call me Dagobert like a brother,' he reminded her, smiling. 'And a good brother looks out for his little sister.' The tenderness in his voice, January reflected, was anything but brotherly – but it was just as clear to him that his relative wasn't aware of this.

Her small hands closed around the silver. Excited cries from the children on the deck below made January turn his head, to behold above the trees the stumpy red belfry of the Church of St Charles on the Destrehan plantation.

'We'll look for you at Cresson's, Mamzelle,' promised January. 'I take it this little voyage is to fool your pursuers into thinking you've left town, if they did manage to follow you to Carrollton?'

Her self-command returned at the prosaic analysis of logistics, and she managed a smile. 'And no,' she added, placing two fingers to Dagobert's lips as he opened his mouth to speak. 'You gentlemen must disembark here at Red Church – yes, please, I insist. I cannot risk having you followed to me. I shall make my way back to town from Bayou Sara—' Her little fist tightened around the silver as she named the next likely stop. 'I shall send you word. But believe me' – she straightened her slender shoulders – 'I will not leave New Orleans. I will not leave Louisiana, so long as my father's name is scorned as the name of a traitor.'

The white blink of flag among the trees signaled that yes, indeed, there was something – cargo or letters – to go upriver from the Destrehan landing. January felt the change in the *Eclipse*'s rhythm as the engines slowed. At this time of year it was a near certainty that a signal was out for a downriver boat as well, to take some of the Germans of this neighborhood to town, though heaven only knew how long before one arrived.

'I will not leave so long as my home remains the stolen property of my father's enemy. I owe it to him, to my poor mama, and to Paloma . . .'

Her voice broke a little, and she looked aside, knuckles pressed to her lips. Then, meeting Dagobert's eyes again, she continued steadily, 'I will remain.'

A break in the clouds flung spangles of sunlight on the sloshing wake behind the *Eclipse*; touched the tears that still beaded her lashes like chips of diamond. Dagobert fell to his knees beside her, gathered her hands in his, pressed them to his breast, exactly – January reflected suddenly – like the hero at the end of act one of a melodrama.

'So what is it,' inquired Hannibal Sefton the following day, huddling deeper in the folds of the plaid shawl he had wrapped around his shoulders over a threadbare greatcoat, 'about the whole situation that puts sand in your back teeth?'

'I don't know.' January considered the question. At this hour of the day – as the extended hour of French Creole 'Sunday dinner' and its afternoon sociabilities were drawing to a close – Rue Dauphin was still relatively quiet: quiet for a Sunday afternoon during Carnival, and St Valentine's Day at that. Whenever they crossed a street, the jangle of music and song blew upon them from Rues

Bourbon and Royale, where young gentlemen were already parading with their friends in costume: Greek gods, imps from Hell, conquistadores with Indian maidens in tow.

They had just finished two hours at the Miragouin townhouse on Rue Chartres, where a children's dance had been given in honor of seven-year-old Marie-Isobelle Miragouin with every child from every dance class in the French Creole world of the French Town attending in miniature costumes (more Greek gods, conquistadores, and Indian maidens). The uptown American Protestants would expire with indignation at the thought of such an event sullying the Sabbath, Valentine's Day notwithstanding. In two hours they were due at the old Théâtre St-Philippe – now converted full-time into a ballroom – for a subscription ball to raise money for the new St Patrick's church in the American sector. With any luck, they would find leftover gumbo waiting for them in the kitchen at Rue Esplanade. Madame Miragouin did not believe in sharing even the leftovers of an entertainment with the musicians.

On top of Mass that morning, it had made for a tiring day. And tomorrow morning – early – was the duel between Evard Aubin (who'd been Bastien Damoreau's most ardent supporter) and Gontran Mabillet (who didn't really care about the now-deceased M'sieu Couvillier but whom Bastien Damoreau had insulted a few weeks previously over a hand of cards). But, January reflected, together the surgeon's fee and the children's dance would cover the cost of firewood for the remainder of the month.

January thought back over yesterday's meeting on the *Eclipse*. On what it was that had triggered the sense that something wasn't right.

That Mademoiselle de Cedillos was being less than straightforward with her two knights errant.

Or one knight errant and one large, black, and unwilling Sancho Panza.

'Her handkerchief,' he said at last.

'Ah,' said the fiddler. 'And was there magic in the web of it, like Desdemona's? Were the worms hallowed that did breed the silk? Was it dyed in mummy wrought from the preserved hearts of maidens? A disgusting thought and scarcely conducive of amour . . . have you ever *seen* "mummy"?'

'I have no idea,' returned January gravely. 'But the handkerchief looked almost new: unstained and un-yellowed by laundry soap. Very fine lawn, almost gauze, with an inch and a half of black lace border, I presume for her mother, and for her sister Paloma, back in Spain. And delicate. Not the kind of handkerchief a woman who has been slaving for pennies in Seville for twenty-six years would buy. Her gloves weren't brand new, but they were expensive kid, and they hadn't been re-dyed or mended.'

He frowned as they turned the corner on to Rue Esplanade, where a couple of very drunk Biblical prophets – one of them appropriately Noah, dragging a line of wheeled toy cows, horses, elephants, and camels on a string – greeted them with a whoop and hurled handfuls of flour over them. Dodging these, he and the fiddler proceeded in the direction of the swamp (and of January's house), and as he dusted flour from his sleeves, he cast back in his mind, almost hearing the voice of his first wife, the beautiful dressmaker Ayasha . . .

'Her bonnet was an older style but hadn't been re-dyed or mended either. The plumes, and the ribbons, were new. And those old-style tight curls around her face take a lot of effort to achieve. They looked freshly done, too.'

'What, those little snail shells over the forehead?' Hannibal fluffed beneath his hat brim and at his graying temples. 'That's an hour at least with a curling iron. Not bad, for a woman who was being pursued by hired bravos.'

'Completely aside from her forethought to pack her curling tongs as she fled for her life,' said January, 'it's the style her sister favored back during the war. I suspect she adopted it deliberately, and I don't believe Dagobert even realized quite why he saw in Mamzelle the reflection of his lost love.

'She's thirty-two,' he went on, as they mounted the stair to the gallery of his house. 'By her own account she's been living in dire poverty, first in Havana and then in Seville, for twenty-six years. A woman that age living in dire poverty almost always loses teeth. And her face would have been more lined. Her skin would have a different tone.'

In the parlor, when they entered (quite properly through January's study on the river side of the house), Rose was saying to Germaine and Aglaëa, 'Well, obtrunco implies a slashing or chopping-into-little-pieces sort of slaughter, whereas decido means a beating or clubbing-to-death activity. There's gumbo and rice in the kitchen, optime dilecte, and what's left of the king cake . . .'

She gestured with the papers in her hand, presumably the girls' translations from yesterday's lesson.

'The Romans liked to be accurate about such matters,' agreed Hannibal, as January removed his hat and bent to kiss his scholarly bride. 'I expect their readership truly wanted to know. And a woman can work for her living,' he added, as he and January passed through the French doors at the back of the dining room and across the back gallery, 'and still accrue sufficient funds to afford Olympian Dew and crushed strawberries to keep her complexion unlined and her smile dazzling. Particularly if beauty is a requisite of her job.'

In the kitchen, the boys flung themselves on their father, so Hannibal crossed to the great brick hearth where a Dutch oven had been three-quarters buried in smoldering coals, and hunkered down to fill two yellow-ware bowls. Dinner had been over an hour ago, and while January and the fiddler ate – with one eye on January's silver watch – at the worktable, Ti-Gall, Zizi-Marie, and Chou-chou came and went around them, finishing the washing-up in the scullery.

'Wash the forks and spoons,' ordered Professor John, toddling purposefully after his ox-like cousin-in-law. 'And fold up the napkins . . .' The tin whistles, thankfully, had disappeared. (*I owe the Virgin Mother another candle . . . Did the Christ child drive her insane with a toy whistle when He was three*?)

'I may be doing Mamzelle de Cedillos a great injustice,' said January, when he and Hannibal finished and crossed the courtyard again to the back gallery ('Wash your dish, Papa,' his son called imperatively after him. 'Hannibal, you wash your dish, too . . .'). 'And Dagobert a greater one. But . . . she looks like a woman who's been well looked after. And that's not the story she's telling.'

It was growing dark by this time, and candlelight glowed from the kitchen behind them, from the parlor, from the windows of the house next door. Rose was reading out loud to the girls from *Le Figaro* but lowered the paper with a smile as January bent to kiss her again. 'Are the directors of the ball this evening going to make you dress up as cupids?'

'Would you insist on such a costume if you knew Cochon was going to be playing?' January countered, and her quicksilver smile flickered into a genuine laugh at the thought.

'Don't mention it to him – you know he'd revel in it . . .'

'Madame Miragouin had all the servants at the children's dance dress as fairies,' said January. 'We had a narrow escape there—'

The girls giggled at the thought as January ducked through the bedroom door, pulled off his coat, and threw open the armoire.

'Mamzelle de Cedillos has all the mannerisms of a sweet young girl,' he continued, as Hannibal shut the bedroom door against Rose's quiet commentary on the French King's architectural taste. 'Almost too sweet . . . Like an actress who's slightly too old for the role she's playing.'

'Ah,' said Hannibal. '*Look like the innocent flower / but be the serpent under 't.*'

Shivering, January slipped into shirt and waistcoat, and fastened his cuffs. Brought that lovely oval face again to mind, those adoring brown eyes. 'There's something about that vow to clear her father's name – to foil his enemy and reclaim the family plantation – that strikes me as . . . improbably naïve. Especially for someone who says she journeyed alone in the poorest class on an immigrant ship to get here. It's the sort of thing you'd read in a three-volume novel by someone who's never actually been on a plantation. Or something you'd see in an opera. She's too old – and she impresses me as being too intelligent – not to know how much money she'd need to bring a neglected sugar plantation back into production. Particularly one that small.'

'She could want it to sell.' Hannibal broke off in a spasm of coughing, one hand pressed to the ribs January knew were still unhealed.

For a time, January was silent, watching him worriedly while his hands automatically wrapped and tied the white linen of his formal cravat. 'She could,' he agreed at length. 'But I can't imagine how proving that her father didn't actually organize rebelling slaves to attack Jackson's forces during the battle is going to get the Louisiana courts to take that land – from a Spanish grant by a deposed king – away from villainous Icarus Pelerine and return it to her. Not at this late date.'

He slipped back into his long-tailed coat – after a final brush to get the last of the flour off the lapels – and made sure his gloves were in the pocket. 'And she's too old not to know that it would cost her a fortune to bring the matter to law. Not if she's been raised in poverty.'

'Not to mention' – the fiddler straightened up – 'the question of how a planter could spare men for twenty-six years – especially at this time of the year – to keep guard over his ill-gotten lands.'

'Exactly,' agreed January. 'But she was genuinely frightened – and genuinely startled to hear that Bertie and I had actually been attacked, I think.'

'If someone was watching her,' pointed out Hannibal, 'they could easily have followed your enterprising kinsman—'

'He's no kin of mine.'

'—from town, you know. Has she mentioned money?'

'No.'

'Never trust a woman who doesn't keep her eye on the purse strings.' Hannibal sighed, stood, handed January his tall-crowned silk hat, and picked up his own. 'It is buckler, sword, and sinew – it is, in a word, a woman's safety, and the wise among them know it. Did either you or the trusting Dagobert find money at Alegre?'

'No.' January shook his head. 'At least not in the strongbox under the belvedere.' He studied the mirror for a moment; settled the tall silk hat on his head. 'And I can't imagine a planter would be holding any substantial sum even in the weeks after harvest, once he'd got his debts paid off. It was pretty clear that what she wanted from the first was for someone to search the house while she herself stayed in hiding.'

'And what did Young Lochinvar discover in the attic?'

'Household accounts, he said. I'm not sure what they could tell him, unless de Cedillos hid a note of some kind in between the pages.' He gathered up his greatcoat and music satchel, then stepped through the bedroom door long enough to blow a kiss to Rose—

'. . . *chosen to cover the walls of this monument with approximately a hectare of images of caracoling horses and dying men* . . . Be safe and stay warm, Benjamin, Hannibal . . . *including tributes to the Revolution that killed half his family* . . .'

—and ducked back through the bedroom and out on to the gallery, Hannibal at his heels with his violin case under his arm. The party that afternoon had exhausted him, January could see, and there was all the night to get through yet.

'My instinct is to wash my hands of the whole business,' January went on as they descended to the banquette. 'In spite of the fact that there's nothing visibly amiss about Mamzelle de Cedillos, except the handkerchief and gloves. I would do it,' he added with a sigh, 'if I hadn't already given twenty-five of the thirty dollars Dagobert Janvier paid me to Jules Gardinier.'

'*Ay, there's the rub*,' agreed Hannibal and sidestepped a marching gang of what appeared to be very drunk Crusaders, singing '*Ching-a-ring-a ching ching* . . .' 'And no chance of talking sense into Dagobert Janvier?'

'You've never met Dagobert Janvier, have you?'

EIGHT

Despite his inclination to believe that Friday night's attackers were in fact simply slave stealers, January took obscure comfort in the fact that men who spoke in the rough accents of Kentucky river-rats probably wouldn't be admitted to the St Patrick's Valentine's Day subscription ball. But of course whoever had the money to hire Kaintuck assassins to pursue Mademoiselle de Cedillos would certainly have had the price of a one-dollar ticket. And under the masks, who could tell?

From behind a screen of potted plants in a corner of what had been the stage of the old Théâtre St-Philippe, January looked out across a dance floor built above the former parterre. Chandeliers shed an intimate golden light and dripped beeswax on swaggering cavaliers and Columbines, periwigged courtiers and fairy princesses, Harlequins and Walter Scott Highlanders and an extremely unconvincing counterfeit of Andrew Jackson.

He didn't need the recollection of Bastien Damoreau's embittered tirade to know that any of them could have been an imposter. There were rumors every Carnival season of passionate flirtations by wealthy matrons which had ended in the mortifying realization that they'd been making sheep's eyes at somebody's octoroon cook.

As usual, he recognized a good half of the maskers by their costumes. The banker Mr Chew, though masked and conservatively clad in his old militia uniform, could be immediately identified by the clusters of financiers and planters who kept coming up to him – January had seen their costumes every Carnival season for the past six years. Bernard Marigny retained the gold-and-crimson habiliments of Jove, with his shining thunderbolt and a beard and wig like the Golden Fleece. Tonight he had added the delicate figure of a swan, like a pharaoh's cobra ouraeus to his jeweled crown, and swan's down now trimmed his bullion-crusted sleeves.

'. . . *and shew'd how Leda lay supinely press'd*,' murmured Hannibal, with a nod towards a voluptuous, heavily masked and wigged lady in chiton and himation nearby, cradling a small, stuffed silk doll of a swan in her arms, '*Whilst the soft snowy swan sate hov'ring o'er her breast . . .*'

Whether 'Leda' was white or the fairest of fair musterfinos was impossible to guess, under a vizard mask and a solid maquillage of rice powder and carmine. In either case, Marigny's contribution to St Patrick's building fund would have guaranteed silence on the part of the ball's organizers. Madame Marigny – clothed inevitably as Hera with a crown of peacock plumes so high it threatened to ignite every time she passed a chandelier – didn't give 'Leda' so much as a glance. With the stately grace so frequently remarked by poets from Hesiod to Byron, she moved grandly through the clusters of non-dancers along the fringes of the chalk-patterned dance floor, introducing a young lady (*Hebe*? speculated Hannibal, observing the slim form in the white robes. *Hestia*?) to every influential woman in French Creole society. 'M'am Marigny's niece,' identified Cochon Gardinier, between a gavotte and the Lancers Quadrille. 'The one getting married on Mardi Gras.'

'Ah,' said the fiddler. 'That would explain Hercules over there by the punchbowl.' He nodded towards a spindle-shanked young gentleman in a lion skin and a tunic liberally stuffed with wadding and buckram at the shoulders. 'Hebe's prospective bridegroom . . . One wonders if we behold a preview of the nuptial costume.' He glanced inquiringly at January, who only sighed and shook his head.

'I wouldn't put it past Marigny.' Rumors were already flying about the proposed fête – scheduled opposite the Janvier festivities in honor of Governor Roman – and the beautiful Madame Marigny's determination to make her niece's wedding the event that people would talk about in years to come, when they spoke of the Carnival season of 1841. God knew they were still talking about the solid-gold dinner service the little planter had ordered when he'd hosted the Duc d'Orléans – later to become the current King of France . . .

'I hear tell' – Cochon brought up a bent-willow chair that creaked alarmingly under his weight – 'that Marigny's going to have his guests ride through the streets in a procession, so I'm guessing that we're going to see Hercules in that outfit at some point that evening.'

'A *parade*?' Young gentlemen, of course, were always forming impromptu processions in costume, but this sounded like a full-dress, planned spectacle.

'Down Rue Esplanade.' The fat man grinned. 'Ten coaches full of flowers and the Orleans Parish militia's marching band.'

January briefly covered his eyes with his hand.

Jacques Bichet put in, 'I hear M'am Marigny was fit to bust a corset string when she heard we was already booked to play at M'am Janvier's that night. She went and stole some French feller from the opera, and had to chase all over town to get two German violin teachers and Damien Jouet to play for him . . .'

'Food at Marigny's'll be better, anyway,' surmised Philippe duCoudreau. 'Marigny's got that French chef, but he went and hired Antoine Alciatore from over to Rue St-Louis for the evening. Look there,' he added, nodding to where the beautiful Hera was talking to the clearly flattered Madame Fortier – Marie-Hélène Janvier's most socially prominent friend. 'She's been asking every one of M'am Janvier's little coven—'

'Five cents says Madame Janvier calls Madame Marigny out,' offered Hannibal, amid general grins, and January played an opening riff on his piano, warning them it was time to get back to work. But January could tell the exact moment when someone broke the news to Madame Marie-Hélène, upon her entrance in a plum-colored velvet houppelande and a jeweled henin taller than some footmen January had seen, that her gala event would now be in competition with a parade down Rue Esplanade in honor of *that Spanish woman* (as Madame Marie-Hélène generally referred to Madame Marigny) and her commonplace niece.

If looks could kill, there would have been nothing left of Madame Marigny but a pile of ashes and a couple of peacock feathers.

With a flourish, he led the music into the quadrille.

And beyond the dreamlike hall with its lines of private boxes around the walls, beyond the gambling room and the marble-flagged vestibule and the dark-red curtains, January was very aware of the foggy darkness that awaited him outside when the music would finally circle to its close. The streets that had been illuminated by lighted windows and cressets burning in the carriageways when he and Hannibal had walked to the Théâtre at seven would, at four, be dark between the wide-spaced, feeble glow of the lanterns hung at the intersections. As dark as the shell road out to the dueling ground beneath the oaks on Bayou St-John at five.

If not slave stealers, who?

He recalled the drunken Noah coming up to him and blowing flour in his face, a traditional Mardi Gras prank. The man could just as easily have wielded a pistol. Who would be the wiser? Or even be sober enough to notice?

I'll find the money to pay my way out of this somehow.

With a final flourish they concluded the Lancers Quadrille – the last before supper – and the sets broke up, chattering and laughing. Beer and sandwiches, the stout major-domo informed the musicians, awaited them in what had been a rehearsal hall on the other side of the building's small rear courtyard.

'Ben!'

For an instant January thought the skinny form that sprang up from a table in the ill-lit hall was Gabriel. But in the next moment he realized it was Olympe, in her son's clothes, her hair skinned back under a cap.

A disguise to pass unnoticed . . .

Why does she need . . . ?

His heart lurched in his chest, turning him almost sick. 'What's happened?'

'It's all right,' said Olympe. 'No one was hurt.'

Shit . . . He felt as if he'd stepped off a curb in the dark. *Or a cliff . . .*

The building had no kitchen. The Théâtre's servants – free and unfree – passed around them, carrying out refreshments to the paying patrons from the line of hampers along one wall. Chatter drifted into the court every time the door opened, like the morning squabbles of birds.

'Men broke into your house.' Olympe kept her voice quiet, but January was aware of the other musicians – and the two members of the St Patrick's Altar Guild in charge of the musicians' table – covertly watching them. 'Rose woke and heard them on the back gallery before they started trying to force the doors. She woke Zizi and Ti-Gall; got the girls out of there before the men broke in. Everyone's over to my house, babies and all.'

Three-quarters of a mile, January thought. *Cloaks over their nightdresses . . . The streets still crowded with maskers, drunkards, gamblers . . .*

And every one of the twenty men in the First Municipality's City Guards fully occupied keeping order in the barrooms and bordellos of the levee and Rue Chartres.

He could feel the blood hammering in his ears.

'When you're done here, come back to my house,' Olympe went on. 'I came straight here to tell you: don't go back to your place 'til daylight. But everybody's safe and well.'

January said, aloud this time, 'Shit.' He felt queasy with shock. His sister's dark eyes held on his face, reading his thoughts.

'Is this just thieves?' she asked after a time. 'Or you piss somebody off?'

'I don't know.' He was astonished at how normal his voice sounded. 'I suspect I pissed somebody off. But I don't know who or why.' He leaned down a little to kiss her: very like their mother, with their mother's dark, cynical intelligence in her eyes. 'Thank you,' he added. 'You get somebody to walk you home, and I'll see you just after sunrise.'

The dark eyes gleamed briefly, then shifted past his shoulder as the ballroom's major-domo appeared, his impeccable evening clothes a rebuke against the frivolity of white folks. 'Madame.' That gentleman bowed and signed to one of the St-Philippe servants. 'Elijah here can walk you home.'

Even the most fair-complected and respectable of the French Town's gens du couleur librés, reflected January, returning to his table and the beer that Hannibal was guarding for him, no matter how stuck-up, knew to stay on the right side of the voodoo Olympia Snakebones.

Tired as he was, he found he could eat nothing. Afterwards, though the others told him he played as well as ever, he had very little recollection of the rest of the ball.

Rose was awake when January reached Olympe's house. As he'd suspected, the ball went late, though he had regretfully sent a message to Evard Aubin – he knew he would be the tallest person on the dueling ground, easily spotted from the trees along the bayou. Every time he shut his eyes, he saw Edouard-Georges Couvillier spinning as if pushed, the pistol falling from his hand . . .

His wife was in the kitchen, helping Gabriel cook grits in a pot set in the coals of the old-fashioned hearth. In Carnival time the restaurant where Gabriel worked stayed open into the small hours, for a hundred intimate post-ball suppers. January knew his nephew would be back cutting up onions in M'sieu Alciatore's kitchen by nine. He still wore the white jacket of a cook, the sleeves turned up over thin, strong arms.

'I'll go to the house with you, Uncle Ben,' offered the young man. 'Then I can run back here and tell Aunt Rose the coast is clear—'

'You'll stay here and get some rest,' ordered January, crushing Rose in his arms. 'You're not going back there—'

'We have to.' She leaned back a little from his convulsive grip. 'Can you imagine what would happen if word went around that hired bravos broke into the house – the school – in the night?'

January opened his mouth to retort but didn't. Couldn't. He knew perfectly well.

Germaine, coming into the kitchen in Olympe's red dressing gown and one of Hannibal's old shawls, finished for him, 'My father would have fifty fits. He'd pull me out – and then he'd find some reason not to send me anywhere else, except to my aunt Marine's in Cloutierville.' The tone of her voice amply provided everything her listeners might want to know about Aunt Marine in Cloutierville. 'Madame Corbier' – that was Olympe's respectable name – 'says we can come here to sleep at night. But Mrs J is right, sir. We can't let anyone know there's any danger at the school.'

'I'll go with you,' offered Aglaëa, almost dancing with eagerness. 'I can run back here and tell everyone—'

'You'll do no such thing.' January looked sternly down at the child. 'I'll make Hannibal do it.' He embraced Rose again, desperate at the thought of what could have happened that night. 'Save us some grits.'

He had planned to breakfast before reconnoitering the house on Rue Esplanade, but he knew Rose was right. To reveal that the school had been broken into, or closed in the face of some threat, would be to lose what few pupils remained. He half-suspected their parents would welcome the excuse to cut expenses. They had to make the show of staying open in the daytime as if nothing had happened – he couldn't imagine where his extended family had slept, or were going to sleep tonight, in Olympe's four-room cottage along with Olympe and her husband Paul, eight-year-old Ti-Paul, Chou-chou, and baby Zéphine. ('We double-dog swear in blood we'll never tell,' both pupils had assured him, in cane-patch French that their parents would have fainted to hear.)

He knew before he climbed the back gallery steps and saw the broken door standing open that this had not been thieves.

They hadn't searched the house (*Thank God*!) for the modest cache of money buried in the oil jar. Had that been gone, January thought that he would, like Job, sit down, curse God, and die. But the mattress of his bed – and of every bed in the house, from Baby Xander's cradle to the attic cots of Germaine and Aglaëa – had been cut with an X, the springy gray-green moss trailing over ticking and sheets. Standing in the doorway between bedroom and nursery, almost sick at the simple violence of those acts of ruin, it was as if the warning had been written on the wall in blood.

Quit what you're doing, nigger. You know damn well what it is.

NINE

'You see!' Dagobert cried in triumph, when January – after grits but before sleep on the mattress that Chou-chou and Zizi-Marie promised would be the first one mended – disclosed to him the events of the previous night. 'Pelerine is behind it! I knew it!'

January saw nothing of the kind. What he saw was that something was going on, beyond Mamzelle de Cedillos clearing her father's name and getting the American courts (*How*?) to reverse their earlier decision and return Alegre to her (*After twenty-six years*?). January doubted they'd even try.

'So what is happening?' he asked Hannibal, when he returned from the Janvier townhouse shortly before ten. 'Since copies of the grant still exist in Pelerine's possession, why threaten us? And if Pelerine suspects that further evidence in favor of de Cedillos is hidden somewhere in the house at Alegre, why not simply burn the house down? Or tear it apart stick by stick? It's on his land, and he can have his men put up a new store shed in a week. And if this doesn't concern the ownership of Alegre – or clearing de Cedillos's name – what does it concern?'

Hannibal, propped cross-legged on a stool in a corner of the bedroom sewing a patch over the slashed X in Xander's tiny mattress, paused to spread the fingers of one long hand. 'So what did happen at the Battle of Chalmette?'

What did happen at the Battle of Chalmette?

Was it something that happened?

Or something that didn't?

1814

'If the British take New Orleans' – Gilles Gignac spread the narrow yards of bottle-green wool over the worktable, then smoothed invisible wrinkles with a practiced hand – 'you know France is going to try to take it back. And they'll send money and men to stir up the Americans to do their fighting for them. It'll be like two dogs fighting over a dead chicken. Whatever happens, it won't be the chicken that wins.'

Two years older than Ben, Gilles had been one of the first friends he'd made at the St-Louis Academy for Young Gentlemen of Color. From a thin, rather gangly boy he'd grown to a tall, rangy young man with sharp features of the acceptable 'free colored' shade of dusky honey. *High yeller*, the Americans would say.

He returned his attention to the green wool, placing the muslin pattern pieces and tracing the outlines in chalk, pins being seventy-five cents a box. Since childhood, January had enjoyed watching his friend work, first as an assistant to Gilles's mother Odile – the dressmaker to January's own mother – and later as apprentice to the tailor M'sieu Fazet. There was talk these days of Gilles going into partnership with Fazet, and marrying the man's fussy, demanding daughter Bertrille.

'Major LaCoste is recruiting men for his battalion.'

'I'm hoping,' January said at length, 'that if the British succeed, they'll keep us from being flooded with Americans. It was bad enough when they were just coming downriver on rafts to sell their pumpkins. Now they've got steam-powered boats on the river – another one docked last week. I've read there's even a steam-powered ocean vessel . . .'

'British,' pointed out Gilles. 'And just because the Parliament outlawed the trade in slaves doesn't mean British companies won't bring Africans in by the shipload if they get control of the river. You notice the British outlawed the *trade*, but they didn't outlaw *keeping* slaves. Not in Jamaica or Barbados or anyplace they can raise sugar. Do they – or you – really think plantation owners are going to start paying wages to cut cane?'

With his minute ivory tailor's tape he measured the differences between the pattern pieces and his notes as to the shape of the buyer's shoulders; the man's declared preferences as to fit. The windows stood open to Michie Fazet's courtyard, but the only sound came from the fountain there. Beyond the high walls, the French Town drowsed under September heat.

'And the other thing they've got running by steam now besides ocean vessels is spinning machines,' Gilles went on. 'Also carding machines and looms. And if you think Parliament's going to abolish slavery in a country ripe for the growing of cotton – or that the Americans wouldn't keep flooding over the river to try to take that land back no matter who they kill doing it—'

'No,' said January quietly. 'No, I don't think that.'

'If they take New Orleans, they will have a foothold.' Gilles stepped back to consider the chalked shape: British wool superfine was expensive (and nobody asked how it had come to be purchased from the enemy's country or brought into New Orleans). 'And now the emperor has been exiled, they can send as many troops here as they can pack on a ship. They need to be stopped.'

Everything his friend said, January knew to be true.

Instead of going home when quick tropical twilight dimmed the windows of the shop, January accepted Gilles's invitation to share dinner on the gallery of his friend's room above the rear courtyard. Smudges of lemongrass and gunpowder were lit, Gilles fetched lemons and sugar from his cupboard shelves and water from the kitchen down below, and January made lemonade. Gilles's younger brother Davy, newly apprenticed to a barrel maker, came through the courtyard passway a few minutes later with an onion and some crayfish from the market; Digo Salazar and Theo Le Fou, fellow musicians working the wharves for the summer, appeared, with Digo's sixteen-year-old daughter Mandie and a watermelon. Shanny the Cook, when Davy went down to beg a pot and some rice in the Fazet kitchen, contributed the carcass of the family's chicken, which still had plenty of meat on it, and the aforesaid chicken's giblets (she had a soft spot in her heart for Gilles). Mandie's friend Callie Medoc brought a pail of beer from her father's grocery.

An evening like a thousand other evenings. Friends sharing food on the little gallery, laughter and talk: the treasures of January's life. He knew his mother would be entertaining St-Denis Janvier, who in the summers returned to the cottage on the Rue Burgundy, to live with his beautiful plaçée as they had before his remarriage. (Madame Marie-Hélène and the children were in the country with her family.) He knew she wanted him elsewhere. The musicians passed Gilles's guitar around among them, and Digo's banjo.

The smoky light of the smudges, of candle lanterns on the table. Dominos. Cards. Talk of gossip and politics. The easy laughter of friends.

But the subject of the militia companies – the existing battalion under LaCoste and a new troop being recruited by a man named d'Aquin from among the refugees from Saint-Domingue – arose as well. Callie Medoc came to sit on the gallery's bare planks beside January, legs hanging over the edge: 'Will you sign up?'

'I don't know.'

She sighed and leaned against his shoulder. She was a big girl, fleshy without being flabby, quick-witted and surprisingly well-read for a child of parents who hadn't the money to send her to school. At seventeen she kept the books for her parents' store and had been one of the little circle of Gilles's friends for three years: like them, a part of the framework that January had built for his life. 'I keep hoping nothing's going to come of it. But I know it will. I know you're not supposed to say it, but I'm afraid . . . My brother and my daddy signed up with d'Aquin. Blanco's sixteen – and Daddy's got arthritis in his shoulder so bad he sometimes moves like he's sixty instead of forty. I know I'm supposed to be happy they're so brave, but I can't imagine what it would be like, to have them . . . gone. Not alive anymore. I look at Gilles, and the Fou . . .'

Her eyes went to January, as if she would have spoken his name, too. But her hand only tightened over his. In the settling darkness of the courtyard below, Shanny called down extravagant African curses on the kitchen boy, then limped out to pluck herbs from the vegetable beds by the reflection of the kitchen lamps. Crows flapped down, to sit in a line on the edge of the tall wooden cistern. The drumming of the cicadas was like the beat of the sea.

'A year from now,' said Callie softly, 'I don't want us to be sitting together like this someplace and everybody saying, "Jesus I miss Digo – remember how he used to play 'Highland Mary'?"'

January said, 'No,' and put his arm around Callie's shoulders. 'But it could happen in a fever summer, or falling down a flight of stairs . . .'

Working with Rubal Gomez, he knew all about summer fevers, and falling down stairs.

'I know.'

January knew, too. Looking from face to face in the dim juddering glow, he told himself that nothing was eternal, save only the love of God.

But not so soon.

* * *

'Don't be silly, Benjamin,' his mother said. At thirty-six (she claimed thirty), she was one of the most beautiful of the ladies of Rue des Ramparts (her cottage actually stood on the next street towards the river, Rue Burgundy). She moved as gracefully as if her claim were true. In public, she generally wore gloves of the most expensive procurable French lace, to hide the scars left by cane knives and lye soap. 'Major LaCoste is a perfectly respectable person, and he's related to the Dutillets, who are received everywhere . . . and the uniforms are quite handsome, I will admit. But with all this talk of the British coming, if you joined now, you would do nothing but musket drill and marching.'

'That is the point, Maman.'

'There are plenty of men' – she sipped her coffee, a green-and-bronze Sèvres ware cup as exquisite as the rest of her bright-yellow, sunny parlor – 'who can march and shoot muskets, dear. But they're only foot soldiers, when all is said. You'll earn just as much taking the position I've arranged for you as clerk at Relf and Chew, and with your education—'

'I have no desire to be a clerk,' said January patiently. 'I'm happy working with M'sieu Gomez.'

'Happy and poor.' Delicate fingers broke a praline in half, then one of the halves in half, to dip into the bitter heaven of the coffee. 'You make more playing the piano than you'll ever earn as a surgeon, and God knows that isn't much.'

'And what would I earn as a clerk for Mr Chew?'

'It's not what you'd *earn*, Benjamin.' Her patient tone added an unspoken, *you poor silly dolt*. 'You're well spoken and can add and figure – thank heavens St-Denis saw that you were taught that. Mr Chew is not only on the board of directors of the Bank of New Orleans and the Bank of Louisiana. He represents the Phoenix Fire Insurance Company . . .'

'Aren't they a British firm?'

'Don't interrupt your mother, dear. The war won't last forever. What I'm getting at is that everyone in the city owes him favors. And in other places as well.'

January was almost certain this accounted for those rolls of green British superfine in Michie Fazet's tailor shop despite the American naval blockade against British ships.

'If you impress M'sieu Chew with your work, he'll move you

into positions of greater responsibility. You know how to keep your mouth shut and you're willing to work hard—'

'I'm willing to work hard,' said January quietly, 'to learn how to help people. To set bones when they break, so that men can go back to work and support themselves and their families. To heal wounds, and cut out the growths that plague the body and shorten the lives of both women and men. I'm not willing – and I don't think I'm capable of it – to work at a desk calculating the compound interest of other men's wealth, or copying loan documents to finance buying land from the government or bringing in shipments of slaves through Cuba and Mexico to sell to Mr Chew's friends. I would run mad in a week.'

'Nonsense.' His mother brushed the words aside as if they'd been floating tendrils of cat hair. 'You'll get used to it in a week and become indispensable to your employer inside a month. You'll meet people of consideration—'

'No.'

She set down the untasted fragment of praline and pursed her lips in annoyance. The daughter of a Yoruba woman who'd been raped by a crewman on the slave voyage to America, Livia Janvier had had the good fortune to inherit delicate Caucasian features and coloring like roasted wheat. She was darker than most of the New Orleans or Caribbean plaçées but so beautiful that most men scarcely noticed that richer hue. She knew all about willingness to work at being indispensable: January was well aware that his mother regarded her position as the plaçée of a wealthy sugar broker as a job, entailing no love but a meticulous attention to the details of making her protector *feel* loved.

What she herself might feel was profoundly and purely secondary.

'I think I know you better than you know yourself, Benjamin,' she said, an observation frequently made. 'And I know what's good for you. Mr Chew has gotten specie and foreign loans for every bank and business in town. I've told him of your education and abilities – it isn't often that they take on couleur libré clerks, and never one as old, or as dark, as you. How old are you now, Benjamin? Seventeen?'

'Twenty-one,' he corrected her. 'I'll be twenty-two in November.'

'Hmm.' She considered him for a moment, beautiful eyes narrowed as if she suspected him of lying. Then she shook her head.

'How many men in Louisiana do you think would even *hire* a surgeon of your blood?' she went on. 'The French Creoles and the Spanish Creoles twitch if a buck so much as picks up a walking stick, let alone a scalpel—'

As always, January felt his neck heat: as a child he had felt it as shame, and now he knew it for anger. He wondered if his mother had ever called his father the names the whites used for blacks: *sambo, nigger, buck.*

In New Orleans, as in the sugar islands of the Caribbean – Martinique, Guadeloupe, and up until twenty-three years ago Saint-Domingue – *colored* implied 'free.' *Colored* meant owning a house or a shop or often a plantation (worked by slaves darker than oneself). It meant money and connections with the whites (like St-Denis Janvier or the ingenious Mr Chew) who held political power. Blacks were slaves. Blacks were Africans. Blacks – even mulattos, quadroons, octoroons who were prized as house servants, as well as griffes and sambos of mixed blood whose owners/fathers hadn't had the decency to free them – could be bought and sold and mortgaged to the bank like mules. Blacks were without power.

And power was what mattered.

Of course his beautiful mother would deny to the death that she'd ever been the 'woman' of a full-blood Wolof cane-hand with 'country-marks' scarred into his face (even as she'd deny to the death that she was thirty-six years old). That she'd ever borne such a person two children.

'I told St-Denis it was a stupid waste of money to apprentice you to Gomez. With that nose and those lips and that hair, few whites hire him, no matter how much Spanish blood he's got . . . or says he has.' She eyed him again, judging his massive shoulders, his six feet three inches, the beau noir lustré (as the dealers described the true African blackness): the legacy of his father. 'Do you think even the librés in this town will hire somebody who looks like a cane-hand?'

He took a deep breath, repeated to himself what his confessor had said to him, more than once: the words Christ had spoken, alone and dying in agony on the Cross. *Father, forgive them. They don't know what they're doing.*

'I don't know, Maman. That's in God's hands. I suppose I'll find that out.'

'Well, don't expect me to support you while you do. And what am I supposed to tell Mr Chew? I'd arranged for him to meet with you Wednesday morning.'

It was the first January had heard of it. He couldn't keep the annoyance from his voice. 'Tell him I had a previous engagement. Please extend my apologies.'

He bowed to her, put on his hat, and left the cottage. By the angle of the sun above the low, pastel houses of Rue Burgundy, it was well before noon, and M'sieu Gomez would be wondering where he was. Still he made his way down Rue St-Ann to the cathedral, the streets summer-quiet and summer-stinking, clouds of mosquitoes hanging above the reek of the open gutters. Only those who had to be out and about in the rising heat passed him: laundry-women chattering of husbands and sons, baskets balanced on their voluminous calico tignons; the vendor pausing before every door to cry, 'Le-mons! Fresh le-mons!' The creaky rattle of a passing cart.

January had only a few half-pennies in his pocket – most of his piano pupils were out of town with their families – but he separated one out with his fingers as he came into the Place d'Armes. He would light a candle to the Blessed Virgin, whom he had revered since first he'd understood who she was, and that she cared for everyone. Light a candle and ask for her guidance. About the militia. About Callie Medoc (Would a virgin, even a heavenly one, understand about not knowing if you were in love or not?). About his mother's efforts to lead him (push him?) on to a better-paying pathway than that afforded by Gomez the surgeon.

For like Gilles, she was perfectly right. Whites – and many of the well-off librés of the French Town – always did prefer to deal with a white, or at most with fair-complected and delicate-featured octoroons. There were no lawyers, no physicians, no teachers, no engineers in the French Town as dark as himself. Certainly no priests – the only other profession in which he had ever pictured himself. (And he had abandoned that idea at the age of fourteen.)

Should I go back to her? he asked himself, as he entered the blessed coolness of the dark vestibule; passed into the gloom of the aisle. *Apologize for my rudeness and say that yes, I'll meet with Mr Chew Wednesday, at least to see what he has to say?*

He wouldn't interrupt Gilles, who would be well into stitching that bottle-green wool coat in preparation for a fitting by this time of the morning. *This evening I'll go by Fazet's and see what he has to say . . .*

He dropped two half-pennies into the box before the Virgin's statue and took a candle; lit it from the earlier prayers of some other seeker, wedged it on one of the spikes in the bank of glowing lights. *Blessed Mary Ever-Virgin, the Lord is with thee.* He felt in his pocket for his rosary, blue beads and a steel crucifix, the touch of them like the touch of God's hand, reassuring. *Blessed art thou among women . . .*

He thought then, as if someone had whispered it in his ear, *If I join the militia, I'll be given that 160 acres of enlistment bonus.*

And then I can choose.

TEN

1841

His mother's response to his note explaining his reasons – and his arrangements – for meeting her in secret was a small rectangle of expensive pale-yellow notepaper, ostentatiously bordered in black. Christophe Levesque – the carpenter she had married following St-Denis Janvier's death in 1822 – had himself passed away in 1830, and Livia Levesque, as she was now known, had worn mourning for him for precisely a year. Black, she said, did not become her. January had no recollection of his mother ever mentioning Levesque's name – his sister Dominique had written to him in Paris informing him of the wedding. On the Feast of All Saints she would drop a few flowers in front of his wall tomb in the free colored section of the new cemetery, before going to pay her respects to the Janviers.

But she still insisted on being called The Widow Levesque, and a lithograph of a woman in deep mourning lying prone across a fresh grave adorned the wall of her parlor, framed and draped in black. A lock of Levesque's grizzled hair, tied with black ribbon, lay beneath it . . . Only sometimes it was a lock of St-Denis Janvier's. A few years previously, when she had left the parlor for a moment, January had checked the drawer of the little pedestal table that supported this shrine and had discovered the alternate memento there, waiting to be substituted depending on who was coming for coffee.

Her note said:

> *If you insist upon such nonsensical melodrama, I suppose I must oblige. Please see that decent coffee and fresh pralines are available, if possible. L.L.*

The rendezvous took place at nine p.m. at Alciatore's Restaurant on Rue St-Louis, in one of the small, vacant bedrooms of the boarding house Antoine Alciatore operated above the dining rooms. January arrived dressed as a working man delivering a basket of oranges; Gabriel, who was a sous chef in the kitchen, sneaked him upstairs. Resplendent in jeweled wig, full-face white Venetian mask, Spanish farthingale, and an Elizabethan starched-gauze collar the size of a mainsail, his mother entered the restaurant shortly thereafter and was guided up to join him.

Gabriel made sure that the coffee was decent – ambrosial, as a matter of fact – the pralines were fresh, and a small fire crackled in the little room's hearth.

'Honestly, Benjamin—' She removed her lace-and-kidskin gauntlets, set aside her mask, and perched on a stool as if she'd served at the court of Good Queen Bess half her life. 'It isn't as though anyone is going to murder me for talking to you.'

'I don't know that,' said January. He folded her green velvet cloak and set it aside. 'I still don't know who's behind this, or what he – or she – is trying to accomplish or prevent. I don't know what the stakes are, and I don't want to take chances.'

'That's very kind of you, dear.' He'd heard her use the same tones when one of her cats presented her with a not-quite-deceased lizard. 'But I'm afraid it's only to be expected, when you take on these errands from goodness knows who—'

'It's Dagobert Janvier!'

'Well, there, you see?' She dropped a fragment of sugar into her coffee, inspected the spoon for tarnish, stirred and tasted the coffee, then set it aside as well. 'Had you invested your money properly when you got it, back in 1835, before the crash, you wouldn't be having this problem.'

January drew breath to explain for the five hundredth time in the past six years that under no circumstances would he invest in slaves to rent out by the week to the sugar mills or lumbering companies ('They cost nothing to feed and mine bring in twenty-five dollars a week!' she had said at the time.) Then he let it out, said, 'You may be right, Maman.' *In the Flying City of Laputa, or the Lunar Realms as described by de Bergerac, you may be right . . .*

'And as for dragging poor Rose, and your sons, into this problem—'

'It's why I need some information.' He sat opposite her, on the other side of the little table that he'd drawn up to the hearth while waiting for her, and poured out coffee for himself. 'Dagobert Janvier hired me to help him clear the name of Bartolomé de Cedillos.'

Her eyebrows skated almost to the pearl-edged wig. 'De Cedillos! Good luck with that!'

'What do you know about him?'

'Well, he vanished during that last battle, you know. Rumor had it that he fomented rebellion on the Doux-Malheur, Dufresne, and Carrière plantations in the hopes that the rebels would then fall on the American troops from the rear . . .'

'Is it true?' January asked, and she moved her head a little, glanced at him sidelong.

'I have no idea. They were such small places to begin with, I hardly see why anyone would bother otherwise.'

'Who was he?' January asked. 'I remember seeing him at parties and balls before the war. As I recall, he was tall for a Spaniard, and dark, with a mole on his chin.' Half-unconsciously he touched the spot. 'He always looked well turned out. He had a plaçée . . .'

'Mélusine,' provided his mother promptly. 'And if the girl flirted with one man, she flirted with fifty. She's lucky he didn't turn her into the street, daughter and all – if it *was* his daughter . . . A sillier little piece I never laid eyes on. She was well served when it turned out he hadn't gifted her with that cottage of hers after all: he'd only been leasing it. So she got no good of it.'

'Is she still in town?'

'She died in the cholera, just before you came back from Paris, she and her daughters, all three.' She shrugged. 'Which was just as well, since I understand she left about ten dollars.'

Only his mother, reflected January, would remember that piece of information. 'And his . . . father? Grandfather? . . . had the plantation of Alegre by grant from the King of Spain?'

'Father. When Spain took over, old King Carlos handed out land grants like a Protestant preacher passing out temperance tracts. Michie Fourchet' – she spoke casually the name of the planter who had bought her, owned her – raped her – as if he'd been a chance-met business acquaintance – 'got grants for two plantations, just for renouncing the French king and marrying that Spanish merchant's daughter. Michie Janvier's father got I don't know how many acres in Avoyelles Parish, and I understand that the American governor of the territory tried to get a hundred thousand acres around Natchez out of His Majesty in exchange for military secrets and assistance.' She smiled her serpentine smile and sipped the coffee with the air of a woman who hopes to find it wanting. 'Honorable people, the Americans.'

January rolled his eyes. 'And I take it the Spanish grant overlapped with the grant given to Icarus Pelerine?' He remembered Pelerine from those days as well. An older man than de Cedillos; tall like the Spaniard but thin, an ageing Don Quixote. Even in that long-ago autumn of 1814 his hair had been silvering. His unscarred face had been somberly handsome, like a Jacobean portrait.

'Pelerine's grandfather had the land along Bayou Joyeuse,' his mother went on. A pity, he reflected, the Cabildo had never employed her. Every detail of every transaction – if they'd involved money, land, or somebody's social misconduct – glittered at her manicured fingertips, as if they'd taken place the previous week. 'He was related to the French foreign minister, and got grants in Louisiana, Martinique, and Saint-Domingue. Icarus Pelerine managed the Saint-Domingue lands, and came here in '91, only to find Bartolomé de Cedillos growing sugar on about a third of his land. He sued, but de Cedillos had kept a copy of the Spanish king's land grant and argued that Pelerine's documents were a forgery. Between the revolution going on in France, and the war between France and Spain, the judge believed him.' She shrugged again. 'The judge was a Spaniard, of course.'

'Of course.' January sighed. No wonder Pelerine hated de Cedillos. 'So de Cedillos had a copy of the Spanish grant?'

'He did. I understand Pelerine produced his own French charter, but it had been chewed by rats and was almost unreadable.'

If the arable land on Sept-Anges was as narrow as that of Alegre, January reflected, presumably the sugar fields crowded the house there in the same fashion, with the same results.

'And he was burned . . .?'

'A fire in the stables in '29. His son and grandson were killed.' She might have been describing a failed attempt to grow geraniums. 'His daughters are married—' Her eyes narrowed as she moved on to more interesting topics than the loss of someone's child. 'One of them married a Picard; another a Trepagier, and died in childbed in 1817. I think the youngest girl married into the Roman family and went to live in St James Parish—'

His mother's encyclopedic knowledge of a thousand tiny details, January reflected, was precisely that: an encyclopedia, save where any of those details might affect her own affairs. Any one of those details, he reminded himself, might be the key to what had taken place last night. And, it now seemed, Friday night at Alegre—

'—and there are Pelerines in Rapides and Pointe Coupe Parishes as well. So they would get the land, when old Icarus finally dies.' The dark eyes sharpened as they returned to the matter at hand. 'Why is that knot-head Dagobert suddenly hiring you to help him clear de Cedillos's name? So far as I know, the Janviers weren't related to them.'

Amused malice made her look very like her daughter Olympe. 'Don't tell me the fair Paloma de Cedillos is back in town? Or would it be her daughter? It would,' she went on thoughtfully. 'Paloma would be forty-two if she's a day. For all Dagobert made a mooncalf of himself over the girl before the war, I doubt he'd spend . . . How much is he paying you, Benjamin?'

'Thirty dollars.'

She made a face.

'Of which I owed twenty-five to Jules Gardinier, when he took his daughter out of the school.'

'If I told you once, I told you a thousand times – and I told Rose – putting time and money into a school, much less one that spends hours on worthless pastimes like Latin and history—'

'You did tell us, Maman,' said January. 'And we were grateful for your insights into the risks.'

'I was only thinking of your children, Benjamin. And if you'd gone to work for Relf and Chew to begin with . . .'

January knew to his marrow that this was a lie. His mother had been thinking of consolidating her own assets with a partnership and hadn't given either of his sons so much as a christening cup to mark their births. But he knew also that to contradict his mother would only prolong a fruitless discussion. 'Thank you,' he said. 'And it's Paloma's sister Felicita who has returned to New Orleans.'

'At her age? She must be all of thirty-two . . .'

'Dagobert is forty-three, Maman.'

'At that age, the girls get younger, not older. Is she beautiful?'

Like the holy flame in a lamp of alabaster. 'She is.'

His mother sniffed. She was friends, January knew, not only

with all the women who had been plaçées in her own salad days, but with their elders, their mothers of the previous generation, both in New Orleans and in Saint-Domingue before its savage insurrection. Friends, or friends with their enemies, their hairdressers, their dressmakers, their relatives who would gossip all the more about them in malice. He wondered if she still paid small sums to the maids of other plaçées, for tidbits of information that might come in useful.

From the Rue St-Louis below the windows came the clamor of singing, the bang of tin pans: young men bound for an entertainment of one sort or another. In the twenty-four hours since the St-Patrick Valentine's Ball, rumor of the Marignys' proposed parade had gone through the French Creole community like fire over the arid grass of the western plains. On his way to Alciatore's, January had encountered two parades which now included horsemen and carriages – poor, small affairs of a few decorated fiacres and a clutch of young men playing the guitar and singing 'Old Zip Coon' – and Dagobert, between meetings with M'sieu Morrell and the representatives of Bastian and Son Importers, had sent January word that there would also be a Grand Cavalcade in connection with his mother's reception and ball on Mardi Gras night. (*What a surprise*!) January and his fellow musicians would be expected to play in it.

'And was de Cedillos's Spanish grant produced when Pelerine sued to get his land back after the battle?'

The pearls dangling from the curled red wig danced as Livia shook her head. 'The judge didn't even ask for them. He just ruled that Pelerine was the rightful owner of the whole of Alegre – and who wouldn't, in the face of the rumors that de Cedillos was a traitor? It was an American judge, at that second trial. I recall the first lawsuit went on for years, on and off, before the Spanish alcalde came down on de Cedillos's side. Pelerine tried to bring it to court four times after the Americans took over, and it never got anywhere. Then after the battle it got settled in his favor in about a week.'

'Because de Cedillos was gone.'

'It's only what you'd expect, with the whole town screaming that he'd encouraged a slave rebellion to help the British.' Livia readjusted a pleat in the puffed parakeet-green silk of her sleeve. 'And Victoire de Cedillos had left town, too, by the time it came to court.

Stupid as a box of bricks . . . And whether she'd been here or not, she couldn't raise the wind for a lawyer. Can the fair Felicita?' Her eyebrow tilted, but her eyes stayed on his, like a lawyer herself, testing a witness's story in the dock. 'Or is she going to get Dagobert to pay for one?'

'I don't know,' returned January doggedly.

'I imagine Marie-Hélène will have something to say about that.' She sounded pleased.

'I heard Pelerine threw Madame de Cedillos and her daughters out of Alegre. Is that true? We – d'Aquin's men – patrolled the woods along Bayou Malheur immediately after the battle, but . . .'

'I expect he did.' Her eyes narrowed – *Remembering*? January wondered. Putting together rumors she'd heard, the way Olympe did, calculating what had been the most likely chain of events? Then she waved the thoughts, whatever they were, aside. 'Pelerine was vindictive that way. And he would have done anything to secure possession of those lands. He had that son of his, and his family, in Alegre before midsummer. I expect money changed hands somewhere.'

Played out, Dagobert had said of Pelerine's lands. January recalled the sodden, disused fields past which he'd ridden in the darkness of Friday night. Sugar was a hard crop on the soil, and he had heard from every merchant and plaçée in town how the two catastrophic hurricanes in August of 1831 had destroyed the sugar fields from Pointe à la Hache to Baton Rouge. If money had changed hands, Pelerine had not gained much profit from the bargain.

'Did Mistress Felicita have any account of what happened to them?' His mother spoke casually, but there was an avid edge to her voice. 'Mélusine – Bartolomé's plaçée, you know – was always bragging about the family's wealthy relatives in Spain. I expect they went there.'

Two years of backbreaking hardship, Dagobert had said . . . the *last fragments of her mother's jewelry . . . the few remaining reals her sister had saved . . .*

To buy a gauze hankie?

'I have no idea.' And since she looked as if she were about to reply, *Of course you have, Benjamin. She has to have told Dagobert, and if the man can keep his mouth shut about anything, I have yet to hear about it . . .* he asked, 'What do you think happened,

Maman? Those plantations were burned, but nobody attacked the American lines from the rear. Do *you* believe de Cedillos was a traitor?'

'Good Lord, no!' Her dark eyes snapped. 'If Pelerine promised the field hands on those three plantations that he could get Pakenham and Keane to give them their freedom for drawing off the Tennessee troops, they'd have done it. They wouldn't have needed much convincing. Briard – the owner of Doux-Malheur – was an idiot, and his overseer was selling three-quarters of the niggers' food to the swamp trappers and putting the money in his pocket. The lot of them were ready to do murder.'

She stood, shaking out her acres of skirts and farthingale, and straightening the lace of her gloves again as she drew them on. 'Pelerine would win either way, you see. If the British won, Pakenham would have the suit brought back to court and the land awarded to Pelerine for his good service. If things went the other way, Pelerine knew he could make accusations against de Cedillos that would carry an American judge against the man, since de Cedillos wouldn't be around—'

'And how would Pelerine know that?' January rose and gathered up her cloak. Even a few feet from the fire, the room was bone-chilling.

She gave him again her small, pitying smile. 'How do you think? Really, Benjamin . . . When one has money – especially in the confusion of wartime – making sure someone isn't around is usually possible. And in either case, Pelerine would still have the money the British paid him, and certainly none of the slaves would stand up to testify one way or the other. Of course I don't know any of this for certain.'

She spread her hands, like a conjurer demonstrating that he really has nothing up his sleeve. Then her eyes hardened again. 'Pelerine is the Devil incarnate, Benjamin. Mean as sin for all his wealth, proud as Lucifer and hard as flint. He would have done anything to get that land back. Beware of him. For years he tried to sway the court against de Cedillos by means of rumor and gossip, slandering the man's name to anyone of influence who'd listen – and the names of his girls and his wife. Between what he paid the judges, and the burning of those three plantations, there was no interest whatsoever in anyone going out to re-survey the old Alegre lands.

Certainly none in reviewing the documents of the case. It was enough to know that de Cedillos was a traitor.'

She picked up her mask, as January settled the cloak about those exaggerated satin shoulders: an old-style full-face disguise, smooth and inhuman, held in place with a button between the teeth. January took her arm and led her down the stairs.

ELEVEN

'Am I being watched?' January asked, two mornings later, as he and Hannibal slipped quietly aboard the side-wheeler *Sarah Jane*, bound downstream for the tiny settlement of Belle Chase. 'Is the house being watched? I haven't seen anyone, but I don't know.'

Winter was the low water season, the river's powerful eddies complicated by the dense, sugar-smelling fog. January had arranged – carefully, because one of the several things he didn't know was who was passing information to who – with a man named Ti-Jon, who straw-bossed work gangs on the levee, to slip him and Hannibal aboard in the early hours, when it was less likely that the men who'd broken into the house would even be awake. The boat itself wouldn't leave, he guessed, until the mists had thinned with the rising of the chill and distant sun.

Even at this hour, there was a great deal of coming and going between the gambling establishments along Front Street and the levee. Traces of music clattered from saloons like the Liberty Bell and the Andrew Jackson, mingling with the blur of lantern light. Blasts of drunken argument burst from the doorways like buckets of thrown slops. All the way down Rue Esplanade, January had strained to distinguish between the half-guessed shapes of gamblers, stevedores, and homegoing drunkards and the unknown possibility that he was being followed. Had fought to hear what couldn't be heard under the mist-muffled brangle of voices cursing their luck or protesting the high price of quim. The fact that so many were masked added to his sense of nightmare unreality.

Hannibal had been waiting for him, chatting with a small-time river trader named False River Jones, in the doorway of the Happy Englishman, beneath a sign depicting a miser in a powdered wig counting his money. Fifty cents that neither of them could afford had guaranteed them a place in the *Sarah Jane*'s hold, behind barrels of salt pork and parched corn from the farms of Kentucky. All they could do now was wait.

At least the hatches were open. Gray light leaked down, allowing January to see the rats that scratched and chewed (and pissed on) the containers of food destined for the slaves of a hundred downstream plantations.

Better than listening to them in darkness.

'I take it Lieutenant Shaw is too much occupied with the general festivities to be of much help?'

'I haven't even asked him,' returned January quietly. 'We're down to two boarding students and two day-students. We can't let word get about that the school isn't safe. Ti-Gall and I walked the neighborhood, last night and the night before. But with the fog coming in . . .' He shook his head, spread his hands.

'I can—' Hannibal began to offer, then pressed his forearm to his mouth, his hand to his side as he was shaken with coughing. After decades of Soothing Syrups and Universal Household Remedies, he had sweated through the agonies of turning his back on both their dangers and their benefits and, unlike Orpheus, wasn't about to look over his shoulder. He held up a hand against January's protests, then finished weakly, 'I can take my turn on those watches, whilst you and your worthy nephew-in-law mount guard indoors.'

'They'd murder you the first time you coughed,' January pointed out, and Hannibal sighed.

'I can convincingly transform it to the sound of a dog barking. It might even frighten them away.'

'It might.' January's voice conveyed both his disbelief and his kindly refusal. He felt sufficiently guilty over asking Hannibal to accompany him this morning as it was. But when he'd penned notes to his mother on Monday morning, and to Gilles Gignac, now a tailor in Vicksburg, his nerve had failed him at the thought of going five miles downriver to the battleground plantation of Chalmette. As at Alegre on Friday night, the black servant of a white man would be relatively safe with his 'master' along, in the soggy wilderness around Bayou Malheur. But every slave stealer and river pirate in the swamps would regard a black man on his own as fair game.

Silence returned.

In time, feet drummed the deck overhead. More bales, more barrels were lowered in the deck crane's net. 'Nigger cloth' and cheap 'nigger shoes' from the mills of New England. German linen and pottery oil jars from Spain. More salt pork and parched corn –

January recalled those tiny gardens at Alegre, and how his father and the other men on Bellefleur Plantation had risked whippings and worse to hunt and fish for fresh meat. A small crate containing (the label said) quality mustard from Lyon, France. Another crate of wine bottles. Men dropped from the deck above, shoved the freight to the sides of the shallow hold, and reached up to guide down another load. January listened to the sounds of preparation overhead: the creak of the crane, the voices of the deck boss cursing, the stevedores singing half-African songs about love and food.

The light broadened, though the clammy cold in the hold didn't abate one degree. Hannibal coughed again, but either the noise of departure was too loud, or Ti-Jon had had a word with the deck-hands. Nobody came down to look. Though the fiddler was the best in New Orleans, frequent illness had kept him from teaching lessons which would have made the difference between mere indigence and the poverty in which he lived. Listening to the sounds above them, January tried not to think about whether the parents of little Flora McCullen or the Savonnière girls, whose lessons today he had postponed, would as a result seek another instructor for their children. Rose, his sons, the girls who remained at the school . . . They needed that two dollars a week.

Light in the hold dimmed abruptly as the hatchway was dropped in place. Distantly, the pilot's voice could be heard: 'Secure them ropes, you puke-faced slush buckets! What the hell you think you're doin', knittin' a sock? Back her! Back her, God damn it, you suck-arse bastards think we got all fucken day . . .?'

January felt the shudder of the ship's engine in the bones of her hold.

Travel downstream was twice as fast as upstream. At this season of the year, there would be parched corn and salt pork for pretty much every plantation in Plaquemines Parish, including the de Macarty property whose 'big house' Jackson had used for his head-quarters. January remembered the place well – rebuilt now, after the British had shelled it to pieces. Almost before they were underway, he heard the clang of the boat's bell, the pilot's curses switching from 'Put on some speed, you bunch of fucken donkeys!' to 'Slow up! Back her! God damn it, you want to run us into them towheads?' There was clearly a flag out on the de Macarty landing.

'Let's go.'

Men were picking up sacks, rolling barrels from the pile set closest to the rail even before the *Sarah Jane* glided the last dozen yards into the Macarty wharf. The supercargo as well as the pilot yelled curses, but the men themselves worked with skilled speed . . . And not a single one of them looked in January's direction when he and Hannibal stepped from the shelter of the companionway. Men gazed off in all directions as the pair crossed to the nearest barrel, turned it on its side, and rolled it – following the other stevedores – as the gangway was thrown into place. January had come on this excursion in his oldest wool trousers and a tattered jersey, and it was the first time in his life he'd seen Hannibal clothed in anything other than his usual sorry-looking long-tailed coat and silk vest.

Nobody gave them a glance. *There's fifty cents well spent . . .*

They rolled the barrel down the gangplank, set it up among the others at the end of the wharf, and walked away, Hannibal pointing down the shallow levee as if calling January's attention to something, in case de Macarty's straw boss was watching.

He didn't seem to be. They scrambled down the levee to the batture – only a few yards wide at this point and choked with swamp laurel and young trees – and under this cover headed with casual celerity downstream.

January could hear the pilot cursing again as the *Sarah Jane* was poled from the wharf, headed into the current again where her paddles began to turn. Presumably the man would continue to blaspheme all the way down to Pointe à la Hache.

In time he said, 'Here.' The ground had grown marshy underfoot, and the levee to their left lower, ruinous, thick with saplings and weeds. Foliage choked the break in the levee beside them, making it nearly invisible. For a moment, he heard again the thunder of the *Louisiana*'s guns, smelled the grit of powder smoke, as if it had lodged in the back of his throat twenty-six years before and never quite dissolved.

Over a thousand men died here, far from their homes. I killed some of them.

'A man named Rodriguez owned a few arpents between de Macarty's land and the battleground,' he went on after a moment. 'He ran a sawmill here during high water and made a deliberate crevasse in the levee for the water power.'

'His neighbors must have loved him.'

'He wasn't the only man who did it. I remember there was some kind of lawsuit over the land downstream – my mother could give you the details, chapter and verse. But when the British dropped anchor in the Gulf of Mexico, this ground belonged to a Frenchman named Chalmet.'

He shoved and thrust his way up a yard or so of steep slope, to the mucky nadir of what had been Rodriguez's Canal, and extended his hand down to help Hannibal follow him. A quarter-century later, the place still seemed to hold, for him, the stench of death.

'This was all sugar.' He gestured downstream to land now covered with clumps of hackberry, stands of maidencane, black gum and tupelo saplings. From the bottom of the ditch it was impossible to see over the ground cover to the house that the St-Armand brothers had built when the war was over, but he knew what it looked like: like every other French Creole plantation on the river, including Alegre. Wooden, one story and an attic over a high foundation that might or might not be enclosed, embraced by a gallery. Brightly painted, orange or yellow or blue. (Only the Americans painted their houses the less expensive white.) A couple of garçonnières in the rear and a little slave village beyond that. Being on the river, the arable had stretched back nearly a mile.

The kitchen garden and, as at Alegre, the formal garden closer to the levee, were wider, the 'shell-blow grounds' large enough to supply the families in the quarters with sufficient fresh vegetables to sell as well as to eat.

'Louis St-Armand still owns the place, but they don't farm it anymore. The land's played out and not worth the cost of keeping it in production. Louis – or his sisters and their families – use the house to get away from the city in the summertime. Just before Christmas of 1814, the British came in from the Gulf by way of Lake Borgne and through the back swamp. Nobody in town knew a thing about it until they came out of the woods and seized the Villeré place – less than ten miles below the city. They took over Chalmet's house as their headquarters, and of course it was torn to pieces and burned after the battle. They say Chalmet died of grief at its loss. Or despair, I suppose, at the thought of starting all over again.'

'I had a cousin who was killed in battle here.' Hannibal took the snake stick January cut for him and followed gamely through the thick foliage that choked the old canal. 'Perfectly nice fellow. Made it all through the wars in the Peninsula without a scratch and nearly bankrupted my uncle in the process with his gambling debts. Sera parsimonia in fundo est, alas. Is that Louis de St-Armand who used to host the balls for the Faubourg Tremé Free Colored Militia at his townhouse?'

'It is.' As a member of the board of the Free Colored Militia and Burial Society, January had worked with the brothers Louis and Hilaire de St-Armand, well-off merchants and mainstays of the French Town's free colored society. 'Everybody will be in town for Carnival, but there isn't a lot to see here. Except that.' He pointed to the upriver side of the ditch, where the ground rose sharply in an escarpment of about eight feet, now overgrown – like everything else in that old killing ground – with clumps of gum and tupelo, tangles of creeper and briar.

I stood there. I pointed my musket down at men trapped in the ditch at the bottom, breast deep in water . . . Shot them, like shooting fish in a barrel, my only thought that if I didn't kill them, they would somehow get to the top and kill me.

And they looked up and saw me with my musket pointed down at them and knew they were going to die. The thought turned him sick. *Hannibal's cousin was one of them.*

Hannibal shook his head. 'Even *I* know better than to charge uphill into emplaced artillery,' he said thoughtfully. 'It never ends well.'

A mile from the river, the ground declined into the murk of the ciprière, the cypress back swamp that lay behind all the plantations and New Orleans itself; an extension of the trembling lands that ran all the way downriver to the Gulf. The larger bayous like St-John and Gentilly-Sauvage, and even some of the smaller ones – Joyeuse, Chien-Mort, Ouaouarons – were navigable, leading eventually to the river or to the lake, or in some cases to canals dug for the purpose, and small plantations dotted the ciprière where the ground was high enough to sustain a crop.

'The American line followed the canal into the swamp.' January pointed back over the shoulder-high ocean of half-grown de Macarty cane, inland of the old Chalmet field, to the gray-green wall of cypresses and the stagnant gleam of water. 'The Tennessee militia held this section. They'd built up redoubts of earth and cotton bales, curving around their left to protect them from the British simply going around the end of the line. The swamp beyond is nearly impassable at this time of the year, especially to men who don't know it.'

'I daresay.' Hannibal leaned on his stick, his breath like a rusty saw.

'According to my mother, Icarus Pelerine convinced the slaves on three small plantations – Dufresne, Doux-Malheur, and Carrière – that if they rose in revolt in favor of the British, he – Pelerine – would speak in their favor once the British had taken New Orleans and see to it they were freed. Those three plantations lay along Bayou Malheur, about five miles from here, which connected with the lake, or at least it did at that time.'

They moved on, breasting through the cane as well as they could. January whispered thanks to the Blessed Virgin that these rear fields of the de Macarty place, like those at Alegre, had been harvested a year ago, and the second crop of ratoon cane growing up wasn't yet thick enough to tear their clothes and flesh with sharp leaves. And, he added, that de Macarty kept his slaves up to their work of weeding the field. They'd all be at the sugar mill now, he calculated. Roulaison was nearly over, and de Macarty was rich enough to have installed modern vacuum-pan boilers, instead of the old system of endless open cauldrons boiling over infernal flame. Smoke rose far off, and the misty air still smelled of burned sugar, but here in the green wilderness of the cane, all was still. Cane rats scrabbled in the weeds, and the hawks hung motionless overhead.

As they walked, he outlined all he'd learned from his mother about the quarrel between Pelerine and Bartolomé de Cedillos. 'Once the battle started, the slaves were supposed to burn the Bayou Malheur plantations—'

'Causing the Tennessee heroes to desert the battle line and go crush the rebellion,' finished Hannibal. 'Some of them anyway would probably do it. Nothing stirs a good Tennessee man to wrath like a slave revolt. *Contention, like a horse / Full of high feeding / Madly hath broke loose* . . . And at that point, presumably, the British would breach the Tennessee defenses, swarm through, and take the Americans in the rear all the way along their line?'

'I've heard Pelerine later put it about that de Cedillos was going to guide them through the swamp around the Americans' left,' said January. 'De Cedillos certainly disappeared afterwards. Either way, the desertion of the Tennessee troops would leave that end of the line fatally weakened. They outnumbered us,' he added. 'I heard later they had about twelve thousand men: regulars, professional soldiers. We were fewer than four thousand – I've heard it was as few as three. Over half of us had never been in battle before. There.' He pointed. 'Bayou Malheur.'

They had entered the trembling lands in earnest, bare gray cypresses and tupelo letting through chilly winter sunlight. The brown waters of Bayou Malheur lay at the bottom of a trough of land some ten yards across, but these days, January judged, there wasn't enough water in it this far from the lake to float a pirogue.

A half-mile further along its brim brought them to what was left of Carrière.

After two and a half decades, it was impossible to determine the boundaries of the little plantation's sugar fields. But it was clear that there wasn't enough high ground between Malheur and the surrounding marshes for the place to have made much of a profit in any case after its first few years, and now the land was soggy and nearly worthless. January guessed that even in 1815 Carrière had been undermanned. More work for everyone, especially at harvest.

Leaving Hannibal to sit on the granite mounting block before the house itself, he walked through the quarters, broken hut timbers buried now under decades of brown weeds. Places where men and women had lived and died. Where children had played, until they were sold away like half-grown colts. He could count only six cabins in all.

Even with two families per hut, and two or three men of working age per family . . .

'That's odd.' He waded back through the weeds to where Hannibal sat sipping ginger water from one of the gourds they'd brought from town. The fiddler raised his brows; offered him the vessel.

'The house wasn't burned,' said January.

His companion turned on his stony seat, studied the faded walls with their curtain of shaggy creepers. 'No charring.' He rose to follow January to the remains of the steps up to the gallery. 'That is curious.'

Resurrection fern had split the stucco that sheathed the tall piers of the foundation, and rain had crumbled the soft Louisiana brick. One end of the house sagged heavily, like a camel frozen in the act of getting to its feet. January pushed aside the feathery leaves; peered up at the cypress timbers of the floor over his head.

Cautiously – the piers were not in good shape anywhere – January moved around the perimeter of the building. A little smoke-blackening was visible near the back stairs, nothing more.

'It looks like someone just chucked a torch on the ground under the steps and ran for it.'

'Yes, doesn't it?' January turned to scan the ruined brick chimney and weed-choked timbers of the kitchen. 'None of the cabins were burned. The roofs of the stables and one of the barns have what looks like fire damage, but not much.'

'Sloppy.' Hannibal shook his head disapprovingly as they returned to the front of the house. 'Can't even do a proper job of an insurrection. Would the family have been here at all, what with rumors of a British landing? It's a little far from town for comfort.'

The gallery steps creaked ominously beneath his scrawny weight as he ascended.

'Probably not,' called January up after him. 'But it was sugar-boiling season – the source of the whole year's income. And we're a good five miles from the British lines, and that five miles is through the back swamp. Michie Lafrennière might have been here, with an overseer, but the family would have been in town—'

'Bloodstain up here.' The fiddler stopped at the top of the steps. 'Quite a large one.'

Keeping to one side of the steps to let the risers take his weight, January followed him up. The cypress beams, he guessed, would survive Judgment Day, but the piers themselves, damaged by weather and flooding, had all shifted over the years and seemed ready to shift a good deal more under human weight and human movement.

The house had obviously been looted, the French doors and shutters of every room carried off long ago by the neighbors. But it was difficult to tell whether this had been done on the day of the battle or by the neighbors, days or weeks later. Swamp folk never let hinges, windows, doors go to waste, and Carrière, like most plantation houses, had been the family's place of business and little more.

The bloodstain on the gallery planks looked large enough to have been fatal, January thought.

And yet . . .

Standing in the open aperture of what had been a French window, he said, 'It wasn't the slaves who did this.'

Hannibal had gone to kneel beside the hearth bricks, which had concealed a hidey-hole, empty now save for a single tarnished earring: he swiveled on his heels. 'Did someone leave a card?'

'No broken glass on the floor.' January picked his way carefully over the lopsided planks to the double doorway that separated parlor from dining room; peeked from there into the pantry, where the floor slanted dangerously in the direction of the bayou. 'Nothing damaged—' Three cautious steps brought him to the door of what would have been the plantation office. Reduced to mold-black blocks of hardened pulp by twenty-five years of rain, account books, ledgers, the remains of boxes of receipts ranged along the wall where they'd been tossed when the shelving had been pried off the wall and carried away.

'Insurrectionists would have destroyed everything in sight,' he explained. 'If they were angry enough to stay and set fire to the house – instead of simply running away into the swamp – they would have done more damage. There would be broken dishes in the pantry. These papers' – he gestured, as Hannibal tiptoed to his side – 'would have been hurled all over the room, or more likely piled up in the middle of the floor and burned. But somebody just wanted the shelving. The desk, too, I think—'

The floor rocked warningly under his feet as he edged across to the crushed, nearly unrecognizable patches of debris: ink bottles, the black stains of spilled ink, the remaining grit where blotting sand had been dumped. String and bits of sealing wax, broken quills, an old-fashioned pencil and bits of chalk, though the slates that had served for figuring accounts were gone.

'If men and women that angry – angry enough to risk capture by staying to destroy – had been in this room,' January continued, kneeling carefully to stir the clotted detritus with his fingers, 'the furniture wouldn't have survived to be carried off. And if later thieves had taken broken things away for firewood, we'd still see the splinters and scraps too small to carry off. We'd see bits of stuffing, torn scraps of cloth.'

'It's the same in the parlor.' Hannibal looked around him at the room, and out through the gaping window-holes at the foliage of a quarter-century of neglect. '*Sævitque animis ignobile vulgus,* as Virgil observes. *Jamque faces et saxa volant* . . . It doesn't look like anything in there was actually smashed – though of course neighbors who have very little will snap up anything that can be used or sold or burned to heat the house. At least the villagers in County Mayo would, if they had the misfortune to rent from my family. So – what happened?'

January stood and wiped his hands on a bandana taken from his pocket. Like Hannibal, he studied the room again, trying – as he had done with Mamzelle de Cedillos on the *Eclipse* – to fit together what he had been told with what he saw.

'Not what people think.'

TWELVE

Dufresne had been burned.

It was past noon by this time. While January investigated the ruins – half-familiar, from his long-ago patrol after the battle – Hannibal, exhausted, slumped on a broken pile of bricks that had been a kitchen chimney, where an oak tree had taken root to provide shade. Foundation piers still supported the Big House's cypress flooring, and though the roof was gone, and several of the rooms showed signs of the blaze, the house had not been gutted. Looted, January guessed, before the fire took hold.

'Before?' Hannibal frowned up at him, shading his eyes against the light. 'Why would slaves who were going to head for the swamp steal chairs and dishes? Silverware, maybe, to sell—'

'Sell to who?' January shook his head at the gourd the fiddler held out to him – the last of the three they'd brought. It would be a long way back to the river. In the ciprière, even the water from plantation wells was customarily filtered. For the whites it was anyway. He remembered how many babies he'd heard of, in his early childhood, dying of 'bloody flux.' 'Any man of color who came offering silverware to any pirate in the Barataria would find himself in irons on his way to the slave exchange in Cartagena before dinnertime.'

'Ah. Ab alio expectes, alteri quod faceris—'

'There were no charred or broken pieces of furniture in any of the rooms – not even where the floor and walls were smoke-blackened.' He had noticed that, he recalled, when the Second Battalion's patrol had been here immediately after the battle, but he'd thought little of it at the time. 'No pieces too badly damaged for later looters to carry off. Nothing. The doors were taken off their hinges – which says to me that someone took the time to hitch up the plantation wagon and had a place to sell the doors. Not even the screws were left.'

'Well, they cost a fortune, back then.'

'That's not all. You can see where fire scorched the door frames where the edges of doors would have protected them.' He demonstrated with his hands. 'There was fire-blackening in the sockets of the hinges as well—'

'And no broken glass?'

'No.'

'That sounds more like my family's rent collector back home than a gang of outraged slaves.'

'It does,' said January softly, 'doesn't it?' He wondered a little why he hadn't seen this on that long-ago, earlier visit: *Probably because I was only twenty-two*. And, he remembered, night had been falling when the patrol had arrived.

Hannibal was silent for a time, thinking about that. At last he said, 'There seem to be more things in Heaven and earth – or at least going on here – than are dreamt of in our philosophy, Horatio. And I'm rather curious about what they are.'

In the years since 1815, the house at Doux-Malheur had been rebuilt, but like Chalmette, the little plantation was no longer a working farm. Its current owner, a well-off libré merchant, divided his time between New Orleans and Natchez. January knew the man – Aristide Peychaud – only by sight but knew also from meetings of the FTFCMBS that he was in town for the Carnival season. That evening, after seeing the fiddler to Olympe's cottage on the Rue Douane (he knew if he returned him to the Keelboat, its proprietress would force him to either make music for the customers or deal faro for the house), he penned a letter to Peychaud, asking for a meeting in absolute secrecy.

> *This is for your safety as well as mine. I will not hide from you the fact that I believe that someone is trying to discourage me, by threat of violence, from making inquiries about a so-called plot to betray the American forces at the Battle of Chalmette by means of a slave uprising. If you do not feel that you are able to take the risk of meeting me, please say so. I will not be offended, and ask only that you speak to no one of receiving this letter . . .*

Peychaud's reply came the following afternoon.

My dear Janvier, all my life I have waited for the opportunity to sneak to a clandestine rendezvous in disguise! I fear I cannot tell you much about the old house at Doux-Malheur, but what I know is absolutely at your disposal. I will be at one of the tables near La Violette's coffee-stand in the market at six o'clock tomorrow morning (as I assume you will be playing at the Faubourg Tremé Colored Militia and Burial Society masked ball this evening and I know such festivities customarily run on into the small hours). I shall be clothed entirely in yellow. I will have kept a chair at my table vacant.

(January was well aware of how difficult it was to find a vacant seat at one of those coffee-stand tables at that hour during Carnival.)

If you ask if that seat is free I will make a fuss about my companion of the evening having deserted me, and will assent. However you are disguised tonight, please wear multiple plumes on your headgear so I will know that it's you. A.P. FMC.

That would, January knew, make for another very long day. In addition to making up yesterday's missed lesson with little Flora McCullen, he had a lesson out in Carrollton with the Walters children at three, followed by a brief meeting at Bernadette Metoyer's chocolate shop with a harried-looking Dagobert Janvier.

'Saturday— no, Sunday – I insist we look again at those three plantations. I am positive there is something there, something that will tell us . . .' Janvier sighed a little as he spoke. 'Tomorrow I'm meeting with Daugherty and Sons – the brokers for the Villeré plantation, you know – at the Exchange, and I hope that will finish this lawsuit about my father-in-law's 1838 shipment discrepancies.' He looked both exhausted and peevish, his mouth bracketed by the same grooves January had so often seen on the face of St-Denis Janvier.

It crossed his mind, as he walked back from Metoyer's shop to change his clothes for the masked ball, that it was no wonder his mother's protector had sought a beautiful mistress whose very demands had been frivolous. Dresses, ear-bobs, evenings at the Salle d'Orléans . . . Anything to take him away from the demands of business, of juggling available specie against some English merchant's promissory note, of nailing down the commitments of Planter A while investigating rumors of the likelihood that Planter B's crop would fail and engender obligations that could not be met without a bank loan. At least, January thought, everybody at the dance tonight would bring excellent food and not be stingy about sharing it with the musicians. Balls at the back of town were always more fun.

He had already made arrangements with Pierre Davis to borrow the largest of the supernumeraries' costumes from last season's performance of *I Puritani*, complete with a Cavalier's curly wig and bucket-top boots. He coupled this with a full-face Devil mask left over from *Orpheus and Eurydice*, and borrowed plumes from the hats of every woman he knew, to obfuscate his formidable height. When he slipped out of Dominique's kitchen – where he changed clothes after escorting her home from the festivities at a quarter past five – if not unobtrusive, he was at least unrecognizable.

The only person in the crowded tables beneath the brick marketplace arcades dressed entirely in yellow was a stout, tightly corseted white woman gowned as a medieval princess. January had to look three times at the rice-powdered face, painted eyes, and ridiculous blonde wig – and the fact that the empty chair beside her was the only empty chair on that side of the market – before he crossed to her: 'Is that seat occupied, m'am?'

'It *should* be occupied,' she retorted in a falsetto squeak, 'by my good-for-nothing cousin, who *should* have been here an hour ago. Serve him right if he *does* come now and finds he's not the only fish in the sea. Do have a seat, M'sieu.' She simpered as she gestured with her fan. The multicolored explosion of feathers on January's hat nodded like a forest in the wind as he swept it off in a profound bow.

In the jumping orange glow of the cressets, the features could have been a white's or a fair-complected octoroon's, a woman's or a man's, beneath that layer of maquillage. As January took the chair, his companion gave him a saucy wink.

The heavily bejeweled hands, January now saw – curved around the cheap tin cup of coffee – were big, the hands of a man. And it was a man's voice that whispered, 'I'm at your service, M'sieu. What a *fetching* hat!'

'Borrowed it from the opera house. Thank you for meeting me.'

'So who is making threats of violence about my house?' Peychaud sipped the coffee and pretended to scan the clusters of late-walking revelers gathered around La Violette's steaming cart. 'I bought the place from a man named Desdunes – he's some kind of a relative of the Forstalls, who had it from one of them, a brother-in-law or nephew or something. I think it was the Forstalls who built the house, after they bought the land. I'd heard it was a plantation back in Spanish times, but it's not really big enough to make a profitable go of sugar. And the bayou silted up so badly during the hurricane of '31 that you can't get more than a pirogue through from the lake on it, if you're lucky.'

Something in the way he said it – and lifted one plucked eyebrow beneath the rim of a padded escoffion the size of a wagon wheel – made January wonder if the house on that shallow bayou had been purchased as a depot for smuggling. The cipriѐre stretched behind the town and behind the plantations that lined the river as far south as Pointe à la Hache, in a labyrinth of small bayous and shallow lakes, clear to the Gulf. Jean Lafitte and his brother Pierre had organized hundreds of small operatives to bring in goods from Spain in defiance of American tariffs – wines and guns, lead and slaves – and the breakup of their network in 1823 had not touched these capillaries of contraband.

And if that's the case, can I trust anything this man says about the house and the events of 1815?

'You've heard the rumors that the original house was burned in a slave insurrection at the time of the battle at Chalmette?'

'I've heard it happened.' All the gems of Peychaud's rings glittered as he spread those big hands. 'The two places up the bayou were burned, too. They're part of my property now, but even together they're not enough to get a crop worth harvesting. You can't get a boat up the bayou anymore past Doux-Malheur.'

'Have you heard anything about that insurrection?' asked January. 'What triggered it, whether any of the rebels were captured or killed? Whether anyone helped them? Whether they escaped into the cipriѐre or joined the British?'

'I can't imagine why they'd have done that, if they could just hide out in the woods,' Peychaud pointed out. 'I gather that was a good deal easier back then. My brother swears half the swamp trappers from the river to Mobile have doors, windows, and wagon wheels looted from those plantations, and up until about ten years ago – according to M'sieu Desdunes anyway – there were four or five regular little villages of runaways in the back swamp, on islands where nobody could find them.'

The sausage curls of his wig caught the orange fire glare as he shook his head. 'Though how *he'd* know I have no notion – the man never leaves town. As for what triggered the revolt, I expect the darkies thought it was a good time to get away in the confusion. Maybe they thought the British would help them.'

'Have you ever heard that the uprisings were coordinated?' asked January. '*Did* all three happen on the same day?'

'Like the lawyers say, I don't know it of my own knowledge. My grandpa Peychaud was in town then and says so. He also claims it was the Spanish who organized it – the Spanish who were still furious that Spain did some secret deal with France to give Louisiana back to France, and then France sold it to the Americans. Americans who were doing secret deals with Spain the whole time, selling American secrets for Spanish silver, and what did the Spanish get out of it, who'd lived here in Louisiana all those years, eh?' He chuckled. 'We kids would get him going on it just to hear him curse. But it was true. France didn't wait three years before passing Louisiana on like it was a plate of cookies.'

'You ever go out there yourself to stay?' January was aware of how many of the smaller plantation houses – including the one at Chalmette – due to either flooding or soil exhaustion, were used now merely as country residences by those who wanted to get out of the stinks and noise of New Orleans. He sensed, too, the lively energy that lurked under those layers of daffodil silk, woven ribbon, and avoirdupois.

'In spring before it gets too hot,' agreed Peychaud. 'And in the autumn. The air's better, and the duck hunting superb.'

'Is there anything left of the old house? Or was it burned completely to the ground?'

'No idea. My boys go exploring in the ciprière, and they never mentioned a ruined house. I've certainly never seen one. M'sieu Desdunes might know, or old Matthieu Forstall, who was the one bought the land from Jacques-Pierre Briard in the first place. It might not be safe,' he added, raising his head as if he'd sighted someone in the Place d'Armes beyond – throughout the conversation, he had not looked at January, speaking softly, and often behind his fan. January, for his part, had gazed vacantly out into the market archways, chin leaned on his hands as if he were a reveler still three-parts drunk.

You never could tell who might be watching.

'You said somebody threatened you – for just asking?'

'I don't know,' said January. 'A threat was made, just after I started asking questions. Since I don't know exactly what I'm supposed to stop doing or asking – or what might happen to the people who answer my questions – I think keeping my mouth shut and my head down might be a good idea.'

'Damn Americans.' Peychaud gathered his cloak – what seemed like five acres of lemon-hued 'Dutch velvet' – around plump shoulders. 'Or damn Spanish because I swear to you we haven't heard the last of them, with Americans waltzing into their northern territories to trap fur and into California to grab land. If you care to come out to Doux-Malheur and have a look around the place for yourself, you're welcome to do it. There's nobody out there now and the house is locked up, but you might find where the old house stood and have a look at that.'

'I may do that,' agreed January. *How did he know my attackers at Alegre were American?* Or was that just a guess?

He watched the gaudy figure disappear – with disconcerting quickness – into the thinning crowd.

'That chair taken, sir?' a voice asked immediately to his left, and with a good imitation of a half-dozing start, January turned and saw a Bedouin in robes of orange and gold with a pink-draped odalisque on his arm.

'Be my guest, sir.' January rose, offering his own seat to the giggling houri.

The foggy dark – and the late-walking crowd – were both just thinning as he made his way, carefully, up Rue Dumaine, aware again of just how difficult it was, in pre-dawn mists, to tell if he were being followed or not. On Rue Bourbon he turned into a doorway long enough to stuff his cloak and mask, wig and plume-bedizened hat into the sack that the cloak had hidden (*Minou will never forgive me if I lose her ostrich plumes . . .*). He removed his gloves and unstrapped the lace-cuffed Cavalier boots – they were actually leggings buckled under the insteps of his shoes – and waited until a group of market women passed by, with their baskets of carrots, leeks, and Caribbean oranges on their heads, before slipping out in their wake.

As he crossed Rue Bourbon, passing beneath the wooly yellow ravel of the streetlamp's glow, for an instant he saw . . .

What?

Something that flagged his attention, among a group of home-wandering revelers on the other side of the street. But when he looked again they were already barely more than cut-out forms in the mist beyond the streetlamp, with a Devil's red tail dragging on the banquette from the seat of someone's trousers. Voices lifted in a woozy chorus:

> *Run, nigger, run, for the patrol will catch you . . .*
> *Run, nigger, run, for 'tis almost day . . .*

My boys go exploring in the ciprière, Peychaud had said, *and they never mentioned a ruined house . . .*

January wondered how old those boys were. Old enough to flee from slave stealers? Or white enough to be unsalable goods? The merchant himself he judged to be octoroon, with one great-grandparent out of eight of African blood – or with some mixture of more distant ancestors that amounted to the same percentage. Marriage with a woman only slightly darker than himself – and January knew that the fairer-complected musterfino families of the French Town frowned mightily upon their offspring wedding those who were more obviously African descended – would produce children who could 'pass.' Unless of course they had the misfortune of inheriting African features, as poor M'sieu Couvillier had been accused of doing.

Clearly, this had never occurred to Aristide Peychaud. His money, January guessed, had protected him. Money and parents related to one of New Orleans' well-off white families. He might well have been sent to school in Mexico or France, and hadn't had to grow up glancing over his shoulder. Just as his money – and possibly a closer connection than he'd admit with the smugglers of the Gulf – would protect his sons.

Even Gilles Gignac, January reflected, hadn't understood, as Rose – the daughter of a white man and a free-born plaçée – didn't understand. As the girls in the school didn't understand what it was to never be quite free.

Callie Medoc had understood. Callie had been born in slavery. Her father, a free grocer, had bought both Callie and her mother when Callie was six.

I could have married Callie.

The thought wasn't new to him. Callie had lived on Rue L'Hôpital near the Gignac family and had been part of that little group of friends who had hunted frogs in the gutters, played marbles and rolled hoops in the hot summer evenings when everybody's chores were done. January had loved her, though not as he'd loved – with passionate desperation – the beautiful Catherine Clisson, whose plaçée mother also lived on Rue L'Hôpital. But when Catherine had broken his sixteen-year-old heart by becoming plaçée in her turn – to an elderly planter with more children than he had teeth – Callie had been there, friendly and kind.

Other than a couple of whores on the levee that he, Gilles, and Davy had gone to one evening after bragging and daring each other, Callie had been the first girl that he had lain with. For a time, when he was seventeen, he had thought he was in love with her, which turned out not to be the case. ('*Oh, come on, Ben, why play all that old stuff? Play something that a body can sing!*')

But he knew he could have married her.

He had been thinking of it, that hot autumn of 1814, when Jackson offered that 160 acres of newly acquired government land to any man of color who would join the militia. Even the other musicians, when he began to play at balls and parties, were married, with families. At the time, he had thought it a necessary part of becoming an adult.

Of being free to live his own life.

The market-women turned away down Rue St-Philippe. There were fewer people here, and the darkness had thinned, like a poor woman's twice-diluted tea. Several of the lanterns that hung above the intersections had burned out. Looking around, January could see nothing of the Devil's dragging tail. *What made me look twice to begin with? Something . . .*

Recollection teased him, and the awful sense of danger narrowly avoided.

The people on the banquettes were peddlers now, like the market women: fish, soap, callas. ('Hot callas, *hot*!') Or men on their way to work on the wharves, any of whom could be . . . not what he seemed.

But *why*?

And if I went out to Doux-Malheur, he wondered, *would I make it back to town*?

. . . *imagination bodies forth the forms of things unknown*, says Theseus, in that most beautiful of Shakespeare's plays. *In the night, imagining some fear / how easy is a bush supposed a bear?*

And how many men had died, January wondered, with the words, *Oh, don't be silly, it's only a bush*, on their lips?

THIRTEEN

He had gone partway down Rue St-Philippe in the wake of the market women, in the hopes of shaking possibly imaginary bears off his track, when across the street he saw a shabby market vendor with a great basket of fish balanced on his head. The man called out, 'Fishes! Fishes for your dinner! So fresh they bite your fingers!' in a rough, deep voice, nasal accents exacerbated by the fact that in place of his nose he had only a boiled-leather sheath, covering where that missing organ had been.

January stopped on the banquette—

'Fishes from the Gulf! Fishes from the ocean—'

—then plunged across the street, the old man turning sharply at the anomalous tread coming up behind him, curiously like the fencing master Mayerling. As if the echo of past dangers lived on in his bones.

'Cut-Nose!'

The gargoyle face wreathed itself in a grin. 'Piano Player!' He swung the fish basket down from his head, threw his arms wide. 'Long time since we met!'

'Too long.' January returned the enthusiastic embrace. 'You're selling fish now, sir? What happened to the vegetable stand in the market?'

'What, for three bunches of onions and a basket of kale, this time of year? Even my grandson Jean can take care of that one! Ursulie – my granddaughter – she's having her baby, so I tell her husband I take care of the fishies today . . .' He paused, dark eyes suddenly sharp as January turned his head at the movement of a shadowy figure on the other side of the street. 'Somethin' wrong, Piano Player?'

'I don't know.' The next instant January identified the waddling shape as Old Lupita, as the stout, black-clothed woman emerged from a carriageway with her buckets of milk. 'That's one reason I'm so glad to see you—'

'Other than to look at my handsome face, eh? Or to buy my

beautiful fishies? You break an old man's heart.' He pressed his hands to his chest in a gesture of grief and laughed. 'And how's the beautiful Rose, eh? I hear nothing but good of her, teaching that school of hers. Teachin' about real things, like the clouds an' storms an' how to make gunpowder, an' the glories of ancient Rome.' Old Cut-Nose might have been uneducated, but as an Italian he knew all about the glories of the Caesars.

And, January reflected, was probably an expert in his own right as to the precise distinctions between obtrunco and decido.

'I will buy some of your beautiful fishes,' promised January, 'if you'll come and have a cup of coffee with me and tell me a story about fighting the British at Chalmette.'

There were coffee stands near the canal's turning basin, on the other side of Rue des Ramparts from where they stood, that were open at this hour, to serve the men who worked the barges and the men who'd spent the night in such local doggeries as the Flesh and Blood and the Nantucket. But January guessed that too many people in that neighborhood would recognize Jean Lafitte's former lieutenant. Instead, he suggested Auntie Houlette's, at the far end of the levee market from La Violette's, and the old man gave him another sharp sidelong look.

'You want that I meet you there in half an hour?' he asked, and gratefully, January said:

'That sounds like a good idea.'

There were many things that didn't have to be explained to Cut-Nose Chigizola.

January stopped at his house long enough to drop off the opera company's Cavalier disguise, change his jacket and his boots, and borrow fifty cents from his nephew Gabriel (encountered in the kitchen taking rolls from the oven) for the promised fish. Not, he reflected, that he could be missed, if someone were watching him – or watching the house. The plumed hat had obscured any exact idea of his height, but at six feet three and just over two hundred pounds of solid muscle, he knew a mere different-colored jacket wouldn't cause anyone to think, *Nah, that can't be him . . .*

But the rear corner of the slightly crooked courtyard behind the house backed on to the passway between two houses that faced on to the Rue Burgundy. Rose – also in the kitchen – helped him fetch a ladder and climb over the wall in that corner. 'Ti-Gall walked around the house before it got light,' she reported, as she steadied the rungs. 'He saw no one, except a gentleman personating one half of a horse, searching for his forequarters. But of course anyone could switch costumes.'

January said, 'Exactly,' and paused to kiss her before ascending. She smelled of soap, ink, and chemical experiments, her cuffs damp from washing up during the preparations for breakfast. 'And whoever it is who broke into the house the other night, I'm taking no chances.'

He reached Houlette's coffee stand a few minutes later, set up under a rough shelter along one wall of a warehouse on the dirt road that skirted the wharves, just short of the Pontchartrain Railroad's terminal shed. Railroad workers, stevedores, sailors, and well-dressed merchants crowded every table set nearby, with not a costumed reveler in sight. Like Dagobert's negotiations with plantation factors and British merchant houses, this was serious business. Even the rough seas of winter didn't still the deep-water trade coming up the Mississippi from the Balize and the Gulf.

The only seat vacant, in fact, was the one occupied by a large willow basket of fish covered over with a layer of wet leaves. Seated on the other chair at the tiny table, Cut-Nose had removed the leather sheath that covered the flat mass of scar tissue where his nose had been, effectively guaranteeing that no one was going to come and ask him to move his wares. It was a sight not conducive to good appetite.

January purchased a tin cup of coffee – in between customers, La Houlette rinsed the cups in a bucket of what looked like river water beside her cart – and looked around at the crowded tables with an expression of diffident exasperation. Heaving a sigh, he made his way towards the spot with the wet fish and noseless gargoyle. 'Do you mind if I share your table, M'sieu?' he asked, for the benefit of the brokers on both sides.

'Ovviamente!' Cut-Nose lifted the dripping basket and plunked it on to the table itself, whipped out a bandana from his pocket to dry the chair, and, as January seated himself, added, 'Mi scusi, mi scusi,' as he dug in his pocket for his nose. Though he spoke perfectly good French, the old pirate said, in clumsy English as he tapped the side of the replacement proboscis, 'A duel, capisci; pirates, eh? Blackbeard, Morgan, Jean Lafitte . . . Lafitte himself, he cut it off, whoosh!' He made a slash with his hand that would have removed January's own nose, had the old pirate been armed.

January mimed astonishment. Cut-Nose leaned close to him, gestured persuasively, then seized him by the lapel of his jacket and pulled him forward, seemingly to inspect the contents of the basket. The tables around them were noisy enough to cover a quiet conversation.

'So who you think following you, eh? At this hour of the morning?'

New sunlight splattered the surface of the brown Mississippi like treasonous gold.

'I don't know,' returned January, in the undervoiced combination of French and what Italian he knew, in which the pirate had addressed him. 'But just after I took a job for a man who's seeking information about what happened – or didn't happen – behind the lines at the battle of Chalmette, men broke into my house and cut up the beds where my wife, my sons, and my family had been sleeping minutes before. And men attacked me, when I went out to the plantation of the man who's supposed to have made a deal with the British back then—'

'What, that Spanish fellow?'

'Bartolomé de Cedillos?'

'Somethin' like that.' The old man adjusted the set of his nose, then drew January back down to look at the fish again. With a proud flourish, he turned back a blanket of wet Spanish moss to reveal an immense yellow hogfish. 'Fellow was run around just when the British bringin' their men in across Lake Borgne, roundin' up Spanish that worked on the wharves, or trapped in the swamps, or hauled goods from the lake into the city—'

'Spanish? Did you see him doing this? Or speak to anyone he approached?'

Cut-Nose shook his head. 'I was down at Grand Terre, where the Boss' – this was what the Barataria pirates had called Lafitte – 'had his headquarters. I heard this from a couple of Chamoflet's men.' He named one of the smugglers currently operating in the marshes of the Barataria. 'Maybe it was from some of the girls, the ones with family in the town.'

A rumor, then? The Boss and his captains, January knew, had mistresses, mostly free women of color, but some Spanish or French.

White and colored alike, these women were looked upon with scorn by the plaçées of New Orleans itself.

'It was long time ago, you know?' The old pirate unveiled another portion of his basket, shining silver snappers wreathed in a garland of sardines. January mimed dazzled admiration. 'What I heard was, this de Cedillos – if that was his name – he was all agonized over that France sold Louisiana to America. Well, so was the government of Mexico, you know. They knew – same as every Spaniard in Louisiana knew – that the Americans was already all over the border into northern Mexico and talkin' about, why don't we just go on through and invade Mexico for the silver mines they got? I don't blame 'em.'

Chigizola shrugged. 'You read any newspaper today an' you see. The Americans, they take over all of Texas now. It ain't that far to New Mexico and the Santa Rita mines. Anyhow, I heard later de Cedillos put together a crew of about eighty Spanish and maybe thirty Choctaw an' Chickasaw that didn't trust the Americans as far as I could pick up an' throw a hogshead of sugar – an' you read any newspaper about that today, an' see who was wrong bein' suspicious of who. These Spanish boys was supposed to burn a couple plantations near town, an' then run to Jackson's soldiers just as the British was attackin', an' tell 'em the slaves was risin' up, which always makes Americans tutti pazzi, eh?' He tapped his temple with a thick brown forefinger. 'Then when half the Americans go runnin' back to see what's happenin', this Spanish militia marches through the ciprière an' jumps what's left of the American line from behind.'

'Nothing about the slaves themselves rebelling?'

'Not that I heard.' The old pirate frowned. 'But I heard all this later, see, when the Boss and all of us moved down to Campeche.'

'And what happened to de Cedillos?' January asked curiously. 'Obviously the plan didn't come off. Why not? What happened? Did he get killed?'

'Well, he was a planter.' Cut-Nose thought about it for a moment. 'Those swamp trappers, an' the guys that hauled cargo by the wharves, an' maybe a smuggler or two – maybe the blacks, too, I don't know . . . I think de Cedillos was in over his head. Any one of those bourreaux, you give 'em a cataplasm about how they're not followin' your orders, they'll turn around and hit you with whatever they got in their hand.'

He rearranged the leaves over his fish, frowning again as he pulled together recollections decades old. Men ran down the wharves, bearing rope or sails to some of the boats. From others, casks and bales were being unloaded, barrels lowered in nets from the holds. The morning was growing bright as the last of the fog burned away.

'And the Spanish were paying him for this? How? In silver?'

'Everybody talks about pirate treasure.' Chigizola shrugged. 'But that much silver . . . that's a lot of metal to be luggin' around. The Boss, now, he'd fix it up with bankers in town. Whatever he stole, he'd sell right off and get credit papers, or bills of exchange doctored up so no one would ask questions. There was always some banker who'd sign and not ask questions.'

He turned his head quickly at the sound of commotion on one of the wharves. A crate had somehow gotten knocked over the edge into the river. From where he was sitting, January half-saw, half-guessed at movement in the water below the planks, and the gleam as somebody reached out from the glistening shadows with a hooked pole, to fish the floating crate quickly out of sight.

The men on the wharf itself paid no attention. When the boat's supercargo came storming over, heads were shaken: *Current got it, sir – pulled it right down out of sight . . .*

Another thing, January reflected, that happened when the City Guards were all recuperating from a night-long tangle with drunks outside the saloons of Gallatin Street . . .

'Maybe them Indian boys didn't trust him to pay them, and there was trouble over that,' the old pirate went on at length. 'Maybe he tried to break up a fight he shouldn't have messed in. I heard about those three plantations that got burned, but I didn't hear about nobody runnin' no five miles through the swamps to tell the Americans about no slave rebellion. Sure nobody ran to attack a bunch of hard-assed Tennessee militia from the rear, British or no British.'

'So nobody ever found de Cedillos's body.'

'From that swamp?' The thick eyebrows wrenched a whole landform of scar tissue upwards. 'You got a corpse you want nobody to find, that country out between town and the lake, or downriver of town between the river an' Lake Borgne . . . Everybody knows it's a lot less work than diggin' a hole, an' sure a lot less like to be found, if you just slit your man's belly or weight his feet. You like them fish?'

'I do.' January was glad he'd borrowed Gabriel's fifty cents but felt painfully aware that in spending what was left of Dagobert Janvier's money, he was now in no position to return it and back out.

'Take this big boy here.' Chigizola slapped the hogfish's plump side. And when January hesitated – the thing must have weighed twenty pounds and was far more than fifty cents – he waved a dismissive hand. 'Nah, take him. Give the Signora Rose my love, an' this fish for her an' your boys. Caught him fresh this mornin'. I never did get anythin' for you when your boy John was born, an' now you got Xander, too. You name him for Alexander the Great, no?' (In fact little Xander's official name was what Hannibal had been called, long ago in another life.)

'I'm behind on gifts. Please,' the old pirate added. 'In eleven days it's gonna be Lent. Those boys of yours, they gotta get used to likin' fish, and this one's the best! Houlie!' He half-stood and waved to the tiny, pug-faced woman beside the coffee cart. 'Lemme have a couple newspapers, eh? To wrap up some fish.'

She came across with them and gave him a smile. January had observed that pretty much everybody in New Orleans was happy to oblige old Cut-Nose, who in addition to manning the cannons on Lafitte's ship during the battle of Chalmette had helped the pirate procure cheap goods – and smuggled slaves – for most of the people in town.

And he still knew people who might 'oblige.'

January went home carrying the hogfish in his arms like a dripping baby, fresh and smelling of the sea.

A make-up lesson for the Savonnière girls would be at two o'clock. Though the streets of the French Town would be no less lively with revelers than usual that evening, there were no large entertainments being given by the French or Spanish Creole grandees, and concerned as he was about the family finances, January felt a sense of relief.

The uneasy feeling of being watched had not left him. Lack of sleep exacerbated this: he knew his senses were less sharp than they should be. Twice, walking quickly along the Street of Frenchmen away from the wharves, he glimpsed a small form on the other side of the street about a hundred feet behind him, gaudily costumed as a gypsy and carrying a basket on her head. He noticed her because she was masked as well as costumed – neither usual for marchandes in this neighborhood at this time of the morning. The second time he noticed her, he observed that her tignon wasn't wrapped correctly, too close wound and knotted in the back. Not like the tignon of any market woman he'd seen anywhere in his life.

He turned right on Craps Street (*Only Bernard Marigny would pick that name for a street*!), heading downriver, then left, towards the swamps, along the dirt embankment of the railway line to the lake. Left again on the Street of Good Children . . .

When he looked again, the market woman was gone.

A woman, he thought. Little and bony and walking with the tough grace of a fighter.

God knows there's plenty of them along the waterfront . . .

But he'd seen her before. He knew it.

He turned half a dozen more times before he made for his house.

Two notes waited for him when he slipped cautiously down the passway into the yard, to ceremoniously present Chigizola's gift to the bemused Rose.

One message was tidily sealed with red wax, stamped with the mark he recognized from his childhood: the stylized head of the two-faced Janus, the Roman god of doorways and beginnings, like old Papa Legba with his keys. *Janus. Janvier*. He'd seen the signet ring thousands of times, on St-Denis Janvier's finger. The ring wouldn't fit Dagobert's bigger hand, so he'd had it remade into a fob that he wore on his waistcoat chain, to seal the business correspondence of the family firm.

This wasn't business.

> *We must arrange to meet at Alegre again. I have spoken with Mademoiselle de Cedillos and she is positive that proof of Pelerine's complicity remains somewhere in the house. Her room on Crozat Street was searched yesterday, and she stands in fear of her life.*
>
> *Please come on Sunday at noon.*

January reflected resignedly, *I guess an expedition to Bayou Malheur is off, then . . .*

> *Conceal yourself in one of the shops along Rue Royale and send me word of your whereabouts. I will slip from the house unnoticed—*

With three maids, two gardeners, a butler, and your stepmama, I'd give a lot to see you try . . .

> *—and meet you. Do not fail me, my Patroclus!*
> *– Achilles*

January briefly calculated his prospects for leaving his own house unobserved at noon tomorrow – when everyone in New Orleans would be promenading in costume in the mild winter sunshine – and opened the second note.

The sight of the handwriting – characteristically sprawling, unlike Dagobert's cramped, careful script – made him smile, before he even read the words.

> *Ben – We're here in town, at Papa Medoc's place. Will you be at Passebon's party Monday night? – Gilles*

1814

Sleeping that morning – his mind divided between the Savonnière girls' lesson and how he and Rose would slip away unnoticed to Medoc's Grocery on Rue de l'Hôpital the minute it grew dark – January dreamed of starlight on the lines of tents before the de Macarty house. Of the smudgy yellow blear in two of its windows as the men assembled. Of the wet pong of the back swamp, the crunch of his boots in the mud and clamshells of the road.

Dreamed of silence, and the weight of a musket on his shoulder. Of how it felt to have his heart no warmer than the bitter air.

The day after tomorrow is Christmas.

You're going to have to kill a man. Maybe several men. Or die yourself.

Gilles walked beside him in the column of men; young Davy on Gilles's other side. The brothers he had never had. He recalled those Christmases of his childhood, when he'd gone with the boys and their mother to midnight Mass, his own mother being too busy entertaining her protector to even ask if he was on the premises or not.

I might not see Christmas.

His hands ached from rifle drill. Blisters from powder burns on his fingers smarted. He told himself not to think.

Père Antoine, the rector of the cathedral, had come out to the camp that afternoon, to hear confessions, say Mass and give the men the blessings of the Prince of Peace. 'Men do what they have to do,' he said.

January thought of the five years he had spent, learning ways to keep men from dying. To keep them from living in pain. Thought of music that he wanted to play. New tunes that he wanted to write, seething like a cookpot, overflowing his heart.

Where does music go, when its composer dies leaving those tunes unwritten? Does someone else write it?

I will do what I have to do.

A few rows ahead of them, at the head of the company, Captain Savary moved in tireless silence, the silence of a man who has marched to battles without count. *Who has done what he had to do . . .*

Though a man of color, Savary had been a lieutenant colonel with the French Army when the French had tried to quell the slave uprising in Saint-Domingue. Most of the Second Battalion were free men of color who had fled Saint-Domingue during the revolution in 1791. Many of these, like Savary, had sided with the whites of the colony in that hellish conflict and had been targeted by the rebelling slaves. Thousands had been killed. Major d'Aquin, nominal commander of the free colored forces, was from Saint-Domingue also. A white man – naturally.

But it was Savary who led.

The night bore the smoke from a hundred sugar mills, where men enslaved, like his father – *if my father is still alive* – carried cane to the rollers, stoked the fires beneath the cauldrons. Prayed for the end of the harvest season so they might rest. Even so, he could smell the British camp, six thousand men cooking, shitting, throwing away garbage for the rats. Across the moonless dark, pinpricks of torchlight.

Do no harm, he had sworn when he'd begun his training with Gomez. Gomez who was behind them in the camp, waiting for the wounded to be brought in.

I will do what I have to do.

The fight itself was chaotic, savage, disorganized, and nearly blind. January's dream splintered it into fragments like a broken wine glass. He'd bayonetted two men – even after twenty-six years he saw their faces – but told himself he'd already fired into the tents, so they weren't the first he'd killed. He didn't know why that was important to him – that they weren't the first. *Do no harm.* Beat another over the head with the clubbed butt of his musket; ducked, thrust, clobbered, and kicked men who came at him out of a confusion of firelight and smoke. He could still taste the bestial intensity of battle fury in his heart, a fury almost outside himself. The yelling around him went through his skull like an axe, but it only added to his own shouts of rage and terror. He remembered he'd been wounded, but this did not happen in his dream.

He thought he'd wake, wanted to wake before he was killed (*But I didn't die . . .*). Instead, there was that stumbling retreat across the dark fields when more redcoats had come up. Drums like thunder in the darkness, beating the signal for retreat.

Icy cold in the camp, and the crush of blinding weariness as the lines re-formed along the mill race. He'd watched across the field by the light of the new-risen moon, to see if the British would counter-attack. Savary walking along the line: 'You did well . . . You all right? Just hang on until morning . . . No sign of 'em yet . . .'

And Jackson's harsh voice, 'Tomorrow we get back to work on those redoubts. We'll yet push 'em into the Gulf!'

But the man next to January in the line of watchers growled, 'And guess who'll be doin' the shovel work on them redoubts. Not the blankittes – nor them stuck-up yellow mulattos.' He realized that the man mistook him for one of the five hundred slaves Jackson had 'negotiated' from the plantations to fight.

His mother was always telling him he looked like a cane-hand. Evidently the real cane-hands around him agreed.

'We gonna have to leave the state, when they frees us?' asked someone else softly, and a deeper voice replied:

'That land they'll be givin', that'll be what Michie Hickory took from the Creeks. It's only over in Alabama. It ain't that far.'

Like them, January understood that he wasn't fighting for who would rule Louisiana. He was fighting for himself. To be free.

FOURTEEN

1841

Marie Laveau lived in a cottage on Rue St-Ann, around the corner and across Rampart Street from the open ground variously known as Circus Square or Congo Square. January considered waiting until late Sunday afternoon – when the informal market there would be ending, the slaves of the surrounding plantations, who came to town to sell their own small vegetable crops, or eggs from their chickens, or Spanish moss they'd gathered in their own scant free time, would turn to drumming, dancing, eating the gumbo that somebody would always be selling there cheap. The voodooiennes and root doctors would come to that market as well, to sell herbs and candles, or the blessings of sacred smoke or water splashed with bunches of tobacco and sweetgrass. Shifty river traders, black and white, like Natchez Jim or False River Jones, would lurk in the shadows, surreptitiously buying or bartering for pilfered coffee beans or items 'lost' from the masters' laundry. With twilight, blankittes would linger by the gates of the square to stare. Especially during Carnival, a lot of people would be coming and going.

Good cover, thought January, for him to slip into the voodoo queen's residence unnoticed.

And by that time I'll have met Bertie on Rue Royale and presumably have convinced him that we practically took Alegre apart and found nothing . . .

But he knew also that Mamzelle Marie would be a part of that afternoon gathering, dancing on a platform made of goods boxes with her great seven-foot king snake; African dances learned from her mother and her grandmother. He knew, too, that at such times the power of the loa, the ancient gods (in which he had been carefully taught not to believe anymore) was in her, filling her flesh and her soul like all-devouring flame. She would almost certainly return to her home physically and emotionally spent.

So he rose, and washed, and dressed in the dark before dawn

(*I'll sleep when I get home*), and made his way to the cathedral (dodging the occasional revelers still at large), to kneel in the side aisles among the market women. To murmur the responses and receive the Host. And over the bent heads, the flower garden of bright-hued tignons and the bared, scruffy pates of workmen and vendors, he saw one dark-red tignon worked into seven points.

The time and the place were scarcely more appropriate than after an exhausting afternoon, but caution still pricked him. Like him, Mamzelle Marie went to the altar rail to receive the Host, her thirteen-year-old daughter beside her; they were among the last to rise and leave after the priest's dismissal. January was the first. He waited in the shadowy arcade of the court building, watching as the men and women came down the steps.

She was, again, behind the others. He guessed she'd stopped to light a candle to the Blessed Virgin for the sake of the four children she had lost in their infancy, even as he would light them (whether he could afford it or not) for friends now departed. For M'sieu Gomez and M'sieu Kovald his old piano teacher; for the father he'd been taken from when he was nearly eight. For the beautiful Ayasha. Another good reason, his heart reproached him, not to trouble Mamzelle Marie now. As she walked towards the shadows of the arcade, a man came up to her, a blankitte, and well dressed – January hadn't seen him in the church itself. He spoke to her, putting his hand to his breast pocket. She did not reply but stepped back from him, and even at that distance, January could feel the snake-cold darkness of her eyes.

She stepped around her would-be client without a word and walked on, her daughter hurrying in her wake – plainly dressed in her best black wool, as befit a respectable wife, mother, and daughter of the Church. Even the tignon with its seven points was respectably dark. Ashamed of his impatience, January retreated into one of the court building's doorways to let her pass. When you pray for those you loved, he knew, your heart wears silence like a veil for a time. You are still close enough to smell the scent of their hair. The last thing you want is yet another person asking you to use your power on their behalf.

Yet she stopped opposite the doorway where he stood, regarded him with eyes that saw the heart and the dreams, and smiled. 'Michie Ben.'

Young Marie-Euchariste stepped back.

'I don't want to trouble you,' he said.

'It's no trouble. I hear you're the one with the trouble these days.'

Of course, he thought, *she'd talked to Olympe*.

Or maybe she hadn't. The voodoos knew everything.

'I need to know who's threatened my family,' he said quietly. 'And why. I'm pretty sure it has to do with Mamzelle Felicita de Cedillos coming to New Orleans to clear her father's name of treason, back during the war, and to get his plantation back from Icarus Pelerine. I've heard old Bartolomé de Cedillos tried to stir up a slave rising at the plantations along Bayou Malheur. Then I heard it wasn't a slave rising at all but an attack by a Spanish militia. I need to know the truth of what happened – and I need to know who's behind the attacks now, on me, on Dagobert Janvier, and on Mamzelle de Cedillos herself. Who's behind them, and why.'

'I heard Mamzelle Cita was back.' The voodoo queen tilted her head a little. Still beautiful now in her forties, the blood of the American tribes mingling with African and whites in her features. 'Staying at Cresson Joubert's and staying out of sight. She was only little back then. I was older – fourteen – but my mama, she wouldn't let me walk out in the streets then, for the Americans all in the town. She made gris-gris for the men, though, and went out one night to put the cross on the enemy's camp. Even that Major d'Aquin, he came to her for gris-gris.'

January reflected that it seemed to have worked.

'While the plot to burn the plantations was being put together, I was in the militia camp,' he said, remembering his dream. 'The men Jackson had commandeered from the fields thought I was one of them. But I heard nothing about anyone trying to stir them to rebellion. The slaves from Carrière and Dufresne got clean away, I think, in the confusion; Dufresne and Doux-Malheur were both burned. But whether that was the Spanish militia, or the slaves themselves, or who if anyone was behind it, I had no idea. Those of Doux-Malheur—'

'They got away.' There was no doubt in her low, deep voice. 'Most of them went to the Choctaw villages or made it to Florida to join the Seminole. Maman kept me at home then—' She glanced back, with a flicker of indulgence in her lips, to her own daughter, as if she saw reflected in that coltish form her own image.

'Was de Cedillos behind it?'

'I've heard it all kinds of ways.' She tucked the dark-red folds of a bandana she wore, scarf-wise, closer around her neck as cold wind veered among the archways. In the Place d'Armes, a woman passed with a creaking cart and called out the virtues of *hot chocolate, hot*! 'You come to my house tonight,' said Mamzelle Marie. 'Right when the curfew cannon sounds. We'll talk then.'

After returning home, January slept for a few hours, his usual Sabbath chore of escorting Rose and their pupils to church for the later (and more fashionable) Mass being excused during Carnival. He woke to the soft music of the parlor harp, and Hannibal's voice: 'Remember to bend your wrist, Mamzelle . . . So. Give the note a minute to let the sound fade of itself . . .' and blessed Rose and Zizi-Marie for sending the boys to Olympe's house that morning. Even Professor John, always a preternaturally silent, studious child, was of the age that found it impossible to play without running and shrieking. Xander, at two, seemed already to aspire to the warrior athleticism of his Macedonian namesake.

The little camel-back clock in the parlor spoke ten, silver in the quiet.

Dagobert, he thought. *Damn.*

January slipped from the house through the boys' room rather than disturb the lesson and found hot water in the kitchen (and the remains of last night's hogfish dinner stewing with shrimp in a gumbo). He was bathing in the laundry room when Rose tapped at the shutters: 'Ben?'

'Enter at your peril,' he warned and intercepted her as she came in. He'd wrapped a towel around himself more to keep from splotching her dress with water than from modesty, but large portions of her striped chintz frock got damp nevertheless before they let each other go.

'This came for you last night.' She put her spectacles back on and took from her apron pocket what looked like one of the torn-out endpapers of an octavo volume, somewhat moist. It was sealed with an assortment of pink and yellow wafers. 'It was pushed in through the parlor shutters. I didn't find it 'til I opened them this morning.'

Unfolding it, January found the single word *Esmeralda* followed by another string of hyphenated numbers. He and Rose returned to the house, where with a little calculation and his dilapidated copy of *Notre-Dame de Paris*, January deciphered the plea that he and Dagobert meet Mamzelle de Cedillos on the *Fleur-de-Lys* (or the *Lily* – he recalled there was a steamboat named the *Madame Lily*) that morning at sunrise, that her peril was desperate.

'I presume it's to both of us,' he guessed. 'I can't imagine she would address me as "vous" if she meant me alone.'

He glanced at the clock on the mantle. 'So much for Rue Royale at noon. Thank God for small favors. If Mamzelle de Cedillos delivered one of these to Dagobert, he'll be long gone, and it will take him hours to return to town.' January folded the coded missive and tucked it into his waistcoat pocket. 'But since Old Madame Janvier can't stand Sunday dinner with Madame Marie-Hélène's family any more than I can, I'm guessing I'd be able to find her at Maman's.'

And at least I won't have to talk Bertie out of another trip to Alegre . . .

This proved to be the case. Zizi-Marie and the boys returned from Olympe's in time for an excellent Creole family dinner at two – Gabriel had put together the hogfish gumbo before leaving for Alciatore's – and they walked en famille as far as the pink cottage that St-Denis Janvier (or, technically, M'sieu Morrell) had given his beautiful plaçée in 1803: January and Rose, Zizi and Ti-Gall, the two little boys (their hands firmly gripped by their father and cousin-in-law), Germaine and Aglaëa on either of Hannibal's arms. While January and Rose quickly ducked down the passway to the yard – even in her widowhood, Livia Levesque would have slapped her son silly had he dared to enter her house through the front like a white person – the rest of the household proceeded to Rue Dumaine to spend the afternoon with Dominique, playing tric-trac and drinking coffee.

Only the acerbic presence of Sidonie Janvier – who was sure to provide an account of Madame Marie-Hélène's reaction to her stepson's desertion, if nothing else – reconciled January to his own program for Sunday afternoon.

'So far as I ever knew' – the elegant old lady dabbed butter on a fragment of brioche and offered it to Thisbe – 'what Icarus Pelerine felt for Bartolomé de Cedillos was contempt rather than hatred. I certainly can't imagine him going to the expense of hiring bravos to skulk around your neighborhood waiting for the opportunity to murder you.'

'And yet—' began January, and stopped as a name returned to his mind.

Esmeralda, he thought. *Esmeralda the gypsy . . .*

The character whose name had pointed him to the tale of the hunchback's grieving love.

And he suddenly knew where he'd seen a thin little woman with that cocky walk before. He thought she had been killed, two years before, in South America. She'd been one of the wharf-side gangs of bully boys who made their drinking money doing favors for the moneylenders, publicans, and pimps who ran the taverns along Tchoupitoulas Street. The rumor had been that they had all been killed.

And if she hadn't been killed, then the men who'd been hired to warn him off could very well be—

'I wouldn't be so sure of that.' His mother's voice pulled him back to the subject at hand. 'You didn't know him as I did. The man could be astonishingly vindictive.'

'I wouldn't have said so.' With two long, white fingers, Madame Janvier slid a bronze-and-green Sèvres plate of pralines – red with cochineal or white with coconut – across to January. It was one of the peculiarities that January's Paris friends had shaken their heads over, that whereas no white person in Louisiana (with the disreputable exception of Hannibal Sefton) would be seen in public eating or drinking at the same table with even the palest of musterfinos, should that white person be invited into the home of even full-blooded Africans, it was then considered perfectly acceptable to have a meal with them.

Presumably, reflected January, white feet honored the floorboards to such a degree that inviting blankittes to dine was no more than their due.

'The Pelerines were related to the Duc de Choiseul, and were cousins to that crooked fox Genêt, his assistant,' Sidonie Janvier went on. 'Cedillos's great-grandfather was a wool merchant' – she deliberately omitted the noble 'de' on the man's name – 'who put his son through university and settled five thousand reals on some minor scion of the de Hurtado family in exchange for marriage with one of the man's daughters. That's where that "de" comes from. I would have said that Pelerine would have considered it a disgrace to lie to the courts. But of course,' she added with a shrug, 'that was to Spanish courts and judges who were *actually* descended from noble families in Spain. He may have considered it a worse disgrace to lose six hundred acres of timber to the grandson of a wool merchant.'

'Considering the mess there was in the records when France handed Louisiana over to Spain,' sniffed Livia Levesque, 'I'm not surprised that imbecile Governor Ulloa signed a land grant over without looking at a map. For one thing, I doubt the man could read one. For another, he'd have handed his own mother over to anyone who'd support him against his new formerly French subjects.'

Old Madame's brows lifted. 'To say nothing of the official records going up in smoke in 1788.'

'Wasn't the transfer to Spain a secret or something?' inquired Rose. 'Thank you,' she added, smiling as her mother-in-law delicately poured coffee into her cup again.

'If I'd made such a hash of the affair, I'd try to keep it a secret, too,' the older woman responded, as she set the Bow-ware pot back on its little frame above the spirit lamp. 'Four years before Spain even sent out a proper governor. No wonder Pelerine's father considered himself king of the land between Bayou Sauvage and the lake. Nobody else was ruling it.'

'So, would an American judge even be able to sort out the French and Spanish grants these days?' Rose nudged the sugar bowl in January's direction. 'Always supposing they'd survived the fire at the Cabildo. Or, at this distance, would he care?'

'I'm sure he'd find a reason not to.' The Widow Levesque rubbed her fingers together, like a merchant counting out coin. 'Cita Cedillos may not even want the land. She may just want the threat of a lawsuit, to push Pelerine into giving her money to go away.'

'She'll catch cold at that if she does.' Old Madame Janvier's dark eyes glinted. 'Whatever else you can say about him, Pelerine's as proud as any Légitimiste nobleman at the French king's court. I should think if blackmail's her goal, it will have no effect but to stiffen the old man's resolve to have nothing to do with her.'

'But would he actually have her *murdered*?' Rose looked from one lady to the other.

'By what I've heard' – her mother-in-law selected one of the apricot tarts January had taken care to bring – 'it wouldn't be the first time. He certainly lost no time in putting Victoire de Cedillos and her girls out of the house.'

Madame Janvier looked shocked and disapproving, but did not contradict.

Of Jacques-Pierre Briard – who had married into the Forstall family and been sold the plantation of Doux-Malheur – Sidonie Janvier had clear recollections: 'An idiot,' she said. 'He was in New Orleans when word came that the British had come out of the woods just a few miles below town. He'd gotten some cousin of his wife's for an overseer – a bully and a fool. Whether Cedillos was behind it or not, nobody was surprised when the darkies took their chance, burned the place down, and ran for it when they heard the British were on their way.'

'What happened to the overseer?' asked January curiously and bent to hold out a conciliating finger to La Duchesse de Gateaubeurre as that fluffy, overfed cat minced into the parlor. With a hiss of scorn, the animal turned her back on him and levitated weightlessly to a corner of the mantlepiece.

'His body was found in the ruins of his house.' Livia passed Rose a plate of petits fours. 'Nobody was surprised about that either.'

'What about the man who has the place now?' January straightened, accepting La Duchesse's snub. 'Aristide Peychaud? Anything interesting about him?'

'Only his taste in waistcoats.' Livia sniffed.

'He lets smugglers bring in cargoes from the lake down Bayou Malheur. You hush, Madame!' Old Madame added, as Thisbe loosed a salvo of barks at La Duchesse. 'Such language! One would take you for a cur on a street corner! French and Spanish wines.' She turned back to January, her long fingers hooked through her pet's diamond-studded collar. On the mantlepiece, La Duchesse yawned.

'Best quality Spanish oil, French and China silks. Lead, gunpowder, guns, and decent tobacco from Cuba. The usual things. Goods easily handled, that you can buy cheaply if you know the right people. I don't think Peychaud even knows what they are or who lands those boats on moonlit nights. The Canal and Banking Company tells Peychaud what nights they expect him to stay in

New Orleans – he doesn't even keep servants or an overseer out there – and Peychaud makes twice the money he'd get trying to keep a sugar crop in production these days.'

Livia said, 'Hmph,' disdain utterly failing to mask her regret that she didn't own land on some minor but navigable bayou out of sight of neighbors. 'Mr Chew tells me that half those smugglers and swamp traders are cheats, and you're getting Virginia grape juice for the price of Bordeaux, and cotton sleaze warranted as silk.'

'Is that the half of those smugglers that don't broker their goods through his friends?' Madame Janvier raised her brows.

'You just ask your daughter-in-law about the quality of smuggled silk,' retorted Livia. To Rose, she explained, 'I gather Madame Marie-Hélène is not only paying for a parade down Canal Street and across to the townhouse at the same hour as Madame Marigny's parade down Rue Esplanade, but she's paying for royal robes and crowns for herself and Beatrice and that imbecilic stepson of hers . . .'

'She'll have to go farther than that,' purred Madame Sidonie, malice sparkling in her eyes. 'Hadn't you heard? Evidently Anna Marigny has persuaded her husband – not that Bernard ever needed persuasion to make a spectacle of himself – to organize a jousting tournament down the middle of the Street of Frenchmen, as part of the festivities when she marries off that nigaud—'

'Good heavens, m'am!' exclaimed Rose. 'The betting alone is going to guarantee an army turns out to watch!'

'I assume' – the older woman broke off a fragment of tart to offer her affronted pug – 'that is the point. It has prompted my daughter-in-law to poach M'sieu Davis's prima soprano to give a recital at the reception for Governor Roman – in retaliation for the appearance of Signor Biagi at the wedding of Anna Marigny's niece that evening—'

January made a show of clutching his temples like Faust beset by demons in act two.

'Mr Chew was fit to be tied over the expense.' Deep satisfaction tinged Madame's voice. 'Ever since Dagobert mislaid a bill of lading two years ago, Marie-Hélène has had Chew look over the books, although I will say for Dagobert that he's quite as clever with the business as his father ever was. And M'sieu Morrell said that the bill of lading was the fault of that imbecile copy clerk at Bastien et Fils. Which reminds me, Livia, Morrell's in a state over his son's marriage . . .'

'I suppose that means,' sighed Rose, when she and January eventually walked on – a trifle warily, broad daylight on the Sabbath notwithstanding – towards Dominique's, 'it's only a matter of time before you're going to be asked to play arias from *Figaro* and *Lucia di Lammermoor* for . . . that would be Madame Scarlatta, wouldn't it? Do you suppose the poor woman will be obliged to ride on a parade wagon in the Grand Cavalcade?'

'I wouldn't put it past Madame Janvier to require it of her.'

'Unless of course Madame succeeds in persuading Mr Chew to sanction stealing members of M'sieu Davis's orchestra as well.'

'Davis hires the whole orchestra en bloc in France these days,' said January. 'And Madame Marie-Hélène actually can't tell the difference between Purcell and patty-cake. Back before I went to France,' he reminisced, 'Maman tried to get me to convert to Protestantism, so I could join the church Mr Chew was active in. Even in those days he had enough influence with the insurance companies and the Bank of Louisiana to get the customs authorities to turn a blind eye on slave cargoes being brought in by his fellow churchmen. It would introduce me, she said, to the notice of important and influential men.'

'I can just hear her.' Rose's quicksilver smile flickered into being at the thought. 'Did she explain that Protestantism wasn't so very different from the Roman Faith, and God probably didn't care as long as you worshiped Him devoutly?'

'Something along those lines.' He could still taste the dry disgust, like a physical film on his tongue, during those arguments with his mother. *You'll never make anything of yourself as a surgeon. If you'd use even half the hours you spend fooling around on that silly piano learning something useful – making useful connections – you could be of more help to me . . .* Not that the annuity St-Denis Janvier had arranged for his beautiful plaçée was less than princely *. . . I thought when that old German piano teacher turned up his toes, you'd be over that music business . . .*

She never so much as looked at him, or spoke to him, when he and the other musicians of the French Town would play for the

Blue Ribbon balls in the old, pre-fire Salle d'Orléans. Tightened her lips when he'd hand over three-quarters of his earnings to her, and then not have money for coffee.

In those days, his heart had lived on the golden light of music and the laughter of his friends. When Gomez would say to him, 'I can only teach you what I know, Ben. I wish you'd think seriously about going to Paris,' he would nod and find another excuse.

Even to himself, he'd felt like a fool, sitting on the gallery outside Gilles's rented room, drinking coffee or illegal beer, playing dominoes. Sometimes they'd all pick up guitars or banjos or improvise drums from gourds or spoons. They'd play off one another's music, handing the melody line back and forth like children playing with a whirligig. Or they'd sing, wrapped in the magic maelstrom of what it felt like to be making music perfectly in tune with dear friends . . . And he would think, *I can't leave this.*

It had felt sometimes that even to save his own life, he could not have walked out of those groups, those rooms, with the knowledge that he might never see those people again.

When Gilles had said, 'Davy and I are joining Savary's company,' it had seemed the natural – the only – thing to reply: 'I'll go with you.'

Had Patroclus gone to Troy, he wondered, only so as not to be parted from his friend?

Then movement flickered in the corner of his eye and the memory of that time, that place, of the young man he used to be, vanished like the blowing out of a candle and he thought again, *Esmeralda . . .*

A man was walking down the other side of the street, visible as only stocky shoulders and dirty ginger hair smeared over them . . .

And January knew him. Rumored dead, with the woman Esmeralda, in South America, on the looting expedition whose planning nearly two years ago had come close to costing January his own life.*

Catastrophe Watling. He was gaudily masked with Red Indian paint and still trailing his red Devil tail, but January recognized the jacket he wore, gingery brown Mexican rawhide with white Mexican stitching on the sleeves. He remembered the garment as clearly as

* See: Murder in July

he remembered Watling's cheerful willingness to kill whoever he was paid to kill.

January wondered how many others of the man's gang had survived the debacle two years ago. Or had he found new 'boys' when he and his lady friend made their way back to the States?

This was a neighborhood where neither of them had any business, where neither had ever come before. There were no saloons or whorehouses on this stretch of Rue Dumaine.

There was only one reason that either of them would be here.

Someone hired him to keep the secret of whatever it was that had happened at the Battle of Chalmette. To get rid of anyone who might learn . . . whatever it was.

FIFTEEN

'It was the Spanish.' Enrico the charcoal vendor glanced sidelong at Mamzelle Marie. 'Spanish and the Indians, that had got run out of their land along the river, with the Americans all comin' in, grabbin' every square foot of land from the river to the lakes. French, they could deal with the Choctaw villages. They'd let the tribes hunt in the ciprière back from the sugar fields, and camp sometimes just back of the quarters.'

Across Rue des Ramparts, the gates of Circus Square – Congo Square – were closed and locked now. The smell of the charcoal smoke from the carts of the coffee vendors, the gumbo ladies, the sellers of hot callas, still hung in the air, with the trace vapors of spent torches and spilled tafia. But the background clamor of the saloons along Basin Street continued, punctuated by the shouts of revelers on their way to balls or parties or gambling halls.

All the silence in the town seemed to have gathered in the dark parlor of the house on Rue St-Ann, yielding the streets to the racket with the indulgence of an adult letting a child play with a tin whistle.

January had lived through enough fever summers in New Orleans to know what it was like when the silence returned.

Marie Laveau sat in the light of twelve candles, her hands folded, a part of that stillness. From the altar shelf against one wall, as in Olympe's house, statues of the Virgin, of St Peter and St James watched him, sharing space with juju candles, mouse bones, little dishes of salt and graveyard earth.

'The Spanish, bad enough after the French king give them that land, to cheat the English out of having it,' Enrico went on. 'They all come up and settle, and get land grants from the king. And then their children got told one fine day they was gonna get handed back to France, just like that.' He snapped his crooked, calloused fingers. 'Then three weeks after all the papers got signed and everybody got used to that idea, they hear, *Oh, no, Napoleon just sold the whole tambouille to the Americans for money to invade England with . . .*' The old man shook his head. 'You don't wonder they was ready to go over to help the English run the Americans the hell out.'

'Did someone try to bring the blacks in?' asked January. 'Try to get you— *them*,' he corrected himself, since he wasn't supposed to know that the old charcoal man had been one of the slaves on Doux-Malheur, 'to burn the plantations?'

'Oh, they tried – or so I hear.' Enrico cocked his gray-fuzzed head. 'I forget who I hear it from. But I hear Abo, that was head man on Doux-Malheur, told them, *We love Marse Briard. He treats us good. We got rum at Christmas and don't got to work on Sunday. We'd never hurt him, nor his home, nor his family. You get on out of here!*' The glint in his eye told January – as it was meant to – that this was a lie: *What the hell you think I'm gonna say, Piano Man? After all these years living free?* 'When the fightin' started, an' we heard the drums, an' the shots, we— they, I mean – somebody told me they just headed for the woods. They knew they'd get the blame whatever happened, see.'

January saw.

'So who was "they"?' he asked. 'Who tried to bring Abo and the others in on it? Do you remember?'

The old man shook his head again. 'I don't remember. And anyway, the fella who told me didn't say. Just that it was a blankitte. I think he might have been Spanish.'

'Do you remember who told you?'

'No. And anyway he's dead.'

January knew better than to pursue that contradiction.

'You let it rest, Piano Man,' Enrico said, his voice almost gentle. 'Whoever it was, that planned to get the Americans to leave the battle line, and to lead the British around the end of that line through the trembling lands, some of those people may still be around. Maybe they don't like it, if some black man come around wavin' proof that they tried to stir up people to rebel just when the British were attackin'. Maybe best you let it be.'

January said, 'Thank you,' and looked across at Mamzelle Marie. Her face reminded him of the images of certain saints, less impassive than compassionate towards both the evil and the good. Understanding that things could not be otherwise than they were. She had brought Enrico here to tell him what the old man felt able to tell him, but wasn't about to threaten or push. Enrico was as much a friend as January was.

She fetched a tray of sand from a table in the corner and traced a design – a vévé – in the sacred dust with the end of a rooster's quill, then scattered a handful of dried beans over it. She studied the pattern of them before she said, 'You go home now, Enrico. You be all right.'

January noticed that she let the charcoal man out the back door of her house, and guessed that, like his own yard, the property contained a way through into some other yard or stable or passway, so that Enrico would not emerge on to either Rue des Ramparts or Rue St-Ann.

Returning to the candlelit parlor, she said, 'Wait a little, Benjamin. Give him time to get clear.'

'Was I followed here?' he asked, remembering Cat Watling and Esmeralda.

She shook her head. 'But it's good to be safe. And he's innocent, and got nothing to do with any of this, except that he was in the wrong place, at the wrong time, all those years ago.'

'Was it the Spanish?'

'It's what I heard.' She sighed and went back to the dresser where the sand tray had been. Took from the top drawer a bottle of whiskey and two glasses. Returning to the table beside which they'd all sat, she poured him a little and herself the same. 'You hear all kinds of things, you know? I heard, too, it was the slaves that rose up and looted and burned those houses. But with the battle lost, and the British driven back to their ships, what would the Spanish say, except that it was those nasty rebellious blacks that done it, while the Spanish that hated the new American governors stood by wringing their innocent pink hands in distress.'

Her dark glance slid sidelong to him, like Enrico's had: *What the hell you think I'm gonna say, Piano Man?*

After a time, she went on, 'In those days, the Mexicans were still trying to do what the Spanish had done for years: stir up the Kaintucks and the men from Tennessee and get them to break away from the United States and join Mexico. Or set up their own country, between the United States and Mexico, so the Americans wouldn't just come right over into Mexico from their own doorstep. In Mexico just then they were fighting each other in the hills, but the new King of Spain was friends with the British, who helped him get rid of Napoleon. They may have figured if the British took Louisiana, they'd hand it all back to Spain rather than see the Americans keep it. And then with silver from the Santa Rita mines, Spain could shut down the Mexican rebellion for good.'

She sipped her liquor, the gold of the candles wavering in her eyes. 'The blacks, what the hell did they stand to gain from burning those three houses? The British were all over the countryside already, men sneakin' away from the quarters every night with their wives and their children, and who's going to stop them? I've talked to some Spanish who were here at that time, and some blacks. But you know, nobody's going to tell the truth.'

January drank also – it was extremely good liquor. Instead of the morning's sober dark dress, Mamzelle wore what she'd had on an hour ago in the square, a blue market woman's bodice and a skirt made of red bandanas. The seven points of her gold-and-scarlet tignon framed her head like static fire. All that she told him now, January had heard before, from one person or another, over the years. He'd been a schoolboy when New Orleans – a very much smaller New Orleans in 1807, still surrounded by a defensive palisade – had been clapped under martial law by the territory's military commander General Wilkinson in response to (Wilkinson's own unsubstantiated) assertions of a Spanish plot by former Vice President Aaron Burr. And this hadn't – if he recalled correctly things St-Denis Janvier had told him – been the first time the Spanish had tried (in collusion with some fairly high-ranking politicians and land speculators in Tennessee) to detach the western territories of the United States and glue them into New Spain.

'Was Pelerine behind it?' he asked at length. 'Do you know? I've heard de Cedillos disappeared the day of the battle.'

'With de Cedillos gone,' pointed out the voodoo, 'and the whole town stirred up over the battle, Pelerine would have been a fool not to say he was responsible, when he brought the suit back to court. There's few men who wouldn't have done the same.'

'What did Madame de Cedillos have to say to that? Or had she been forced to leave town before it ever came to court? I hear Pelerine lost no time in putting his son into Alegre.'

'Victoire de Cedillos had nothing to say to it.' Mamzelle Marie set down her glass and regarded him then in surprise. 'She and her daughters disappeared the night after the battle as well.'

For several days after that, to January's intense relief, he heard nothing from Dagobert Janvier. He kept to the house on Rue Esplanade, sleeping in one of the two tiny chambers he had made behind a moveable wall in the storerooms of its raised foundation as accommodation for the runaway slaves he – and the local 'Underground Railroad' – assisted towards passage to the North. Daytimes, while Rose taught their few remaining students, he'd slip over the back wall like a thief, to teach his own piano pupils. He cautiously eschewed his second early-morning engagement to play surgeon, at a duel between Bastien Damoreau's friend Adrien Lafrennière and a cousin of the Romans who claimed Damoreau was a liar about many things, and the two evenings on which he had paid work, he sneaked out of the house in disguise.

When he'd return, Rose and the girls would already be gone.

Never in that week did he see evidence that anyone had entered the house while he slept. None of the friends, who walked the neighborhood periodically in the evening, had seen anyone watching the place, though with the streets aswarm with false Ivanhoes and poor copies of Harlequin and Indian chiefs, it would be hard to tell.

Yet even in the streets, in broad daylight, he found himself looking over his shoulders. And when, during a performance of *The Castle Spectre* at the St-Charles Theater, some jolly soul in the audience set off a firecracker, January was halfway under his piano before Cochon signed that it wasn't a murderous attack.

Confronting Cat Watling, he knew, would get him nothing. Though he had dealt amicably with the man two years ago, he had been very careful to give the impression of being unlettered, slightly stupid, and completely harmless – no threat to Watling or to those who had hired him. Though the river-rat had, he thought, taken a liking to him, he was well aware that Watling was a professional killer who, if paid to do so, would shoot him on sight ('No hard feelin's, Ben . . .'). Not someone he would risk leading to Mamzelle de Cedillos's hiding place, no matter what he thought of the lady himself.

And not someone he wanted to have knowing where he himself was, or anyone that he cared about.

(He did wonder what the man charged for his services and wished he could ask him. Rose would want to know.)

His one note to Dagobert, asking what Mamzelle de Cedillos had told him of the circumstances of her departure from Louisiana in 1815, went unanswered. This did not surprise him. Dagobert Janvier was a sugar broker, and the harvest season had just concluded. Every plantation from Baton Rouge to the Gulf was presenting invoices, demanding prices, dickering over offers from New York, London, Bordeaux. In any case, there was always the chance that Madame Marie-Hélène, seeing his handwriting on the outside of the sealed note, had simply put it into the fire. (Quite possibly after reading it herself . . .)

After three fruitless visits to the Cabildo, January finally tracked Abishag Shaw down at the room he rented over Valentine's Livery Stable. The policeman promised to do what he could, but January knew that with only twenty guardsmen on the First Municipality force, there wasn't a great deal that he *could* do. 'I'll keep a eye on your place when I can, Maestro.' Shaw leaned a bony shoulder against the railing of the stairway that led from the stable yard up to his room. 'Sounds like you're doin' all I'd tell you to do in the meantime, havin' your family out of there at night, an' you sleepin' in the storerooms down below.' (January didn't mention the extra-legal sleeping arrangements concealed behind the wall.) 'We got seven days left 'til Mardi Gras, thank the Lord. After that I'll start trackin' down folks on the wharves what might have heard somethin', either about this de Cedillos jasper or whoever it is that's got a hard-on for you. It's all I can do right now, an' that's a fact.'

'I know that, sir.'

The lieutenant looked considerably more war-torn now than he had two weeks previously on January's front gallery, a black eye and a knife cut on his forehead augmenting the previous battle scars. Like Dagobert, this was his busy season. 'I heard already Watling's back in town. Helps to know *that* war'n't just a rumor. I'll ask around.'

Hannibal, Ti-Gall, and Paul Corbier took turns escorting Rose and the girls to Olympe's house to sleep, though January guessed that Hannibal was the only one of them who would recognize Cat Watling or any of his gang. Other members of the Faubourg Tremé Free Colored Militia and Burial Society volunteered for these duties as well: Mohammad LePas the blacksmith, Isaak Jumon the stonecutter, and Ti-Gall's Uncle Ghis, and even old Digo Salazar. Other friends as well: Ti-Jon and Parnassus Sam from the wharves, the carter Fly-Trap Novain and his sons, and the uptown musicians Preacher, Bill, and Four-Eyes.

It was an uneasy week. But there were nights of laughter in that season as well, like the little chénier islands in the morass of the back swamp. Nights when nobody had a paying gig and everyone got together at somebody's house, January would sneak in disguise to meet Rose and Olympe while Paul stood guard back at Olympe's house and the girls all giggled together in the attic. Nights when everybody whooped with laughter over Hannibal's account of Madame Marie-Hélène's attempts to enlarge her Grand Cavalcade to twenty-five carriages and a troop of mounted militia (Madame Marigny was reported to have acquired, in addition to twenty carriages full of the cream of French and Spanish Creole society, six actors from the St-Charles Theater to perform scenes from Shakespeare and a pageant wagon that rivaled the jeweled hearse of Alexander the Great).

Nights when everyone brought pots of greens and 'dirty rice,' spoon bread and sugar-dusted king cakes (and illegal rum for tafia punch), when everyone would play and sing and talk and forget what bills were owing.

Those evenings – and the solid friendship, even to the brink of danger – brought back to January the joy that had been so intense in the years of his youth: loving and being loved, in a wide-flung quasi-family where people cared for and depended on one another. Intense, he understood now, because in those days of being young and living in his mother's house, he had needed it so. *How can I leave them? How can I leave this?* he had wondered then.

He recalled as if it were yesterday his sense of panic, at the thought that by the time he returned – if he ever returned – it would all have blown away like autumn's dry leaves, leaving him with nothing.

It was good beyond words to see Gilles again, down from Vicksburg on the steamboat *Vermillion* and accompanied by Callie, filled with stories about their children and their tiny grandson, and tales of the outrageous behavior of the wealthy Americans of that town. In many ways it was as if they'd only been parted for a week. Gilles was thin and gangly these days from fever last summer, his molasses-colored hair reduced to a middle-aged tonsure but the happy brightness of his smile undimmed. Stout, laughing, Callie was talkative as ever and as always ready to flirt with anyone. ('You behave yourself, woman, or I'm gonna have to call that Michie Sefton out . . .')

One evening, January asked Gilles about the battle, about whether he'd heard rumors of slave revolt – or a Spanish conspiracy – at the time. Gilles thought about it, sitting with January in a corner of Crowdie Passebon's small green cottage on Rue Burgundy, while Hannibal demonstrated card tricks and everybody else recovered their breath after nearly three hours of dancing.

'You mean those three places on Bayou Malheur that got burned out during the battle? I always thought it was the field hands taking their chance to run for it and make everybody believe the British done it.'

'You never heard anything about, that somebody stirred 'em on to do it?'

'You mean Lafitte's pirates, eggin' them to revolt and then layin' in wait for 'em in the swamp? That crossed my mind, that night we camped out near Dufresne, and saw the places. It would be like Lafitte – or like some of the black hearts who followed him – to think up something like that. I always did think it was a little fishy,' he added, turning a gilt-rimmed punch cup in his hands. 'Him – the pirate chief of the whole Barataria! – turning up like that with an offer to help, after our navy had attacked his base and captured all those ships and men. And to hand General Jackson a sloop, a gun crew, and that pile of guns and gun flints into the bargain! He worked for the Spanish, too, after the war.'

A different way of looking at those bits and pieces of information, reflected January . . . which was one of the problems with putting together a mosaic of small facts. It would make sense of Enrico's comment that *Some of those people may still be around.* Certainly old Cut-Nose was. Where had Cat Watling been in 1815?

And yet . . .

He returned to Crowdie's six-octave pianoforte shortly after that (nobody was ready to quit dancing yet), and across the room, to his surprise, he glimpsed, flushed and shy, Cosette Gardinier, hand in hand with a young man whom he recognized vaguely as the son of his mother's business manager M'sieu Morrell.

And later, over king cake and punch, when someone recounted how they'd taught Jean Lafitte to cheat at backgammon, Crowdie said, 'I heard Lafitte didn't die at all back in '25. That what they buried at sea was a bag of rocks.'

'I heard it was a feller named Lucius Robinette,' put in somebody else.

'An' *I* heard he was seen only year before last in . . .'

January had heard all this before, too. The number of variations on how and when the pirate 'Boss' had faked his own death, and where he had gone afterwards, rivalled Cut-Nose's accounts of how he'd lost his nose.

Loud cheers, from everyone who'd been part of those gatherings on Gilles's gallery in that hot autumn of 1814, as Gilles grimaced and spat out the traditional king cake bean.

'So when you throwin' the next party, Gilles?' whooped young Jean-Xavier Morrell . . .

But if Lafitte is living in Missouri under an assumed name, why would he be afraid of whatever I might have found under the ruined belvedere at Alegre?

And who would have told him about that?

Two days later, on his way home from Flora McCullen's lesson in the Faubourg St-Mary, January made it his business to walk past the white, solid block of Charity Hospital on Common Street, and ask one of the nursing sisters if Dr Ker was free for a few moments. Rather to his surprise, he only waited in the dingy, whitewashed lobby for twenty minutes.

'I dunno what's worse,' muttered the Scot as he came in, wiping his hands on a rag that had probably been clean that morning. 'Fever in the summer or blame fools callin' each other out over four whiskeys an' who's bribin' the King of France this week. What can I do for you, January?'

'First,' said January, 'you and Madame Ker can come to dinner on Sunday, and I promise you that the feast will include neither the banging of tin pans nor the serving of a king cake—'

'Weel, thank God for that!'

'Second,' he went on, 'I heard a strange rumor the other day about the Spanish raising militia troops during the British assault on Louisiana at the end of the war, and I wondered if it had really happened. It didn't sound very likely . . .'

'Gah.' The older man waved an impatient hand. 'Don't look to me for word of it, man; I was fair done in tryin' to keep the eejit they gave me from droppin' my equipment overside into the lake. I was in the first lot they rowed across the lakes from the Gulf – five hours for the boats to reach that pawky little sandbar where we made camp, and then back to the ships for another lot, like an idiot kitchen maid tryin' to bring in a pipe of wine by carryin' it one teacup at a time. We were camped on that island six days while they rowed the men across that lake, an' I think in that time I'd have heard—'

Ker paused then, frowning as if at some distant sound, still straight and trim in his early sixties as he'd been when January had seen him first in the infirmary tent, ordering the New Orleans ladies who'd come to help with the wounded as if they were a squad of newly recruited farm boys. The future Madame Ker, January recalled with a smile, had been one of them, boiling water and threading up needles by lantern light long after most of her compatriots had gone back to their beds in town.

'Now you speak of it,' the surgeon said slowly, 'some of the men did say the Spanish, and the Choctaw, would be helping us out. I wasn't paying much mind because I'd heard nothing of the matter from our officers, and soldiers are always feedin' each other rumors. I had a Dutch private the day before the battle joined at Waterloo tellin' me how the Belgian officers were set to mutiny against Wellington. I don't remember rightly what that Spanish rumor was, but some of the men said there'd be help from the Spanish – or maybe it was from a revolt at one of the plantations – to break Jackson's line.'

At that point, one of the junior surgeons appeared in the inner doorway, and January bowed a little to Ker. 'Thank you, sir. What you've told me will be helpful.'

'Will it now?' The Scot's sharp, dark eyes scanned his face. 'That water's been and gone under the bridge a long time ago, to be askin' questions about now.'

'It has,' said January ruefully. 'And it may or may not have any importance, whether it's true or not. If I could ask you not to speak of it, sir—'

'This have somethin' to do with you gettin' potted at out on Bayou Joyeuse, t'other night?'

January hesitated, more annoyed than shocked, knowing how rumor fleeted through New Orleans. Still . . .

'Madame Janvier,' provided Ker, reading the expression he thought he'd hidden. 'Molligrantin' over tea to Madame Ker, that you've led that fair-haired boy of hers into danger—'

'*I've* led—?'

The surgeon raised a quelling hand and stifled a grin. 'He's her lad, for all he's got sons old enough to vote and chase ladies who don't run so fast. And she says, he wouldn't have the brains to get himself into a scrape if he didn't have you to tell him where he ought to go next. And maybe that's his trouble.'

'He fought at Chalmette,' January pointed out quietly. 'And risked his life on the redoubt, the same as I did.'

'He fought at his father's side,' returned Ker. 'As his father's son. Fought as a boy and not a man. And he's been at his father's side ever since, in his business, in his family, for all the poor man went on to his reward near twenty years ago. He never left Louisiana, as you did. 'Twas too easy for him to stay and have his stepmama, and his wife, to look after him. He hadn't the courage to see what lies down the river and out over the sea.'

As he watched that soldierly form disappear, trailed by the junior surgeon, back into the hospital's corridor, January understood that he was right. He had never thought of it in those terms before, but indeed, Dagobert Janvier had stepped seamlessly into the running of his father's affairs. Trained to watch the shipping news and read the reports of each plantation's prospective crops, to advise the sugar planters in the downriver parishes about prices and credit for the coming year. To negotiate with the banks that held the specie, with customs officials and moneylenders and the representatives of the English trading firms. And he was, January knew, competent and well regarded throughout the three municipalities. Good at what he did, despite his stepmother's carping: conscientious, hard-working, and the treasure of Marie-Hélène's jealous heart.

But January guessed that St-Denis Janvier had never asked his son – as he had asked the son of his mistress – whether this was what he wanted to do.

What would he have replied, January wondered, if he had been asked? And if Dagobert had replied that he wanted to be a soldier, or an engineer, or a lawyer, and not a sugar broker who also managed the American side of a wine imports firm?

January shook his head, for the first time oddly sorry for his exasperating relative.

But Ker was wrong about one thing, he thought. It hadn't been courage that had turned his own steps down the river and out across the sea.

'Lafitte worked for the Spanish, sure enough,' agreed Gilles, when he and January met again on Saturday night at the house of Fortune Gérard. Gérard's shop on Rue Chartres sold only the finest (and most expensive) coffee and tea, and his house, on Washington Avenue, stood in its own grounds, close enough to the river to be more or less safe from floods, and surrounded by a hedge of sweet olive and roses. Though large for the Marigny district, the house itself was typical of the Caribbean Creoles, plainly furnished, its walls glowing with colors, daffodil, persimmon, and spinach-green.

Playing for Gérard's guests wasn't so much a job as part of the party, though Gérard had slipped January, Hannibal, the Bichets, and a dozen others who'd brought instruments a dollar apiece. He treated them like the other guests, and they came and went from the musicians' corner as they chose, sometimes dancing, sometimes playing dominos or cards with friends, or joining the feast on gumbo and oyster pie.

This was fortunate, since January had arrived at the party seething. That afternoon a note had come to the house, sealed with red wax and the mark of Janus – from Dagobert, he had assumed, until he broke the seal. It had been, in fact, from Madame Marie-Hélène, informing him that his services would not be required on Mardi Gras night.

'Είς κόρακας with her, then,' Hannibal had said when informed. 'The only piano player in town still without a job that night will be Herr Hatch who plays for drinks at the Blackleg – and Madame will be obliged not only to engage him – and to keep him relatively sober if possible – but to find two violinists, a cellist, and men on clarionet and flute of equal excellence . . .'

'No—' January had waved aside the words, though he felt touched, knowing that Hannibal, Cochon, the Bichets, and Philippe duCoudreau would indeed quit, something they could ill afford to do. 'Don't do that, please. For me, it's just as well,' he'd added with a sigh, as some of his anger fizzled down into simple irritation: *Why am I surprised? Of course she'd dismiss me . . .*

'It lets me out of spending the evening having her glare at me – not to mention that every time she saw me, she'd start off again telling her guests what a low-down zinc-plated cow I am who can't play worth the four paws on a dead dog.'

'I wonder what her mother-in-law will have to say to her,' mused the fiddler, a remark which cheered January up considerably.

They'd gone inside then – this conversation had taken place on Gérard's front gallery – and January bowed with regal acknowledgment to the whistles and applause that greeted him: he hadn't returned the Cavalier togs he'd borrowed from *I Puritani* the previous week and had worn them for the occasion. It was that kind of party. When Aristide Peychaud appeared clothed as a Musketeer, January had immediately signed for Hannibal to take over 'The Basket Quadrille' mid-bar and had leaped to his feet to challenge the 'perfidious Frenchman' to a duel. (Wine corks at ten paces.)

Peychaud, no mean performer on the pianoforte himself, then claimed the defeated January's place in the ensemble, donned the over-plumed Cavalier hat ('Oh! So *that's* what became of my pink ostrich tips!' had protested January's neighbor Virginie Metoyer), shoved Hannibal from the piano stool and dropped straight into the quadrille's melody without a pause.

January asked Gilles now, 'But why would Lafitte join Jackson, then? Let alone give him weapons and men to turn the *Louisiana*'s guns on the British troops?'

His friend shook his head. 'Who knows what he planned? Maybe he didn't even know, if he was taking orders from someone. That crooked snake General Wilkinson was taking Spanish money the whole time he was governor of the Louisiana Territory, for God's sake – and I daresay half the time *he* didn't know why he was doing the things he was asked to do. And you notice within a few years the Americans and the British joined together to run Lafitte out of business. He may have just been trying to buy himself a little time, or a little credit.'

'Your mother tells me, Benjamin' – Hannibal appeared at January's elbow, a plate of king cake and a cup of ginger water balanced in one hand and another cup of lethally powerful punch in the other – 'that it was her friend the ingenious Mr Chew who put his friends in the Department of the Treasury on course to chase Lafitte out of the Caribbean, presidential pardon be damned. Mr Chew was smuggling at least as much as Lafitte—'

'More,' said Gilles with a grin. 'He was the port customs inspector then.'

January sighed. 'My mother was right. I did go into the wrong business.'

'But nobody invites the man to all the best parties.' Solange Souchet, Peychaud's serpentine lady friend, slid an arm around Hannibal's waist, and with the other hand removed the plumed Cavalier hat from his head and dropped it on to Gilles's. 'I hear he's a dead loss even at an Episcopalian Church tea.'

Gilles laughed, took the velvet cloak that Callie had brought to him ('Your mama's been ready to go for a half-hour now, sweet potato . . .'), and flung it with a theatrical flourish over his shoulders. 'I challenge anyone to show me how one can sparkle at an Episcopalian Church tea! Yes, Maman, I'm coming.'

He kissed his hands to Madame Gérard, nodded thanks to Plançon – the Gérard butler – and as the servant opened the door stepped out into the night to help his womenfolk down the gallery steps. Turning on the threshold, he took off the plumed hat, flung it back through the door to January . . .

. . . and in the next instant January saw beyond him the yellow flare of a muzzle flash in the darkness; heard the crack of a rifle.

Gilles threw up his arms with an expression of blank surprise before crumpling in the doorway.

SIXTEEN

Rose grabbed January's arm and with a strength that astonished him dragged him back. Callie had already hurled herself through the door and to her knees at her husband's side; Odile Gignac's scream drowned out Callie's gasped, 'Gilles!' and by the dim flare of the candles in the parlor January saw the glint of his friend's eyes as they were opened, as his head turned. Saw his hand move; convulsively grip Callie's arm.

Rose shoved January violently into Hannibal's grip and threw herself through the door, shrieking, 'Ben! Oh, God, Ben!' at the top of her lungs.

Callie darted one glance out into the night, the next down at Gilles, and another back at January before firmly holding Gilles down when he tried to move, and raised her voice in a desperate wail, 'Ben!'

Which told January that his friend was conscious and the wound – allowing for the darkness, the candlelight, the confusion – did not appear mortal.

Olympe was through the door next, and January dropped to his knees and prudently crawled after her. 'Get back inside, fool,' she hissed, though January was fairly certain the attackers had already made tracks down Washington Avenue.

Olympe's husband Paul, Fortune Gérard and his son-in-law Isaak, and five other members of the FTFCMBS nearly trampled them rushing out the door, armed with pokers, fire shovels, and in two cases completely illegal firearms. At the same moment, January heard others emerge from the rear doors of the house, spread out into the starry darkness, like warriors on a half-forgotten battlefield. Cochon, Hannibal, Fly-Trap Novain, and the stoutly formidable Bernadette Metoyer eased Gilles on to a blanket, carefully pulled him back through the door, leaving a smeared trail of blood over the door sill.

'You stay down, fool,' whispered Olympe and kneed January into the house before her as if he'd been a dog.

He understood immediately what Callie and Rose had done, in the instant they'd realized that Gilles wasn't dead.

Someone fetched blankets and pillows. Every candle in the house was brought close within seconds, as January kneeled at his friend's side. Scissors were pushed into his hand. 'Water be here in a second,' promised Christophe Glapion, Marie Laveau's husband and the only other white man, besides Hannibal, at the gathering. Even as he spoke, January heard the clonk of feet on the dining-room floor, coming in from the rear yard, and a pannikin of hot water – prudently kept steaming in the kitchen boiler in readiness for a late-night session of dishwashing – was set down at his side.

All this took less than a minute, while January cut Gilles's old-fashioned court coat free. The bullet had taken him high in the left shoulder as he'd turned to toss the plumed hat back into the house, breaking the head of the humerus and lodging against the scapula. Had he not turned when he did, it probably would have torn the subclavian artery or gone into a lung. Face ashen, Gilles had lapsed into merciful unconsciousness; January washed the wound while Olympe and Mamzelle Marie returned to the kitchen for herbs.

'It's the men who've been after you, isn't it?' whispered Callie, kneeling beside January to take Gilles's hand. He saw Gilles grip the strong, dark fingers convulsively, and Callie returned the pressure. 'It's all right,' she added, bending close to her husband's ear. 'You're all right. You'll be all right.'

January knew the havoc a bullet could make of the complex bones of the shoulder and felt sick at the thought. *Not Gilles. Virgin Mother of God, not Gilles . . .*

Olympe kneeled at his side, a steaming bowl of poultice in her hand. Now, by candlelight, was not the time to go digging for the rifle ball.

'It true?' Madame Gignac – Gilles's mother – hunkered down at his other side. 'He be all right?' He heard anger tremble in her voice; glancing sidelong, saw it in her eyes. It had only been chance, and silly horseplay with that plumed hat, that had made Gilles the target, for of course one of Watling's boys must have followed him – January – out to Marigny tonight.

Damn it . . . Damn it . . .

He knew, as he packed pad after pad of torn sheeting on the wound, that there was a good chance that his friend's left arm would be crippled for life. Knew, too, that the stout seamstress had never gotten over Davy's death – Davy who had marched to Chalmette with his older brother Gilles, with January, wild with excitement to be going into battle like the hero in a play.

'I don't know.' Because one never did. He saw her mouth twist, her furious eyes accuse him, because she had to accuse somebody.

She rose abruptly and walked away.

Damn it . . .

Madame Gérard went after her, for by that time everyone understood, almost without speaking, that they'd all have to participate in the deception. Even those who'd never been slaves – and most of them hadn't – and whose parents had never been slaves, knew instinctively: tell the story that it was *January* who'd been wounded. Uphold the deception that would leave him free to search for the truth, of what was happening, and why.

Whether Gilles died or not.

Dear God, please don't let him die.

Virgin Mary, Mother of God, pray for him. Pray for Callie, and for their children.

And as he prayed, the part of him that had never ceased to be a surgeon, the part that had tried to revive the half-ruined corpses of children or cleaned gunshot wounds at the Hôtel Dieu in Paris, felt only the cool concentration of doing the job before him, in partnership with the mercy of God.

The note that waited for him at home – when he finally reached the place – read:

> *They have tried once more to murder ~~Felicita~~ [crossed out] Mademoiselle de Cedillos, by poison this time. She has taken refuge at the house of Speranza Rocher on Marais Street near the Turning Basin*

(Put this in the letters column of the Louisiana Gazette *while you're at it,* reflected January, turning the sheet, with its broken seals, over in his fingers.)

'That wasn't me, Uncle Ben,' protested Zizi-Marie, coming into the tiny, secret room in the house's foundations. 'Those seals were broken when I found that letter stuck in the crack of the door.'

and is in desperate fear.

'And well she should be,' murmured Rose, reading over his shoulder, 'with an idiot like Michie Dagobert on her side.'

January brought the paper closer to the lantern which Rose held up. For four years now, he had played host to men and women fleeing their enslavers, men and women hiding out for a night, or two nights, or a week. On the night he'd been asked to be part of the Railroad, he had dreamed a dream of the Blessed Virgin in her blue veil, urging him to extend that perilous assistance to the fugitives: *Did you think gold was given to you to use for yourself alone?*

And now he was a fugitive in earnest.

Had the Mother of God known?

Of course she had . . .

Gilles Gignac had been put to bed in the guestroom at Gérard's and a doctor ostentatiously summoned. ('I'm not going to die of a broken arm,' Gilles had whispered, half-stupefied on laudanum, as Dr Ker was cautioned to tell everyone that it was January who had taken the bullet – January who lay near death . . .) Only after Ti-Gall and Olympe had stealthily guided Germaine and Aglaëa to Olympe's house, and Parnassus Sam and Ti-Jon had checked the now-quiescent streets round about, had January returned, warily, to his own house to sleep. Zizi-Marie had been there still, with Dagobert's note.

Mademoiselle de Cedillos has been through all of her father's papers that we retrieved from Alegre and has not found what she seeks. This is, she tells me, an account of the events surrounding the Battle of Chalmette and documenting her father's reasons to suspect Pelerine's activities in the days leading up to the battle. He told her that he saw men coming in secret to Pelerine's house on the twelfth and thirteenth of that month, bearing three iron chests.

'Money at last!' cried Hannibal.

Among the papers she tells me that she found a coded letter to her and her sister, saying he would pen such an account and conceal it beneath the floorboards of his room, but Mademoiselle de Cedillos believes that at the last minute he concealed it elsewhere in the house.

I will search the house again tomorrow, as soon as it grows light, approaching it in secret, through the old cane fields and the swamp on the lake side.

'I trust he's made his will,' remarked Rose.

'I bet he means he'll go through the fields of the old Gemme plantation,' guessed Zizi-Marie, who in her younger days had followed her mother into the ciprière on herb-gathering expeditions at the dark of the moon. 'There's paths in back of the fields from Little Bullfrog Bayou that you can get to pretty easy, and Michie Bertie doesn't sound to me like a man who'll let his shoes get wet.'

(*Or a man who'll do any heavy work without assistance*, thought January, recalling those stored heaps of lumber, tools, and disused impedimenta in the old house at Alegre. He could already see what the note was leading up to.)

I will be there at daybreak. If ever you cared for me, Benjamin

Here he used the pronoun 'tu' as to a childhood friend.

meet me there. For if ever I needed a Patroclus, an Oliver, a Horatio, I need one now! – Achilles.

'Who's Pat Rockless and Oliver?' Zizi-Marie wrinkled her nose.

'Men in legends who let their friends talk them into messes they couldn't get out of.' Hannibal took the note from January's hand and studied it. His own thin fingers shook slightly. 'Shall I come with you, amicus meus?'

All the evening at Gérard's, January had uneasily observed how at intervals his friend would step into the deeper shadows away from the candles, lean against the wall, and fight for breath. Helpful as it would be to have a Patroclus of his own guarding his back as he made his way out to Alegre tomorrow morning (*This morning*, he corrected himself with a groan – first light would come in barely three hours), he suspected that now at the end of the Carnival season, it was the fiddler who would need watching over, as well as Dagobert. *And I will not*, he told himself grimly, *put another of my friends into the hand of death over this.*

'I'd rather you stayed here,' he said quietly, 'and kept an eye on Rose and the girls.'

Hannibal hesitated, as if he read January's thoughts.

'They think I'm dying over in Marigny,' January added. 'They'll have plenty of time to let Pelerine know this – or whoever is behind this. I'll be all right.'

'Ti-Gall—' began Zizi-Marie.

The loyal and well-intentioned Ti-Gall was, as the children said, something of a turkey, and January had no intention of letting his niece become a widow five weeks after she was wed.

'I'll be all right. Hannibal, I would take it as a favor if, when you've escorted these ladies to Olympe's house, you'd come back here and wake me at five . . .'

'*Since I cannot prove a hero*,' misquoted the fiddler, with a sweeping theatrical bow, '*I am determined to prove an alarum clock*—'

'Oliver would be proud of you,' Rose approved.

But when January closed his eyes, in the locked darkness of the hidden room, all he could see was Gilles, in his extravagant cloak and that silly mountain of a feathered hat, turning in the doorway of Fortune Gérard's house. Saw the way his body jerked, spun, at the bark of the rifle in the darkness. Like that poor Frenchman – *What had been his name? Couvillier* – beneath the oaks beside Bayou St-John.

And only because he had been a shape silhouetted by the candle-light inside, his height disguised by the hat . . .

And when he'd turned his head, the glint of sick terror, of bitter hatred, in the eyes of Gilles's mother.

1815

Then he was on the redoubt above Rodriguez's Canal again. His hands shook as he stuffed rag and ramrod down the barrel of his musket, clearing out the fouling; fumbled ball, powder, wad from his patch box, guns thundering in his head. Gilles shoved his own ramrod down his musket barrel beside him – Gilles was always quicker at loading than him – and shouted something to Davy, over on his other side. From his right, on the river, the *Louisiana*'s guns split even the din of the British fire, the yells of the men trapped down in chest-deep water in the ditch below the escarpment. And somehow in his dream January knew that Cut-Nose Chigizola – whom he wouldn't meet for years – was doing just this: ramming shot down the barrel of a cannon, squinting through the rising light. Blasting at men who were trapped between river and redoubt, men who didn't want to be there and couldn't get away. Like Couvillier, standing up in another chilly gray dawn to be shot at—

Gilles ran the few short yards to the line of cotton bales that topped the escarpment, gun in his hand. The iron of January's own weapon was hot in his grip as he checked the flint, dropped in a pinch of powder, the miasma of powder smoke and fog and dust burning his eyes. Davy, blazing with excitement, dropped his patch box and cursed as he scrabbled for the scattered musket balls in the dirt. January scooped up three and smacked them into the boy's hand, the men over on the other side of them leaping to their feet to run back to the barricade.

Men down in the ditch below the American lines shouted – screamed – as the Americans above them shot down into the packed, jostling mob.

And clearly as if the fiddler stood at his side he heard Hannibal say, 'Even *I* know better than to charge uphill into emplaced artillery . . .'

He saw – as if looking at two paintings hung side-by-side on the same wall – what was going on a mile and a half away, beyond the dark wall of cypresses on the edge of the swamp. Smoke rising from two burning plantations. Men yelling as they broke through those doors, as they looted, knowing they'd be able to sell the stuff without being sold themselves . . . Other men, women, and children, disappearing into the fog that still hung on the trembling lands.

Three iron chests, Dagobert had written . . . Mademoiselle de Cedillos had said . . .

Then he was crouched behind the line of cotton bales at the top of the escarpment, wet earth soaking into the knees of his breeches, the roar of the guns, the yelling of the men below like the din of

Dante's Hell. He stood up, knowing he had only seconds – knowing he stood for only seconds on that cold day. But it was as if he looked down at the ditch below for leisurely minutes, seeing every detail: the advance guard shoving to flee, having no way to get up the escarpment, the men behind them crowding to advance, not knowing yet of the danger. The black soldiers of the West Indian regiments falling side-by-side with the Waterloo veterans . . . *Let us make incision*, says the dark Prince of Morocco in the *Merchant of Venice*, . . . *to prove whose blood is reddest, his or mine* . . .

But there was no difference, and the water of the canal was only a horrible blackish-crimson, mud mixed with blood, as men trampled one another, floundered, and drowned. Other men, further back, milled and shoved, having no orders, evidently, either to advance or retreat.

Knee-deep in ooze, an officer, in fury and frustration, threw rocks at the American line.

Men's faces below him. Dr Ker – though his waking mind knew that Ker was at the infirmary tent at LaCoste's plantation downriver, listening to the guns as to far-off, terrible thunder. Hannibal's cousin, who had made it through Waterloo and the Peninsula War, only to die in America . . .

And another man, whose face he briefly recognized from waking life, and thought, *Of course* . . .

He'll know . . .

But he fired into the mass of those trapped men, as the men on either side of him fired, and felt a musket ball rip his sleeve, the burning brush of hot lead on his flesh. He ducked down and turned his head in time to see Davy Gignac run up to the parapet, musket in hand and eyes wild and joyful with battle. January yelled, 'Get down, Davy!' and heard beside him Gilles yelling, too, their voices drowned in the shouting of the men all around them, the pounding of the guns. Davy stood up behind the cotton bales, aimed down – too young to remember you can't aim a musket as you can a rifle – trying to hit this man or that.

Then his body arched backward as he was struck, his arms flung wide, his musket falling with the slowness of dream. January knew – as he had known that morning – that Gilles yelled, 'Davy!' though he couldn't hear him over the guns. Both young men flung themselves forward; scrambled along the trampled ground. Both knowing

Davy was already dead and that it didn't matter if they reached his body or not.

Gilles scooped Davy's body into his arms; shouted his brother's name over and over, louder and louder, as if so doing could call him back.

But it couldn't.

1841

January woke. Falling asleep, he'd heard far off and small the desultory noises of the tail end of a Carnival night: women's laughter, the clatter of tin pans and carriage wheels. Somebody singing: *You heard of the battle of New Orleans / Where General Jackson give the British beans . . .*

Now there was nothing, save the scratching of a rat's feet in the greater cellar outside. The candle within the pierced tin sleeve of the lantern put burning speckles of gold on the lathe walls, the huge cypress beams of the ceiling.

Faintly, a footstep creaked on the planks overhead. Someone on the gallery.

One person, moving stealthily. January's heart seemed to compress within his ribs, his breath halting in his lungs . . . *They've figured out I'm here. Or at least they think there was something amiss about my 'injury.'* The next logical step for Watling would be, of course, to fire the house.

A cautious tap on the shutters, inaudible save for the deep stillness of what he knew to be a blackly foggy morning outside.

Then, within the house, a lighter footfall (*Hannibal's – it must be later than I think . . .*), and a hoarse cough. A moment later, the slight creak of the shutter opening.

January got to his feet, took up the lantern, and slid the bolt back on the hidden door of the chamber. *If Hannibal knew whoever knocked – whispered – and let them in, it has to be news . . .*

Dagobert coming here?

I have to meet him at sun-up . . .

He slipped out beneath the back gallery, into the yard – as he'd suspected, fog and utter darkness. The smell of the river, and the last lingering traces of sugar boiling and smoke. Roulaison was over. Carnival would end Tuesday at midnight, in the silence of ashes and Lent. The planting of next year's crop had already begun.

Swiftly he climbed the steps and unlocked the shutters of the French door to the dining room, which he knew would be unbarred.

Candlelight within, and Hannibal emerging from January's study, a folded paper in his hand.

'What is it?' January looked past him into the study's darkness, half-expecting to see Ti-Gall or Gabriel. Or, worse, someone from Fortune Gérard's household . . .

The fiddler shook his head, and his mouth twitched in a grin. 'Ignosce, amice mi. I'm sorry that woke you – it's nothing. A note for Germaine, from Cosette, trapped like Cinderella at her Gran'mère Poucet's in Spanish Fort.' He dropped the folded paper on the corner of the sideboard. 'Though how a douce maiden like Cosette came to know such a reprobate as False River Jones even existed—'

'That was False River Jones?'

Like a fragment of a broken plate, he remembered his dream, of the faces of the men trapped in the muck of the Rodriguez Canal. Upturned, covered in mud and blood and sweat, looking at the American guns pointed down at them.

Men who'd come to this place to fight and die.

And some of them, like Dr Ker, had not died . . . and had not left.

Before Hannibal had even nodded, January was striding across the parlor, through his study and out through the French door and down the gallery steps. He was aware of the fiddler coming behind him but outdistanced him. Barely a ravel of yellow around the streetlamp above Rue Burgundy, but he guessed that the river trader had turned towards the swamp rather than the river. *He'll have left his pirogue in the Basin or at Bayou St-John.* Not a whisper of light, from any of the houses, though far-off traces of sound from the gambling dens near the waterfront: Armageddon wouldn't have silenced them.

Into the darkness he called, 'Jones!' and hoped the Watling boys weren't hiding behind the trees of the neutral ground of Rue Esplanade. 'Jones!'

Long stillness.

Damn it . . .

Like a thickening of the darkness, a figure seemed to congeal from the fog just beyond the narrow radius of the hanging lantern's light. A man's form – and at his heel, like a little goblin, the smudge of a small black dog.

Then Jones came forward, his shape resolving itself into a flapping coat stitched from a striped 'trade' blanket, long gray braids plaited with blue ribbons, more blue ribbons tied in bows in a gray wilderness of beard. Across three waistcoats, one above the other, of the finest Chinese silk, fobs glittered on several gold chains, and the bright black eyes smiled as he reached January and held out his hand.

'Not dead, then?'

January said, 'Come in the house, if you would, sir,' and Jones's grin widened in the beribboned whiskers. 'You wouldn't happen to have heard who paid Cat Watling to take potshots at me, would you?'

'Alas, I can't help you . . . Cat Watling, you say? He's usually a better shot than that. I'm pleased to see the rumors lied.' The Welshman followed January up the steps to the gallery, where Hannibal stood in the darkness beside the shuttered door. 'I can ask about for you—'

'Maybe.' January half-opened the shutter, then stood back while False River Jones slipped like a snake through the French door before him, his black dog a little shadow at his heel. Inside, a single candle burned on a corner of January's desk, touching only the dimmest outlines of shelves, books, ledgers with threads of gold, and gleaming in the dog's demon eyes. 'Since I have no idea who's behind these attempts, I wouldn't ask it of you, sir. Whoever it is – they are – they have the money to hire men. What you can do,' he added, gesturing Jones to the more comfortable of the room's two chairs, 'is tell me – did you happen to fight in the Battle of Chalmette?'

SEVENTEEN

'A sorrier mess I never did see in my life.'

Only after the dirty lanterns of the saloons that surrounded the Basin – and the grimy agglomeration of tents, sheds, whorehouses, and barrooms that dotted the sodden ground behind them – had given way to canebrakes, cypress trees, sheets of water, and the occasional huts of swamp trappers and slaves who 'slept out,' did False River Jones take up his story of the events of the eighth of January, 1815. Even during Carnival, the gambling and drinking establishments of the Basin and its surrounding thoroughfares quieted down in the cinder-gray hours between first light and sunrise. Clinging fog made it even less likely that anyone would see the tall river trader, and his still-taller companion, as they threaded their way through the backstreets of Tremé, to where Jones had left his pirogue tied in the canal near the Flesh and Blood saloon.

Mists lay thick over the water as January settled into the narrow dugout, and the smell of sewage stuck in his throat like poisonous glue. But there were few other craft on the water this early. Even the piano players in the whorehouses were silent. Where a few candles still brightened the windows of taverns, January guessed that the only customers there were the hardened men intent on their games, or the sorry gamblers for whom the pat of shabby cards, the clatter of dice, and the glint of gold and silver in the dim light were like liquor to a drunkard, something you didn't leave until you passed out from exhaustion.

Silence folded around them, and the grit of smoke from the first breakfast fires.

'Daresay you've heard how the lot of us had to be rowed across Lake Borgne in those damn bitty boats, on account of the lake being too shallow for the ships of war, and the river passes defended. Six days it took, while your lot had all the time in the world to build up that redoubt above the canal, and get the pirates on your side, and put up a wall of cotton bales. That's not to speak of Pakenham dithering like a schoolgirl when first we attacked your line, and pulling our men back, which only gave the enemy two more weeks to bulk up his defense – tcha! It was after that I left.'

Jones shook his head, looking back – as January had for over two weeks now looked back – on that younger self, in his red jacket and black trousers, lying in the tents around the Villeré house while January and Gilles and all those friends of their youth in d'Aquin's battalion moved inexorably towards them in the darkness.

'I heard tell of it later. You'd think, if a regiment's been tasked with making ladders and bundling up fascines because everybody in the damn army knows by that time they're going to have to wade fifteen feet of head-high mucky water with naught but slime underfoot, and then climb up a seven-foot parapet with men shooting down on 'em, the bloody idiots would *remember to bring the damn things with 'em* on the day of the attack, wouldn't you?' But the anger faded from his voice, replaced by a sadness worlds deep. 'Forgot 'em. Left 'em behind like a pair of gloves. If Wellington had been with us, the lot of you would never have stood a chance.'

The faces came back to January – from his dream, from all his dreams over the past quarter of a century, more than half his life. Men trapped below the parapet, raked by musket fire from above and shredded by the guns on the *Louisiana*, with no defense for them. Remembered that single, furious officer throwing stones at the American lines and cursing helplessly as grapeshot ripped his men to pieces, tears running down his face. In his dream, he'd seen Jones among them, hair ribbons and all, though he knew the man hadn't been there.

Quite quietly, he said, 'I know.'

'I had friends in the Ninety-Third.' Jones sighed and bent his back to the pole, against the silent obsidian waters of the canal. 'Dear good men and true as forged steel. I felt a swine and more than a swine, sneakin' out of camp that night, with all the powder and ball, all the camp knives and liquor and pistols I could carry, and half of the lot I had to trade to some villain of a Choctaw, to sell me his pirogue and guide me away into the marshes – and damn lucky the man was a Christian and didn't just cut my throat and take the lot. But I knew my friends – Danny Mullin and Red John Dannaher and Tommy Barton and the rest. They wouldn't have deserted for a pension.'

The canal debouched into the wider dark of Bayou St-John. On other pirogues tied to the banks among the cypress knees, or hidden by swamp laurel and palmetto onshore, or in the occasional white wooden American houses beyond the levee, lights showed. A dog barked, and Cú Sidhe – Jones's little companion – put his forepaws on the gunwale, sharp ears pointed, but made no sound. Once January smelled bacon.

'For all I know they died that day,' Jones went on after a time. 'Or in the days after the battle, when our lads retreated with fall of dark, as far as they could get – four or five hundred yards, it must have been. They made huts out of cane, lashed together with gear straps and belts and twisted grass, just for a place to lie down in. I was hid out in the back swamp by that time and dasn't to come close, part because of the gear I'd stolen and part because through all that time, all those ten fooking days it took for our ships to get our men out of there, your lot kept shelling the camp, though you didn't dare come on for an attack.'

'We hadn't the strength,' said January. 'Even with your numbers reduced, we were still no more than a few thousand.' He didn't add, *And why would we have attacked, seeing your makeshift camps diminished every day as one unit, and then another, were drawn back?*

Jones said, 'Tcha,' again, then for a time was silent. They tied up the pirogue on the batture below the Widow d'Hebecourt's land, crossed over the Bayou Bridge and along the old Indian trail between a little cluster of dancehalls and gambling parlors, sleepy and three-quarters deserted, like a village on the outskirts of Hell, where lights still burned. January glanced behind him half a dozen times, but here, as on the bayou, the fog made a ghostly curtain. The only thing that moved were two men staggering along the other side of the roadway, singing incoherently of the loves of Rory O'More.

In half a mile they reached the soggy bottomlands of the Bayou Gentilly. Another pirogue, larger, was tied there among the cane and alligator grass. Little Cú Sidhe ran ahead of the two men and leaped inside, eyes gleaming like those of his ferocious namesake; January waded calf deep in the freezing water, to help push the vessel into the clearer stream.

Dark trees closed them in. Cocks in some distant plantation yard began to crow.

After a time, January asked, 'What about the Spanish?'

'Naught about the Spanish.' Jones sniffed his contempt. 'Half the camp was trading rumors, all the week before, like lads swapping marbles. The slaves would rise up in revolt someplace behind the enemy lines, and a troop of Spanish militia come out of the swamps to fall on Coffee's Tennessee men that was holding that end of the American line. Some of the girls said they'd heard this from the swamp trappers, how the Spanish sent twenty thousand pesos to a secret Spanish militia force to buy weapons, though how they'd smuggle that much silver in – let alone the guns to buy with it – is another story. Some of them had Spanish pesos – or pieces of them – to spend around the camp. And I will say those bits looked as if they'd been fresh chopped.'

'How would they have bought the guns?' January remembered what Chigizola had said about bank drafts – and what his mother had commented about the ingenious Mr Chew.

'The usual way.' Jones shrugged. 'Somebody arranged for some merchant in Mexico or Cuba to get the money, in specie or more like in a bank draft, to one of the smugglers, D'Aury or Beluche or one of the Cubans. They'd buy the guns in Havana and bring them in through the Barataria, and let the militia know where they'd leave them, on one of those little islands, those chéniers, in the swamps. You know the Barataria, Ben. South of English Turn, once you get off the ridge of the river itself, it's nothing but a hundred little bays and lakes, and a thousand ponds and swamps and bayous that appear and disappear and change their course, like the promises a girl makes to you in a dream.'

January nodded. He had moved through the Barataria, on foot and by pirogue, and knew that place was not called the trembling lands out of romantic fancy. The back swamp between New Orleans and the lake was an echo of it, a wet, green world of cypress trees emerging from the water like the pillars of some endless Byzantine cistern, a world where you could lose yourself and die of thirst before you came to clean water. A world where if you stepped off your boat on to what you thought was an islet, you could find that it was only a flottant, a floating mass of vegetation that would sink under you: crotch deep, neck deep, drowning deep as your feet entangled in submerged roots, or clinging weeds, or the rotted trunks of cypresses sunk a thousand years ago.

That had been the world at the inland end of the American line. The world through which the British troops would have been unable to pass, had they attempted to circle the end of Jackson's forces. The world through which the Spanish militia would have guided them – or *someone* would have guided them – to prevent the men who'd survived the Peninsular War and Waterloo by grit and courage from drowning, ignominiously, in the deadly muck of the Louisiana swamps.

Away from town – away from the Faubourgs of Marigny and Montreuil, from the hopeful developments of sugar planters who could no longer make a profit by their cropped-out lands, from the brickyards and cotton presses closer to the river – the ciprière was as it had been, under the growing light of dawn. January wondered if Dagobert would actually be waiting for him, at that half-ruined plantation house on Bayou Joyeuse, or if – *God help us!* – he'd managed to lose himself in the swamps in an attempt to come to Alegre by stealth. *And how long do I wait before I start to search for him?*

It was one reason he'd bargained with Jones to accompany him to the place (with money he devoutly hoped he'd be able to borrow from Dagobert . . .) – completely aside from his own need to reach the old de Cedillos plantation through the wet mazes of the ciprière.

Or will he have just overslept?

No, thought January. No account books could compete with the vision of Felicita de Cedillos, doe-like eyes wide with terror for her life, begging him – her Roland, her Achilles, her Theseus – to help her clear her father's name.

Rather to his surprise, as he and False River Jones approached the old house through the shoulder-high rows of the cane fields on the lake-ward side, he found his relative waiting for them on the gallery. Dagobert had clearly gotten a start on searching the place, moving stacks of barrel staves, old buckets and shutters, tangles of hoes and God only knew how many disused baskets and looms. His clothing, face, and hands were smutched with filth and spiderwebs, his hair dark with sweat and his old (but stylishly cut) jacket torn on one sleeve.

But his face was alight with enthusiasm as he bounded down the steps and clasped January's hands. 'I knew you'd come!' He turned startled eyes to Jones, while January introduced them, and shook his hand with equal pleasure. 'Do you know anything of de Cedillos, then?' he asked. 'By what Mademoiselle de Cedillos has told me, there has to be more to it than just Pelerine cooking up a slave revolt to throw rumors of treason on to Mademoiselle's father so he could turn the American judges against him. Who else would have sent three chests of money – it has to have been money! – to Pelerine, if not the British or the Spanish?'

'Pelerine?' The river trader's white brows jerked together. 'You mean that old fuddykin was behind it?'

'He has to have been!' Dagobert drove his fist into his dirt-blackened palm, face ablaze with enlightenment. 'And that's the reason he has hired ruffians to kill poor Cita – and us, for aiding her! De Cedillos must have found evidence of his treason, and that's what's hidden, somewhere, in the house! I have been searching the house since it was light enough to see—'

'It has occurred to me, sir,' said January, 'that we might start our search at the other end of the trail. If M'sieu Pelerine was part of the Spanish conspiracy to retake Louisiana – if he was behind the plan to draw off the American forces and strike behind them, as my mother thinks, with either a Spanish militia, rebelling slaves, or both – he'd need to provide his forces with guns. And if the attack didn't come off – if de Cedillos learned of the plan, went to speak to Pelerine or to the mutinous Spanish themselves, or if he set out to warn Jackson of the attack and was intercepted – might his murder have caused the Spanish militia to lose their nerve? That would be why there was never an attack—'

The merchant's mouth and eyes made a repeating symphony of Os in his face. 'You're right!' he exclaimed. 'You're absolutely right! That would explain everything! And if we can but find his body—'

'You'll not do that, sir.' Jones fished in his pocket for his pipe. 'Not after all those years you won't. If he was dealing with desperate men, mutineers or rebels or what-all, you'd not have found it after twenty-four hours, let alone twenty-six years. It's easy enough, to lose a man's bones forever out there.' He nodded towards the gray wall of trees, and Dagobert's face took on the desperate expression of a hero with his back to the wall.

'We must.' He clenched his fists. 'Surely—'

'What we *can* do,' said January, 'sir, is look for the guns themselves. Michie Jones here says they'd likely have been hidden on one of the chénier islands in the swamp. Or at a guess, more than one, if the shipment was brought in several lots for better concealment. If de Cedillos was murdered by the Spanish militia, they may well have panicked. Took what they had and left the rest of the shipment behind. Whatever they left may give us proof as to who paid for them.'

They found the guns on the fourth chénier they searched.

As January had suspected, the arms had been cached in several places. The box they found contained six muskets, heavily coated in grease now long hard and rotted, and wrapped in oiled canvas. It had been buried under the shell midden of what had been first a Choctaw or Houmas village, and later a camp of runaway slaves, deep in the swamplands between the river and Lake Pontchartrain. A land, as False River Jones had said, of a thousand little ponds and pools and bayous that appeared and disappeared depending on the season, the weather, and which direction you thought you were facing.

Jones knew the country, and knew where the old camps had been, the old villages. Cut-Nose knew it, too, as did every smuggler and slave stealer who brought their wares into town for cut-rate prices: slaves from Africa, prime wines, lead and silk on which no tariff had ever been levied for the benefit of Northern factories. Spanish silver coin, at a time when silver in America was scarce. Doubtless the men who lived on the edges of those swamps could also have found their way about them, if they were men who enjoyed hunting deer and geese and, back in those days, cougars. ('Mademoiselle de Cedillos said that was how her father originally stumbled on Pelerine's plans,' Dagobert affirmed.)

And any slave quickly learned where the bigger chéniers lay, the islands where oak trees had taken root on chance-formed sandbars, where silt had further accumulated, to make proper foundation for the huts of Indians and swamp trappers, the hideouts of fugitives before New Orleans grew large enough to support organized action against such groups.

Twenty-six years ago, January marveled as he gouged the thick-packed accumulation of oyster shells, fishbones, pottery shards and raccoon skulls that rose eight feet high behind the cluster of ruined huts. Before the land was so settled up, it was still possible for men to hide within ten miles of the slave owners with their guns and their dogs. Possible for men to steal back to the plantation quarters at night to visit their wives and their friends. As few as six years ago, a man named Cut-Arm had headed up several villages of fugitive blacks and a sprinkling of white thieves and ne'er-do-wells. According to the runaways January sheltered in those tiny rooms below his house, some were doing so still.

The guns hadn't been buried deep. Trees and grass grew over the place, but not so thickly as over the rest of the mound. It was easy to find.

Dagobert cried, 'I knew it!' as he pointed to the roughly stenciled word *HAVANA* on the crate's side. With his shovel – he'd brought two, with his original intention of digging beneath the house at Alegre if necessary – he cracked open the wood, then dragged at the board-stiff folds of the canvas.

Interested, Jones – whom Dagobert had paid five dollars for his help and continued assistance – leaned close. 'Brown Bess.' His voice rang with pride, as he tapped a clotted gunlock nearly encased in putty-hard residue of grease. 'Beat the Spanish 1752s all hollow. Threw a bigger ball, they did, and twice the distance. Any guerrillero in Spain would trade his sister for one of these. Some of them did just that.' Carefully, he began breaking off the decayed wood of the crate all around the crumpled block of hardened cloth and crumbled grease. Little black Cú Sidhe sniffed at the wrapping, then drew back in disgust. Jones pulled his hand away as well, when Dagobert produced a chisel and attacked the rectangular lump like Hephaestus forging the armor of Achilles, his unprepossessing face transformed by the ardor of his quest.

Searching, January guessed, for an invoice that no smuggler would ever have included in such a shipment. (*What does he expect? 'Delivered to Icarus Pelerine, Orleans Parish, Louisiana, fifteen muskets, at the cost of twelve Spanish dollars per, delivered to the account of . . .' Of who*?)

But all that January found – prodding and scraping the whole of the dug-in area around the crate – was a single Mexican peso, black with tarnish, bearing the head of King Ferdinand VII and the arms of the Spanish Bourbons.

Dagobert showed signs of spending the remainder of the afternoon – it was already four – leveling the entire shell mound and if necessary digging up the whole chénier, in quest of further evidence. But January pointed out that only the seven-foot rectangle of vegetation around the hole showed any sign whatsoever of having been excavated.

'We have the proof we need,' he said, rolling down the sleeves of his shirt and taking his threadbare brown corduroy jacket from the bush where he'd hung it. 'There was a conspiracy; the rumors were true about the Spanish militia being armed—'

'But we knew that!'

'*We* knew it, sir.' January entered the mental caveat that he, personally, had only believed it since his conversation with Jones that morning, but that still counted as eligible for the use of the past tense. 'But remember, in order to help Mamzelle de Cedillos, you have to be able to prove the existence of the plot in a court of law. It's now' – he checked his silver watch – 'a quarter past four, and it will take us at least an hour, maybe longer, to reach the river road. Michie Jones' – he turned to the trader – 'would you be able to guide us in further search through the ciprière tomorrow, or later in the week?'

His glance went to Dagobert, who nodded eagerly, a promise of payment that made the older man incline his head.

'I'm your man, then.' The ex-soldier dug again in his pocket for his pipe.

'And you wouldn't,' went on January, 'know of a place where we can keep these guns, would you? Where they would be safe and undiscovered until we have the rest of the information we need?' He didn't really expect the trader to volunteer his own hideout, wherever it was that he cached his stock-in-trade of smuggled gunpowder, antiquated firearms, napkins and shirts pilfered from plantation laundries, and liquor of all grades surreptitiously traded to every plantation quarters along the river. He wasn't surprised when Jones frowned and thought deeply before replying.

'You might try the old sugar mill at Alegre,' he said at last. 'Pelerine stripped the machinery and kettles out of the place years ago, but never had it torn down, and it's far enough from the house that it's been swallowed up by the forest. It's easy enough to get to and get away from, through the back swamp.'

Dagobert looked disappointed but agreed with a sigh. 'I know there's more guns still hidden in the ciprière,' he said, as Jones and January steered the pirogue – now low in the water with the weight of the contraband – through the marshy fastnesses, back towards Bayou Joyeuse. 'There must be hundreds of chéniers . . . I've found nothing so far at Alegre, but de Cedillos's account of Pelerine's treason – of who paid him for his perfidy – has to be *somewhere.* Why, Mademoiselle de Cedillos showed me his coded note!' (January carefully refrained from rolling his eyes at such 'proof' so opportunely discovered.) 'We may even find his body—'

'With that much water in the swamp' – Jones paused his paddling long enough to blow a line of smoke – 'I can promise you, you're not going to find Cedillos's body.'

'And there must be something, at one of those chéniers, that will serve as proof of what was planned. Pirates wouldn't just have . . . have handed those guns over to Pelerine's co-conspirators. Not without papers of some kind.'

There, thought January, *speaks a merchant.*

'If they had papers,' the river trader reminded him patiently, 'they wouldn't have left them with the goods. And papers or not, you generally didn't try to cheat Lafitte, or Beluche, or any of those wise lads. They had long memories.' He bent to fish the last pottery bottle of ginger water from the little cache of empties in the bow. 'And very accurate ones.' He held the drink out to Dagobert first, a gesture more towards accepted custom in Louisiana than from regard for the man. Dagobert being Dagobert, he had neglected to bring anything resembling lunch on his expedition to Alegre that morning (heroes in romances generally had their minds on higher things), and had cadged half the bread, cheese, and sausage that January had packed, wrapped in clean newspapers, before leaving the house with Jones in the cold of pre-dawn.

The winter daylight was graying over the water as the three men made short portages, from one pond to another, from the last shallow dribbles of some nameless bayou to another one half-hidden by walls of palmetto and cane. ('Just a hundred feet,' encouraged Jones cheerfully, and in fact it was. January hated to think how he'd have fared trying to guide Dagobert through this sodden labyrinth.) Under the double burden of the pirogue and the crate of muskets, they sweated, and January felt keenly the effect of the reduced rations and shortage of fluids. Only cautious listening, as they approached the Alegre sugar mill, kept him from the sleepiness he felt gnawing at his attention and his strength.

They left the pirogue tied in what January thought, in the gathering gloom, had to be Bayou Trois Fous, under Cú Sidhe's prick-eared guard. January prickled like a cat as Jones casually hacked saplings to put under the crate and bear it inland.

If nobody attacked Dagobert at the house this morning, he told himself, *he can't have been followed there.*

But he didn't entirely believe this, and his relative's chatter about what his stepmother would say to him if he missed this evening's session with Madame Arthemise, Madame's seamstress, to fit his costume as King of the Grand Mardi Gras Cavalcade Tuesday evening – grated on his nerves. He was just trying to think of a tactful way to say *Shut up* to a white man, when (*Thank God*!) Jones lifted his hand, whispered, 'It's about a hundred feet. Let's keep it quiet.' January could have embraced him.

As Jones had said, the sugar mill had long ago been stripped of every fragment of equipment, as well as the tiles of its roofs and its hearths. Stored wood – presumably cut in the back swamp for the mill at Sept-Anges – stacked one wall twenty feet deep and head high, and the gold eyes of possums and foxes gleamed at them from out of that dark. The three men concealed the guns in the remains of one of the great hearth platforms, where the charred wood of the last of the roulaison fires had not even been cleared out following de Cedillos's disappearance, that long-ago day of the battle. Jones cut another sapling from the forest of young trees that had grown around and within the derelict walls, to sweep away their footmarks as they left the ruins.

The trader – who had put away his pipe at the approach to the Alegre lands – had to shush Dagobert three or four times, as the merchant showed a tendency to discourse on what they still needed to seek, and how this would surely help Mademoiselle de Cedillos's cause.

In the softest of undervoices, Jones said, 'I'll take Ben here back to the Bayou Road the long way around, through Bayou des Ouaouarons. Might be best if you come that way, too, Janvier.' They paused on the edge of the trees. Across the rows of cane, the gleam of the ditches, the dim shape of the house glimmered in the dusk. 'The town'll be lit up and dancing in the streets – I hear tell Henri Mabillet and his friends are having a parade down the Champs-Élysées tonight, to advertise *his* party—'

'Oh, that's not necessary,' returned Dagobert cheerfully. 'But thank you. I left my horse and chaise just the other side of Bayou Joyeuse—'

'You did *what*?' January stared at him, forgetting even to add, *sir*.

'I made sure he was baited and near water,' explained his relative defensively. 'He's perfectly—'

'You *drove* out here?'

The other man bridled. 'It's seven miles! I had spades and chisels with me – I wasn't going to *walk* . . .'

And from somewhere in the dark wall of trees, three rifles spoke with the crashing of doom.

EIGHTEEN

False River Jones turned on his tracks like a rabbit and vanished into the tangles of foliage and dusk. Dagobert lunged to grab him, and for good measure yelled 'Jones!' at the top of his voice before January could stop him. Another shot barked, and Dagobert staggered, then fell with a cry. January reached him, and Dagobert seized his arm, tried to stand, and his right leg buckled again. 'My ankle . . .'

No blood, no hole in his boot – January's mind registered these facts automatically as he pulled the other man to his feet. *Sprain or break . . .*

Taking Dagobert's weight on his own shoulder, January pushed through the wall of coarse, fan-shaped leaves, and tried to recall in which direction that tiny bayou lay and failed. Palmetto, hackberry, then they emerged into a wide space of crotch-deep water that he'd never seen before in his life, studded with the goblin shapes of cypress knees.

Thank God the gators are all asleep . . .

In the dusk it was impossible to judge direction. Underwater snags and branches tore at his legs as he waded across the shallow pond, Dagobert clinging to his arm.

We'll be lucky if we don't get turned around and walk smack into Cat and his men.

The water shallowed to mud, walled by a forest of canes. Then dry land, shaggy-barked oaks and knots of laurel and swamp maple. January listened desperately, but the sound of his own legs slashing through the alligator grass, of Dagobert's sobbing breath, covered whatever noise of pursuit there might have been. *Three of them at least*, he thought. *Give us a minute's lead, for them to reload – if those are rifles rather than muskets – another half-minute for them to cross the open ground to where we were last seen . . .*

It went through his mind that if he left Dagobert to fend for himself – Dagobert who, like an idiot, had come to Alegre openly, in a chaise! – he could make better time while their pursuers ran down the easier prey. He, January, would have time to hide . . .

But he knew he couldn't. Much later, it occurred to him that it wouldn't have done him any good anyway, since the hunters would split up to follow them both, but that wasn't the reason.

(*Roland and Oliver be damned, even Sancho Panza wouldn't have done that.*)

He simply couldn't.

Not to the son of St-Denis Janvier.

Not to anyone.

Dagobert gripped his shoulder like the Old Man of the Sea, gasping in agony. Having broken his own ankle a few years before, January didn't blame him in the least.

In half an hour it would be full dark. January half-dragged his burden through another stretch of standing water – deeper, this time – skirted the first canebrake that he saw and plunged into the heart of a tangled 'hell,' as they were in some places called, of swamp laurel and trumpetweed. There he sat Dagobert down, propped against a clump of canes the thickness of his arm . . . *What now*?

His own strength, great as it was, wouldn't be sufficient to outrun their attackers for long. *We have to go to ground. Once it gets dark, we won't be able to move . . .*

Will they track us in the darkness?

Hannibal coming back into the parlor with Cosette's letter to Germaine seemed like a dream he'd dreamed in childhood. The dark shape of False River Jones in lamplight, the demon gleam of Cú Sidhe's eyes in the fog, something that happened weeks ago. Even if the fiddler told Rose he'd gone off with False River Jones in the small hours of the morning, what good would that do? There were fifty square miles of back swamp between New Orleans and the lake, and hundreds downriver of it. No one in their right mind would search them by night. Certainly not anyone of African descent. False River Jones – if he hadn't been shot – would be gliding away in his pirogue as fast as he could work the pole, headed for wherever it was he hid out in this wet, empty world of water and silence.

Dagobert had slumped back, teeth clenched against thin gasps of pain. January checked his ankle again, but no blood stained the leather of his boot. It bulged tight, though, on his swelling ankle, putting excruciating pressure on already damaged tissue. He felt the white man's pulse and hands, clammy and cold. His breath was a thready keening . . . *Damn it*! January was familiar with the condition that surgeons at the Hotel Dieu had called 'choc' or 'shock,' that often accompanied wounds or pain. This condition alone, they said, could sometimes kill a man, particularly one who was cold and wet.

Voices. Barely a whisper, confused by the wind rustle in the canebrakes. On the other side of the water, the gleam of a lantern pierced the darkness, lost at once.

Hail Mary, full of grace, the Lord is with thee . . . pray for us sinners . . .

Then the eerie silence of the winter swamps, impossible to tell if it boded the presence of strangers.

Another rustle, sharp, different (*Is it different*?) from the wind.

Dagobert stirred, whispered, 'Paloma?'

'It's all right,' breathed January. 'Hush.' *I'll give you Paloma . . .*

The sugar mill was right beside Bayou Joyeuse, two hundred yards from the Big House of Alegre. January estimated they'd come inland into the swamp four or five times that distance, but it was impossible to be sure. If he'd curved parallel to the bayou, they could be only yards from the Big House. Could have overshot it and be somewhere in that tangle of weeds and palmetto that had overgrown the quarters.

Voices, this time clearer. A crunch of undergrowth. Scarcely louder than the lap of the bayou among the reeds, Dagobert whispered, 'Where are we?'

'Too close. We need to—'

Sudden thrashing, not a dozen feet away. A harsh American voice: 'You hold up your hands and come out, nigger—' and a gunshot crashed. Two more shots followed immediately; January slid his shoulder beneath Dagobert's arm, and the two men slipped and scrambled away from the sound, following the line of the thickets that January could now barely see.

Come out, nigger. That had not sounded good.

The clash of men running towards them. January ducked back into the thicker foliage, the sharp leaves of palmetto cutting his face and Dagobert's bulk and weight hampering his every move. But cane rattled in the brake behind them, and the sudden flare of a lantern glared blindingly in the dark.

'You stand still if you know what's good for you,' snapped a man's voice, in French this time. Another lantern thrust through the thicket, light gleaming on the barrels of a shotgun, and in the eyes of the men who stepped out with the light. January raised his free hand, spread the palm of the other – hooked around Dagobert's waist – to show it empty.

Two other men came out of the canebrakes behind them.

Not Cat Watling at all. Nor any of his henchmen (or henchwoman) as far as January could see. The man with the lantern was lighter than the others, quadroon or octoroon, his tough square-jawed face horribly pockmarked and his dark eyes cold.

The rest were nearly African-black. All wore the coarse, cheap garments of field hands.

The pockmarked leader glanced at Dagobert and asked, in English, 'How bad's he hurt?'

'His foot is sprained or broken,' January replied in the same tongue. 'How bad I don't know. I'll have to wait 'til daylight to see.'

The quadroon – who held a pistol as well as his lantern – signed to the men behind him, and two of them stepped forward, took Dagobert's weight from January's shoulder, and half-carried him back a few paces. Dagobert made as if to struggle, but his leg buckled under him and he would have fallen, teeth clenched against a cry. A third man took a pair of manacles from his belt and clipped January's wrists behind him while the man with the shotgun kept the weapon trained on him.

'Let's go,' said the quadroon. 'Michie Pelerine's gonna want to talk to you.'

The slave jail at Sept-Anges Plantation was, like most such structures, brick, four cells built side-by-side and equipped with iron wall rings, latrine buckets firmly locked into place, and small iron-barred windows that could not be reached if the occupant were chained to the wall. Optional amenities included a sort of shelf, like a Turkish divan, across one end of the room for the prisoner to sleep on, a mattress stuffed with straw (clean), a blanket (also clean), a big jug of water and a bowl of cold congris (*Whatever else becomes of me, Virgin Mother of God, I will die praising your name for this*!). The jail was mounted, like all the buildings on the bayou, on brick foundation piers, these some four feet high. Many planters didn't bother with this and built their jails – and in most cases the slave cabins as well – at ground level. Who cared if the niggers got their feet wet?

Though he ached with exhaustion, when they started to lead him up the steps to the jail, January pulled back and asked, 'May I take a look at my friend's foot? I'm a surgeon—'

He spoke French from reflex, and the quadroon answered, also in French, 'I get my wife to tie it up. We gonna have to cut that boot off him.' And to the men still supporting the barely conscious Dagobert, 'Take him to the sick house. Michie Pelerine see him there. Go,' he added, switching to English, his dark eyes glinting as January showed signs of arguing. 'You caused enough harm.'

The man had a truncheon hung on his belt as well as his pistol, and he looked more than capable of using it. The man with the shotgun followed January's two guards up the steps and stood by the door as they pulled off his boots and spancelled his ankles to the wall ring, leaving enough slack in the chain to let him reach the bed shelf, the food, and the bucket, but neither the door nor the high, barred window.

They removed the manacles and left him with no light, but the waning moon had risen by that time. By its dim glow, January located the water and the food. Between ravenous mouthfuls he listened, but no sound came from the indigo rectangle of the barred window, save an owl's occasional shriek. Cold smells of earth and vegetation drifted in, and all the myriad smells of a plantation: outhouses, the mule barn, banked cookfires, smoldering coals. *If there is any time to escape, that time is now, while everyone is asleep . . .*

But his captors had searched him on the way to Sept-Anges, relieving him of his knife, his matches and candles, his free papers in their oilskin wrapping, the keys to his house, and what little money he had in his pockets – though not, interestingly, of either his rosary or his watch. He could reach neither the window nor the door. By the feel of it, the water pitcher was cheap clay, the food bowl a gourd, and the box it was set on made of cheap slats and tacks. Nothing that was harder than the wood of the window bars or the iron of the door hinges.

Don't lie down, he told himself. The last sleep he'd had had been a few hours' restless doze before dawn in the hidden sanctuary room Sunday morning. He knew that once he fell asleep, even the entry of a boo-hag clothed in the skin of Andrew Jackson wouldn't serve to wake him . . .

He woke up with the thin moonlight in a different spot on the floor, his neck cramped because he'd been asleep with his head on the box beside the empty food bowl. Somewhere in the night – the quarters, probably – a baby cried, then silenced with the soft whimper of content as its mother gave it suck. The words of a lullaby came dimly to him, one he'd heard Olympe sing to her tiny daughter Zéphine:

Michael, row the boat ashore, hallelujah
Michael, row the boat ashore, hallelujah . . .

He rolled sideways with the intention of getting up and investigating what he could of the pitch-black room, and woke – what seemed to be seconds later – to full daylight at the sound of the padlock on the door bolt being unfastened.

The bolt scraped back, and Icarus Pelerine stood in the doorway.

He was as January recalled him from dozens of glimpses across ballrooms over the years, a gaunt man in his seventies with thick white hair neatly trimmed and cold pale eyes. In the morning light, the scarring that covered the left side of his face looked less gruesome than it did at town balls by candlelight. Maybe it was only because it had been some years since last he'd seen it.

Pelerine stepped inside, stiffly, like a man in pain.

Arthritis . . .

'You're Ben Janvier.' He used the polite form, vous êtes . . .

He held up the oilskin wallet that had been taken from January last night. His hands, crippled with the disease like an eagle's claws, also bore the scars of fire.

'I am, sir.'

Pelerine tossed the wallet on to the hard bench beside January. 'How do you fit into all this?'

January checked the wallet. It still contained his papers. 'Michie Janvier hired me to help him find who was behind the burning of those three plantations during the battle here,' he said, guessing that if this man was the villain Felicita de Cedillos claimed, he would know this already. 'And whether there really was a plan to attack Jackson's forces from the rear.'

'Why the hell would that matter at this time of the day?' The old planter sounded genuinely surprised.

'I didn't ask him, sir. I need the money.'

'Don't we all?' Pelerine sighed. 'So who were you shooting at in the woods, back when the moon was new? Noble tells me the six of you was going through the swamp like hornets—'

'That was the four of *them*,' said January. 'Whoever *they* are, going after Michie Dagobert Janvier and myself, when we searched the old de Cedillos place, sir. How is Michie Janvier, if I may ask? He was in a lot of pain, and having to flee from . . . whoever it was only made it worse. I was trained as a surgeon, sir, in France—'

'That's what Noble tells me,' agreed Pelerine. 'Noble's my overseer. Some of the other men go into town Sundays, he says, to sell moss and shingles and go to the dances in Circus Square. They've seen you. And of course I've seen you play. It's been a bad year for everyone all around, hasn't it?' He hesitated, then took a hooked spancel key from his pocket, limped forward, and, rather warily, unlocked the shackle on January's leg. 'Noble's just outside,' he cautioned as he did so.

January stood and bowed. 'At this point, I doubt I could take on even a man of your years, sir,' he replied, 'even were I armed with Hercules's club and King Arthur's sword and had three hundred Spartans at my back. And I wouldn't do it anyway,' he added, as Pelerine broke into a raspy chuckle, 'to anyone who arranged for that feast last night.' He gestured without irony towards the empty gourd and pitcher. 'Thank you. Were any of your men hurt in the shooting?'

'Joe took a ball in the meat of his thigh,' said the planter. 'Sassy – Noble's wife – got it out, but if you are indeed a surgeon, I'd be grateful if you'd have a look at it, after you've seen to Janvier. Sassy says Janvier seems well enough – it looks to be no more than a bad sprain, but those can hurt worse than a break. We didn't wake him. I wanted to hear your side of the story first.'

The Devil incarnate, his mother had warned. *For years he tried to sway the court against de Cedillos by means of rumor and gossip, slandering the man's name to anyone of influence who'd listen – and the names of his girls and his wife.*

He remembered, too, the terror in Mamzelle de Cedillos's lovely eyes.

A man may smile, and smile, Hamlet had observed – groping for his tablets to make a note of the fact – *and still be a villain . . .*

And January was well aware that birthrights had been traded for a mess of pottage, let alone the safety of those who sought to regain land from those who'd stolen it. He still felt gratitude for the pottage.

'I did notice,' said the Devil incarnate, as they descended the short stair from the slave jail and followed the shell path towards the Big House, 'that Michie Janvier's pistol had not been fired. So you contend that you were attacked by persons unknown, two weeks ago at Alegre, and again last night? Persons intent on . . . what? Keeping you away from the old de Cedillos house? I've searched the place half a dozen times, you know, in the years since the battle, and I've never found a trace of it.'

'A trace of what, sir?'

Pelerine halted in his tracks, surprised. 'The money,' he said. 'De Cedillos received almost twenty thousand dollars' worth of Mexican silver from the British, to organize and arm a covert militia of disgruntled Spanish – and as many rebellion-minded slaves as he could muster – and attack Jackson's forces from the rear. But on the day of the battle, he decided to use the general confusion to take the money chests and run for it. I gather the Spaniards got wind of his intentions and marched post-haste on Alegre – presumably to collect what they felt was owed them, since they knew the money was at the house – and de Cedillos took his family and fled.'

They had reached the house by this time, and Pelerine led the way up one of the rear stairways. Like Alegre, Sept-Anges stood on eight-foot piers of stuccoed brick, the main block (if so modest a structure could be called a 'block') facing Bayou Gentilly, with wings extending back towards the lower ground behind. January noted that the wooden walls of the wings badly needed painting, and that broken panes in the French doors of several of the rooms along those wings had been mended with cardboard.

Mean as sin for all his wealth, his mother had said.

The narrow galleries along the wings were clean swept, and the winter-bare garden between them looked well tended. But the whole aspect of the place – like the planter's threadbare jacket and neatly mended linen shirt – was worn with use, age, and straitened means.

Dagobert, he recalled, had described Sept-Anges as 'played out.'

'I doubt he was able to take much of that silver with him,' Pelerine went on, pausing again at the top of the stair. 'There were stragglers from both armies all over the countryside – deserters—'

Like False River Jones, thought January.

'—or men just out to loot what they could in the confusion. That much silver weighs close to three tons, even in sacks. Put it in chests and you need a wagon, or a couple of mules. Not something a man on the run – with a wife and two daughters – could easily hide or take through the ciprière.'

He shook his head, old anger mingling with sadness in his eyes. 'De Cedillos and I never got on. He refused to believe that his father had been granted that land illegally and refused to negotiate any sort of settlement: threatened to sue me, in fact, over half a hectare of marshland that wasn't part of his father's original grant at all. But I knew every plantation in the parish was losing men, with hands running off in the woods knowing nobody would look for them in the confusion. The swamp was crawling with deserters, camp followers, bandits, and runaways . . . Frankly, I was afraid for Madame and the girls.'

He looked around him at the long, rickety wings of the house, seeing, January guessed, the place as it had been on that winter morning, with the thunder of the guns still sounding far off, as Jackson's artillery continued to shell the defeated British in their makeshift camp. January remembered what it had been like to stand sentry duty in the camps behind the canal redoubt, the constant glimpses of furtive movement in the woods. *Deserters, camp followers, bandits, runaways* . . . Shapes that slipped into the camp at night, to steal food or horses . . .

'I knew de Cedillos had ridden out that morning.' Pelerine paused at the bottom of the steps that led up to the gallery along one of the wings. 'Then two of my own men told me they'd met a couple of the Spanish militiamen, on their way to Alegre, once they'd talked to their comrades and figured out that de Cedillos hadn't been at any of the three plantations that were attacked. They added two and two and realized he was going to make a break for it. My sons and I took a half dozen men and rode over there. We got there mid-morning, and they were gone.'

'Do you know what happened to them?' Mentally January held

the story up against the one Felicita de Cedillos had told Dagobert, of lawsuits and land grants and a destitute woman and her daughters being turned out into the road.

'No. There were no signs of violence in the house, though it had been looted by that time. In the bedroom, and the nursery, clothing of his wife and daughters had been tossed on to the bed, as if Madame had sorted it out to pack in haste. There wasn't a trunk or a portmanteau anywhere in the house. I took that to mean de Cedillos had gotten away with his family, and of course there wasn't a bondsman, a horse, or so much as a chicken on the entire property.'

He cocked a sharp, gray-blue eye at January from the wasteland of scars. 'After the battle, there was no sudden appearance of twenty thousand dollars' worth of pesos among the Spanish community, though goodness knows the Americans were spending freely enough in town. The Spaniards in the militia couldn't say anything out loud, of course, but the rumors went around fast, and I guessed that de Cedillos wouldn't be coming back. I moved Jeremie, my oldest boy, and his family into Alegre as soon as I could, and as soon as word came that the treaty had been signed and things were getting back to normal, I started the procedures to have the entire lawsuit over the land revisited in the court.

'For the ten years that he lived there, Jeremie – and his son, and his brother Dom – searched the house half a dozen times and never found so much as a single silver peso. After Jeremie—' He stopped himself, scarred, crooked fingers closing into what would have been fists. For a time he looked aside, then drew breath and went on. 'I looked when we cleaned the place out and found nothing. Dom was gone also by that time,' he added. 'My second son. I suppose I could have had the house torn down, but . . .'

Silence again.

But what? You couldn't tear down the place where your son had lived? Couldn't pull up and burn the floors your grandson had run across to greet you? The gallery you'd sat on in the evening, smoking cigars and laughing with those you loved?

'But I didn't,' the old man concluded and turned to go up the steps to the gallery above. 'What was it made M'sieu Janvier want to search the house again, after all these years?'

'That I don't know, sir,' January replied stolidly. 'He paid me to ask no questions, but just to do as I was bid. But since that first visit to the house I've been threatened, personally, twice – the second time, not two days ago, another man took the bullet that was meant for me.'

Pelerine stopped again, shock and disgust that looked absolutely genuine on his ruined face. 'What had you to do with it?'

'I don't know, sir,' January repeated. 'Maybe only as a warning to Michie Dagobert, the way bullies will kill a man's dog or hamstring his horse.'

'And has your employer been threatened directly as well?'

January shook his head and said for the third time, 'I don't know. But someone seems to know it, when we come to Alegre. And someone seems determined to stop us for whatever the reason, at whatever the cost.'

NINETEEN

January entered the first shuttered room at the top of the steps to find it dim and smelling of herbs and spirits of wine. Dagobert lay on a bed whose sheets looked fresh, as if someone had only put them on last night when he'd been brought in. A tabouret stood next to the bed, and beside it a low stool. Fresh dressings lay folded and ready, beside a clamshell that held three pins. Dagobert's eyes were closed, his foot elevated on a stack of folded blankets, his breathing a slow gasp.

Pelerine frowned with concern as January stepped hastily over to the bed. Without opening his eyes, Dagobert mumbled, 'Papa? Have them put the horses to— We must . . . we must . . .'

With an exclamation of alarm, the old man stepped back out on to the gallery, and January heard him call out, 'Allie? Allie!' His footfalls retreated along the walkway in the direction of the main house.

Dagobert's eyes popped open, clear and without fever, and he gripped January's wrist. 'Why did you tell him all that? About us being attacked? About someone knowing whenever we were going to Alegre?'

'If he was behind it, he'd know that already,' pointed out January.

'*If*? Of course he's behind it! That tarradiddle about the Spanish militia killing de Cedillos because he'd stolen their silver—'

'That isn't what he said, sir—'

'It's what he was hinting! That de Cedillos deserved what he got, that he was a traitor— not to speak of refusing to "negotiate" over the land dispute. It was Pelerine who kept causing trouble with the courts. Ci— er, Mademoiselle de Cedillos says she remembers her father coming back from New Orleans, times without number, almost in tears of frustration, because the old sinner had his lawyers bring it up again claiming the evidence had been at fault—'

'Mamzelle de Cedillos was six,' January reminded him. 'Five, or four, if it was before the invasion . . .'

'She remembers.' His relative's mouth set in a grim line. 'And my poor Paloma remembered, all those years of hardship in Spain. And their poor mother. They told her everything they'd been through.' His grip crushed January's hands. 'Benjamin, don't believe him! Mademoiselle Paloma, and Madame their mother, both knew the man. Both warned Mademoiselle de Cedillos that he was the very Devil, a consummate villain who would stop at nothing to ruin them from sheer spite. Don't . . .'

Shadows fell across the doorway, and Dagobert let his head roll back on the pillow. His hands fell away from January's fingers. In a feeble voice he murmured, 'I'm sorry, Ben. Was I talking nonsense? I dreamed . . . something about my father. Where are we?'

'Sept-Anges.' Pelerine stepped through the door. 'It was the name my wife's aunt took when she entered the convent in Rouen.' Two women followed him in, wearing the head wraps of slaves. One of them, January guessed, would be the pockmarked quadroon overseer's wife Sassy. She was the one who went straight to the sideboard – the only other piece of furniture in the room – and poured liquid from a cheap pottery pitcher into a pottery cup. This she brought to Dagobert's bedside, pausing as she reached it, to look down at January sitting on the stool.

'You'll be the man Michie said was a surgeon?' She held out the cup to him. 'There's 'bout a spoon of laudanum in here, sir. First he's had since midnight. I don't hold with it most times – not after seein' poor Ma'am Nina, that was Michie, 'Carus's sister, like she got – but I can't let him suffer so. That foot's all swole up, but I don't think it's broken. I've been puttin' cold compresses on it all night.'

'Good for you, Ma'am Sassy.' January sniffed the cup, smelling in it not a great deal of laudanum and the fainter whiffs of white willow bark and feverfew, Olympe's preferred remedies for rheumatic aches.

Dagobert took the cup and drank, and gripped his jaw tight as January unpinned the bandages and carefully untied the twine that wrapped the wet compress to hold it in place. Behind him, as he probed gently at the intricate bones of the foot, he heard the other woman – presumably the slender, quick-moving Allie – speak softly to Pelerine: 'I couldn't find but half a dozen more pins, Kobaba.' January glanced back in time to see the old man squeeze her shoulders reassuringly: *It's all right* . . .

Kobaba, he knew, was one of the African words for *Daddy*. He had called his father that, all those years ago. But the glance between them was that of lovers.

The Devil incarnate. There was nothing of that in either the woman's eyes or the man's.

Dagobert's foot was unbroken, though – as Sassy had said – swollen. At this season of the year, the fresh water the women had brought in, with clean strips of sheeting, was cold. While January was rewrapping the ankle, Pelerine came quietly up beside him and dropped five straight pins into the clamshell on the tabouret. 'I hope that will suffice?' he asked, and January nodded towards the yards of stout twine that he'd taken off the compress.

'That should be fine.'

Dagobert turned his head sharply, watching their host as if he expected the old man to snatch up the bindings and garrote the both of them, but, thankfully, kept his mouth shut.

'I can offer you sanctuary here, M'sieu Janvier,' Pelerine said to him, 'if you need it. To you and to M'sieu Ben as well. I apologize for my men treating you like prisoners last night. I had gone into town yesterday to Mass, and met with my daughter and her husband. I've only just returned. I wasn't aware until Noble told me that we've been dealing with two groups of' – he groped visibly for an alternate word for *intruders* – 'of searchers. We just knew that strangers were prowling in the old Alegre fields and woods, and we knew there'd been shooting two weeks ago.'

January opened his mouth to ask, *Strangers prowling since when?* then glanced across at Dagobert, since it was often considered a liberty for a black man to question a white one. But evidently the query didn't occur to his patient. He tried to tell himself that Dagobert had after all just had a spoonful of laudanum but suspected that stone-cold sober he still wouldn't have thought to ask.

In his most diffident voice, January inquired, 'What day would that have been, sir? When first you heard of these men in the woods?'

Pelerine showed no inclination to take offense. 'That same day. Friday the twelfth, it was. Big Pete and his son were out checking their fish traps and heard the shooting near Alegre. The next morning they went out there again and told me someone had dug up something in the old garden where the belvedere used to be – was that you, sir? – and had been through the house. I thought it was strange, since the house had been searched a dozen times already, as I was telling M'sieu Ben here, and we've never found a thing.'

Dagobert widened his eyes innocently and shook his head. 'Really?' With his good foot, he poked January's thigh through the blanket. 'I didn't know others had searched the place before this.'

January held his peace.

His relative heaved a mighty sigh and said to him, 'Well, I guess we've come on a fool's errand, Ben.'

January refrained from expressing how wholeheartedly he agreed.

For several minutes after that, he feared that his employer was going to refuse Pelerine's offer to have one of his men hitch up the wagon to take them back to town – Dagobert showed signs of insisting that he was well enough to walk the twelve miles. But in the end he thanked the 'consummate villain' with a deprecating smile ('I'm sorry, I just hate to be beholden . . .'), and the moment the old planter and the women were out of the room seized January's arm again.

'Do you have a weapon? When they bring the wagon about, insist that you yourself drive us, not any man of his. I'm afraid that will mean you bringing the wagon and team back here this evening, but . . .'

'If it's all the same to you, sir' – with difficulty January kept his voice neutral – 'I had rather not be out driving a wagon down the Gentilly Road on the evening before Mardi Gras. The weather's been fair all this week, half the town will be out, driving or riding or walking, and I have no idea if M'sieu Watling and company were killed, or discouraged, or merely annoyed by the shooting last night. They could be disguised as anything, or hiding anywhere in the woods along the road . . .'

'Oh.' Dagobert's brow creased. 'Oh, you're right, of course. Forgive me, Ben, I'm . . . I'm terribly sorry. It's just that I think of poor Mademoiselle de Cedillos, of her terrible plight . . .'

'I understand.' January felt that if he had to hide his annoyance once more, he would burst into flame. 'I'm sure Rance' – he named the Janvier coachman – 'would return the wagon and could bring along one of your stable men with a couple of mules . . .'

'No!' The white man straightened up in bed, breath hissing as his injured foot moved. 'I mean . . . Well, Maman will have the carriage this afternoon and probably this evening. I know she was going out to the Widow d'Hebecourt's, where they're assembling the carriages for the Grand Cavalcade tomorrow night. You know she hired a second band from the Donaldsonville militia, and two canopied parade wagons? She was concerned about them being ready . . .'

Meaning, January knew, that Dagobert didn't want his stepmother to know anything about last night's adventure.

After a visit to the plantation sick house, to make sure the man Joe's wound was clean and well bandaged (it was), he returned to help his relative sit up, and to remove the mended and faded nightshirt in which he'd slept. Sassy had left many yards of clean, worn-out sheeting at the foot of the bed, and, January now saw, a serviceable crutch standing in the corner by the door. Using one strip of the sheeting as a sort of cross-gaiter, he wrapped on another layer of bandage to immobilize the foot, hearing as he did so the tiny *plink* of a loosened pin dropping to the floor. Like the housewife in the parable, he searched around the bed until he found it (*And when she hath found it, she calleth all her friends and neighbors together and sayeth, 'Rejoice with me . . .'*), and carefully re-pinned that fold of the compress . . .

And sat for a moment, considering that tiny slip of steel, before rising to greet the woman Allie as she came in to ask would Michie Janvier and Michie Ben care for something to eat, while Jonas hitched up the team?

It was Allie who came up with the idea ('If those bad men still followin' you, Michie Ben') of lending January one of Sassy's capacious calico dresses and a tignon, so that, sitting in the back of the wagon beside the prone Dagobert, the portion of him that wasn't hidden by the sides of the little vehicle would be completely unrecognizable. ('That pink is *just* your color, Michie Ben! I swear you look better in that dress than I ever did!') (January curtseyed deeply in thanks.) Even in the balmy forenoon, as January had foreseen, the road along Bayou Gentilly, and even more so the river road, was alive with wagons, carriages, horsemen, and drays, with laughter and song. It would have been impossible to tell which knights and ladies, which Gardens of Living Flowers, which court of sultans and odalisques, might have been assassins. Several of the open carriages were followed by wagons full of musicians, guitars and flutes, banjos and fiddles, to accompany the light-hearted singing of the celebrants.

> *J'aime l'oignon frit à huile,*
> *J'aime l'oignon quand il est bon . . .*
> *(I love the onion fried in oil,*
> *I love the onion when it's good . . .)*

At Mardi Gras, January reflected, people would sing about anything.

He sprang down from the wagon bed the moment they were in the carriageway to the Janvier townhouse on Rue Royale, stripped off Sassy's pink frock and tignon and pulled on his own shirt, jacket, and cap before ringing the doorbell for the butler. 'Remember,' he said as he did so, 'there was a hunting accident yesterday afternoon and we spent the night with swamp trappers—' He dug in his empty pockets and nodded emphatically to Dagobert – several times before his relative caught on and produced a quarter-real piece to hand to Jonas the wagon driver.

'If anyone asks,' said January with a grin.

Jonas grinned back. 'I'll say I'm this swamp trapper's coachman, shall I?'

'Aren't you going to stay and help me in?' asked Dagobert. 'We need to go back . . .' Belatedly, he glanced at Jonas and bit back his plea to continue the search for the missing silver at Alegre. 'Uh – we need to talk—'

'We will,' January promised. 'But do you really want to risk me encountering Madame your stepmother? Or having one of her servants mention—'

As the door started to open – and Thisbe raced out, barking furiously – January touched his cap and strode out of the carriageway before the footmen emerged to bear Dagobert up to his bed.

Rose wasn't a woman to fling herself into his arms sobbing, *Dear God, Ben, I thought you'd been killed!* when he climbed over the wall into the narrow space beside the kitchen and crossed the yard to the back gallery steps. But the violence of her embrace when she came out on to the gallery as he ascended, the way she pressed her face to his chest, her spectacles askew, told their own story. So did the faces of the girls, peering through the French doors from the dining room.

'I'm all right,' he said. 'Is Gilles all right? Are *you* all right?'

She nodded; straightened her spectacles. 'All well. Gilles is back at Medoc's. Ker got the bullet out and set the bones of his shoulder as well as he could—'

'Thank God!'

'The wound seems to be healing cleanly, no infection, only a little fever that first night . . .'

Virgin Mother of God, I owe you a whole shop's worth of candles and will wash the feet of the first fifty lepers that I meet . . .

'Ker says there's a new technique to immobilize broken bones by setting them in bandages wrapped in camphor and plaster of Paris—'

'I read about that in *Lancet* . . .'

'But he says he wants to wait, to make sure there'll be no infection first.'

'I have to see him.'

'You have to sleep,' she said. 'I was there yesterday, and this morning. Gilles sleeps most of the time. Callie's frantic about you. After dinner, I'm going over there with a ratatouille Gabriel made. Ti-Gall can walk there with you once it's good and dark.

'And,' she went on, eyes sparkling with triumph, 'Cosette is back with us! Aurelien Morrell – who will be her father-in-law – wants his son Jean-Xavier's bride to be educated in useful things, like mathematics and composition—'

Her words were interrupted by the shrieks of Professor John and Xander as they toddled out and flung themselves against his legs. Taking his welcome of the boys for license, Germaine and Aglaëa – and, yes, Cosette – ran out also, and it was nearly an hour before January was finally able – with Rose repelling all boarders – to close the bedroom door behind him. Even then, his sons insisted on joining him, swearing they would be quiet and let Papa sleep. (*A likely story*! said Rose's eyes when January gathered them both into his arms and carried them in with him.) But he doubted they could have kept him awake at their worst, and in fact they fell asleep curled against him like puppies, in a rocky welter of lead soldiers and a bilboquet.

He dreamed about pins.

1814

It started with the old dream, the familiar dream of his mother taking him to the store owned by Beverly Chew and his partner Mr Relf, to introduce her son to the banker and, January suspected, to show off his excellent French, English, Spanish, and social manners. *He may look like a cane-hand*, her gracious conversational openings almost shouted, *but he knows which fork to use, and he speaks like a white man.*

Only the prospect of having her son employed in one of Chew and Relf's numerous enterprises – Chew was on the Board of Directors of the Bank of Louisiana, the Bank of Philadelphia, and the Bank of the United States branch in New Orleans, as well as the Board of the New Orleans Insurance Company and the British-owned Phoenix Fire Insurance Company – would have forced Livia Janvier to admit that she had a son twenty-one years old at all, much less one whose ebony blackness hinted at union with a full-blooded African.

Mr Chew, January was well aware – looking around him at the ground-floor rooms where Chew and Relf displayed their mostly legal merchandise – brought in illegal cargoes of slaves from Africa every few weeks, either by his own vessels (registered under a variety of pseudonyms) or for other New Orleans, Cuban, or British businessmen. Standing in the inner showroom of the building while his mother talked to Chew, he was aware of the Virginian's calculating brown glance sizing him up. *A likely boy*, Chew would have called him, if he'd encountered him on the deck of one of his vessels. *Beau noir lustré*, as the French said: a healthy, beautiful black complexion that proclaimed full, or nearly full, African blood. There were many who claimed that the admixture of white ('human,' some of them said) ancestry made for sly, scheming, unreliable bondsmen, with just sufficient intelligence to cause trouble.

Upstairs, he had heard, was the less-advertised merchandise, the drafts on Mexican silver coins for those who didn't trust the ever-fluctuating paper currency of Louisiana, New York, and every other state plus hundreds of private banks and insurance companies. (At the moment, he could hear his mother suggesting that Chew try her son out on the thick weekly binders that contained the latest discounts and comparisons of such notes: 'I promise you, Mr Chew, he can tell how many Rothschild notes you can get for a hundred Bank of New York dollars off the top of his head . . .')

On a table of small goods, among the jars of British mustard and rolls of transshipped Chinese silk (still labeled with the name of the *Glasgow Queen*), he found the printed sheets of one of Handel's harpsichord suites – one he had not heard, one that his late teacher Herr Kovald had not possessed either. Just touching the paper, seeing the notes – transposing them in his mind to the stronger voice of the pianoforte – was like the taste of clean water after long thirst. The sensation of morning sunlight on his face, after an unsheltered night in bitter rain.

I can't. He looked towards the doorway, where that trim, long-faced gentleman conversed with his mother about salaries and favors pending, and he knew he could no more work for a bank than he could stick his hand in a muddy bayou to try to catch an alligator with his fingers.

I can't.

Like a pot-bound plant, he knew his heart would not survive.

His mother beckoned, beaming: 'Mr Chew will be glad to spare you half an hour on Wednesday, Benjamin.' She was dressed like the most respectable French matron in plain silk foulard, her tignon a miracle of intricate folds, softly gleaming silk, and expensively understated ostrich tips. ('Courtesan? *Me*?')

The banker bowed; said in his soft Virginia voice, 'From what Madame Janvier says, Ben, I think we can come to some understanding.'

January shook the firm, gray-gloved hand and mendaciously assured Mr Chew that he looked forward to it, knowing he would write a polite note tomorrow breaking the appointment . . .

Chew said, 'Thank you for the pleasure of your visit, Madame Janvier, and for the introduction to your son.' He took her hand in turn. 'Please allow me to give you a little token of our talk.'

From the table of small goods he took two white cards of pins, fifty cents apiece in those days (they would have been more, January reflected, had any tariff ever been paid on them). Two cards would have paid close to a week's wage, to a servant or a laborer . . . or to a soldier, for putting his life at risk.

His mother beamed and thanked Mr Chew with soft-voiced charm, gloved hands clasped over the precious slivers of hardened steel.

Chew's eyes returned to January. 'I noticed your interest in the Handel pieces, Ben. Please do pick out one of them for yourself, with my compliments.'

'Oh, he couldn't,' effused Livia at once. 'Something so expensive . . . Besides,' she added, turning those beautiful, velvet-dark eyes on her son, 'it's little enough time you'll have to spend twiddling music, once you're devoting your time to helping Mr Chew.'

Her face glowing like that of a child on Christmas morning, she tucked the pins into her reticule.

TWENTY

1841

January woke, hearing Hannibal's light, scratchy voice from the other room. The fiddler spoke softly, barely above the muted background of dishes being laid on the table – the shuttered room was nearly dark, and January could hear the increased rattle of carriages in the street – 'At the risk of offering insult to the Muse Melpomene, had Robert opened his mother's will in act one—'

'There wouldn't have been an opera,' finished Rose. 'Everybody would have said, "Oh, so *that's* what's going on," and exited stage right before latecomers in the audience even took their seats.'

'Exactly. I'm always annoyed by plots that depend on someone doing something stupid, or not asking for an explanation at the beginning which would have solved the entire problem.'

But what he heard in his mind was the fiddler saying, *Never trust a woman who doesn't keep her eye on the purse strings.*

And that brought his mind back to pins.

He had been married to a dressmaker. He had watched Gilles, a hundred times in his youth, laying out muslin pieces of coat patterns – side backs, tails, sleeves, collars – painstakingly measuring additional inches on to the edges, marking the shape with chalk and then basting the garment together. His first wife Ayasha had done the same, times almost literally without number, and he had shared dozens of hunts before and after client fittings in her shop, when pinned adjustments had come unstuck, entailing searches that would have put to shame the widow in Our Lord's parable and her quest for a vanished coin.

Pins were expensive. At least they had been up until a few years ago, before some Yankee had finally invented a pin-making machine . . .

Could a man who had been married – who had daughters – who could afford to hire at least four armed bravos to not only attempt to murder January and Dagobert but to break into January's house and leave a terrifying warning . . . Could such a man not afford to buy pins?

Mean as sin for all his wealth, he reminded himself. He had no idea whether Pelerine's land really was cropped out.

Lying in the dimness of the bedroom, his sons cuddled asleep against his side, he recalled the house at Sept-Anges. Creole French houses in the countryside were almost invariably furnished plainly – the true 'home' for the Marignys, the Mandevilles, the Forstalls and Livaudais, was the townhouse. But his impression over the past half-dozen Carnival seasons was that, like many planters, the widowed old Pelerine stayed mostly on his lands. And why not? His sons were dead, his daughters married to men in other parts of the state. So far as he knew, there was no Pelerine townhouse.

Yet even by the plain standards of the Creole French, the house at Sept-Anges, though scrupulously clean and well maintained, was shabby. Looking back on those occasions on which he'd seen the scar-faced planter at balls in town, he recalled noting – the way marriage to Ayasha had made him automatically note a person's clothing – that the old man always wore the same broad-lapelled, notch-collared black coat that he'd worn in 1816, its dye discreetly renewed as the garment grew greenish with age. Always the same waistcoat, too.

Recalled, too, how Pelerine had taken no more notice of the shabbiness of his raiment than he'd taken of the ruin of his face.

Miserliness? Conviction of his own rightness?

Or 'played-out' lands and straitened means?

At that point, Xander woke and decided it would be hilarious to drop the ball from the bilboquet on to his sleeping brother's nose, so there was no time for further rumination. Rose must have heard the ensuing giggling, rassling, and threats to throw both boys out the window, because when she tapped at the door twenty minutes later, it was to inform him that there was hot water ready in the kitchen, and dinner would be on the table shortly thereafter.

Rose left the house immediately after dinner – bearing a ratatouille, escorted by Ti-Gall and trailed at a distance by Hannibal, in a pointy-hatted Merlin costume Gabriel had worn last year. As soon as full dark came, January followed. Given the circumstances, it was impossible to stick to uncrowded streets. Every street in the

French Town, in Marigny, and in Tremé was a carnival of maskers coming and going, either to or from parties being given by friends or wending their way from saloon to saloon. Minor cavalcades abounded, in imitation and expectation of the greater spectacles promised the following night. Impromptu tourneys and jousts turned intersections into mob scenes.

Mohammad LePas the blacksmith, the stocky little carter Fly-Trap Novain, Cora Chouteau who ran the Buttonhole Café in Tremé, both January's sisters, and Cochon Gardinier had all let January know that they'd keep costumes – Red Indian garb, bed-sheet Bedouin robes, a suspiciously genuine old British uniform, and several of January's own old jackets and trousers – concealed in their yards, which enabled him to change his appearance twice between Rue Esplanade and the Medoc grocery on Rue de l'Hôpital in Tremé. Callie had also sent a sketch map of whose yard to duck through from St-Claude Street to get over the fence into that of the grocery. January actually didn't need this; he'd taken the route dozens of times in his youth. Baptiste Medoc had been known throughout Orleans Parish as a man willing to sell rum out his back door to anyone, black or white or colored, with the money to buy it.

'God, I'm glad to see you better!' He dropped into the bent-willow chair beside Gilles's bed in the tiny back room, grabbed his friend's good hand, and pressed his face to it. The table beside the bed was cluttered with medicine cups and tumblers of rum and cocoa, plates spotted with the remains of ratatouille, dirty rice, and king cake.

'You ever figure out who that is who's after you?' Gilles's voice was slurred, with pain and with the potions to allay it, but his fingers closed strong over January's, and his face had lost the ashy hue of blood loss and shock.

'Yeah, Daddy, tell us a story!' Callie flounced in with Rose from the front part of the house, where the voices of neighbors chattering blew through the door behind her like the scents of sugar and punch. 'We want to hear all about the Spanish, and buried treasure, and Icarus Pelerine's evil henchmen skulking around in the swamp—'

She plumped herself down on the end of her husband's bed in a whoosh of salwars and veils, and folded her arms around her knees.

Rose put a plate of king cake and a clay tumbler of cocoa on the bedside table, and January steadied the plate for Gilles while he ate with his good right hand. He felt as if an iron band encircling his chest had broken. In the other room, someone was singing 'Au Claire de la Lune,' and the door opened again to admit Gilles's mother, Odile Gignac, who crossed to January and took his hand.

'Thank you,' she said, genuine welcome in her face. 'Thank you for coming, Ben. And what the *hell* is that you're wearing?' she added, staring at his Red Indian garb and the Devil mask pushed up on his head. 'I seen better outfits at kids' parties!'

And the memory of her anger Friday night, as it was meant to, dissolved in forgiving laughter.

Ti-Gall and Cochon escorted Rose back to the French Town at around eleven, and January stayed at Gilles's side for another hour. He changed disguises – borrowing a plaid kilt, Scots bonnet, and white Pierrot mask from Cochon – and took a roundabout way back to the old Spanish house. Entering as usual over the back-yard fence, he saw splinters of lamplight around the kitchen shutters and stopped. A moment later, one of the shutters opened, and Rose stood silhouetted against the dim glow of a candle's light, a red bandana in her right hand.

It was an old signal between them: *All is well. This isn't a trap.*

He stepped from the dark beneath the gallery and whistled the first few bars of 'Eine Kleine Nachtmusik,' – another signal – and she met him at a run halfway across the yard.

He entered the kitchen only long enough to take up the candle and close and lock the shutters. Unlocked the doors beneath the gallery and locked them again behind them as he entered the darkness of the storerooms beneath the house. His inspection of those few rooms was thorough but very swift, before opening the hidden chamber at the lake-side end of the house, then locking it again behind them.

When they woke for the first time, cramped together in the narrow bed, in utter dark that smelled of sex and candlewax, Rose whispered, 'What time is it?'

'Who cares?'

After they woke the second time – quite some time after, in fact – she asked again, and this time January turned over and sought his matches and his watch in the discarded heap of clothing beside the bed. He found the candle by touch in the dark. It was just after five.

'Paul will bring the girls over soon,' Rose said.

January kissed the handfuls of her hair that lay on his shoulder. 'Paul and the girls can go to the Devil together.'

She chuckled and sat up a little in the circle of his arm. 'You know,' she said, picking up the conversation of the previous evening, 'I never really believed Icarus Pelerine was behind the attacks on you and Dagobert. He's Coralie Chardin's uncle, you know – on the other side of the family – and she speaks of him with great affection. Your mother probably knows things about him that we don't, but—'

'What bothers me,' said January, 'is the pins. And the state of the house. The state of his clothing.' And he recounted to her his thoughts: 'How much would it cost, anyway, to hire four ruffians to murder me, and Dagobert, and to kidnap Mamzelle de Cedillos . . .?'

'I expect the market varies.' Rose considered the matter as if calculating the expenditure out of the household expenses, candle flame reflecting points of light in those remarkable gray-turquoise eyes. Without her spectacles, she had an unfledged look, literal minded and almost schoolgirlish. 'It would be cheaper now that the town is flooded with them, of course. But how would one find a bargain in such circumstances? Or are there brokers? What surprises me' – she gathered the sheet up under their chins, for despite its stuffiness, the hidden room was cold – 'is that your mother would get Pelerine's financial circumstances wrong. She knows that kind of thing about everybody in the parish.'

'You're right.' January thought back over that conversation in the upper room at Alciatore's, and the one over coffee the previous Sunday. 'I don't think I've ever heard her mistake something about money . . . But why would my mother lie?'

'I don't know. Why *would* your mother lie?'

'For money,' he answered promptly. 'Either immediate or prospective. Or to protect her own interests, if she guessed that someone wealthy, or influential, was involved. Someone whose help or favor she might want later. She might even lie,' he added thoughtfully, 'to protect me, or Minou, for the same reason. She does care for me, in her way.'

Rose lifted her eyebrows at that, but all she said was, 'Ah. *Non sum qualis eram bonae / sub regno Cinarae*?' and January made the gesture of a fencer conceding a point. So far as his mother's concern for him went, things were not even the little that they had been (in ancient times, as the poem said) when he was a child and the neighbors would tattle about neglect.

After a time, he went on, 'If that is the case – if it isn't Icarus Pelerine trying to keep Dagobert from investigating . . . investigating *what*? . . . at Alegre – then who in New Orleans has the money to hire American bravos?'

'Bernard Marigny?' Rose brought forth the obvious name. 'He was in New Orleans at the time of the battle, too.'

'He was Governor Claiborne's aide-de-camp,' said January. 'He was one of the men who helped arrange for Lafitte to meet Jackson with an offer of help. I can't see him taking money from the British to engineer an American defeat.'

'True,' agreed Rose. 'But we have no actual proof that the attacks on you are connected with the battle at all, you know. There could be something entirely different behind them.'

'What? Keeping Madame Marie-Hélène from upstaging his wife with a fancier parade?'

'Well, we *are* talking about a man who ordered a solid-gold dinner service for one meal and then threw it in the river. I expect the servants took careful note of where it went in . . .'

They both laughed at that, and January shook his head. Laughter was one thing. Those murderous Xs cut into the bedclothes of everyone he loved clung like a bloodstain to his thoughts. 'It wasn't just a single occasion,' he said slowly. 'We've been stalked, and fired upon, three times. There have been two attempts that I know about on Mamzelle de Cedillos, one of which included the rental of a carriage . . .'

He paused, considering the implications of that approach to kidnapping.

'It would have to be the villain's own carriage,' pointed out Rose. 'There are only so many livery stables in town.'

'But a private carriage and team could be traced, probably more easily than a rental. Borrowed from someone who owes him a favor?' He tried to fit the elements of such a scheme together, trying to see how it would actually work. 'Borrow the carriage and rent a team, from someplace like Carrollton or Bayou Sara—?'

'That's starting to sound . . .' She paused, frowned, as if groping for something in the dark.

Very quietly, January prompted, 'Like something in a bad melodrama?'

Rose turned her head against the bare flesh of his shoulder, met his eyes. Around them the house was a tangible block of silence. At this hour even the streets were dark and mostly still, though far off he could hear a man's wavering voice singing,

Va chez la voisine,
Je crois qu'elle y est,
Car dans la cuisine,
On bat le briquet . . .'
(Go next door,
I think she's there
For in the kitchen
Someone's lighting her fire . . .)

Doubtfully, Rose said, 'Why would Mamzelle de Cedillos lie?'

'I don't know. I don't know if it *is* a lie – or how much of it is a lie – because I don't know what's at stake. But I'm fairly certain she's been lying to Dagobert all along. What would be worth the cost of paying men to watch this house, to follow me the other night to Gérard's and try to kill me? Every man he – or she – whoever is behind the attempts – every man hired is another potential blackmailer. And to pay Cat Watling and his boys to wait on the off chance that Dagobert was going to come bowling down the street in his chaise headed for Alegre that day? Or to watch him hoping he'd lead them to Mamzelle?'

'And think how much time they'd waste,' added Rose reasonably, 'following your cousin to the Cotton Exchange, or to Au Cheval de la Lune to buy a necktie—'

'In which case,' pointed out January, 'they've had ample opportunity to kill him. And he isn't my cousin. But if he – or she – is paying a spy in the household, that's five potential blackmailers on our—' He hesitated over a word straight off the stage of the St-Charles Theater.

'Our *villain's*?'

'What would be worth that?' repeated January slowly. 'And to whom? It has to be someone who is wealthy, and someone who was in New Orleans at the time of the battle at Chalmette.'

'Not necessarily. He – or she – could have lived upriver – Baton Rouge or Natchez – or in Milneburgh—'

'Baton Rouge was barely a trading post in 1814,' January objected. 'Milneburgh didn't even exist. New Orleans was smaller then, but it was always the center of things in Louisiana. It's the only place you could bring in even ten thousand pesos' worth of silver more or less unnoticed, not to mention boxes of guns. Even if you put half the payment in bank certificates of some kind, you're still talking about over two tons of metal. There were barely a handful of steamboats on the Mississippi at that time, and there wasn't the coming and going between here and Natchez that there is now.'

He fell silent, remembering the New Orleans that had lain outside the door of Rubal Gomez's little surgery on Rue St-Louis. The center of power in Louisiana, even then the key to the whole center of the North American continent, yet curiously isolated in its wilderness of cypress swamps, of bayous and ponds and sheets of water that came and went. Rose, he thought, had not known it: she'd been very young when her plaçée mother had died, and the clearest memories of her childhood were of the barrier islands on the Gulf.

Spanish silver and British guns . . .

Rose kissed him and got up, gathering her clothing by the candle stub's tiny light.

'You could ship sixty barrels of corn and spread the silver among them,' she pointed out.

'You could. But that would mean more containers to collect and transport. And it would increase your chances of something being stumbled upon by accident, or barrels going astray or being stolen.'

He recalled the crate tipped 'accidentally' from the wharf opposite Auntie Houlette's coffee stand: how the long pole had slipped out from beneath the shadows of the pier to drag it immediately out of sight. Soon now, he thought, in Olympe's dark-red cottage on the Rue Douane, his sister would be waking up the girls – the girls he and Rose were responsible for protecting as well as educating. Would be getting the two little boys dressed, ready to return here, to this house marked by Watling and his bravos . . .

The house that would not be safe until this deadly puzzle was solved.

And how long, he wondered, before the truth came out and the school was ruined? Before Olympe and her family were taken hostage? Or 'disappeared' as a warning?

Damn it. Damn it, damn it, damn it . . .

'As you say,' repeated Rose, doing up her corset front.

He got out of bed to pull the laces close, shivering in the cold. Kissed the dusky skin of her back above the corset's rim.

'M'sieu Pelerine has had twenty-six years to search Alegre for that silver and hasn't found anything – and I'm sure that includes the stables, the kitchen, and every cabin in the quarters. The same goes for your friend M'sieu Peychaud and for every planter in Orleans parish: M'sieu Pelerine can't have hired Kaintuck ruffians to shoot at all of them. We'd certainly have heard about it by this time. So why now? What changed? Has Dagobert been assaulted when he wasn't with you?'

'I don't think so.' He pulled on his shirt, his drawers, and folded up the remains of Cochon's immense kilt. 'His stepmother has always hated me, as my mother's son, but I think I'd have known if he'd been attacked separately, as I was. Which doesn't mean much,' he added thoughtfully. 'He's white, and if our attacker is wealthy – and was wealthy enough twenty-six years ago to lay hands on twenty thousand pesos – he probably knows the family. Very possibly he knows Dagobert himself.'

'Could Spain have even raised that much at that time?' Rose found her spectacles, placed carefully in a corner under the bed, and frowned, calculating the value of the silver. 'They'd just gotten rid of the Bonapartes and the country was torn apart because the king wanted to throw out the constitution, and Mexico wasn't having any of him, either. I know it was illegal to ship specie out of the country . . .'

'Not Spain,' January corrected, remembering that single, silver coin as he'd scratched the dirt off it, and the crown and 'GR' engraved on the gunlocks. 'And not Mexico either.' *Spanish silver and British guns.*

Someone who could lay hands on that much specie. And who knew the family.

Rose started to take up this unfinished thought, and he held up one finger for silence. Feet creaked, very faintly, on the steps to the back gallery, then on the floorboards overhead. He heard Professor John's laugh, and Aglaëa's voice call out, 'M'am Janvier?'

Quickly, January kissed Rose again. 'You'd better go up.'

'Shall I make you coffee?'

Farther off – barely a bird's chirp muffled by the thick bousillage of the walls – came the tiny silver note of the cathedral's bells.

Mardi Gras.

He wondered if he'd be able to make the time to go to confession that day and immediately discarded the thought. 'If there's any left from last night,' he said. 'But I need to leave, soon, while all the evil henchmen are still asleep – or hung-over. I need to pay a visit to the one person who will certainly know something about the conspiracy . . . and who has no reason to murder me over what I may have learned.'

Rose looked at him a little blankly for a moment, then said, 'Oh.'

He kissed her again, and hand in hand they slipped from the hidden room and out of the cellar to climb the steps to the house.

TWENTY-ONE

The Scots butler at the house of the Consular Under-Secretary of Great Britain on Rue Royale – resplendent in powder, knee smalls, and buckled shoes – regarded January with disapproval in the cool gray dawn light of the courtyard. 'Sir John does not customarily receive petitioners until after luncheon, sir.'

The cathedral clock was just chiming six.

January bowed his head. 'I was certain that was the case,' he replied, in his most perfect English. 'Believe me, I would never have dreamed of disturbing him were the matter not one of urgency, and were it possible for me to come and go safely at a later time.' From his pocket he took his cardcase – he could see the butler's dismissive glance and almost hear him sniff, *Sheffield plate* – and withdrew a card.

Benjamin Janvier
Musician, instructor of piano, harpsicord
Rue Esplanade, New Orleans
FPC

'If you would wait here, sir.'

January seated himself on the brick edge of a raised vegetable bed. As at the Janvier townhouse a few streets away, neat rows of stakes and strings marked where herbs, peas, and probably aubergines would make their appearance later in the year. Rosebushes, sweet olive, and iris grew at the house end of the garden, where their scent would perfume summer nights. When he had come down the carriageway from the street, and across the courtyard to the kitchen, January had been relieved to see candlelight in some of the upper windows of the main house. His impression that Sir John Oldmixton – formerly secretary to the British Minister in Washington City – was an early riser had been confirmed when he'd seen two footmen bearing silver trays to the main house. Silver-covered dishes on one, a silver coffee service on the other.

It was part of the under-secretary's duties to attend social events. Even the most easy-going of British gentlemen would not, he knew, appreciate being woken at six in the morning during Carnival.

The butler returned, impassive as a freckled Praxiteles Apollo. Opinion about callers at such an hour was clearly beneath him. 'Please come this way, sir.'

The business room was not in the main house but was rather the first room of the wing that ran back along one side of the courtyard, the two rooms behind it housing, January guessed, the under-secretary's servants, grooms, or clerks. Though the morning was brightening, the courtyard was still in shadow – a blessing during the semi-tropical summers – and the room itself gloomy, with its shelves of ledgers, of neatly filed and stacked newspapers, of record books and tomes of law.

Pink-faced, dark-haired, barrel-chested and cheerful, Sir John Oldmixton sat behind the desk, in the dressing gown of quilted violet silk in which January had seen him, upon one occasion, on the doorstep of the British Ministry in Washington some four years previously. Newly shaved, washed, and half-dressed in shirt and trousers beneath the robe: January suspected that had the Apocalypse commenced at two in the morning, it would find Sir John shaved, washed, and not in his nightshirt.

'Benjamin!' He rose and reached across the desk to clasp January's hand. 'I would say how glad I am to see you, but I know you wouldn't call at this hour unless there is something very wrong. I hope you'll tell me how I can help you.' And he gestured January to a wing-back chair. 'Will you have some coffee?' A second Limoges cup, January saw now, had been brought in, and another scrolled and curlicued silver spoon.

'Thank you, sir. And I hope that *I* will be able to help *you*.'

It would be bad manners to imply disbelief by saying, *Do you indeed?* But Oldmixton raised his brows. His function – both in the British Ministry in Washington and now in the consulate – had been, ostensibly, to assist His Excellency Sir Henry Fox, and now the Honorable John Crawford, with the social side of representing Her youthful Majesty's government to the Americans: organizing consular entertainments, managing catering and music, greeting important persons and assisting British subjects who found themselves in difficulties in New Orleans. His actual duties, January was well aware, involved the gathering of information concerning the smuggling of slaves to the United States and Brazil, the smuggling of guns to the insurgent new republics that had formerly been part of Gran Columbia . . . and any other stray bits of information concerning the American Navy or American relations with Mexico and the aforesaid South American republics that he thought might be of interest to Britain.

He probably hadn't been in New Orleans in February of 1815, but January guessed that there was little about those events that he didn't know.

'I was recently engaged,' he began carefully, 'to help locate three chests of Spanish silver, rumored to have been hidden by a man named Bartolomé de Cedillos at the time of the British invasion of Louisiana in 1815.' *Let's keep Dagobert's name out of this. I don't need Madame Marie-Hélène plotting revenge against me as well.*

Oldmixton's face broke into a delighted smile. 'So you know about that?' he exclaimed. 'I've been trying for weeks to find out who Cedillos might have hired before he was killed. I was positive he'd come back for the silver sooner or later . . . Do you know who killed him?'

January could only regard him blankly. 'Come back for the— What?'

'Yes, three weeks ago. He was killed in a duel – you were there—'

'That was *de Cedillos*?' *The beard*, he thought. *De Cedillos had a mole on his chin.* He felt as if he'd been standing under the trapdoor of a hayloft that had suddenly given way, showering him with fodder and enlightenment.

'He didn't tell you, then?'

January took a deep breath. *Not a hayloft*, he thought. A set of shelves, whose contents all had to be picked up, re-sorted . . . and which turned out to be not what he'd thought they were. 'I never spoke to him,' he said at last. 'He wasn't the one who hired me. It was his daughter – I assume. The woman who posed as his wife.'

'Ah!' Oldmixton sat back in his chair, cradling the black-and-gilt coffee cup in deepest satisfaction. 'No wonder the woman never went about with him. I wondered what became of her.'

Never trust a woman who doesn't keep an eye on the purse strings . . .

He saw again that delicate handkerchief. The breathless innocence of her countenance, and the way she'd settled, like a trusting child, into Dagobert's arms. The bright glint of those too-intelligent eyes.

He felt suddenly a great deal better about coming to confide in the under-secretary.

'Mademoiselle Felicita de Cedillos paid me to search the old plantation house at Alegre,' he said. 'She claimed her father had disappeared on the day of the battle, and that with the death of her mother and her sister, she had come back to Louisiana to clear her father's name and, if possible, get the Louisiana courts to reverse the decision that gave her father's lands to his old enemy Icarus Pelerine.'

'Yes, I heard something about that old lawsuit from Pelerine's daughter.' The Englishman tapped the polished marble surface of the desk, as if as an aid to thought. 'It sounded like a perfectly straightforward judgment to me. The first Spanish governors of the territory made a shocking hash of their record keeping, as they did of nearly everything else that first few years.'

'I now realize,' continued January, 'that what she wanted was to find some kind of note about where the silver was hidden. She'd have guessed that the house would be searched many times over the past twenty-six years. She knew that the chests had been left behind: if de Cedillos escaped with his family through the swamp, they couldn't take a wagon, and even laden mules would have aroused suspicion.'

The less said about the box of British muskets buried in the back swamp, he thought, *the better*. Besides, if he knew False River Jones, those guns were in all probability already gone.

'I gather from Pelerine that the men of the Spanish militia, rather than attacking the rear of the American lines, were closing in on Alegre demanding their pay, which de Cedillos had absconded with. I'm pretty sure de Cedillos got part of his payment in the form of bank drafts . . .'

His words tailed off mid-sentence, as if he'd turned over a card while playing patience and found written on it the name of the person who'd hired ruffians to kill him. Maybe, he thought, he'd half-guessed it before. It certainly didn't surprise him.

Like a dream one recalls only a few mornings later. *Oh, yes, that . . .*

'And did you find such a note?' Oldmixton's voice broke his thoughts, and he answered quickly, hoping the man hadn't noticed the pause.

'No.' January did his best to sound innocent. 'But I'm fairly certain I know where the chests were buried.'

He hoped the Englishman didn't guess what else he knew. *That* he knew.

Because that, he knew, would alter everything. And would be his death warrant.

He spent the remainder of Tuesday, the second of March, in a disused chamber in the under-secretary's townhouse, a room which he guessed had once housed a governess. It was on the uppermost floor below the attics, close to the backstair that communicated with the quarters of the white butler and footmen; one of the footmen brought him luncheon and, a little later, tea. With the tea came two notes, one from Dagobert, the other from Rose.

Dagobert Janvier to Benjamin Janvier
March 1, 1841
Evening

Ben,

I know not where you may be hidden; I hope this will reach you ere I must take action. Events have made a surprising turn, and rather than lead Pelerine's hired bravos to you

(Obviously Pelerine's account of the Spanish conspiracy had made no impression on Dagobert . . .)

I have bargained with Mr Jones for his assistance tonight. If you employed him yesterday, I assume he will not betray us, but I would prefer your own judgment and experience in the matter, as well as your physical aid in getting about.

If I do not hear from you by the time of my meeting with Jones at midnight (I will leave this house suitably disguised, and have no fear of discovery), I must trust to the Providence that has looked after poor Mademoiselle de Cedillos thus

> *far. But if you are able, I beg of you to rendezvous with Jones and myself at the City Bridge over Bayou Gentilly. (My ankle improves, but I still need assistance with walking.) Whatever happens, we will need your strong arm in our endeavor tonight.*

(Damn it, groaned January, *when I said stay in bed, I meant it!)*

> *Trusting that you will receive this in time,*
> *Your friend,*
> *Dagobert Janvier*

(Damn it! Jones must have told him something!)

The other note was from Rose.

> *Securi sumus. Plures duae amici felis w Zizi visi sunt. Domus adhunc spectatur. Platea in chaos ob praeparationes ad processio. Confugiemus in domum corvi ante cenam. Cognatus tuus hanc epistulam misit. Hoc accepi illud mane. Amo te.*
>
> (*We are safe. Two more of Cat Watling's friends seen by Zizi. House is still watched. Street in chaos due to preparations for parade. We will seek refuge in the house of the crows* [that is, with Olympe – a 'corvus' or 'corbie'] *before dinner. Your relative sent this letter. I received it this morning. I love you.*)

And January had to smile, since *felis* could mean either *cat* or *thief*.

Damn it . . .

Events have made a surprising turn . . . we will need your strong right arm . . .

Strong right arm was not the phrase that leaped to his mind when he thought of False River Jones. He only hoped that the proposed adventure wouldn't involve another chest of contraband muskets.

And the thought of the confusion of thousands of masked persons milling around Rue Douane outside Olympe's house for Madame Marie-Hélène's Grand Cavalcade made him shudder. Cat Watling and his ruffians could break into the house, kill or kidnap Rose, his children, Zizi-Marie, Olympe, and who would know? Who would hear over the noise of a militia band?

And with two processions going on, the chances that the City Guards would even hear of trouble, much less be able to thrash their way through the crowds to prevent . . .

Prevent what?

He turned his mind away from more frightening possibilities. *Damn it* . . .

Somewhere in the house he could dimly hear the clock striking three. Would a message from him even reach her? Obviously Dagobert's hadn't done so until hours after the rendezvous time. And how many of Watling's usual 'boys' would be out looking for him? Had they recognized him in Sunday night's darkness? Clearly they'd had their suspicions before . . .

'I shall send Sebastian and Mr McAliester to your sister's for the evening,' said Oldmixton at once, when January told him of his concerns half an hour later. 'Suitably masked, of course,' he added. 'And suitably armed. McAliester will be shocked to death, but Sebastian – he's my coachman – has been dying for a chance to don fancy dress the whole of the season and was devastated when I was obliged to tell him that I would not, after all, be participating in either of the Grand Processions this evening.

'I was invited to both,' he went on. 'Mr Trulove' – he named a wealthy British planter who had farmed sugar cane in Orleans Parish since the closing days of the Spanish regime – 'even offered to lend me half a dozen bondsmen to transform my carriage into a fully-rigged man-of-war flying England's flags. I referred him to the Honorable Mr Crawford, who I am pleased to say was appalled, though both he and I will – I hope – attend both the Marigny wedding and the Janvier ball later tonight. I trust' – he glanced at the small window of the room, with its cramped view of the roof next door and a modest slip of sky – 'that our excursion to Bayou Joyeuse will be concluded in time for me to change my clothes?'

'That depends,' replied January grimly, 'on how deep a hole de Cedillos had time to dig before the Spaniards closed in. I wouldn't count on it.'

January crouched on the floor of Sir John's closed carriage as the vehicle clattered out of the carriageway and down the brick pavement of Rue Royale, while the under-secretary himself occupied the seat with an expression of bored unconcern. Even in his cramped position, January could tell the streets of the French Town – and of the Third Municipality on the other side of Rue Esplanade – were crowded, early as it was in the afternoon. He had been able to see nothing from the little window of his chamber, but even in that rigidly respectable house the excitement was palpable.

Two parades of fabled magnificence were promised, one along Rue des Ramparts and down Rue Esplanade to the Marigny townhouse by the river, the other down Rue Douane – though it would start at the house of the Widow d'Hebecourt, which had at one time been the Big House of the plantation of Marie-Hélène's uncle, and would pass through the decidedly unfashionable suburb of Tremé. By the slowness of the carriage's progress along Rue Royale, the frequency of stops and the occasional shouted imprecations of Sir John's under-coachman, January knew Rue Royale – and probably every other street in this oldest part of town – was thickly crowded. The clatter of beaten kitchenware, the shouts of hawkers peddling newspaper cones of candy and nuts, the scraps of music from doorways (and drunken song from the banquettes) told of rising anticipation.

In addition to all this, January knew, half the houses in the First and Third municipalities – and a hefty percentage of those in the Second – would be hosting festivities tonight: king cakes, candy, masks, dancing and confusion. At Olympe's, he knew, there would be thin pancakes, cooked in the kitchen and handed out to friends, family, neighbors in the courtyard: butter, sugar, a little oil to grease the frypan. Beer and rum and tafia punch. At Bichet's at the back of town, at the family home of the Gardinier's noisy clan, in the yard behind Medoc's grocery . . .

He stole a glance up at Sir John's impassive smile as the Englishman looked through the carriage windows, like a man viewing the quaint antics of savages, an indulgent foreigner in a foreign land.

He remembered again why he had turned his back on this world, these friends, this laughter and noise and the distant rattle of drums from Congo Square, on all the family and joy he had known. But he remembered also why he had come back – and that it had not been entirely the black grief of losing Ayasha that had drawn him.

He could have gone anywhere in the whole of the empty world after her death. And he had chosen to come back here.

Sir John had arranged for one of his footmen to meet them near the Bayou Bridge where the road to Milneburgh crossed Bayou Gentilly, with a horse, a riding mule, and a pack mule draped in empty sacks and laden with a couple of rough jackets – though the day was mild, the night promised cold – and a couple of spades. January could tell they were coming close to the place because Sir John, after carefully scanning both sides of the road with those sharp blue eyes, stripped off his well-tailored London coat and unwound his cravat, revealing under them the calico shirt of a laborer. The sides of the carriage had concealed not only January's presence but the fact that instead of his customary dove-hued pantaloons, the consulate under-secretary sported stout corduroy trousers and well-worn boots. January wondered what else he wore them for, since they were obviously his and obviously battered and old.

Presumably, he thought, this was not the first time Sir John had gone masquing as a laborer – and not necessarily at Mardi Gras.

The carriage pulled up. The under-coachman called down in his back-street London accent, 'Road's clear, sir,' and leaped down to open the door. The footman – also out of his customary uniform, with only traces of grayish powder clinging to his hair – brought up the horse and the mules; Oldmixton checked the pack mule's load and swung lightly to the bay mare's saddle. Glanced at the sky, then at his watch.

'Have a bath, supper, and my evening things ready for me when I return, please, Charles. I shouldn't be later than eight.'

It was now four thirty – January guessed the estimate was optimistic. The earth, he thought, would long ago have hardened over the Spanish silver, which might not be in the first place they dug.

'How can you be sure it was buried?' asked Oldmixton, as they followed the shell road along Bayou Gentilly into the grays and browns of the winter countryside. Below the shallow ridge of the bayou road, silent armies of cypress stood like beggars clothed only in the gray rags of Spanish moss, weak winter sun glinting on the ponds and sloughs between them. Where the land was high enough to sustain a crop, they passed open fields, new-harvested and black with ash where the 'trash' – leaves, weeds, cane tops, as well as the 'bagasse' left in the grinding mills – had been burned, preparatory to re-digging and replanting. Opposite the Sauriac place, an overseer – probably a Protestant, reflected January grimly – had already started the backbreaking work of replanting. On this day – Mardi Gras day – the field stood empty, but January could see the network of trenches that crossed the dark soil, the gleam of water at the bottom of the seams where the cut lengths of last year's cane would be laid.

The smell of the wet earth, of the turned mud, slipped past the years of his manhood and hurt his heart like a poison: the heart of a child who knows no world but the world of watchfulness and fear. As a child, he'd carried baskets of those cut lengths – billets, they were called – out behind the men's gang, the cold of early springtime seeping through his wet 'quantier' shoes. He'd heard the men singing, the songs of the Africa they remembered, the world they had lost. Not an easy world, but their own.

Now, as they had then, they had dug the earth, shaped the mounds and trenches and the irrigation channels, prepared the field before the planting started. For the planting went swifter than the digging, and the second gang – the smaller men, the older men, the 'half-hands' and 'quarter-hands' – was needed for the other tasks of late winter: repairing tools, planting vegetables . . .

When he was twenty-one and a free man, he had still asked himself, *Why should I put my life in danger to protect these people?*

'Think about it,' January said. 'De Cedillos knows he can't hide the money in the house. The place will be looted, searched – quite possibly burned. He guesses the Spanish militia will realize he's cheated them and fled. But because of the amount of silver involved, he can't take flight until he has the attack itself to cover his tracks in the confusion. He knows he has to take his wife and daughters through the swamp. In all probability, the slaves have run off. Possibly he let them go, so they wouldn't see anything they shouldn't. But he knows if he buries the silver away from the house, the turned earth will show.'

Oldmixton's eyes went from the turned earth of the cane field to January's face. 'It was just this time of year, wasn't it? The fields would have been dug up – that's cane they're going to plant there, isn't it?'

'It was about a month earlier than it is now,' said January. 'They probably wouldn't have put cane in yet, but the soil would have been dug up ready for it. The earth would be loose and easier to dig in half a night.'

The blue eyes flared with delight. 'My dear Benjamin . . .! How close to the rear of the house would the fields have come? Three chests would mean at least half his payment was in drafts or bills of exchange, and even so, each chest would weigh hundreds of pounds. It would need a barrow, or at least . . .'

'The sugar field comes right up to within a few yards of the house on the lake side,' said January. 'Left, as you face the doors with your back to the bayou. The arable land along Bayou Joyeuse is so narrow, de Cedillos has to have had that field under cultivation. My guess is that he buried the chests in a straight line from the stair, at the edge of the field. With the earth soft, and the trenches dug for planting and irrigation, he – probably his wife helping him – wouldn't have been able to drag the chests across the field itself.'

He turned in the mule's saddle, scanning for the dozenth time the eerie stillness of the ciprière.

'And the daughters?'

'They didn't know. I'm sure the burying was done late at night, and de Cedillos wasn't about to risk the knowledge in the hands – and the mouths – of girls six and sixteen years of age, particularly if the family happened to get separated. He certainly didn't trust Felicita with it when they returned last month.'

No light in the shrouded darkness of woods and cane fields. No sound but the dry, almost metallic shirring of a night breeze through the cane, like the rustle of the Grim Reaper's robes. Horse and mule both had rifles sheathed on their saddles (and to hell with the laws governing firearms in the hands of men of color), but January knew that two men would be no match for half a dozen 'Salt River roarers.' Sir John seemed to feel that his diplomatic rank would protect him. January wouldn't have bet that Cat Watling could find Great Britain on a map, or knew that England and the United States weren't still at war. (Or that the war in question wasn't still the Revolution . . .)

And if he did, his orders might still be to shoot January no matter who he was with.

So far, he had seen no one.

It doesn't mean he's not there, January reminded himself grimly. *He may just be saving himself the trouble of doing his own digging . . .*

* * *

The question, as it turned out, was a moot one.

From the gallery stair, January paced towards the most likely location of the edge of the field – 'And it would have been purely luck that that was the field being replanted that year,' he said to Oldmixton, who followed, leading the beasts with their burden of shovels and sacks. 'In any given year, only one field is replanted, while the others are either still growing – sugar cane takes almost two years to mature – or are ratooned, like this one now, with a second crop or a third growing from the same—'

He stopped. The Englishman halted beside him, both men looking at the gap in the greeny-brown wall.

It was Oldmixton who cursed first. 'Well, bloody hell.'

'I'll second that, sir.'

Exactly where January had calculated the Spanish silver would be buried, the half-grown cane had been chopped off short, and a large hole gouged in the earth.

Dagobert, thought January. *False River Jones must have figured it out the same way I did.* He had to force himself to start walking again, the reddish-gold stalks cracking under his boots. *It's really the only place it could have been dragged to, that particular night, if all the slaves had run off.*

The hole was about three feet deep and six in length, the soil still fresh looking, dug in the early hours of that morning. The newly broken remains of three empty wooden trunks, of the sort that women would keep their winter dresses in, had been tossed back into it, along with two shovels and a torn canvas sack. Why carry them back to town when you had ten thousand pesos to buy new ones?

He kneeled to pick up a split fragment of trunk that lay among the strewn cane. Stained and discolored, the paper that had lined it rotted to nothing with the seepage of water over a quarter-century. *So much for 'three iron chests.'* Any bank drafts or bills of exchange that had been in the chests with the silver would have been reduced to pulp.

But he saw none, either in the hole or among the trampled cane that surrounded it.

'Well,' he sighed, 'at least we were right about where the money was buried. And about who buried it.'

Where the wet earth had been thrown up out of the hole, a man's heavy boot tracks printed the soil, and among them, the occasional track of a narrow boot, and the round pocks of what looked like the end of a pole.

'Is that a crutch?' Oldmixton kneeled beside the place.

The narrow boot was the left foot – Dagobert, favoring his sprain.

January shook his head. 'It's a peg leg,' he said. 'One of our friends has a timber toe.'

In one place, where the wet ground was very soft, he discerned the delicate paw print of a small dog.

Sir John raised his brows. 'A pirate, you mean.'

'A pirate,' January affirmed. 'Or an ex-soldier.' *I'm going to strangle Dagobert . . .*

Sir John repeated, resignedly, 'Bloody hell.'

TWENTY-TWO

In the winter dusk, the crowds had thickened, jostling all along the Bayou Road where it passed the big houses of the Coquets and the Fleitas and the Belleanges, between New Orleans proper and the dancehalls and billiard parlors of the little faubourg of St-John. Anticipation for the Grand Cavalcades ran high. By the time the treasure hunters reached New Orleans again, in the long 'neutral ground' that separated St-John from the six streets that constituted (on paper) the Faubourg Pontchartrain, torches were being lit and half a dozen gentlemen in pasteboard armor or the fluttering robes of Bedouins were staging mock jousts by their smoky and uncertain light. Elsewhere, before the doors of the extravagantly illuminated Alhambra dancehall, half a dozen young men improbably attired as Roman soldiers chorused 'Annie Laurie' in what they assumed to be Scots dialect but wasn't.

January had kept an eye on the road behind them, all the way back to town, and had seen no one following. But it was impossible to tell which of those masked revelers – and there were thousands of them now – was watching for a six-foot-three-inch black man returning along the Gentilly road. He felt as if he rode with a target pinned to the back of his jacket.

It wasn't only silver, he thought, that had been in those chests. Silver is anonymous – *unless of course it's Spanish silver paying for British guns.*

But his heart quickened at the knowledge that three trunks meant that part of the payment hadn't been in silver. *It* has *to have been in there somewhere . . .*

A crowd of men (and possibly women – it was difficult to tell) masked and covered in gaudy robes of 'Indian' feathers pranced across Claiborne Street, surrounding the two horses; black men, January saw, hidden from the eyes of the City Guards by their costumes. Sir John's horse spooked, reared, and while the Englishman was getting the animal under control, January turned his mule's head and spurred into Villeré Street, where the crowds were thicker still. Women on the makeshift balconies of saloons, masked in crimson and black, were executing the newest French dance, the notorious can-can, with delicious abandon, for the benefit of those in the street below. *Benefit*, observed January, because the acrobatics of the dance involved lifting one's skirts and petticoats head high. These dancers did not, as some did in the opera when called upon to wear short skirts, modestly sew shut the crotches of their drawers (a modification which avoided offending the ladies in the audience but made it nearly impossible to relieve nature without getting half undressed). Some of these young ladies wore ordinary drawers – two legs sewn on to a waistband with the crotch conveniently left open between them. Quite a number of them simply avoided the problem by wearing no drawers at all.

Four years on the Board of Directors of the Faubourg Tremé Free Colored Militia and Burial Society had given January a fair idea of the geography of what was called 'the back of town,' and he was familiar, by name at least, with the establishment run by Speranza Rocher. Like Mesdames Joubert and Lemaitre, Mamzelle Rocher had gone into the business of keeping a boarding house after her protector had terminated their relationship. Unlike them, she had discovered that her protector had not, in fact, given her the cottage on Rue des Ramparts that he had said would be hers. His wife's lawyers had sold the property out from under her, the protector himself had refused to answer letters, and his family had threatened a lawsuit on the one occasion she had presented herself on his doorstep. She had sold her jewelry (and anything else for which men would give her a dollar, had remarked January's mother) to raise the wherewithal to buy a shabby cottage made of old flatboat planks on Marais Street, in a neighborhood of grimy bordellos, saloons, and groceries that clustered between the turning basin and the New Cemetery.

There she rented rooms indiscriminately to men and women, taking in addition a cut of whatever the women earned in their rooms from the men they met in the streets. Twice a day, she also served food to those who roomed there or to anyone sufficiently desperate to venture through her door.

January rode into the yard of a livery stable on Rue Villeré, paid the yardman there the last few bits in his pockets to look after the mule, and traded his own jacket, and a cigar Sir John had given him, for the man's coarse woolen roundabout and cap. 'I didn't see nuthin',' said the yardman with a grin and showed January the broken boards in the fence that led from the stable yard through to the yard behind the grocery on the next street. The passway between that yard and the building next door put him into the middle of a crowd of men gathered around a fight outside the Hope in Hell saloon on Marais Street.

From there it was a dozen feet to Speranza Rocher's.

The seven ruffians who loitered outside the three shut doors of the rear wing of Rocher's house made Cat Watling and his cohorts look like choirboys. One brawny individual, bearded like a grizzly bear, stepped out of the group to block his way: 'I think you in the wrong place, boy.'

January was well aware that he was in the wrong place. White men – particularly if they were as drunk as his challenger smelled – had been known to beat a black man to death for presuming to bull the same whore used by every white man in the parish. He bowed, quickly and humbly, and asked in his most cane-patch English, 'I sho' hope not, sir. This Mamzelle Rocher's house? I gots a message for her.'

Two of them pointed to the back door of the house. As they did so, one of the shut doors on the wing opened, and a sailor came out doing up his flies; January heard an argument break out behind him as to whether Grizzly Bear had lost his place in line ('You pussified suck-arse, I was here 'fore you was—') as he climbed the single shallow step.

A thin woman who could have been twenty-five but looked forty came when he knocked on the jamb of the open back door. 'What you want?' She had a pistol in one hand and a black eye, and the kind of scar on her lip that a woman gets when a man hits her hard enough that her own teeth are driven into the flesh.

January bowed again. 'I'm looking for Mamzelle de Cedillos, m'am. I was told she'd be here.'

She glanced past his shoulder into the yard. 'No wagon? Just you?'

January didn't turn, but by the sound of it, the issue of precedence had been decided and someone was telling a long, rather confused story about his initiation into the Iroquois tribe as a boy.

'Wagon's comin',' lied January promptly. 'They told me to meet 'em here.'

The woman waved him inside. Another pistol and a twelve-inch knife were strapped to her waist on a man's belt. 'Upstairs.'

The room that looked out on to the yard had been fitted up as a sort of pantry, cheap tin dishes piled on a counter at one side and shelves of sheets roughly folded at the other. With the coming of evening, an American oil lamp had been lit on a small, square table in the center of the room. A shelf above the counter held liquor bottles, and a small wooden chest labeled *Jardine Matheson & Co* – the largest importer in Britain, January knew, of Indian opium. Even with the lid closed and locked, the musky, sweet smell of it mingled with the reek of garbage, stale booze, the fishy stink of the burning oil, and of piss from the yard.

She walked ahead of him to a narrow door at one side of the room, opened it, and yelled up the rickety stairwell in a voice that could have shattered rocks, 'Porter's here, m'am!'

With the opening of the door, January heard several sharp cracks, of someone pounding something – *hammering nails?* These ceased, superseded by an indistinct reply. In those few moments, January observed a slung shot and eight stacks of silver Spanish pesos beside the lamp on a corner of the table. Interestingly, he saw neither liquor bottle nor glass.

'Go on up.'

Above them, the hammering resumed.

I see I'm just in time.

He bowed one more time. 'Thank you, m'am.' He climbed the stair.

Dirty orange lamplight outlined the open door at the top. When he knocked on the wall beside it, the hammering ceased again and the sweet voice of Felicita de Cedillos exclaimed, 'Well, that was fast!' She straightened up from kneeling by the far wall of the room as he stepped inside. Turned, and stopped, that lovely oval face for a moment comical with shock and dismay.

'Mr Janvier!' Like a startled cat, she scooped a pistol from the top of a small crate beside her and pointed it at him with both hands. There was a frantic glint in her eye, and at that distance she couldn't possibly miss.

January raised his hands at once. On the neatly made bed lay Dagobert Janvier, snoring like all Seven Sleepers of Ephesus in chorus, bandaged ankle raised a little on a pillow. Along the far wall lay a heap of empty sacks, with a scattering of dirt but not a single peso left in sight.

The smaller, stout wooden crates by which she'd been kneeling – six of them – were stacked along another wall, and nails strewed the floor like jackstraws, gleaming in the light of the lamp on another – empty – box from Jardine Matheson near the bed. A hammer lay on top of one of the crates.

No papers anywhere. *Damn it . . .*

A leather satchel lay on the floor beside the bed. On the Jardine Matheson box, beside the lamp, two tin cups still contained coffee, beside a dish of cheap brown muscovado sugar that would, January guessed, be strong enough to mask the taste of laudanum.

He touched the brim of the livery yardman's cap and bowed. 'I'm glad to have found you, mamzelle.'

Her whole slim body stiffened, her defiance worlds removed from the delicate victim of circumstance Dagobert had spent the past three weeks rescuing. 'It's my money,' she said. 'My father sacrificed himself—'

January, hands still carefully raised, shook his head. 'I'm not interested in the money, Mamzelle.' He spoke with gentle reasonableness in his best French, for despite her defiance, the way she held the pistol spoke of uncertainty. He wondered if she'd ever shot anyone before, though the desperation to do so was clear on her face. 'I'm sure your father had his reasons.'

'My father was murdered.'

'I know that, Mamzelle. I was there.'

She lowered the weapon a little, her eyes widening at this news.

'Twenty-six years ago,' January went on quietly, 'your father got himself mixed up with traitors, with the Spanish conspiracy to push the United States back east of the Appalachian Mountains. The Spanish plots to keep America from spreading its domination west into land that Spain claimed for its own. The same way Aaron Burr got mixed up in it, the same way Senator Blount of Tennessee got mixed up in it, the same way the territorial governor of Louisiana got mixed up in it – and others,' he added. 'Some of them are still in New Orleans and are wealthy enough to pay someone to cover their tracks. Do you – or did you – know anything about this?'

Her eyes shifted quickly, and her chin came up. 'N-No. That is . . . No. My father only told me that he'd left money hidden at

Alegre. He didn't say where. Paloma was the one who told me about the belvedere.'

'Was it his idea to come back for the money?' he asked. 'Or yours?'

'His.' The reply came much too quickly. 'He wouldn't tell me where it was.'

He probably didn't trust you as far as he could throw you . . .

'He said that anybody else who knew about the money would be dead by this time.'

Did he? Or did he argue that going back was too dangerous because he would *be recognized?*

'He said Icarus Pelerine still had the land, and the house, and probably wouldn't consent to having him go anywhere near it because of the lawsuit.'

'Someone knew who he was.' January looked past her again as he spoke, one quick glance at a time, his eyes returning again and again to hers. 'Even with the beard.' By the way Madame Rocher had spoken downstairs – by the six nailed-up crates, the canvas sacks heaped along the wall – porters were on their way.

Her eyes went past him to the door, and then to the window, through which the clamor in the yard was almost physically palpable. *Should I shoot him or not?* Or more likely, *Can I get away with it?* In this neighborhood – probably anyplace south of the confluence of the Mississippi and Ohio Rivers – a white woman shooting a black man in cold blood wouldn't raise an eyebrow, but in front of witnesses, it might be different.

'Someone recognized him,' January went on, to keep her listening, and off her balance. 'Someone paid Bastien Damoreau to set him up to be shot. Were you ever actually attacked, Mamzelle? Or was that just to keep M'sieu Janvier thinking he had to rescue you?'

'Well, I needed *someone* to help me, after Father was killed.' There was annoyance, and self-justification, in her voice, and beneath those carefully frizzed curls, that old-fashioned topknot, her face was the face of a woman who has never really had to look out for herself. A clever woman, but one who has never had to fight. 'Papa locked us in our bedroom while they were hiding it, that night before the battle, when the Americans were moving into position. Paloma didn't even tell me that's what was going on until years later when we were in Spain. Papa always said it would be dangerous for us to know where it was, but I never saw that! He should have trusted us! I can keep a secret . . .'

January wondered if she would have kept the secret of that much money if she'd seen some way of getting it all for herself. Her father, who knew her, presumably had had his reasons . . .

'But after we came here, and Papa was killed, I *had* to hide. Whoever killed him, I was afraid they'd come after me as well. I wrote to Galahad over there' – she twitched her head in the direction of the bed – 'begging for his help because I knew he'd been sweet on Paloma . . . One or two people in town had seen me as Juliette, on the levee or at the hotel, so I knew I had to stay out of sight, and I knew I had to keep moving. But I couldn't tell him why because he said *he* was being followed, and I didn't know whether it might be the police or someone from the Army.'

So she knew it was in fact treason when she made up the kidnapping story . . .

'But it *is* my money.' Her eyes hardened again, and she raised the pistol, again aiming at his heart. 'You can't deny me that. And I'll shoot you dead before I'll let you or anyone else touch it.'

'I don't want the money.' Again he held up his hands. 'You can keep the money. And you might want to be careful about bringing all those men up from the courtyard at the sound of a shot. Especially not if that's your only pistol.'

She bit her lower lip in sudden uncertainty. Clearly she hadn't thought of how long it would take to reload. 'Well . . . That won't do you any good if you're dead.'

'No,' he agreed, reflecting that she apparently hadn't given a thought about the safety of those she sent out to do her treasure hunting for her, either. 'Were there papers with that money, Mamzelle? Stock certificates? Bills of exchange? Or do you still have the bank drafts that I found under the belvedere in the garden?'

'Those were worthless. All those banks went out of business, and the bills of exchange would have Papa's name on them. I burned those . . .'

Damn it!

'I sold the certificate from the Phoenix Fire Insurance at a discount to someone who . . . who can cash it in later—' Her unoccupied hand moved protectively towards the pocket of her dress, like a woman with child will sometimes lay a hand on her belly, when she speaks of her state.

January's blood turned cold. 'Who?'

She drew herself up again. 'What is that to you?' Her dark eyes darted once more towards the door and she added, 'Now, you get over there in the corner by the bed. Someone will be here at any—'

'What it is to me, Mamzelle,' he said grimly, 'is what it is to you also. Because if you took that insurance certificate to one of the moneylenders hereabouts this morning,' he went on, as her rosebud mouth popped open to either tell him that he was above himself (or to scream rape and then shoot him, as a convenient way of ending the conversation), 'he will have taken it to whichever banker in town he thinks will keep his mouth shut. And it may be that that banker is the same man who paid for your father's murder. The man who was the middleman for the British, the man who facilitated the whole plan. And since he's looking for you already, he has only to look at the age of the paper to look for the name on it . . .'

By her flared eyes and indrawn breath he could tell she hadn't even thought of that, either.

'For that reason, Mamzelle, I suggest you leave here at once. And that you don't call attention to yourself in any way. Because it isn't the money that concerns Mr— that concerns whoever it is behind these attempts on our lives,' he corrected himself. 'He – or she – thinks we know who he is. Thinks that the treason can be traced back to him through those bank drafts and that certificate of exchange. That's how he's going to trace you. And as soon as he manages to find his hired killer Mr Watling, Watling and his Merrie Men will be coming up those stairs. So if you will excuse me, Mamzelle,' he finished, 'I'll take my friend M'sieu Janvier and go.'

He went to the bed – almost feeling the pistol follow his movement – and shook Dagobert by the shoulder, a token gesture at best. He could tell by the way the man breathed that he'd been heavily drugged, and a sniff of both coffee cups confirmed this suspicion immediately. He sniffed – then cautiously tasted – what little remained in the coffee pot, then added it to the gill or so of undrugged liquid in one of the cups.

He didn't dare look over his shoulder. It was like trying to escape the dog packs Michie Fourchet would use to hunt slaves in his childhood. If you acted like prey, you became it.

He willed his whole body to say, gently and reasonably, *You know and I know that shooting me would be a bad idea . . .*

'Easy,' he said, when his relative coughed and tried to turn his head aside. 'You'll be all right, sir. Drink this up—' Cold and stale, the stuff was almost certainly nasty, but with luck it would have its effect.

Behind him, the woman stammered, 'You're lying. You can't prove any of it! You're just trying to scare me! If you go to the police – if you can *find* a policeman in this town today – I swear I'll tell them—'

'Men's here with a wagon!' bellowed Madame Rocher from the room below, accompanied by a thunder of boots.

Mademoiselle de Cedillos said, 'Shit!' and pushed past him to the foot of the bed. She pulled a cutlass from under the mattress (*Bertie would* have *to be drugged to fall asleep on top of that . . .*) and shoved the weapon into January's hand. 'If it's not Mr Novain, I'll give you half the silver if you fight for me,' she hissed. 'Please . . .'

January raised his voice, yelled, 'That you, Fly-Trap?' as the footfalls clumped the stairway like an avalanche in reverse. Mamzelle de Cedillos looked nonplussed, but Fly-Trap Novain's deep voice echoed up in reply.

'That you up there, Ben?' The carter – all five feet two of him – and his two towering, burly sons appeared in the doorway. January set the cutlass out of sight on the other side of Dagobert's body, and Mamzelle de Cedillos hastily concealed the pistol behind her skirts. 'M'am,' added Fly-Trap, bowing respectfully. 'These the boxes?'

'Yes,' she said breathlessly. 'Thank you. Hurry . . .'

'My pleasure, m'am. The *Alicante*, for Cadiz?'

'Yes. Thank you.' She cast a quick glance back at January, who pretended to be absorbed in feeding Dagobert more coffee. (*Does she think I didn't hear that? Or does she plan to get rid of me before my knowing will matter*?) She paid the carter, January could see, in pale-brown bank notes – whatever her moneylender had paid her for the insurance policy certificate. Fly-Trap pulled a grimy but recent copy of the Bank Note Detector from his hip pocket and thumbed a few pages, then smiled.

They must be from someplace that's still in business, like the Bank of Louisiana . . .

When the three men descended the stair, each lugging one of the boxes ('What she got in here, bricks?' floated back up the stairway), January stood up, reassured – though he knew this was foolish – by the departure of at least part of the treasure. 'I hope, Mamzelle, that you'll stay here long enough to help me get M'sieu Janvier on his feet, out of here, and into a fiacre to get him home?'

'My ship—' she began.

'It's easy enough for you to get another ship down to the Balize, m'am,' January reminded her, in his most respectful tones. 'Ships bound for the East, or for Europe, often wait there for weeks, for other cargoes to come in. You'll have plenty of time.' He turned back for a moment, as Dagobert coughed again and fumbled to rise. 'If M'sieu Janvier is still here when the henchmen of the man who murdered your father arrive, they're going to wake him up and ask him where you've gone – and they'll certainly ask me.'

Mamzelle bit her lower lip again, her eyes fleeting to the door – Fly-Trap and Sons were already reascending the stair. He could almost see her calculating how long it would take her to reload, if she killed him – *Does she even know how to load a pistol?* If, as black men, Fly-Trap and his sons would be unable to testify against her in a murder trial, they would certainly refuse to cooperate about the rest of the chests. And who knew who would come up from the yard to investigate a shot? Or what they would demand?

More quietly, January added, 'If they catch us . . . Well, my employer is a strong man and may very well have the strength to die before he'd betray you, Mamzelle. I'm big, but I'm like a little girl when it comes to pain.'

His eyes met hers, and he added, *And personally I don't give a shit.*

She was still calculating the odds of getting her silver down to the wagon (if she had his corpse to account for) and the wagon out of the courtyard (through the mob of drunken and randy men outside those little rooms in the wing) when Fly-Trap and one of his sons came in, having wisely left the other (and larger) young man down with the wagon and the three chests now inside it. Grunting like a bull, Fly-Trap picked up one chest, his son another, and both cast a quick glance at January. They both knew, of course, that no matter how much his strength would have helped with the last remaining chest, tending to a semi-conscious white man (who was currently dribbling cold coffee down his front in an effort to drink) was universally regarded as a far more important task than helping black men do any actual work.

(*Damn drunk*, said Fly-Trap's glance to his son.)

'Will you help me,' January asked quietly, the minute the carters were through the door, 'or not?'

Panic flickered in her eyes. But at this point, with half of the silver on the wagon, too many things could go wrong.

He could already feel his own heart pounding fast, counting minutes – seconds – *How much time do we have?* – Was someone watching the place? Did whoever paid to have that certificate signed over to him send word to Beverly Chew – *It has to be Chew*—

Chew had been – maybe still was – the New Orleans representative of the Phoenix Fire Insurance Company . . .

How long would it take to round up Catastrophe and his 'boys' and send them this way?

'Two dollars,' said Dagobert suddenly, his voice thick. 'Pay you – dig where you said – Cita, you pay Jones. I don't—' He fumbled in his pockets, his head lolling. 'Give you money later. You pay him – keep his mouth shut—'

January raised his brows. 'Did Jones know what your father buried?'

The uncertainty vanished into sudden rage. 'Puta madre Englishman! He guessed where it had to be. Him and Gilipolas here' – she jerked her head at Dagobert and used the Spanish word for an idiot – 'dug it up, and he screwed me out of two hundred fètido pesos before he'd go away! Your *bobo* cousin—'

'He's not my cousin . . .'

'—was gonna give him *five* hundred, just for where to dig, when *bobo* was the one who had to come up with the horses and the mules and the sacks, *and* he brought it all here to me instead of taking it someplace safe . . .'

'You were lucky, Mamzelle,' said January quietly, 'that it was M'sieu Janvier that Jones went to for the horses and the shovels and the sacks, rather than some others—' *Who would probably have cut Jones's throat, of course*, he reflected, as Fly-Trap and son reappeared in the doorway.

Instantly Mamzelle's face changed, and with an expression of pity and adoration, she rushed to Dagobert's side (tucking the pistol under the pillow where January couldn't easily reach it) and put her hands tenderly to the drugged man's face. 'M'sieu Janvier! Oh, M'sieu Janvier, thank God you're awake! I was terrified. We have to get out of here—'

'Felicita?' His own hand groped to cup her cheek. 'Felicita, I—'

'You were wounded,' she whispered. 'We have to flee, now, at once— Oh, M'sieu Novain!' Suddenly seventeen again in the murky lamplight, she raised pleading eyes to the dray man's face. 'M'sieu Novain, can you take us – M'sieu Janvier, and Ben, and myself – out of this awful place? Can you get him down to Rue Royale? Please – I'll pay you another' – she hastily consulted the slim roll of paper money – 'I'll pay you another five dollars—'

Startled at the sum, the carter glanced at January, who nodded. 'We have to get out of here,' he said. 'Fast. Do you have a blanket or a tarpaulin in your wagon you can cover us with?'

'Sure do. It'll take us a minute—'

January signaled Mamzelle de Cedillos to hand the carter the money – signaled her twice, when she opened her mouth to protest. That done, she snatched her pistol up and followed the carter down the stair with the last of the chests, and January – able to breathe again for the first time in twenty minutes – turned back to the task of getting Dagobert on his feet.

'Ben?' mumbled Dagobert. 'Ben, I – I couldn't find you. Couldn't find where you were—'

'It's all right. I tried to catch up with you at Alegre—'

'Jones.' Dagobert drained the last of the coffee and let the cup slide to the floor. Considering where the water in it had probably come from, January made a mental note to give his companion a purgative later – *If the problem doesn't take care of itself. And if we both make it out of here alive . . .* 'Said he thought he knew where the money was. Said . . . Cedillos . . . Don't believe it. Cita said . . . but if Cedillos got it from Pelerine somehow, that last day. If he found it in the swamp, dug it up, brought it back to Alegre . . .'

He blinked stupidly at January, nodding to himself at his own version of the story.

'We can go over that later,' said January. 'Can you walk?' A stout and very handsome ebony cane stood in one corner of the room, which January recognized as one St-Denis Janvier had often used. Mud from the Alegre sugar field crusted its tip. *Lucky nobody stole it on the way . . .* 'We have to get out of here . . .'

Dagobert fumbled for the cane's silver head. 'M'father's,' he identified owlishly. 'Walk but can't shovel. Just a little. Paid Jones. Paid him – paid him two dollars—'

Completely aside from what Jones had extorted from Mamzelle de Cedillos, January wondered how much extra the river trader had managed to scoop into his coat pockets when Dagobert hadn't been looking.

Mamzelle de Cedillos appeared in the doorway, like a flustered angel, clutching her pistol in one hand and a lamp in the other. 'Hurry!' she whispered. 'Is he all right? Can he— Surely those men won't hurt him. I mean, it's obvious he knows nothing—'

That's been obvious from the start, January almost choked not to say and, rising, helped his relative to his feet. Dagobert swayed – his father's cane was inches too short for him – and draped an arm over January's shoulders. Turning, he stretched out his hand to the woman haloed in the golden aura of the lamp. 'Paloma,' he said softly, 'I love you. I've always loved you. You know that.'

'I know that,' she said, 'but you must *hurry*! Come on – can't you go faster?' She glared up at January as they helped the stupefied man through the door. 'This is stupid—'

For a moment, January had the impression that, in the absence of witnesses, Mamzelle might easily have shot her erstwhile rescuer simply for convenience's sake.

'Mamzelle,' he said quietly, 'I've seen how these men ask questions when they want to find out where something is – or where it's being sent. Or where you're going, since they know you'll have to be waiting down at the Balize for the *Alicante* to sail. And I will tell them everything they want to know within the first two seconds, rather than let them harm my friend here—' He moved his head towards the man who leaned so heavily on him, the man he would cheerfully have brained with a stick of firewood twelve hours previously. St-Denis Janvier's son.

A man who had always treated him decently, even as children. Who had never meant anyone harm.

'All right, all right,' snapped the woman, as if she barely heard. 'But *hurry*!' And she darted down the stairs, then back up as he eased his burden down one steep step at a time . . . 'I can't do this without light, Mamzelle,' he called when she turned to go down again.

She scampered back up to him, like a dog impatient to be walked. And given what January guessed Cat Watling and his 'boys' would do before they killed a woman they were told to kill, he reflected that she was right to be afraid – whatever the hell else she had done.

Whatever the hell I'm *going to have to figure out now, to keep Chew from hunting me down and murdering me . . .*

Because he'll think I saw those bills of exchange. Those bank drafts that he countersigned, and to hell with him being in the militia company in the battle himself.

He couldn't even, he knew, try to enlist his mother to help. That she was a friend of the banker would mean nothing if Chew even suspected that she might know he'd been involved in paying for Spanish militia and British guns with smuggled Spanish silver.

Chew was the only man in New Orleans in 1815 who could have brokered that deal, January knew. Chew, whose ships inexplicably sailed right through the British blockades in the Caribbean without being stopped with their crates of Spanish wines and their bolts of British superfine wool. Chew, whose partner Relf's shop on Rue St-Louis had bulged with British and Spanish goods at prices even Jean Lafitte's smugglers couldn't beat. Chew, who, despite his service in the New Orleans militia, had been perfectly willing to deal with whoever paid him the most.

The man had been customs collector for the port of New Orleans, January recalled. The man in charge of confiscating cargoes of smuggled African slaves – and of selling them for whatever prices he cared to charge, to whoever he chose, allegedly to 'recompense' the American Navy for its trouble catching the smugglers. (*And whose idea was* that *system?* January wondered furiously. *Those kidnapped prisoners ended up picking some white man's cotton, either way . . .*)

Even halfway down the steps he could hear the racket in the streets outside had redoubled. It was full dark now, and men who'd been drinking and gambling all day staggered into Speranza Rocher's yard yelling for whores and forty rod. The noise of men fighting outside those three shut doors on the house's rear wing redoubled, and January winced at the thought of the night those three women would have. Madame Rocher herself, when she briefly appeared in the doorway that led from the little back room into the barroom out front, was followed closely now by a sturdy, red-bearded Irishman with murderous eyes and at least six weapons visible on his person and probably as many more concealed. Mardi Gras – the night of masks – was universally used by the waterfront gangs, and the bands of ruffians attached to one or another publican/moneylender/smuggler, as the traditional occasion for settling scores.

Mamzelle raised the lamp high, to negotiate the last step down and the near darkness of the pantry beyond. Somebody had lighted cressets in the yard (*Here's hoping nobody out there knocks one of them over into the side of the house . . .*). By them January could see that Fly-Trap and sons had turned their small wagon around, Fly-Trap waiting in the back while one son held the nervous mules in check – with difficulty – and the other young man, armed with a shotgun in one hand and a three-foot iron pry bar in the other, stood over the tarpaulin-draped chests. He was watching the crowd in the yard – the black-bearded Kaintuck who'd challenged January earlier was fighting three other men, like a grizzly baited by dogs, and men streamed in off the street to lay bets. Fly-Trap was straining his eyes to see into the ill-lit pantry, glancing now and then over his shoulder.

Mamzelle took three fast steps towards the door, turned back, said, '*Hurry*—'

Someone in the yard fired a shotgun. The charge ripped the side of the wagon, sent Fly-Trap's son staggering back clutching his arm, and made the mules scream and plunge in terror. Dagobert stared in astounded stupidity at the gash ripped by flying wood fragments in the back of his wrist. The man who'd fired was masked – a long-nosed red gargoyle – but January recognized Cat Watling's brown rawhide jacket, with its embroidered sleeves, and his long red Devil-tail. Two other men – masked also – and a diminutive form that had to be Esmeralda, leaped to grab the team's reins or to scramble up to the box.

Mamzelle screamed, 'Go!' and young Novain, streaming blood, lashed with his whip, first at the nearest thief and then at the mules. January shoved Dagobert back into the stairwell, reached the pantry's back door instants ahead of Watling's men, slammed and bolted it and grabbed the lamp from Mamzelle's hand. Madame Rocher reappeared in the barroom door, her eyes met January's, and she nodded towards the stairwell. As January grabbed Mamzelle by the waist, pulled the door open and slung her in on top of the befuddled Dagobert, he saw the proprietress fling wide the door into the barroom. In the same moment, he blew out the lamp, ducked into the stairwell himself and slammed its door behind him.

Mamzelle de Cedillos at least had the brains to keep silent, and, by the sound of it, put her hand over Dagobert's mouth. January heard the smashing of wood and glass as Watling and crew burst into the pantry. Madame Rocher screamed, 'That way!' and boots thundered across the room and into the barroom—

'Wait,' whispered January, keeping a firm grip on Dagobert, who had begun to struggle.

Quick light feet. The stairwell door opened, and Madame Rocher shoved a Bedouin cloak, a golden wig, and a tin of boot-polish in at them. She watched the back door as January yanked the knife from his boot, pulled Mamzelle's hair free of its topknot with a clattering storm of hairpins and hacked it off ('No!' wailed the woman, clutching at his wrists), then smeared her face and slicked down the curled tousle of her remaining hair with the polish. 'Work that in . . . m'am,' he remembered to add respectfully. He tore off his own jacket and shirt (*What the hell, they belonged to that liveryman anyway* . . .), clapped the wig on to Dagobert's head, wrapped his relative's bleeding hand with a clean handkerchief and donned Dagobert's jacket (which was too small) and then swung the cloak over Dagobert's shoulders.

'I owe you,' he said to Madame, as he half-dragged his stumbling employer to the rear door. 'I won't forget.'

'If you don't, you'll be the first, Sambo,' she retorted with a grin.

They plunged outside into the melee around the fight.

TWENTY-THREE

The back of town. *Who can we trust?*

If it was Mr Chew who was paying the Watling boys – and January was virtually certain it was – staying ahead of pursuit was not only life and death to himself and his companions but to whoever he sought for help.

Masks on every side. The hilarity of Carnival was going full cock and fever pitch: the hilarity of Carnival, and the knowledge that murder would go completely unavenged. It would be easier, he thought, if he could just let go of both Dagobert and Mamzelle de Cedillos and make for the Buttonhole Café by himself. But he guessed that clever as she was, Mamzelle would be disoriented in the back-of-town crowd and, black-faced or not, her blue-sprigged gray dress would eventually be recognized and draw closer looks. And Dagobert, of course, was still too stupefied to realize that their pursuers were looking for them towards the river and the French Town, and would set off in that direction himself for home.

Watling would ask him questions until it became obvious that he didn't have answers, and then kill him.

Neither of them deserved what would happen to them, if they were caught.

Not with ten thousand silver pesos at stake.

The Buttonhole was on the other side of the canal and around the corner from the new Tremé Market. Saloons and gaming houses on either side of the wide neutral ground that ran down the center of Orleans Street had all put out extra lanterns, and wood-burning cressets, and groups of gaudy pseudo-Indians, voluminously robed quasi-Bedouins, and Greek and Roman warriors in unconvincing pasteboard armor were holding what looked like duels, with a variety of unlikely weapons, beneath the octagonal cupola in the middle of the market. Dagobert was far from the only person present who needed assistance walking, and on January's other side, Mamzelle de Cedillos clung tight to his arm.

'They'll expect us to head for the river,' January half-shouted to her over the din. The ruckus around the market sounded louder than the cannon at Chalmette. 'They'll be watching for us – and watching for you on the wharves.'

Her panicky grip tightened. 'Where are we going?'

'To someplace we can hide,' he said. 'And think.'

He prayed that Rose and the girls had already taken refuge at Olympe's. That they were having their own little Mardi Gras feast of pancakes and sugar, though it was just as likely Olympe and Paul, Zizi and Ti-Gall were having one last night of dancing, one last orgy of king cake, with friends. Would someone be watching the house on Rue Esplanade?

The Buttonhole, like every other place of public resort that night, was illuminated like the burning of Moscow and crowded with what looked like half a regiment of Cossacks, knights, houris, and members of the Greek pantheon – most of them people January knew from the FTFCMBS or his own neighborhood at the rear corner of the French Town.

Someone in the crowd behind him shouted, 'Benjamin!' and he pushed towards the narrow passway to the rear of the building. The last thing he needed, he thought, was to be recognized . . .

'Benjamin!' Someone grabbed his arm. 'Amicus meus!'

Hannibal, in the robes of a medieval monk, long hair straggling from an assortment of combs and ribbons down his back.

January released his hold on Mamzelle de Cedillos for a moment to seize the fiddler by the shoulder; thrust him ahead of them into the passway, Mamzelle clinging like a creditor to his sleeve. 'I thought you were playing at Janvier's by this time?'

'The procession only started thirty minutes ago.' Hannibal coughed, steadying himself against January's shoulder and nearly tripping over a gentleman dressed as Rob Roy who had retreated to the passway himself to commune privately with a bottle of wine. 'Excuse me, sir . . . Likely we can intercept them at the Claiborne Bridge over the canal. When you didn't return to the house, Rose and I feared you were either in trouble or in hiding—'

'Both.'

'—and I checked at Speranza's—'

'You know Speranza?'

'Oh, gods, yes. Well, speaking Biblically, half the men in the swamp *know* her . . . She described the events at her place, and I guessed this was one of the places you might try to come. Mamzelle,' he added, as they came into the quiet of the Buttonhole's yard, illuminated only by the reflected lights from the upper floor – where the owners lived – and the kitchen. He bowed to Mamzelle de Cedillos and lightly touched her sticky hair. 'Might I assist you with your coiffure? Have they seen that dress? The men who're following you?'

She nodded, panting for breath after the struggle through the crowd. 'I need to get rid of it—'

'Cora will have something,' said January. 'Will you find her, Hannibal? We'll be in the kitchen—'

'*I'll put a girdle round the earth in forty minutes*.' He darted up the back steps of the house, which would lead, January knew, into a pantry like that at Speranza Rocher's. The proprietress, Rose's friend Cora Chouteau, would undoubtedly be there.

'I'm sorry about your hair, Mamzelle,' he said, as he led (and half-carried) his charges across the little yard. 'We had to change the way we looked—'

'No, I understand.' She raised her fingers to her cheeks and forehead, gently working the hastily smeared polish into a smoother finish. It wouldn't have fooled a child in the daytime, reflected January. But at night, in the light of lanterns or cressets, it was enough to make a man looking in a crowd for a white woman go on looking. 'Thank God I frizzed it like Paloma used to.'

Instead of going into the kitchen, where lamplight gleamed from half-open shutters, January led the way around the corner of the little building, to a stair that ascended to a half-story attic above. Cora's cousin Gin – who helped with the heavy work at the café – emerged from and re-entered the kitchen half a dozen times before Hannibal returned across the yard with the thin form of the café owner limping behind him.

'Good Lord, Ben, I heard you were dying!' Cora kept her voice down; seized January's hands. 'Rose said – everybody said—'

'I'll explain later . . .'

He reflected that Madame McCullen and Madame Savonnière had undoubtedly heard this yesterday, too . . . and had sought another piano teacher for their daughters today.

'You're in trouble, aren't you?' The café owner glanced towards the kitchen, from which Gin emerged and strode towards the house with yet another pot of gumbo without giving them a glance. 'I can hide you—'

January shook his head. 'We just need something to wear. As conspicuous as possible – they'll be looking for someone trying to be invisible—'

'Who?'

'Kaintucks from the Tchoupitoulas wharves.'

'Tcha!'

'I can get us to Kate the Gouger's,' offered Hannibal. 'You can hide there while I scout the neighborhood and recruit reinforcements. Kate won't betray us.' He added, a little self-consciously, 'I shall ask her nicely. Recte et suaviter . . . And in case of trouble, she can take care of herself.'

January knew this to be more than likely. He'd met Kate.

'The Claiborne Canal bridge is lined both sides with torches – they'll never get the horses across,' the fiddler went on. 'We shall catch them there, never fear. The ice cream at the governor's reception will be puddles by this time. Madame's prima soprano will have fallen asleep, and Madame will have murdered at least three servants—'

Both Cora and her husband Gervase were enthusiastic maskers – during the whole of their conversation Cora was dressed as an angel, complete with tiny wings on her twisted back and an apron over her pink cheesecloth robe. This being Mardi Gras, the whole Carnival season's worth of fancy dress was still heaped in one of the little bedchambers above the café. It was early enough in the evening that five-year-old Ti-Rose and three-year-old Ti-Ben were still awake, being watched over by Gin's ten-year-old son Tommy ('Double-cross my heart and may the witches ride me three times around the moon if I ever tell anybody I seen you here, Mr J!'); Tommy worked wonders with Mamzelle de Cedillos's shorn hair and his mother's dressmaking scissors.

Fifteen minutes later, two medieval monks – one black and one white – descended the stair, followed by a papier-mâché ogre in peasant rags, assisting a befuddled gentleman in the white coat and toque blanche of a master chef. The three coherent members of the party loaded this individual into Gervase's wheelbarrow – January handed him an empty wine bottle and put three more into the barrow. 'Hold on to that, sir,' he instructed, squinting through the ogre mask's eyeholes. 'Can you sing?'

''Course I can sing.' Dagobert peered up at him. 'Sing better'n . . . better'n . . . that Italian fella Davis had last season, ever'body made all that fuss about.' And to prove it, he flung back his head and began to carol 'Una furtiva lagrima' at the top of his lungs.

Content that nobody would look twice at so un-fugitive a party, January wheeled him into St-Ann Street, making considerably better speed than they'd done when he'd been trying to help Dagobert to walk. And at least pushing the barrow – and walking crook-backed and hunched like an ogre – made his height less noticeable in the crowd.

In anticipation of the long-tardy Grand Cavalcade, every street in the back of town held a crowd. It wasn't solely the hope of concealing themselves in one of the carriages of the Cavalcade that led January to guide his party lake-wards. Maskers jostled along Orleans Avenue on both sides of the Tremé Market, shouting to people on the balconies above the shops on either side of the avenue and wandering in and out of the groceries and cafés. Everybody knew the City Guards would be fully occupied along Rue du Levée and down on Gallatin Street by the wharves, so in addition to the danger of the Basin Street ruffians settling scores, it meant that nobody was enforcing curfew. Neither was anybody watching for slaves who 'slept out,' or keeping track of whether bartenders were selling drinks to white men or black.

In torchlight and masks, who could tell anyway?

On the other side of Claiborne Avenue, the swamp began in earnest – fewer houses, scattered among clumps of cypress, oak, and palmetto, black shadows barely touched by the glare of the lanterns outside the saloons. Moonlight gleamed on sheets of reed-prickled water or in the eyes of rats. The Kaintucks and filibusters who rented rooms there – men who'd come down the river on the flatboats and keelboats – didn't mask but rioted happily among the crowds, picking fights and staggering along the dirt streets with the harpies from the dancehalls and bordellos, every one of whom, it seemed to January, knew Hannibal and greeted him with drunken kisses (and occasional attempts upon his virtue), which further slowed their progress. At one point, as they turned upriver to begin the slow circle around towards the French Town and relative safety, Hannibal recruited a troop of Fat Mary's girls to march in a mob around the wheelbarrow and the four fugitives, completely concealing them, waving fans and hair ribbons and singing 'Ol' Zip Coon' . . .

You heard of the battle of New Orleans,
How old Gen'ral Jackson give the British beans;
Them Yankee boys do the job so slick,
For they catched ol' Pakenham an' rowed him up the crick . . .

Mamzelle de Cedillos, her eyes wide, clutched to herself the satchel which contained her money and travel papers, the monastic robe she'd borrowed at the Buttonhole having no pockets. Her blue dress, crammed into a pillowcase, currently did duty as a cushion for Dagobert, and nothing could have persuaded her that anything in its pockets would be safe if, for instance, the wheelbarrow overturned.

Hannibal had been perfectly right about the Grand Cavalcade stalling on the Claiborne Avenue bridge. Where the little Claiborne Avenue drainage canal ended, and the bridge spanned the dark width of the Carondelet Canal, the open space of Claiborne Avenue was a circus of drunken ruffians and whores, dancing wildly to the two orchestras on the red-and-gold parade wagons. Over a dozen carriages, gaudy with hot-house flowers, were stopped in the muddy street, while coachmen and footmen coaxed nervous teams one by one across the bridge between lines of burning cressets. January could see a dozen more, waiting in the torch glare on the other side for the procession to form up again. In the largest of the carriages, spilling blossoms like a gargantuan flowerpot, he thought he could distinguish Madame Marie-Hélène herself, a thin, awkward figure in a green-and-gold Elizabethan gown (*She'd spit blood if she knew Maman had one exactly like it*!), standing up and watching the scene behind her, presumably with frustration and rage. Around them, the Donaldsonville militia band was also playing what sounded like 'Greenland's Icy Mountains' at full volume.

The situation was not improved when the occupants of a keelboat on the canal, nearly invisible in the flickering shadow and darkness on the lake-side of the bridge, began to set off fireworks. The men and women in the avenue cheered – a number of the celebrants were moved to fire their pistols into the air – and the horses already crossing the bridge between two lines of fire reared and bucked in panic. The ladies in some of the carriages shrank back into their seats and clutched the arms of their gentlemen escorts, and the men who, armored as knights errant, accompanied the procession on horseback, nudged their mounts defensively closer around the vehicles.

January touched Hannibal's shoulder. 'Let's go.'

The parade wagon nearer the bridge – embellished with cardboard turrets and the silken flags of Austria, Russia, France, and England (*Don't tell me they expected Sir John to ride that one . . .*) – held the small ensemble poached from Caldwell's St-Charles Theater, mostly uptown Germans. Like the ladies in the carriages, they gazed nervously around them at the firelit hurly-burly as if seeking an escape route. (*And no wonder* – January guessed that the fireworks were the brainchild of one of the swamp publicans whose 'boys' were now slipping through the crowd picking the pockets of every spectator they passed.)

The other wagon bore January's friends: Cochon Gardinier, Jacques Bichet and his uncle, Philippe duCoudreau, in addition to half a dozen others he'd worked with around the French Town. Pylade Vassage, the Valada brothers, a stout German maestro of the double bass named Herr Pleck, all sat on the sides of the parade wagon, attacking the music as loudly as they could, in the hopes of drowning out the piano playing of Herr Kasper Hatch. Hatch – the worst piano player in Southern Louisiana – had indeed been the only one still unemployed when Marie-Hélène had dismissed January from her entertainment. A spinet piano – gilded and wreathed all over with paper flowers – occupied the front end of the wagon, and in contrast to the uptown Germans, January's friends, as they wailed and tootled and sawed upon the strings, looked around them at the confusion with obvious delight. All of them had played under circumstances more bizarre than these.

Still ringed with Hannibal's lady friends, January pushed the wheelbarrow forward, Mamzelle de Cedillos clutching his heavy leather belt with one hand and her satchel with the other. Cochon caught sight of Hannibal, startled, and January released the barrow's handles long enough to lift up the ogre mask—

'Ben!'

'Hush!' He settled the mask in place and grabbed the tail of the wagon. Hands reached down to him; dragged him up into the potted forest of paper flowers and banana plants.

'I heard you was dead!'

'I will be if I'm caught.' January turned and seized Mamzelle de Cedillos's hands as Hannibal and a hefty she-wolf named Railspike boosted the woman up to them. Without being told, as soon as Hannibal handed her satchel up to her, she dropped down among the festoons of greenery around the musicians; January was already dragging Dagobert up. An armored rider spurred forward with his lance, but Cochon straightened up and signed to the man – somebody's groom, guessed January, who knew the violinist – who reined away.

Six or seven Perdidio Street nymphs lifted Hannibal up to be hauled aboard, like Hylas kidnapped by a particularly slatternly gang of naiads. He was still leaning over the tailboard to kiss them when the wagon jolted forward towards the bridge. January had to grab him by the back of his robe.

Under the red-and-gold glare of the fireworks, January dragged an overturned plant pot to Herr Hatch's side at the piano – ogre mask and all – and joined him in jangling duets as the procession slowly approached the bridge. Hidden among the ivy and camellias, Dagobert joined in on a Chopin mazurka with 'Ten Green Bottles.'

They reached Kate the Gouger's bathhouse without further incident.

TWENTY-FOUR

1815

They marched through the Faubourg Marigny, and up the Rue Esplanade.

Dreaming – remembering – January saw very clearly the crooked house of gray Spanish stucco that he would later live in . . . *Why didn't I realize it then*?

In his dream, he saw himself and Rose, little Professor John and Xander, Hannibal and Gabriel and Zizi-Marie, all standing on the gallery, waving to his twenty-one-year-old self. Telling him that it would all work out. That it would all be all right.

When they marched through the French Town itself – only back then people referred to the French Town, the Faubourg Marigny, and Tremé almost as a single unit – there was little cheering. The music of the Second Battalion's band seemed to echo loud against the Spanish balconies and brick banquettes, the dirt streets that had been paved when he'd come back sixteen years later . . .

But I'm not coming back, he protested.

I am done with this place, this town.

When Jackson's bounty comes through, when I get my 160 acres, I don't care if it's in the middle of the American Desert, I'll go there.

So what am I doing living in the crooked Spanish house?

He turned his head to look back at them on the gallery, but their shapes were indistinct already, distant. His feet, and the feet of Gilles and Digo and Fly-Trap and the other men who'd stood beside them on the rampart, who'd shot down into that seethe of helpless faces . . . They were like the beat of waves on silent rocks. Men – white men – lined the sides of Rue Royale to watch them pass, but they watched in silence.

Damn you. Damn you. Damn every single one of you to hell.

White men, the city fathers of New Orleans had written to Jackson when the victory parade was planned, feared that the sight of black men bearing arms – walking in procession as victors over white ones, even the white enemies of their country – 'might destabilize slavery and lead to a general uprising.'

And Jackson had ordered the two battalions of colored troops out of the city: to dig graves, to excavate latrine pits at the militia camps, to guard supplies. To drive wagons and feed mules.

He saw Davy lying in Gilles's arms by the cotton-bale rampart, the blood draining out of the fist-sized hole in the side of his head. Heard Odile screaming at her elder son, *You couldn't have brung his body home, even . . .?*

Remembered the men on either side of him as they ran across those humps and trenches of sugar field, towards the dark shapes of tents, the dim few lights of dying fires. The men who'd gone down like tripped horses, silent, rolling to a stop that he didn't see because he'd already run on past them. The crackle of musket fire and the tiny sparkle of firefly gun flashes ahead of them. The knowledge that he might be the next man to go down.

Only when he'd got back to camp did he know who they'd been, men he'd shared rations with, shared campfire, shared stories.

'Might destabilize slavery . . .'

By letting the men you've got working in your cane fields – the men who live in fear that they might come back from work one day to the news that you've sold their wife and you've sold their children to some man in town, and you'll never see them again – like my father did . . . by hinting to those men that they, too, can carry guns?

'Destabilize' the ownership of bucks, of wenches, of pickaninnies by letting them realize that they are men, and women, and children just like you?

They were within a few streets of the Café des Exiles, where the men who'd fled Saint-Domingue would gather (*Was that now? Was that later*?) to rehash their memories of the great uprising there, when the men they'd beaten to death, or killed unspeakably so as to instill fear in others – men they'd enslaved and worked until they died – 'destabilized' and took up arms . . .

'Exiles' who complained and sighed, and it never occurred to those men, *not once*, that what they had done for the sake of money – for the sake of the cheap labor that poured wealth into their own pockets – was wrong. Or anywhere close to wrong.

Oh, they're actually better off as slaves, you know . . . He had heard this a thousand times.

Men even pointed out that the Bible instructed slaves to obey their masters. (Those men generally didn't mention Moses . . .)

Captain Savary had refused the order to have his men perform the duties of slaves. Had given them their weapons – unloaded – and had marched them through the streets of Marigny, down Rue Esplanade, down Rue Royale, under the striped and starry banner of the United States.

You'd be seeing men march through the streets under the Union Jack if it weren't for the blood we shed.

Savary's troops passed the tall yellow townhouse of St-Denis Janvier, where Madame Marie-Hélène, and Old Madame Sidonie – her hair then black as a raven's wing – had stood . . . *Yesterday? Last week*? In his dreaming, January couldn't remember. Only that they'd stood on the upstairs gallery to cheer when the white troops marched past in victory. His mother – with him in tow, as she'd demanded he accompany her – had stood then on the opposite side of the street, dressed with the gorgeousness of a golden phoenix. *No wonder Madame Marie-Hélène hates her . . .*

St-Denis Janvier and seventeen-year-old Dagobert had stepped along proudly in the uniforms of Beale's Rifles. So had Mr Beverly Chew. January wondered where Chew had been during the actual fighting. Back at headquarters, in his tailored militia uniform?

Gilles marched beside him today. Fly-Trap Novain, the stonecutter Basile Nobert, Callie's brother Blanco. Silent, proud, brothers now in the kinship of blood that could never be sundered. Where they had been, none of these watchers had witnessed. *How can I leave them?*

I can't imagine what it would be like, to have them gone, Callie had said.

Gilles, furious, had sworn – when d'Aquin had told them about not being allowed to march – that like January, he would take his 160 acres and scrape the mud of New Orleans from his feet, but January guessed that wouldn't be the case. With Davy dead, Gilles would stay near his mother. And he – January – would go. No way of telling, either, whether that land was going to be handed to them by lottery – *Well, Ben, you get lot 21,168 which is on the Godforsaken River five miles from the Mexican border, and you, Fly-Trap, you get lot 13,537 which is in Soggybottom Swamp 127 miles up the Missouri River from Noplace Landing . . .*

I'll find a way to visit. I'll find a way to see them, even if it's only now and then . . .

He pushed from his mind the deadly fevers of the New Orleans summer, the chance that one of those visits could end with his shocked cry, *Died? When?*

When the white troops had paraded, and he'd stood beside his mother, he'd held tiny Dominique in his arms so that she could better see – and so that St-Denis Janvier could see her. (*And how did Madame Marie-Hélène like* that?) *Can I really live with only seeing her as a child of six, and then suddenly a girl of ten, and then not until she's a young lady getting ready for Maman to start taking her to the Blue Ribbon balls?*

To be free? To have land of my own?

Yes.

Yes.

1841

He woke with a headache, and a queasy lassitude that weighed on every bone from his parietal crest to the distal phalanges of his feet. He had meant to stay awake: Hannibal's carnal quid pro quo with Kate the Gouger notwithstanding, he knew better than to fall asleep in a whorehouse crib in the swamp. He was aware he'd slept deeply, more deeply than he should have, particularly since he'd been lying on a mattress on the filthy floor.

He and Dagobert – insofar as Dagobert had been making a sort of sense after three cups of mouth-wringingly bad chicory coffee – had both willingly given Mamzelle de Cedillos precedence of the only bed in the little room. At least Kate – between tricks (she had evidently been engaged in a competition of some sort with Russian Nancy) – had put a sheet on the mattress, out of respect for her guest's sensibilities. (She'd had to borrow the sheet from Big Annie over on Girod Street.) After two cups of coffee, January had settled with his back to the little shack's door.

That was the last thing – other than his dream – that he remembered.

He'd woken lying on his side, a few feet from the door. It was daylight. Distantly he heard the bells of the cathedral, calling all Christian folk to communion with God.

Ash Wednesday.

Long after dawn.

Dagobert slumbered noisily on the floor in the corner, his head on the pillowcase that still contained Mamzelle de Cedillos's wadded-up dress. A rat sat on his hip, nibbling a fragment of the king cake that had accompanied that vile chicory-laced coffee.

January's stomach turned at the thought of where he could have woken, and in what circumstances. He groped instantly for his boot, and his fingers touched the stiff fold of his freedom papers. *Jesus*, he thought. *Jesus*.

And then, *That fucking coffee . . .*

How could I have been so stupid . . .?

Like the goddess Persephone: *Do not* ever *eat or drink anything in Hell. Or you'll never get out.*

He turned his head – which gave a cloudy throb – and saw the bed was empty. The monk's robe in which Mamzelle de Cedillos had escaped from the Buttonhole lay across the foot, but her shoes and her satchel were gone.

Resignedly, knowing what he'd find (or wouldn't find), January checked his pockets. Fortunately she hadn't taken any money – since he'd given his last two bits to that hostler on Villeré Street – but the silver watch he'd bought in Paris was gone. She'd even taken his spare clean bandana. The only reason, he guessed, that she hadn't made arrangements with a slave dealer to spirit him on to a ship bound for Galveston was because she was too afraid of Cat Watling's pursuit to linger.

His rosary – being cheap blue glass and steel – was worth nothing. His confessor had told him, more than once, *When you can't think of anything else to say, say, 'Thank you.'*

His fingers closed around the blue beads, and he whispered, 'Thank you,' and meant it from the bottom of his soul.

He crawled woozily across the unspeakable planking of the floor and shook Dagobert's shoulder. The rat regarded January in deep offense: *And who the hell do you think* you *are?*

Dagobert sighed, 'Paloma,' and turned half-over. The disgusted rat retreated under the bed.

January checked his relative's pockets. No watch, no money, no gold cigar case, no Janus-headed signet ring. He shook Dagobert again, and Dagobert, without waking, pushed his hand pettishly away.

He wondered if Olympe, like Prospero in *The Tempest*, could summon a storm that would sink the *Alicante* and everyone on her to the bottom of the sea.

But that wouldn't be fair, to the crew, to the other passengers, to the families of both.

Surely there's some form of non-contagious dysentery?

And how far would such a spell reach?

I'll have to ask her.

At least, he reflected, he had Mamzelle's dress, which would give Olympe something to work with . . .

In the yard outside, a woman screamed, 'That fucken sow!'

The epithet could have applied to every woman in a half-mile radius, but somehow, January knew to whom it referred.

The door of the shack was wrenched open with a force that could have knocked the house down. Kate the Gouger stood framed in it, sketchily draped in what the vulgar called a 'good-time dress' – a Mother Hubbard many sizes too large for her thin frame – her red hair hanging greasily down her back and a skinning knife the size of a cutlass in one hand. 'Where is that bangtail bitch?'

January sat up and propped his back against the frame of the bed. Something darted across the pillow and out of sight. Given its size, he hoped it was a mouse. 'If she's trying to catch up with the *Alicante* at the Balize,' he said, 'I'd say she's just passing Pointe à la Hache about now.' He rubbed his temples.

'That fucken—'

'What did she take of yours?'

'Every goddam fip in the money box! *And* my good rouge, *and* my purple silk, the only goddam silk I had, and every goddam petticoat I own—'

January hid his astonishment that Kate the Gouger even possessed such a thing as a petticoat, much less a silk dress. He'd never seen her in anything but a Mother Hubbard. He cried, 'Shame!' which made Dagobert sit up, wince as if stabbed, and rub his eyes.

'Palo— uh, Mademoiselle de Cedillos?' He looked around the filthy shed, then at the bed, and his eyes widened with alarm. 'We were drugged!' he cried perceptively. Then, 'Pelerine came in the night and carried her off! Where—'

He looked frantically around him.

'No, sir, it wasn't like that,' said January, since Dagobert showed signs of leaping to his feet and hobbling for Sept-Anges forthwith. 'She escaped. Do you not remember?'

Wide-eyed, Dagobert shook his head. 'We – we found the treasure,' he stammered after a time. 'False River Jones sent me word that he knew where Pelerine had to have buried it, practically on poor de Cedillos's doorstep, where he'd never think to look for it. We brought it back to Madame Rocher's, paid Jones—' He passed a hand across his eyes. 'I don't – I don't remember . . .'

'You helped Mamzelle de Cedillos pack it into boxes, to be shipped back to Spain,' said January. 'One of Madame Rocher's servants brought you up coffee. I talked to the man later – he swears he knew nothing of it, but with the confusion of Mardi Gras, people were in and out of the kitchen. You drank none, but Mamzelle and Jones both partook, Jones more than she. She realized she had been poisoned when Jones collapsed. Four men, masked for Carnival, stormed up to her room: it was a terrible struggle, but when I arrived, three of them – pretty badly trounced already, I could see – fled. I managed to seize the fourth, and he confessed that he was one of the old Spanish militia, hired directly by the King of Spain during the war to help the British defeat Jackson. Pelerine, and the lawsuit, had nothing to do with it at all. Bartolomé de Cedillos told his daughters that it was about the lawsuit because he feared that if they probed into the business further, Spanish agents would surely hunt them down.'

Kate blinked at him from the doorway and said, 'Holy shit,' fortunately in English, of which Dagobert had only a rudimentary grasp. 'Any of that true?'

'Please nod, Mamzelle,' said January. 'This man is an imbecile.'

'That's for goddam sure anyways,' she agreed, nodding vigorously. 'That's a whale of a yarn, Mr J. You should write plays for Mr Caldwell's theater.'

I'll try that before I'll agree to do a job again even for somebody I know . . .

'Thank you, Mamzelle.' He turned back to Dagobert, and tried to recollect how act three of any melodrama at the St-Charles Theater would wind such a story up. 'At that point, Mamzelle de Cedillos noticed that you had been wounded in the affray—'

Dagobert looked, startled, at the scabbing cut on his hand.

'—and the Spaniard gloated that his dagger had been poisoned. She – and I – rushed to get a tourniquet on your arm, and in that moment of confusion, the Spaniard escaped. Mamzelle and I managed to get you to my sister's, where she was able to provide both of you with antidotes, Mamzelle's for the poison she had drunk, yours for the venom already coursing through your veins.'

The white man gazed up at him in an agony of suspense, as if afraid he would be told that in the end he had died before the antidote could take effect.

'She would have stayed with you,' January continued more quietly (*And thank God for all those operas I've seen. I will definitely be saying rosaries until Easter for lying*), 'but it was only an hour until the turn of the tide. You ordered her to take her chests of silver and get on the ship for Spain. To go at once, for though the poison in your blood had been rendered harmless, you could feel the delirium of its after-effects coming over you. You knew that if you succumbed while she could see you, she would remain and put herself in greater danger from the renegade Spanish. I went to summon a carter – when I returned, she was in tears but resigned to your wiser judgment. I could not imagine,' he went on, 'what it cost you to send her away for her own protection, knowing you would almost certainly never see her again.' (*And thank God for that.*)

Dagobert's breath left him in a sigh. Tears glimmered in his eyes. 'Such courage,' he whispered. 'For her to set forth alone—'

'She'll be all right,' January comforted him. 'You were the one who had to be strong. Moments after her departure, you collapsed. Fearing the revenge of the Spaniards, I brought you here, until I can be sure that they have left New Orleans. Madame' he turned and gave Kate her accurate title – 'please permit me to introduce Monsieur Dagobert Janvier. Monsieur Janvier, Madame Kate.'

She executed a little bobbing curtsey, like a servant – learned, he suspected, while in the pit at the St-Charles Theater, by watching the actors onstage. Dagobert rose, bowed deeply to her, and kissed the air about an inch above her knuckles. 'Thank you,' he said. 'Thank you for the sanctuary you have given us in the hour of our need.'

'What-all happened to Jones?' asked Kate of January, again in

English, caught up for the moment in the story. 'If he was poisoned back at Rocher's?'

'He's fine,' said January. 'We gave him some of the antidote, too, and he took his money and left town.'

'Good,' said Kate, returning to reality. ''Cause he owes me six dollars for his last three visits here.'

'I recall none of this,' said Dagobert. 'The dreams—' He shook his head. '*Beyond the wit of man to say* – but thank you.' He clasped January's hand. 'Thank you for standing by me, like the true friend you are.'

January was still trying to adjust his mind to the spectacle of Patroclus pushing a drunken Achilles (in a chef's white toque) through the streets of New Orleans in a wheelbarrow, when Hannibal appeared in the doorway beside Kate, a few ribbons still tangled in his hair and looking decidedly the worse for wear.

'Vale, amicus meus?' the fiddler inquired anxiously. 'Your brother-in-law patrolled the neighborhood of your house earlier this morning and saw no sign of danger, but—'

'That fucken bitch dosed Ben here with laudanum and stole a hundred and thirty-eight dollars an' my purple silk dress!' yelled Kate. 'Now she's took off for Spain—'

'I doubt she'll get far,' said Hannibal. 'Benjamin and I will see what we can do about a new dress – a much prettier dress – for you, Aphrodite of the Cypresses . . .' He kissed her hand, then turned back to January and took a sheaf of papers from his coat pocket – stained with water, earth, and rust; each bearing the red discoloration where a seal had been removed. 'I think,' he said, switching back to Latin, 'these will take care of our problem.'

Dagobert frowned with concentration. His Latin, acquired over thirty years previously, was marginally better than his English, and January prudently switched to classical Greek.

'Those are the documents I found under the belvedere at the Joyous House.' He recognized the penciled notes on their backs and recalled how Hannibal had helped lift Mamzelle up into the parade wagon, and handed the satchel up to her afterward. His Greek wasn't nearly as good as Hannibal's, and he had to grope for the words for Alegre. 'The lady told me she'd destroyed them.'

'The veracity of the lady would challenge that of Ananias,' returned Hannibal – whose own abilities as a pickpocket would

challenge those of Autolycus. 'Most of them are drafts on banks that failed, but I don't think it matters. What matters—'

'Is that the bills of exchange had to be countersigned,' finished January, unfolding the first certificate and scanning the signatures. 'And if the man who countersigned one of them to transfer credit to pay for British guns and Spanish treason is still here in New Orleans—'

'He would do anything to shut you up. I have all the seals, by the way,' the fiddler went on. 'They're intact – I removed them with a hot wire.'

Now that, reflected January, *is truly the act of a friend.*

Carefully, he opened each document, looking at the names of men – most of them probably long dead – who had authorized payment from persons or firms which could be traced to British banks, British companies, or British representatives to Bartolomé de Cedillos or his representatives . . .

'I can replace them easily, so whoever it is won't know that anyone read them.'

'That's fortunate,' said January quietly. 'Because if he even suspected that someone had seen his signature – or had talked to anyone who had seen his signature – he would . . . tidy up the situation.' Again he saw Gilles in the doorway of Fortune Gérard's house, framed against the darkness . . .

'No sense taking chances,' Hannibal agreed.

January unfolded the thickest of the packets – from the Bank of Louisiana – and on the third page found what he was looking for.

The countersignature authorizing payment of ten thousand silver pesos from the account of a British merchant in Mexico to Bartolomé de Cedillos, signed by Mr Beverly Chew.

TWENTY-FIVE

1817

In waking life, January was well aware that of his family, only St-Denis Janvier had accompanied him to the wharves on that day in April of 1817, to take ship on the *Reine de Navarre* for Le Havre. Gilles and Callie Gignac, Digo Salazar and his daughter, John Davis – the father of Pierre, who had been one of the first to hire him to play at public balls. Dr Gomez, who would die of yellow fever in 1829 . . . January realized with a pang of grief. *This is the last time I will see him . . .* These followed him across the wet mix of mud and gravel, past the stacked walls of cotton bales, the head-high platforms of molasses barrels and sacked grain, to the gang-plank, that dark, cold morning. He could still smell the reek of the river, the stink of smoke heavy in the air. Feel the weight of his portmanteau and the small wonder in his heart that this single piece of luggage was all that he would carry away with him from New Orleans.

From the city to which he would never return.

But I did return . . .

But he was twenty-three in his dream, and he couldn't remember why he'd returned. Only that he knew that he wasn't coming back.

Ever.

The reason for that was clear in his mind.

But curiously, in his dream, Hannibal Sefton walked beside him, Hannibal in the robes of a bedraggled monk, as he'd seen him that morning in waking life in that muddy shed behind Kate the Gouger's bathhouse, the morning air stinking of the nearby outhouses, of stale liquor and weeks' worth of sweat and copulation.

'Mr – um – whoever's signature was on one of those bills of exchange,' temporized the fiddler, like January carefully avoiding the name of the man who, at the time of the dream, was the customs collector for the Port of New Orleans, as well as on the board of the Bank of Louisiana, 'is – must be, that is – a friend of Madame

Marie-Hélène,' he corrected himself again. He and January had both seen Chew hundreds of times at balls, parties, musicales, chatting with Dagobert's stepmama over smuggled champagne. 'Of course she'd complain to him when Dagobert took the chaise and sallied forth to meet you at Alegre, or went to assist Mamzelle Felicita with – er – one thing or another.'

New Orleans townhouses were all built with only one exit from their courtyards, to discourage delinquent bondsmen from disappearing out the back when there was work to be done. He could not have slipped away unseen. And seeing the look in his eyes when he spoke – elaborately casual – of the woman, of course she'd guessed.

'She'd complain to anyone who would listen.'

January knew this to be true.

And after the first complaint, a man with treason hanging over his head would thereafter listen closely and watch for his chance.

'It would be nothing for Cat and his boys to pick up his trail. And Madame would almost certainly add,' the fiddler went on, 'to anyone who would listen – that if it weren't for you, her son wouldn't have the faintest idea how to go about finding out the truth of the faked rebellion and the Spanish militia. Eliminate Sancho Panza and Don Quixote would have returned home within a week, if he didn't get himself lost on the way.'

'Of course she would.' January sighed. 'She would blame me if it rained on her birthday. And thanks to my mother, Ch— that is, whoever it was knew me. I mean, he would have known me from – er – hiring me to play at entertainments, if he was wealthy and socially active . . . whoever he is.'

Whoever he is . . .

Hannibal brandished the sheaf of financial documents, each carefully refolded with the original seals glued precisely back in place, proof that neither January nor Dagobert had read them. That neither had seen the signature of the man who'd facilitated the payment of twenty thousand dollars in Spanish pesos and bills of exchange to the credit of Bartolomé de Cedillos – *whoever he is . . .*

'I'll get these to Mr Oldmixton today,' the fiddler promised. 'It shouldn't take him long to inform the – ah – principal in all this that no, you and Janvier are as innocent as babes unborn. Maybe another twenty-four hours to locate the good Mr Watling and cancel the bounty on your lives, and for Watling to impress this fact upon his own underlings. It would probably be a good idea for you to find somewhere else to be for that time.'

'I can manage that.' *Of course I can,* January thought in his dream. *I'm getting on the Reine de Navarre and leaving New Orleans forever; why am I worrying about Mr Chew?*

'I shall let you know, as the smugglers say, when the coast is clear.' And Hannibal walked off, through the confusion of hogsheads and cotton bales, the dark shapes of longshoremen and stevedores, and vanished into the mist. Somewhere along the levee, porters loading a ship began to sing, the wailing call and response of an African song.

Ouendé, ouendé, macaya . . .
Ouendé, ouendé, macaya . . .

Words – he couldn't remember who had told him this – about gorging oneself on food, sung by men who lived on whatever ration their owners thought they could spare . . .

A bell clanged on board the ship. Half-seen in cindery mist, men clambered up the rigging. It was time to go.

'Write.' Gilles hugged him hard. Gilles young, with all his hair, lively and athletic from dances and drilling with the militia. Gilles still able to use his left arm. 'Let us know what you see, what you do. How you are.' He had been taken on as a partner to Fazet that year. Callie was heavy with their first child. 'God, I'll miss you, Ben.'

January took Callie's hands, and she pulled them free to throw her arms around him, to hold him tight.

'And I'll let you know' – Gilles managed a wry grin – 'if the Congress ever starts handing out parcels of land—'

'We'll send a message over to you in Paris,' added Callie, 'in the mouth of a flying pig.'

January agreed gravely, 'I'll be watching for it.'

They all laughed.

After the militia parade, he had waited over a year for Congress to act upon – or even acknowledge – General Jackson's imperative demand that the men of color who had mixed their blood

with the mud of Chalmette be given the land they'd been promised. One hundred and sixty acres, whose possession could make a man free.

One hundred and sixty acres that the government could profitably sell to a land speculator – who was quite possibly a member of Congress.

They'd agreed, at least, to pay the men of Plauché's battalion, and d'Aquin's, the same wage that the white men had received. But even as he'd marched behind Savary down Rue Esplanade, through the Faubourg Marigny and the French Town, January had known that it would go no further than that. The battalion had been ordered out of the city after the parade. Savary – and many of the men of Saint-Domingue who had fought under his leadership – had given up in disgust and gone to Mexico, where Guerrero and his insurgents were still fighting the Spanish troops for independence.

Savary's departure had been, for January, the closing of the door, the moment at which he'd understood that the land bounty would never materialize. That you could spill your blood for the Congress, and the Congress would still bow to the demands of the slave-owning rich.

Savary had asked him, would he go with them? 'I'll wait, and see what happens,' he had replied, and the captain had nodded, accepting. But he had known – and he'd seen it in Savary's eyes – that he was simply whistling for a wind that would never rise.

John Davis gave him thirty Spanish pesos, interchangeable with American dollars: *To go to the opera when you get to Paris. Man doth not live by bread alone.*

Callie, and Gilles, embraced him again. Neither of them said, *Come back.*

How can I leave this? The low pastel city, whose roofs alone were visible above the levee in the slow-clearing light. The memories of all those evenings sitting on the balcony above Fazet's courtyard, of walking along the levee to watch the endless familiar chaos of the waterfront comings and goings. Memories of the music he'd made, the dances he'd played at, the children he'd taught, black and white . . . The faces of his friends.

He'd spent last night in Gilles and Callie's little cottage in Marigny: candlelight and the smell of the gunpowder and lemongrass in the mosquito smudges. Callie's marvelous cooking and the joy of laughter. *It's hard for me to go,* he had said at one point, and – joking and not joking – Callie had responded, *Then don't.*

How can I not?

He had turned and walked up the gangplank and on to the ship.

1841

The following afternoon, Hannibal came up the attic stairs of the townhouse of Augustus and Madeleine Mayerling, where January had slept the previous night, with the news that the duly sealed papers – 'whatever they are,' Hannibal said – had been delivered to Sir John Oldmixton. 'To be sent on to their rightful owner – whoever that might be.' The under-secretary's note had just reached the fiddler, informing him that all was 'settled to the satisfaction of everyone concerned.'

'He found this for you, by the way—' As they walked down the Rue Dauphin, Hannibal held out to him the silver watch he'd bought in Paris. 'It was in a pawnshop in Gallatin Street. He even promised to purchase a purple silk gown for Kate.' They turned along Rue Esplanade, and the dinner that Rose had waiting for them at the house. 'I had a nightmare last night about what that hue will look like against her red hair. And – which I think was just as handsome – Sir John proposes to pay for the removal of the body of Edouard-Georges Couvillier from the Potter's Field, and its reburial, under his rightful name, in the St-Louis Cemetery.'

January wondered if Dagobert Janvier would attend the funeral.

It was Cosette Gardinier's first evening back at the school – giggling with Germaine and Zizi over her proposed engagement to Jean-Xavier Morrell, and her grandmother's discomfiture. Callie was there also – Gilles could not yet rise from bed in his father-in-law's house – and joined in the game of thinking up ways that January and Dagobert could have sneaked through the streets of New Orleans in disguise the previous day, now that Carnival was done. What was fairly simple subterfuge on the night of Mardi Gras had been much less easy on Ash Wednesday when nobody was wearing a mask. Speculations ranged from being packed in coffins and trundled in a hearse ('Madame Marie-Hélène really would kill me if I delivered Michie Dagobert to her door in a coffin!') to disguising as women ('Two women over six feet tall are not as

convincing in daylight, Chou-chou.') or wearing potato sacks over their heads ('We thought of that, Professor, but Dagobert was afraid of what would happen if we met someone who liked potatoes.' 'Oh,' said the three-year-old, frowning as he reviewed this logic.)

The truth had been less colorful. Olympe's husband Paul had hitched a rented horse to the wagon in which, before the bank crash, he'd customarily delivered the furniture he used to upholster, lashed a tarpaulin over it, and two of the girls who rented cribs behind the bathhouse for business purposes obligingly staged a spectacular fist fight in the empty ground on the other side of the Eagle of Victory saloon. This drew the riveted attention of any watchers who might otherwise have spotted January and Dagobert clambering aboard (and of nearly a thousand other gentlemen). ('Think if we advertised, you girls could do that for money next week?' Kate had asked, viewing the size of the dispersing crowd. Russian Nancy and Railspike had nodded enthusiastically.) ('During *Lent*?' cried Aglaëa, shocked when Hannibal recounted this sequel to the escape. 'They're Protestants,' Zizi-Marie reassured the girl.)

It was good, January reflected, to be home.

He did not expect to receive any acknowledgment from Dagobert and wasn't disappointed. He saw his relative the following morning, at Mass, kneeling between his stepmother and his long-suffering wife.

'Numquid voluntatis meæ est mors impii? dicit Dominus Deus . . .'

Have I any pleasure at all that the wicked should die, saith the Lord God.

'. . . et non ut convertatur a viis suis, et vivat?'

. . . and not that he should return from his ways, and live?

As Bartolomé de Cedillos had turned from treason, January wondered, and lived another twenty-six years in Spain with his daughters – and presumably, for a time, his wife? Had poverty, or debts, or some other money trouble finally convinced him to return to New Orleans in search of the Spanish silver he'd been paid for his treachery? Or had he – or his daughter Felicita – simply grown tired of pinching pennies?

Was it Felicita who had said, *Oh, come on, Papa, after all this time nobody will care anymore!*

Having dealt with the woman, January could easily believe that version of events.

And when it turned out that after all this time somebody *did* care about the danger of being exposed, she had sought out the man who had loved her sister. The man in whom she saw the perfect cat's paw.

'Si autem averterit se justus a justitia sua, et fecerit iniquitatem . . . numquid vivat?'

But when the righteous turneth away from his righteousness, and commiteth iniquity . . . shall he live?

January remembered Chew speaking to Bastien Damoreau at the Blue Ribbon ball – Chew to whom paying three hundred dollars' worth of gambling debts was a small investment. Plus whatever he paid someone – probably Cat Watling – to lie in the trees beside Bayou St-John with a rifle, that February morning . . .

He was well aware that both he, and Dagobert, were fortunate to be alive.

He did not go to the altar rail to communicate – confession wasn't until tomorrow, and he had sufficient lies on his conscience (to say nothing of evil thoughts regarding Mamzelle de Cedillos) to raise blisters on his lips if they touched the Host. But he remained in prayer as others went up (Dagobert, he noticed, abstained as well), and when Père Eugenius gave the congregation leave to depart, he lingered, to donate his last few pennies to the purchase of candles: for the souls of his dear friend Davy Gignac, of Ayasha, of St-Denis Janvier, and Rubal Gomez. A candle of simple thanks, that he'd survived – that Gilles had survived. A candle for the soul of Bartolomé de Cedillos, and another (he grudged this one but knew it was what Père Eugenius would instruct him at confession tomorrow) for the safe voyage of that no-good slatternly bitch Felicita de Cedillos back to Spain, damn her.

He was turning away from the Virgin's altar when a woman behind him said, 'Benjamin?'

It was Marie-Hélène Janvier.

He bowed, and she held up her gloved hand, as if to silence his greeting. To block any words that would distract her from what she had to say.

'Thank you,' she said. And then, drawing a deep breath, 'I'm sorry. I have held a grudge against you for all the years of your life – since you were a little boy. But you were only a little boy, and it was not your doing.'

'You had been sorely hurt, m'am,' he returned quietly. 'And I'm sorry that my mother was party to that.'

She looked aside for a moment, then made herself return her gaze to his. 'Thank you for saving Dagobert,' she went on simply. 'Friends' – he wondered if she meant Sir John, or whether Chew himself had circuitously reassured her – 'have told me that the men who threatened my son over this disgraceful business have been appeased; that he will have nothing more to fear.'

She couldn't keep from glancing over her shoulder, to where the daylight outside splashed across Dagobert's well-tailored shoulders as he limped upon his cane. Across his wife's lace bonnet and red-and-gold Norwich shawl, her head bent to listen to his every word. His two grown sons, January had seen, had also been in the church.

'He tells me that you recounted to him the events of the other night, events that he doesn't remember – how he bade farewell to that . . . that *frightful* hussy who got him into all this trouble to begin with. Whatever actually happened' – her voice thinned as she spoke the words, and he guessed that she didn't believe a syllable of what her stepson had said – 'thank you for . . . for ending his infatuation. I presume the woman has left the country.'

'She has, m'am.' January bowed again. 'If you'll forgive me for saying so, I suspect your son's infatuation hasn't ended. I think he'll always cling to that dream. But a dream is all it will be.'

Her sigh, and the tightening of her lips, told him – and he wondered that this hadn't occurred to him before – that this hadn't been Dagobert's first quest to assist a romantic, though probably completely platonic, attachment.

And given what he knew about the other man's nature, he supposed that like Don Quixote, Dagobert needed a Dulcinea in his life. A dream to sweeten the days at the counting house and the warehouses, the evenings totting up entries in ledgers and writing letters to business contacts in Havana, Seville, Cartagena, and Bordeaux.

I love what I do, thought January. *I went to Paris to seek my freedom, the freedom I'd hoped to get from possessing land. The freedom to deepen my learning about how to heal and save lives. Coming back, I make people happy, like Rapunzel spinning the straw of notes written by men far away or long dead into the gold of present beauty, present joy.*

In his heart, does Dagobert hate what he does?

He recalled what Dr Ker had said: *He's her lad, for all he's got sons old enough to vote and chase ladies who don't run so fast . . . He hadn't the courage to see what lies down the river and out over the sea . . .*

Or does he not even realize it, except in his dreams?

Awkwardly, Marie-Hélène went on, 'I owe you a great deal, Benjamin. And if in the past I did, or said, anything that . . . that hurt you . . .'

If?!?!

He closed his mouth on the word and saw only in her face what that thanks, and that apology, cost this woman.

'That water went under the bridge a long time ago, m'am,' he said. 'It's miles out to sea by now.'

He waited a little, standing in the cathedral doorway on the down-river side to give her time to catch up with her stepson and his wife, her grandsons and her mother-in-law. He was still watching them – these people whose family money had paid for his education, for the house he'd grown up in, for his sister Dominique's music lessons and pretty dresses and for the fact that he had been able to grow up a free man at all – when a man crossed the flagstone paving before the cathedral towards him, and he turned to see the neat, powerful form of Sir John Oldmixton at his side.

'Sir!' He bowed. 'I was just going to call on you this afternoon, to thank you for . . . for dealing with the . . . misunderstanding concerning the affairs of M'sieu Bartolomé de Cedillos. I hope, as Mr Sefton informs me, that matters have been settled to everyone's satisfaction.'

'Perfectly, sir. Perfectly.' Oldmixton held out his gloved hand for January to shake.

'Did you send word to the Balize, to intercept the crates Mademoiselle de Cedillos sent aboard the *Alicante*?' This had been part of Hannibal's message to Oldmixton on Wednesday morning.

'In fact,' sighed the Englishman, 'the *Alicante* was delayed sailing, so we were able to take possession of the crates before they went on board. Unfortunately, the crates turned out to contain nothing but bricks – I believe there's a brickworks within a hundred yards of Mrs Rocher's establishment. I can only assume that Miss de

Cedillos had arranged for the labels to be switched on the wharf, and the actual silver to be sent on another vessel – or possibly to be deposited in a bank in exchange for credit to her name. We are currently checking on that possibility.'

Good luck with that . . .

She probably deposited it back with Mr Chew.

'And Mademoiselle de Cedillos herself?'

Oldmixton shook his head. 'I'm fairly certain she took ship early Wednesday morning, under an assumed name. She certainly wasn't on the *Alicante*. I will make inquiries at the Balize, of all ships going down the Pass to the Gulf, but with what could she be charged?' He spread his hands. 'Shipping bricks to herself? Visiting the home of her childhood? I would be cut forever from New Orleans society,' he went on smoothly, 'if I attempted to apply pressure of any kind to a respectable broker like M'sieu Janvier. After Madame's Grand Cavalcade and Mardi Gras ball, the family stands extremely high in the regard of every French Creole clan in the state. Given my position at the Consulate' – the bright turquoise eye caught January's: *And you know jolly well what my position there really is* – 'I would be a fool to alienate so many valuable connections in what would be a futile errand at best.'

January bowed again. 'I don't envy you your position, sir. But however the case may be, thank you, with the whole of my heart, for . . . arranging things with whoever was the true owner of those papers . . . Whatever they were.'

Oldmixton gravely returned the bow, acknowledging January's discretion. *We won't even admit you knew they were bills of exchange, much less who signed them or where the funds came from.*

'Not at all,' he said. 'My pleasure.' He clasped January's hand again. 'I hope I shall have the pleasure of working with you again, M'sieu January.'

And he strolled off across the Place d'Armes, a straight, dark figure in the wan wintry light. January watched him go for a few moments, listening to the cries of the market women, the yarking of the gulls. Horribly aware that he now owed the British spymaster a favor.

Then he turned his steps towards home, knowing that whatever the future payback was going to be, he was not going to like it.

[illegible] just an suggestion [illegible] on the [illegible] of the [illegible] to be [illegible] to [illegible] or [illegible] at the [illegible] [illegible] checking on [illegible]

[illegible]

[illegible] with Mr. [illegible]

[illegible]

[illegible] up [illegible] the [illegible] of all [illegible] not with [illegible] said. [illegible] but [illegible] I [illegible] [illegible] and [illegible] the family [illegible]

[illegible] And [illegible] many [illegible] would be [illegible]

[illegible] your [illegible] [illegible] with [illegible]

[illegible]

Not [illegible] he said. [illegible] I hope I shall have the pleasure of [illegible] of [illegible]

And he [illegible] the Place d [illegible] [illegible] of the [illegible] in the [illegible] of the [illegible] of [illegible] [illegible]

Then [illegible]